More from Laurie Bell's
Stones of Power
The Butterfly Stone
The Tiger's Eye
The Crow's Heart

More from Wyvern's Peak Publishing

The Recalcitrant Project
by Lauren Lynne

The Secret Watchers
Visions
Whispers
Insights
by Lauren Lynne

Charlie Sullivan and the Monster Hunters
The Varcolac's Diary
Witch Moon
Council of the Hunters
The Dragon Gate
by D.C. McGannon & C. Michael McGannon

THE SERPENT'S KISS

THE SERPENT'S KISS

WYVERN'S PEAK PUBLISHING

An imprint of The McGannon Group, LLC

The Serpent's Kiss

The Stones of Power, Book 4

Written by Laurie Bell – www.solothefirst.wordpress.com

Copyright © 2025 Laurie Bell

Published by Wyvern's Peak Publishing. 2025
An imprint of The McGannon Group, LLC

Cover by C. Michael McGannon

The Serpent's Kiss / by Laurie Bell – 1st Ed.
Summary: Tracey Masters undergoes challenges she never imagined, weathering the storm of an internal battle while trying to track a mischievous stone protector and trying to avoid the vicious hunt by a third, all while trying to keep her friends and family safe from the chaos.

1 2 3 4 5 6 7 8 9

ISBN-13: 979-8-9869817-1-0

To Emily and Hannah – My biggest fans!

Also to Taylah, Skye, Mark, Bree and Amy, Mia & Isabel, Chloe & Bryce, Elsa. Lisa, Jenny and Kathy. And to you, Elise! Thank you for waiting.

Be kind.

Magic is inside all of you.

Be amazing!

-Laurie Bell

PREVIOUSLY

Tracey's uncle was tasked with finding a missing butterfly necklace. He enlisted Tracey's help to find it. Turns out, the missing necklace was in fact a magic stone once owned by Tracey's ancestor. Tracey's search embroiled her and her friends in a battle to find the necklace before the menacing Shadowman could find it and use its power against the world.

Tracey discovered that the Butterfly Stone was just one of many. Other magic stones were out there and she needed to find them all before the ghostly spirit of Timothy and a mysterious Dust Devil could track them down. Tracey and her friends discovered that the Tiger's Eye was trapped inside a terrible curse. Every time they learned something new about the Tiger's Eye, they forgot it. They learned that Tracey's new friend Jilly was the key to locating the second Stone of Power.

But Timothy's stone was still out there, and that meant Timothy was still at large. To stop him, Tracey was forced to make a terrible bargain and Kylie, another new friend and the sister of Tracey's crush, suffered as a consequence. Kylie now held the Serpent's Kiss.

With three stones now in their grasp, Tracey's investigations took her and her friends to London to find the fourth Stone of Power. Fighting off giant clay men, Tracey and her friends learned the tragic story of Millicent Flowers and through mazes of mystery at last discovered the whereabouts of her stone, the Crow's Heart. Tracey found a way to save Kylie from the Serpent's Kiss, but her choice may be her undoing.

Now Tracey Masters and her friends are in a race to find all **six** Stones of Power before the evil Timothy Hart can get his hands on them. They have **four** stones. The Butterfly Stone, The Tiger's Eye, the Crow's Heart, and the Serpent's Kiss.

There are **two** more to find …

My Dearest Friend,

I appreciate you allowing me to read
the excerpt of your manuscript.
It is very good.

1

Prince Henry's dejected figure walked away down the concourse alone. When he was out of sight, Tracey pulled the Serpent's Kiss out of her pocket. The stone was the blackest of blacks with a rich, blood-red snake swirling down the center. Depending on which angle she held it at, she imagined she could see a pair of snake eyes staring back at her. She pulled the chain over her head so it would nestle next to the Butterfly Stone. As the stones touched, the Serpent's Kiss and the Butterfly Stone screamed.

Tracey opened her eyes in a dark place — a black worse than night. There was no moon or stars or even lamplight to break the nothingness. A shadowy man appeared in front of her, glowing red from within. A man she recognized.

Timothy's face creased in a grin.

"Hello Tracey."

Her heart thundered as panic set in. Strobing vision blinded her from her surroundings. She forced a slow deep breath, and then another. What had she expected? She wore his stone. Her ancestor, Stephanie, never hesitated in sucking Tracey inside the white room of the Butterfly Stone to speak with her. Why would Timothy not do the same?

The tremble in Tracey's fingers faded as her vision returned. She stared up at the man before her. Timothy was a tall, weedy man with dark hair, thinning at the temples and a slight wave below his ears. There were more lines on his face than she recalled seeing in Stephanie's Vision memory. His long nose, when he tilted his head up, made his glowing red eyes shrink. He sneered down at her. It gave her the willies, but at least she knew he couldn't hurt her in here.

He wore an olden style white suit and stood evenly balanced, his hands held loose by his sides. He examined Tracey as if she were something equally fascinating and irritating. Her gaze flicked around the room. She stood in one circle of light. Timothy stood opposite. The rest of the room was black. Just black. All around them. Pitch black. Like the bottom of the darkest cave. Underwater.

"What am I doing here?" she asked. Her voice only wobbled a bit.

"You came to me," he said.

"No, I didn't."

"Tracey, you chose the Serpent's Kiss — my stone. You let me in." His voice crawled over her and she shivered in revulsion.

"Only to save Kylie."

He tilted his head back further. "She was perfectly safe. You ensured I could not communicate with her. You did not need to take my stone as your own. So why did you?"

She hadn't even thought about it. She had just acted. "Kylie didn't have a choice. The curse on the Stones of Power prevented her from removing it. The spell that locked the stone's magic away wouldn't let her use magic. Not having magic is horrible. So, when the chance came to help her, I took it."

"You made the decision for her?" He hummed. "You took away her choice."

Tracey shook her head violently. "No. I helped her."

"Did you?"

"I did." They all knew that at his first opportunity he would have taken over Kylie's body again. It was far too dangerous to leave the stone around her neck. Tracey did the only thing she could do. As soon as she could take the Serpent's Kiss away from Kylie, she had done so.

"And now, you cannot remove the stone. My stone. You put yourself in her place."

"I did what I had to do. She's only a kid."

"As are you."

Tracey straightened and thrust out her chin. "I'm stronger. I can handle it."

"Can you?"

Another shiver swept down her spine as if trying to hide from the intensity of his stare. "Yes. You can't do anything to me, unless I let you. I must give you permission. And I won't."

"You will. One day soon. Sooner than you think. You will give me control."

"Not a chance. You're trapped in here and I'm not scared of you."

Timothy smiled, though his gaze remained stormy. "Of course. You have defeated me before. Still, I have much knowledge of magic, Tracey. I could be useful to you."

"Useful? I don't want anything from you. I took the stone to protect Kylie. That's all."

"So altruistic."

Tracey was pretty sure that meant doing something without expecting anything in return. "Exactly!" But even as she said it, a nagging voice in the back of her mind — the one that sounded a lot like her sister Sarah — reminded her of her desperation to keep her promise to Kylie's brother, Damian. She wanted Damian to like her and that wasn't altruistic at all. Still, she saved Kylie, so she *was* a good person. "You're trying to trick me." It was awful that she couldn't freely move in this place. She pictured herself moving away from him and was frustrated when nothing happened.

"What makes you say that?"

"That's what you do. Spin lies into truths. Make people do what you want them to do because you're evil."

"You have a hard opinion of me."

"Because you're horrible."

His forehead creased. "What makes you believe that?"

"Stephanie told me. She *showed* me what you did to her."

"What did I do?"

"You brainwashed her. Made her think she loved you."

He shook his head. "Tracey, I cannot make a person fall in love. That is magic not even I can control."

"You're lying. I *saw* you wrap her up in your magic and she changed her mind. That's not love. Love is not hurting other people. It's not lying to them. You don't know what love is. You hurt her. That's not love. That's control."

"And what do you know of love, little girl?"

"More than you," she growled. She had witnessed the truth of his actions against Stephanie. *Ugh, why am I even arguing with him? He's pure evil.* Tracey shut her eyes and ordered herself to wake up. When she cracked her eyes open she was still in the black place and Timothy stared down his nose at her — his lips curled in a sneer.

"I take it Stephanie was able to show you her memories somehow?"

Tracey nodded.

"A memory is a moment in time captured like a painting. Who is to say things truly happen the way it is remembered?"

"It's Stephanie's memory," Tracey argued. "Obviously it happened."

"Have you never remembered something a little differently to what actually happened? Perhaps you were slightly taller, used slightly different words from what you actually said in the moment, remembered an event that happened but the timing is off. Perhaps you were embarrassed by something you did and don't want to remember it properly? Do you swear that everything you recall is completely one hundred percent accurate?"

"Are you saying Stephanie's memories are not real?"

"Not at all. I am merely asking you the question. What if our memories are not the whole truth? Your opinion of me has been formed by what you have seen and what you have been told. But has Stephanie told you the truth?"

Of course. "You're trying to trick me."

"You are a smart girl, Tracey. I don't care if I hurt you, but I will always tell you the truth."

Tracey shook her head. She refused to believe anything Timothy said. He was the bad guy. She peered around the black room, frustrated she wasn't learning anything new. It was time to get out of this black place and return to her friends.

"What about your teacher, Agent Malden?" Timothy continued. "Did he always tell you the truth?"

How much of Kylie's knowledge and experience had Timothy been aware of when she held his stone? Tracey assumed Timothy knew what Kylie did. How else could he have known about Agent Malden's betrayal? Oh, but she didn't want to think of Agent Malden. Her once-friend kidnapped Tracey, Jilly, and Kylie for the power of their stones. All to restore his beloved Agent Striker to life. His betrayal hurt Tracey and her friends, and she could never forgive him for it.

Unless Timothy didn't know and was just guessing to get Tracey to reveal the truth. "I'm not going to fall for your lies," she said.

"Of course not. We are nothing alike, am I right? Agent Malden, Stephanie, your friends and family, they always tell you the truth. And so do you, Tracey. I am sure you always tell the truth."

"I do."

"Even if it hurts the ones you love? You have so much magic, Tracey. You could be so powerful if only you would do what needs to be done —"

"Oh my God, seriously?" She threw up her hands. "Good try, but yeah, I am smart." She laughed. "You really think I'm going to stay here listen to you babble on? You're evil."

"You are tempted, Tracey. I can sense that. The Serpent's Kiss can give you everything you want. You have only to ask."

Ugh. She wouldn't listen to anymore of this. "All I want is to find the stones and destroy them. And you can't stop me." She slammed her eyes shut and willed herself back to reality.

Timothy's voice filled her head. *You will change your mind on that, Tracey. I will always tell you the truth. And you will ask. One day soon, you will ask for my help. I will be waiting.*

You simply must go ahead with
your publishing dreams.

2

Tracey opened her eyes and blinked, momentarily dizzy, and searched the airport boarding terminal for her friends. They sat sprawled over several hard plastic seats waiting for permission to board their airplane back home. Had they noticed her odd pause? She knew that while she spoke with the spirit inside the Stone of Power, it appeared to those around her that she froze like a statue. Her shoulders and neck muscles agreed, feeling tight and sore like they had been locked in place for hours. Tracey relaxed her shoulders and loosened her fists.

No one appeared to have noticed her mental absence. Of course not. Her confrontation with Timothy occurred inside her mind. No one knew she held Timothy's stone. *That's a secret I can tell no one.*

Tracey's sister Sarah laughed at something Jilly said and the two girls leaned in toward Laura as she showed them something on her cell phone. All three were dressed in comfortable travel clothes, jeans and T-shirts, their hair hanging loose around their shoulders; yet somehow all three looked super stylish. Tony and Jonny, also dressed casually in hoodies and track pants, stood near the window absorbed in the planes taking off and landing in the distance. Someone's perfume burned Tracey's nostrils. She twitched as a gaggle of travelers walked past, dragging or carrying their carry-on luggage, chatting on cell phones or shouting over each other. It was like being slammed by a wall of noise after the silence of the black room.

Tracey looked for Damian, Kylie, and Mrs. Carter stopping only when she remembered they took an earlier flight. Mom sat beside Grandma. Both held takeaway coffee cups, though they didn't appear to be drinking from them. Numerous strangers crowded the waiting area. Tracey caught suspicious glances as passengers noticed her, flicking to her wrist and the emerald light shining from her Mage-kind identification bracelet. Scowls formed on several of those faces. Tracey's shoulders hunched, uncomfortable with the feeling of being judged without cause.

Grandma focused on Tracey, pursing her lips. Tracey tore her gaze away, not wanting her grandmother to realize anything was wrong. Overhead speakers crackled with a boarding announcement, calling for the front rows to board first, and anyone with babies or wheelchairs. Tracey's group were seated at the back of the plane. It would be a while before they were called. Tracey plopped down on an empty blue plastic seat beside Dave Two. She figured if anyone was likely to ignore her it was him. The football jock held his cell phone in front of his face. She spied his eyebrows rise above the device. "What?"

"What?" she snapped back.

He shrugged. "You don't usually sit near me. Not on purpose."

She rolled her eyes. Dave was an unusual friend — not the sort she hung out with normally, but he was growing on her. Kind of like a wart. She grabbed her cell and typed out a text message to Damian. He wouldn't get it until he landed, but at least he would know she was thinking about him. She pictured his dreamy, perfect, warm brown eyes and charming smile and sighed softly as her tummy flipped. *He kissed me!*

Tracey's sister Sarah leaned forward drawing Tracey's attention. "What did Prin — Hank want? Where'd he go?"

The last her friends and family knew Tracey had walked away talking with Prince Henry. "He went home. We're getting a new agent."

Every conversation cut off as they tuned into Tracey's words. She was suddenly aware of how public the terminal gate was. Anyone could overhear them. The woman with the super strong floral perfume stood pretty close to Laura, Jilly, and Sarah. "I'll, ah, tell you all later."

Their seats were called and Tracey led her large party onto the plane.

Jonny, her oldest and bestest friend and ever the gentleman, let Tracey have the window seat again. She thanked him with a smile and closed her eyes, blocking his handsome face from her tired gaze. She leaned her head back against the seat rest and awaited take-off. Her brain and thoughts were turning muddy and slow now that the adrenaline from their trip was fading. If only she could sleep for a week, then she might have clearer focus.

Cracking open an eye, Tracey caught a glimpse of the silver chain around Jonny's neck. Jonny wore the Crow's Heart, Millicent Flowers's Stone of Power. Millicent, a member of the Sect of Six was Tracey's ancestor's best friend and her Stone of Power, the Crow's Heart, was the stone

Tracey and her friends traveled all the way to London to find. And none of the adults with them knew they found it.

Tracey's hand drifted to her neck and the two stones she wore tucked beneath her shirt. That wasn't the only secret she was keeping. Not a single one of her friends knew she held the Serpent's Kiss alongside the Butterfly Stone. With Jilly holding the Tiger's Eye, Tracey and her friends held four stones out of the six they needed. It was good, but it wasn't good enough.

She forced her eyes open and stretched into a half stand to see where her friends ended up throughout the plane. Jonny's mom sat in the aisle seat on Jonny's other side. She looked immaculate. Her hair a riot of braids and perfect make-up. Tracey was only a smidge embarrassed by her own barely clean t-shirt and the same jeans she had worn all week. Jilly and Laura sat directly behind Tracey and Jonny. Tracey's mom picked the aisle seat next to Laura, and in front of Tracey sat Dave and Uncle Donny. She peered further back. Tony sat next to Sarah and Tracey's grandma. Tracey plonked her tired body down in her seat and sighed.

"Are you as exhausted as I am?" Jonny asked. He pushed his glasses higher up on his nose and bent to tuck his gaming devices into the seat pocket in front of him, jamming it in beside his phone — on Airplane Mode — his tablet, and several comic books. Tracey's phone and Millicent's diary were in her carry bag, tucked safely under the seat in front of her.

"So tired," she agreed.

"You should sleep," he said, nudging her shoulder with his arm.

"Yeah, I'll try." Tracey shuffled around so she could stare at him without straining her eyes. "How's the — uh — you know? Is it quiet?"

"I haven't heard a peep from it," he confirmed. "Don't worry, I'll shout the second Millicent says anything to me."

Tracey smirked.

"So, what did Hank tell you?" Jonny's teeth shone as he grinned, ever hungry for gossip.

It was still funny to Tracey that a prince who was an actor and also a Mage-kind M-force spy, was their friend and mentor. He remained in London to deal with the fallout from being exposed as Mage-kind. His fans were pissed he had lied about who he was. "He didn't say much. Agent Malden's been taken in for questioning. Hank thinks Malden will go to prison. Maybe. M-force were not happy he tried to take the stones for himself. Supposedly, they will take his mental state into consideration."

Flight attendants shuffled down the quietening aisles, checking overhead locker doors and closing the ones still open. Tracey pulled her sleeves over her wrists while Jonny pushed his hoodie off and smiled as the flight attendant walked past.

"What about the new agent? Will they let us search for the next stone?" Jonny asked.

"He didn't say much. Only that we'll meet her when he flies over to introduce her next week. She has to let us find the remaining stones so we can destroy them all before Timothy can get his hands on them."

"What do we need another M-force agent for anyway? We've done all of the hard work finding the stones ourselves."

"In case anything happens or if people get hurt? I dunno. To help us if we need it?"

"We don't need 'em." Jonny grumped and leaned closer. "What about the next stone? Any clues about where it might be?"

"I don't want to think about that yet. I just want to sleep."

"But we *are* looking for the next one, yeah?"

"We have to," she blurted. "I mean, we've gone so far. We can't stop now." She peered around searching for anyone who might have heard her outburst. Laura and Jilly wore noise canceling headphones, but Mom stared at Tracey with a curious raised eyebrow. Tracey shook her head and slumped back in her seat.

"Right, right," Jonny said.

Tracey glanced out of the window beside her elbow and watched the little men in the empty baggage carts race each other away from the plane. For a moment all was silent. Then the engines revved as the plane backed away from the airport hatch. Tracey's attention returned to the stones around her neck. Only a few months ago, she helped her uncle investigate a missing necklace and now she was in a race to find all six stones before Timothy could use their power to take over the world. The last two stones could be anywhere in the world. How was she supposed to find them when they were cursed not to be found?

She could —

"Hey Tracey?"

She tilted her head. Jonny's hands twitched around his neckline. She couldn't tell if he wanted to pull his hood back on or if he wanted to tug the stone out from under his shirt. "Hmmm?"

"Where do you think the Serpent's Kiss went?"

Tracey sat up straight. "Uh, what do you mean?"

"We weren't in the church basement with you, Jilly, and Kylie. Kylie wore it when Agent Malden's mumble kidnapped her and when we found you, it was gone. Did Agent Malden get it off somehow?"

"I don't know. I mean …" Her hands twitched. She fought not to touch the black stone hidden beneath her shirt, clamping her fingers tightly around the seat arm instead. The plane coasted to a gentle stop. A moment later the engines roared and she and Jonny were thrust back in their seats as the plane raced down the runway. The nose lifted and the plane launched into the air.

Tracey used the distraction of take-off to formulate a story her friend would believe. Jonny could always sniff out the truth. She found it impossible to lie to him.

So, don't lie. Timothy's voice curled deep into her ears. *You don't have to give him every detail. You know Kylie was wearing it prior to Agent Malden's spell. When the spell was over, it was gone. All of this is true.*

Tracey shook her head. She couldn't argue with Timothy in front of her friend. Jonny wanted to know what happened. She knew what happened, and she knew where it was now. She just couldn't admit it.

Tell the story as you know it. Choose your words carefully.

The plane leveled out and the engine's roar settled into a low humming vibration. Jonny grinned widely. "I love take-offs."

"Yeah." Tracey bit her bottom lip hoping he wouldn't remember his question. As Timothy said, it wasn't a lie. She would just neglect to tell him everything. It didn't make her heart or stomach ache to imagine what they would do if they ever found out the truth.

"What do you think happened to the stone?" he asked again.

"When I woke up Agent Malden was doing a spell. There was so much magic in the room. It hurt. And then I was fighting Agent Malden. I don't know. Maybe it fell off?"

"Fell off?" One of Jonny's eyebrows rose.

"Agent Malden's spell was on all of the stones. I was focused on him and the magic dug into my brain …" She shrugged. "If it fell off we might not have seen it. The stone is black, it was dark …" Tracey struggled to hold his eye contact.

Well handled, Tracey, Timothy whispered.

"Did Hank say anything?" Jonny pressed.

Tracey's cheeks heated. Why was he still asking about this? She grit her teeth together and forced her words out slowly and with care. "He said they haven't found it."

"Maybe one of the searchers found it but claimed they didn't. I feel sorry for whoever has it."

Tracey's fingernails dug into the hard plastic of the arm rest. "Why?"

"Well it's evil, ain't it? They'll be corrupted by it."

"Kylie was —"

"You saved her." Jonny leaned back in his seat and closed his eyes. "You convinced the stone's guardian to lock up her magic so Timothy couldn't use it."

"I … yeah. I did," Tracey said.

"So, don't worry about it. We'll find it. After we get the other stones. Whoever holds the Serpent's Kiss will be caught and we'll break the curse. Timothy will never possess anyone ever again." Jonny's eyes popped open as he reached into the seat pocket in front of him for his game device. "We'll find 'em, Trace," he said and turned it on.

The Serpent's Kiss lay cold against Tracey's clammy skin. Timothy's voice was silent now, but she could feel him smiling. "Yeah. We'll find them," she muttered. She forced her hands to relax on the seat arms and pressed her head back into the cushion. She stared up at the plane's ceiling as her chest tightened. "We'll find them."

I am astonished at the wild and
extraordinary characters you have described.
Oh, how I wish I were a Dreamer.

3

Tracey jolted awake at a hard tug on her forearm. "What?" She squinted up into Jonny's unusually bright — almost bluish glowing eyes. The look on his face was unfamiliar. He gave her a gentle, soft smile. His head tilted to the right and Tracey was overcome by a strange sense of recognition. "Jonny?" The hairs on the back of her neck quivered.

Her friend's smile softened further. He held a finger to his lips. "Hello, Tracey."

The stone around Jonny's neck pulsed faintly violet beneath his hoodie. Tracey straightened. "Millicent?" The spirit inside the Crow's Heart possessed her friend! Tracey remembered how horrible it felt when Stephanie had taken over Tracey's body. She was unable to feel anything while the spirit controlled her movements and her voice. Eventually, she worked out how to push herself forward but possession was not a thing she would wish on her worst enemy. She rose and glanced around the darkened plane. Most of the passengers were asleep or stared zombie-like at their screens. The imaginary closet door held closed over Tracey's magic trembled, wanting to be thrown open so her magic could spring forth and protect her. Tracey's fingers glowed with silver light. "Let him go."

"I won't hurt him."

"If you do anything, I'll stop you."

Jonny — no — Millicent nodded.

"Don't wake his mom," Tracey whispered.

Jonny's head twisted to examine the sleeping woman on his other side.

Questions filled Tracey's mind. Only one required an urgent answer. "Did Jonny give you permission to take control?"

"He is asleep. He does not know I'm here."

"It's not right that he doesn't know what you're doing. You should ask. Or at least ask me to ask him if it's okay."

Jonny took Tracey's hand. Or — well — technically Millicent did.

How confusing.

"I will not stay long. I only wished to speak with you."

"What do you want?" Tracey leaned up out of her seat again to check no one was listening. She caught the roaming flight attendant's eye and ducked down out of sight. *Don't come over.*

"Jonny does not know where the Serpent's Kiss is."

Tracey's hands twitched as she tried to pull free of Millicent's tight grip. "Oh, yeah I know."

"You must do what needs to be done."

The desperate need to keep her secret extended even to Millicent. "It's on my list."

The flight attendant's head appeared beside Jonny's mom, looking over at Tracey. "Did you need something, love?"

"No, sorry. I was just stretching," Tracey whispered hoping not to wake the sleeping woman. She pressed a wide smile onto her face. The flight attendant's dark eyes twitched. "All right, love." He walked away. Tracey sighed and fell deeper into her seat.

Millicent stared at the back of the plane seat. "Goodness, what is that?" she said pointing to the black panel in front of her eyes.

"A display screen — for in-flight movies and stuff."

"Movies? In flight?"

Tracey smiled "We're in an airplane. A flying machine. We're traveling high above the entire world."

"Goodness." Millicent shook herself after a moment. "Timothy is very dangerous. Whomever holds that stone is in mortal peril."

Tracey swallowed hard. "Yeah, he's evil. I get it."

"I feel an urgency I cannot quite explain. Jonny feels this too. He is very intuitive. Listen to him, Tracey." The higher pitch of Jonny's voice was jarring but Millicent's worry came through clearly.

"I — I will, but —"

"There is dark intent focused on you."

"Me?" Tracey tugged uselessly at her hand again. "Your magic? Can you use it when you're in control of Jonny's body? He's a Norm but I remember Timothy was able to use magic when he possessed Officer Jameson."

"Norm?"

"It's what we call non-mage people."

Jonny's game controller twitched in his lap and floated upward. Tracey snapped her hand free and grabbed the controller. "Stop that!"

"I can use the magic stored within my stone like this, yes. Someone is paying close attention to you, Tracey. You must be careful."

"Is it … Timothy?"

"I cannot see for certain. As you know, my strength lies in predicting death. But something is different now. Perhaps it is this boy whose body I inhabit? My feelings, all of them, are so much stronger. I do not see your end. It is something else. A loss of control. You must be careful."

Millicent's power was to witness how people died. "I will be careful." Tracey rubbed her tired eyes then pressed hard on her temples. Should she tell Millicent the truth? That she held Timothy's Serpent's Kiss? The hairs on the back of her neck quivered. No. No she couldn't tell anyone. It had to remain secret to stay safe. If no one knew she held it then *no one* would try to take it from her. "Do you have any ideas how to find the other two stones?"

"I cannot tell you much. I can say that Stephanie and I were the only women in our group."

"What was the group formed for? Why did you create the stones in the first place?"

"To explore our abilities and to strengthen them," Millicent said.

To increase our power, Timothy whispered into Tracey's ear.

"What happened to you all?" Tracey asked over the top of Timothy's voice. How much could he hear? She would have to figure out a way to block him if she wanted to keep anything secret.

You cannot.

Millicent let out a little smile. "Stephanie and I were close. The bestest of friends but —"

"— but?"

"I knew, deep in my heart, that she did not view our friendship the same way that I did. There was a — distance between us on her side. I believe she was not completely honest with me. She kept secrets and I do not know what they were. Though she denied it, I believe she looked upon me as her lesser for my lack of a family name."

"I'm not sure what that means."

"I had no living relatives. My parents died shortly after I was born. I was given to the orphanage and no records were ever found. I had no family name. There was always a pause when Stephanie introduced me as her companion. I would see her eyes twitch. She assured me it was only in my imagination; that I heard things she did not say, saw things she did not intend in her behavior. It led to her keeping things close to her chest. In contrast, Matthew — her promised — was an open book. A lovely man who was desperately in love with her. If Stephanie could not fully trust me, then she certainly kept secrets from him. Matthew's friends, however, she trusted them implicitly."

"You didn't like them?"

"It wasn't that I did not like them. They made me uncomfortable."

"Why?"

"Where Stephanie attempted to hide her attitude toward me, those men did not. I know they did not accept me. They would not let me touch them. I could not see their end and therefore I could not see their truth."

"Did you see Stephanie's death?"

"No. That is why we became such good friends. I never did witness her end. She was blocked to me or perhaps that was simply her magic. It was so much stronger than mine."

"What can you tell me about the men — Matthew's friends."

"You have met Jing? Charles was another. A rather hateful man. Intent on gathering great power. He was very dangerous. Jonathan, though, he was different. Creative. Clever."

Jonathan? "Why was Stephanie friends with them?"

"As I said. She trusted them deeply and she —" Jonny blinked and shook his head. His voice dropped back to his normal register. "Oh man, I just had the weirdest dream."

"Millicent?"

"Nooooo?" He scrunched his nose. Tracey hid a sigh. By waking up Jonny had pushed Millicent out of control. She debated telling him what Millicent said while he was asleep, then thought better of it. That information would freak him out, and she didn't want him to refuse to wear the stone. Jonny holding the Crow's Heart protected Millicent. Besides, the stone's guardian chose him. Tracey didn't trust anyone else to hold it.

"How long was I asleep?" Jonny asked.

"Don't know. I just woke up myself." She was getting pretty good at this lying by not lying thing. Millicent *technically* woke her up. Timothy laughed softly in the back of her mind.

Tracey stretched her arms high above her head and stood up. Jonny shuffled sideways, squishing his long legs into his mom, disturbing her rest. Tracey apologized to Martha and squeezed past, stumbling into the aisle. The plane cabin was dark, lit only by the aisle lights simulating night time. Tracey shuffled and stretched again before she wandered off toward the bathroom. On her return she stopped beside Uncle Donny. Her uncle occupied the aisle seat and there was an empty seat next to him. Dave had somehow scrunched his large body into the window seat. His mouth hung open as he snored loudly. A bit of drool dripped onto his shoulder sleeve. Tracey hid her smile and gestured to the empty seat. "Hey."

Uncle Donny shifted to the middle seat and Tracey slid into the aisle seat. "Hey, kiddo. Did you get any sleep?" His cheek was creased from his hand where he had leaned against it while playing with his tablet. His curls stuck up high on the right side of his head. Orange juice stained his shirt beneath the top button.

"A little. It's hard to sleep sitting up." They both glanced at Dave and chuckled. "What about you?" she asked.

Uncle Donny shook his head. "My mind is whirring," he said. "I'm still angry. It's hard for my head to settle."

"Agent Malden?"

"He was my friend, Tracey, and he put you in danger. You, and Jilly and Kylie. You are just children. I will never forgive him for breaking my trust. He swore to keep you safe."

"He was devastated over Agent Striker's death," Tracey reminded him.

"That is no excuse, Tracey. None." Uncle Donny slammed his hand against the arm rest. "To put another person in danger — any person — is unacceptable. I need you to understand that." A rumble of *shhhhh's* and grumbles about disrupted sleep filled the air, hushing her uncle. It didn't shift the sourpuss expression off his mouth or the deep lines from digging into the skin around his eyes.

This was the most serious she had ever seen him look and it made her squirm. *I can't tell him about the Serpent's Kiss. Even if I wanted to. Look at him. He's so angry.* Tracey's face heated and she stared down at her hands, twisting her fingers together.

"I understand," she whispered. The stones around her neck were heavy, weighing her down. She forced her shoulders back and straightened her spine. "That's kinda what I wanted to talk to you about."

"Oh?" He dropped his voice and scooched lower in his seat, bringing his ear toward her face.

She leaned in. "What do you do when you have absolutely no leads in a case?"

"Ah." He pressed his head back into the seat and tapped his lips with his fingers. "It depends on the case. I take it you are looking for where to start in the search for the next stone?"

"We have no clues. Nothing."

"Not entirely true, Tracey. We have your poem, and we have two stones already." Uncle Donny didn't know they held Millicent's stone. He had asked her once to trust him to look after her. She did. He might not be all that great at his job but he was her uncle and he loved her. She couldn't tell him about the Serpent's Kiss or that she wore it, but she could be honest about other stuff.

Tracey pushed up on her elbows and peered around the darkened plane. Mom and Grandma's eyes were closed as they slept off the busy trip. There were no flight attendants in sight and no passengers peered in her direction. Would Uncle Donny tell Mom about the Crow's Heart if she shared the secret? As much as Agent Malden's betrayal angered her uncle it also made Tracey afraid to tell him a partial truth. But this was her uncle. If she couldn't trust him, then she couldn't trust anybody.

Perhaps, if she told him about the Crow's Heart and Millicent it would be easier to keep Timothy's stone a secret?

"You can't tell Mom," she said, lowering her voice even further. "You can't tell anyone."

His lips pursed. He raised his two pointer fingers and tapped them together. "What can't I tell her?"

She stared into his eyes. "We found another stone."

"What!"

Heads stirred. "Shhhhh!" she hissed.

He slouched back down. "You did find Kylie's stone?"

Tracey sucked on her teeth for a moment, trying to figure out how to word it without actually lying.

Tell the truth, Tracey. Timothy urged softly. *Just don't tell him everything.*

Tracey poked her finger into her ear and jiggled it. "We found Millicent's stone," she said instead. "The Crow's Heart."

Uncle Donny's whole body relaxed with a shudder. "Where did you find it?"

"In the maze outside the Manor House. Millicent still wore it. She was hidden by a spell. Actually, I used your spell, the one you cast in the bell tower, the 'show me her last moments' spell and we found her."

"What, alive?"

Tracey shook her head.

"Of course. Oh, that's rather sad," her uncle said. "So much time has passed. She'd be ancient if she was still — oh wait, my spell worked?" He sat up straight, his eyes widening. "What did you see? You saw her death?"

"It was an accident. She was asthmatic or maybe had some other breathing problem and that led to a seizure. She was out of breath and fell. She died after she hit her head on some concrete."

"And no one buried her?"

"No one could find her. There was a spell on the maze that hid her body."

Uncle Donny held out his hands and clenched his fingers in a *"gimme"* motion. "Show me?"

She jerked her head back and twisted slowly, staring between the gap in the seats at Jonny. He had fallen back asleep and his mouth hung open, like Dave's. He breathed out little snorts.

Uncle Donny's eyes narrowed. His sharp gaze darted from Jonny to Tracey back to Jonny and back to Tracey again.

She nodded.

"Jonny?" he mouthed. Tracey nodded. Uncle Donny sucked in a deep breath, and rested his elbows on the arm rest. He placed his chin in his hands.

"Uncle Donny?"

"I'm processing."

She watched him in silence. After a moment he shook his head. "Can he take it off?"

This was what she had hoped he wouldn't ask. She held her uncle's stare and lied right to his face. "No." Inside Tracey's head, Timothy roared with laughter.

Uncle Donny sighed. "That's unfortunate. I suppose it is to be expected. Okay, so you have three stones."

Tracey's head pounded with one word. *Four. Four. Four. Four.* She shot him a tight smile. "How do we find the next one?"

"Back to basics, Tracey. We gather all of the information we have and search for clues. It will be a painstakingly slow process and will probably involve a lot of dusty research and analytics. We need to look at the problem like we would a cold case. Treat it as though all of the previous evidence was destroyed. In the meantime, you keep training. You're meeting your new handler, ahem, M-force liaison in a few days, correct?" Tracey nodded. "She might have some ideas on how to proceed."

"And we just go back to school?" Tracey grumbled. "Pretend everything is normal?"

"Yep."

She let out a huge sigh. "Sounds boring."

Uncle Donny's eyes flashed. "Oh no, you've done it now."

"Done what?"

"Tempted fate."

Tracey rubbed her face with one hand. "That's silly, Uncle Donny."

"Is it? Industries all around the world will tell you, anecdotally, that whenever someone says it will be quiet, it will be anything but quiet. The ambulance service for example. Retail is another."

Tracey rolled her eyes. "It won't be that bad."

"Oh dear," he said again.

Tracey snorted.

Her uncle laughed softly. "Go and get some sleep. We'll be back home soon and in a few days we'll meet up at the office to brainstorm our next moves. We will get all of our cards on the table … or well, whiteboard."

Tracey stood up. Her hand drifted to cover the stones beneath her shirt. "Sure. All of our cards on the table."

Your creation of these fantastical myths and the tales contained therein of extraordinary abilities are as entertaining as they are exciting. I do hope your manuscript will be a success.

4

The airport was near empty when they landed in the early hours of the morning. Tracey blearily blinked under the bright lights and stumbled along behind her family and friends. Her thoughts were slow and plodding, just like her feet. Janitors wiped over every surface with strong smelling chemical sanitizers which didn't help her lack-of-sleep headache. Tracey's mom waved happily as she spotted her husband and the takeaway coffee he held for her. A few other people stood nearby waiting for their friends or family, holding up signs and squealing in delight when they caught sight of them.

"Thanks for picking us up, hon." Tracey's parents shared a brief kiss and Mom took the coffee from his hand with a happy moan. Tracey turned on her phone, checking for messages. Nothing. Maybe Damian hadn't seen her text? She sent a quick, `We've landed`, but there was no response.

"Hey kids. I hear it's been an eventful trip," Dad said smiling over at Sarah and Tracey.

Both girls nodded.

Tony's parents stood near the ceiling-high windows and greeted Tony with a warm hug. Laura's dad picked Laura up in a big embrace and he swung her around. She laughed as his lips smacked her cheek with a loud, *"Muah!"*

"I'll grab an Uber and take Dave home," Uncle Donny called. "Anyone want to come with us?"

"Yes, Donald. We'll come with you." Martha herded Jonny toward Dave. "Tsee is working the early shift at the hospital. We have to make our own way home. This is a better offer than the bus!" Jonny flicked his hand in a sad wave at Jilly, his shoulders slumping as he trailed after Dave, dragging his and his mom's bag behind him.

Jilly stopped next to Tracey. "My mom should be close. You do not need to wait with me."

"Nonsense, Jilly. Of course we'll wait," Tracey's mom said.

Tracey and Jilly waved goodbye to Tony and his family. Tony mimed phoning Tracey later with his hands. She nodded. Jilly's feet shuffled back and forth beside Tracey's emerald wheelie bag. "Did you sleep much?" Tracey asked.

"A little. I was listening to an audio book most of the time. Honestly, Tracey, your family does not need to stay here for me."

"My mom is not going to let you wait on your own. It's fine." Tracey smiled but Jilly didn't. "What's wrong?"

"My mother knows who you are. She is aware you are a stone Protector."

Tracey's mouth dampened. She swallowed and shoved her hands into her pockets. "Is that bad?"

"Please do not be offended by anything she might say. She is not used to people remembering us. She is … still adjusting."

"Okay." Tracey followed Jilly away from the windows to a strip of cold metal seats. They wheeled their suitcases along behind them. Tracey's mom and grandma stood close by, explaining to Dad all about the trip home. Sarah cut in several times, adding details they missed that she deemed important.

"Your mom is a powerful mage-kind, isn't she? I remember you said that," Tracey said to Jilly.

"Yes. Rated Significant, like your grandma. She spent many years searching for the Tiger's Eye with no success."

"You never said if she was happy that you found it."

"I don't really know. She is normally quiet — always watching and listening. It is her superpower. She has amazingly sharp hearing. I *think* she is happy, though she would never come right out and say it."

Tracey fiddled with her suitcase's wheelie handle, pushing it closed and pulling it open again. "It must be odd to her, to your whole family, now that you are remembered."

"It is. I desired for it for so long, and then after it happened …" Jilly turned to stare out through the window. They watched passengers shove their bags into open car doors and trunks before the cabs screeched away one after another. "Tracey, I have always felt I was special, you know? No one knew who I was. If I could break the curse and rescue my family name then everything would change, be better somehow. I dreamed that I would be the one to find the Tiger's Eye and break the forgetting curse. I felt destined for — it's odd to say — but …" A boarding announcement blared over the speakers above their heads. They flinched at the loud sound. Jilly's gaze drifted to a squealing family hugging happily. "I felt destined for greatness if only the curse could be broken. I was desperate for a "normal" life. And then … it happened. We broke the curse and I got the life I'd always wanted. And honestly? It is a little boring."

Tracey laughed. Jilly's eyes widened. Tracey shook her head and waved her hands around. "Sorry, no. I didn't mean to laugh at what you said it's just, I mean *'normal?'* We were chased around the UK by giant clay monsters. What's normal about that?"

"That is not what I meant." Jilly grinned. "I mean — oh, it is hard to explain — things like homework and shopping and friends. I wanted it all for so long. Now, I realize my life is not that different to what it was before."

"Apart from not having to introduce yourself to everyone each day?" Tracey said.

Jilly's face flushed. "Yes. I suppose that's true."

"Things will settle down. Once the other stones are found and we break the curse on them everything will be boring again." Tracey's eyes grazed the ceiling as she stared hard at the rafters. "I should tell you … I, ah, I told Uncle Donny about Jonny. He promised he won't tell anyone else."

Jilly's face pinched with unhappiness. She nibbled her bottom lip. "I thought we were to keep the Crow's Heart a secret?"

"We are. It's just I think we're going to need Uncle Donny's help to find the next stone and as a detective he needs all the data we have."

Except that he doesn't know everything. Does he, Tracey? Timothy's sarcastic voice made Tracey twitch.

"Jilly!"

Both girls' heads snapped up at the soft call. A stunning woman dressed in a lavender suit wearing super high crimson pumps strode toward them.

Tracey would have known Jilly's mom was a Significant even if Jilly hadn't already warned her. Her skin buzzed from the woman's mere presence despite her inner closet door remaining closed over her magic. The woman was electrifying.

"Mother." Jilly pressed a gentle kiss on her mom's cheek. "Thank you for coming to fetch me." Jilly turned to Tracey's mom and grandma. "Thank you for waiting." She gripped her wheelie suitcase handle and tugged her mother away.

Mrs. Cho stopped and turned back, staring intently at Tracey. Tracey felt the touch like a prickle over her skin. Jilly wavered on uncertain feet. "Come on, Mother. We should go."

"You are Tracey?" Mrs. Cho asked.

Gulping, Tracey nodded. "Yes ma'am."

The woman's long black hair swung like a pendulum as she strode forward on those ridiculously high heels. She stopped an inch away, her eyes fixed on Tracey's face. Tracey wondered what she was looking for and wished she was a little less wrinkled and travel tired.

"Mother, come on. We should get going," Jilly tried again.

Mrs. Cho didn't move, her face remained still and as smooth as marble. Tracey shuffled awkwardly on her feet, unsure of what she should do. She spotted her mom approaching and relaxed. Mom would know what to do. Mrs. Cho tugged Tracey forward and embraced her tightly. "Thank you."

After a split second of shock, Tracey returned the embrace patting the woman awkwardly on the shoulder. Her body was all sharp angles and smelled of strawberries.

Mrs. Cho pulled back as suddenly as she lurched forward, nodded sharply, and turned a sharp one-eighty. "Daughter, come." She strode away with sharp click-clacking sounds. Jilly sighed. She shrugged her shoulders at Tracey, her cheeks brightly flushed and raced after her mother.

Tracey caught her mom's eye.

"Well." Mom chuckled, shaking her head. "Come on, let's go home."

They decided on a lazy Sunday. Tracey napped as soon as she got home and no one in the family woke her. Apparently, they all wanted a quiet day.

Tracey dragged herself out of bed just before midday and pulled on her ancient. Threadbare. flamingo-pink robe. It was too short for her arms. She found her slippers under her bed and stumbled into the kitchen for food. Sarah eventually emerged from her cotton cocoon, hair a tangled mess, and found Tracey pouting down at her soggy cereal.

"What's wrong?" Sarah asked.

"Too sleepy. I made it but I got distracted by my phone and now it's gross."

"L-O-L," Sarah said. She grabbed a mug and the milk carton from the fridge. "Want hot chocolate?"

"Ooooo yeah," Tracey said, a grin running ear-to-ear. It died quickly. Her phone lay beside her hand. There was still no message from Damian. She refused to worry. Much. Maybe his mom stopped him from messaging? She texted him again just in case. **Hey, how are you? Did you** see my texts? How was your flight back? She stared at the silent phone, willing it to beep with a return message.

Sarah grabbed a second mug and the cocoa, spooning way too much of the mixture into each mug — the way they both loved. Mom appeared as Tracey yawned into her empty bowl. "Ugh. Jet lag is the worst. Good thing it's the weekend, right girls?"

"Where's Dad?" Sarah asked.

"Took the boys out to let us sleep. What are you planning to do today?"

Tracey shrugged and then raised her eyebrows at Sarah. "Wanna go to the mall?"

Sarah brightened. "Sure. As long as we don't have to walk."

"I'm doing laundry so you might as well pop out." Mom sighed and pulled a sad face at Tracey and Sarah.

"Do you want to come with us?" Tracey asked.

"Gosh yes," Mom said making them laugh. "But, I'm the grown up so I have to do the laundry. Still, how about I drop you off? I'll grab a coffee and come back."

Tracey pushed to her feet and let out a giant yawn. "I'll go get dressed."

I hesitate to write the advice I now offer as I am unsure of how you will take it.

5

Not long after, Mom parked her car outside their favorite coffee shop on Main Street. "I'll be back. I want a drink too," Sarah said following Mom inside.

"I'll go look at the books. Come get me," Tracey shouted, pointing to the bookshop in the distance. Sarah waved and Tracey headed down Main Street alone, shoving her cell phone into her back pocket. The last song they listened to before Mom flipped the car engine off bounced around inside her heard. She hummed and bopped along to it as she walked.

The sun was out despite the cooler air and it warmed her face as she glanced into window displays marveling at how different her hometown felt after their overseas trip. Everything was brighter, slower, and a little kitschy, a bit like a rom-com movie. She walked past boutique clothing stores, touristy new age knick-knack gift shops, and the Miltern Falls confectionary. The magic stones under her shirt buzzed softly. Tracey stopped dead in the middle of the sidewalk. A soft curse and a grumble erupted behind her as a figure walking past swerved to go around her. She pressed her hand to her neckline. The Butterfly Stone only buzzed if magic was being used nearby. She couldn't see anything out of the ordinary. A few shoppers with green lit bracelets wandered the streets, peering through shop windows as Tracey was doing, or stood chatting with each other, crowding the sidewalk. A pretty typical Sunday morning.

But Tracey's skin itched.

She couldn't pinpoint where the "not right" feeling was coming from or what it warned her against. Narrowing her eyes against the glare of the sun, Tracey tried to figure it out. Was it just her imagination? In the distance, a cackling laugh echoed down Main Street. It didn't get any louder but it also didn't fade away. Someone was certainly having a good day. Tracey huffed out a breath and shrugged. Weird.

Turning right, she headed toward the bookstore. A car thundered past, splashing dirty puddle water all over Tracey's shoes and soaking her socks. She darted back, letting out a screech of horror and surprise. Her face heated as nearby shoppers laughed, catching sight of her plight. She threw up her hands. "Oh, come on!" What caused that puddle to form? The sun was out and she was sure it hadn't rained this morning.

There were no other visible puddles in the street. Just that one right in the absolute worst spot ever. She jumped back further as a second car drove past a fraction too fast, sending up another drenching dirty wave.

"Ugh, gross!" Cold brown water stained her lime green socks. She imagined she could hear her toes squelching as she scrunched them inside her soaking wet trainers. The laugh in her head sounded louder now and younger. It wasn't Timothy. *Are they laughing at me?* If the water was some kind of practical joke she literally walked right into, she would be furious.

Tracey spun on the spot, searching for the culprit. *Oh, I need to take off my shoes and socks!* She hunted for a seat, but every street-side seat was full, even the ones up near the joint double door entrance to the council building and the library. Tracey hobbled closer. *That's odd.* The council office doors were open. Unusual for a Sunday morning. Still, the timing was perfect. She could sneak inside and go to the bathroom to dry her feet.

The council building was a three-story, imposing, white-painted building. Tracey climbed the steps and entered the dark marble foyer. To her left was the library, to her right the council chambers and the desk where people went to pay fines. The only time she had ever been on that side was when her dad got that parking fine. He had been so mad at himself and his mood tainted the whole experience. Hopefully, there would be paper towels in the bathroom she could use to dry her feet. If she hid in a bathroom stall, she could even use her magic to heat her shoes and dry them out.

"Hello?" she called out. "Is anyone here?" Her squelchy footfalls echoed on the tiled floor. She spotted the sign pointing to the bathrooms down the corridor between the council offices and the library, and pushed open the single swing door. It was a long room with an exit at either end. Shutting the door of the first toilet stall she slipped off her shoes and socks and whispered her heating spell, holding her silvery glowing hands over the damp items until they dried. She glared at the silver sheen. Her magic used to glow with golden warmth, but since taking hold of the Serpent's Kiss her magic was this unusual shiny silver color. She hoped it wasn't a bad change.

The vibration of her necklaces buzzed aggressively beneath her black superhero t-shirt. Her gaze sprang to the closed stall door. "Hello? Is someone out there?"

Greeny-gray, foggy smoke seeped in beneath her stall door. It smelt icky, like a gas station that had dead rats in the ceiling. Tracey grabbed her shoes in one hand and her socks in the other and backed toward the toilet, not wanting the smoke to touch her. *What the …?* Her instincts screamed to get away from it. She leaned over the fog and popped the stall door open, jumping the foggy tendrils that were drifting closer over the stall floor. She stood in the outer bathroom near the sinks gasping softly in the cool air. Her heart pounded faster as the smokey fog gave off a slight hissing sound and grew thicker, like someone had switched on a theater smoke machine and pressed it right against the bathroom entrance door. The fog crept further into the bathroom, surrounding all of the stall doors, and inched toward the mirrors and sinks, seemingly headed straight for Tracey's feet. *It's like it's … coming after me.*

Tracey shuffled back until her spine pressed up against the exit door on the opposite end of the bathroom. This exit would take her to the council offices. With luck, no one would see her and she could sneak back to the foyer and make her getaway. Tracey shoved her socks into her pocket and jammed her feet into her shoes, eyeing the fog crawling ever closer. Before it could brush the tips of her laces, Tracey tugged open the door and pulled it shut behind her. *That will stop it.* As she watched, the green fog seeped beneath the door in a whisper-thin stream. *Fruit tingles!*

Tracey raced down the unfamiliar hallway and reached a crossroad. *Crud. Which direction is the foyer?* The fog swept along behind her in a thick roiling cloud. *This is crazy!* Gray marble stairs rose up in front of her and she ran up them as fast as she could. The fog licked at her heels as she pushed open the door at the top of the stairs and tugged it shut behind her. The slow release on the door pulled against her hands. Fog slipped through the gap while she pulled and tugged on the handle. It flowed in tendrils, stretching out to try and snake around her ankles. She hoped back, jumping over it like a weird ghostly skipping rope. *What do I do now?*

As if suddenly sick of this keeping's off game, the ends of the fog tendrils formed hands and zoomed toward her. Tracey shrieked and raised her shield bubble against it. The fog hands flowed straight through her protection as if it wasn't there. Tracey ducked the long reach and dragged her shield closer to her body, projecting magically, electrified hands of her own, using them to slap away the fog hands. There was a spark when her magic connected with the strange substance. The fog sizzled and Tracey's magically formed hands dissolved in silver sparkles. She ducked again as the fog hands snapped out once more. She pushed her weight against the glacially closing door and heard a cry. The fog pulled back sharply as the door slammed shut. Tracey panted and sank against the wood. *What the heck was that?*

"Can I help you?" A snotty, posh voice boomed from another set of stairs to her right. About halfway up stood a round man who looked about her uncle's age. He had thinning, muddy brown hair and a double chin. Sharp gray eyes stabbed into her, raising the hairs along her neck and down her arms.

"No. I'm sorry," she said. There was no one else around and her voice echoed in the cold dimly lit hallway.

"Are you feeling well, young lady? You seem rather out of breath." The man ran a hand over his green tie to straighten it. The pattern was like the skin of a dinosaur and there was a picture at the bottom. Tracey couldn't make out what it was from this distance. He tucked the tie neatly beneath his suit jacket.

"I'm okay." She sank to the ground and clutched her knees. "There was a fog."

His brow furrowed. "A fog?"

"It tried to grab me."

"The fog tried to grab *you*?" The man's bushy eyebrows rose. "Let me call someone to come and get you. Can I fetch you a glass of water?"

Tracey pushed to her feet. "I'm fine. Really." The dim darkness of the hallway was exacerbated by the black floor tiles and gray wall paint. There was no sign of the fog.

Did I just imagine it? "I have to go," she muttered and popped open her inner closet door to let her magic out. She drew it down her arms and gathered it into her hands. The silvery glow around her fingertips grew stronger. If she threw her search spell up into the air it would tell her if the fog was lurking nearby. Her spell fizzled out as soon as she launched it. She tried again. And, again, her magic failed.

"Young lady, what are you doing?"

Tracey's eyes popped wide as she realized she was using magic in a public place. A council building would be spelled against Mage-kind magic. She dropped her hands. "Ah, nothing. Sorry." Mom would kill her if she got caught using magic in public.

The man's gaze dropped to the Mage-kind identification bracelet dangling from her wrist. They darted back up to meet her eyes and his head rose. "You should move along now, young lady. The council chamber is closed."

"Yes, sorry." Tracey turned left and moved rapidly to the end of the hallway following the exit signs hanging from the ceiling. Her gaze swung in every direction searching for any sign of the creepy green fog. The man followed, as if making sure she did actually leave. The hallway turned a corner and Tracey found herself standing at the mouth of the stairs leading down to the entrance foyer. The double ornate doors were shut. Tracey ran down the stairs and tugged on the left side door handle. The door didn't budge. She repositioned her fingers and pulled again. "It's stuck," she called.

"Hmmmm. Let me assist you." The suited man approached and Tracey backed up, wondering why she still wanted to run. "Let's see here." He gripped the handle and Tracey spied a thick wristband with a green light in the center.

"You're Mage-kind?" she blurted.

His stare returned to her face. "You sound surprised."

"I am. I didn't think we could go into politics."

He smiled. The expression gave her the willies though there was nothing actually wrong with it. His teeth were white and perfectly straight. "Perhaps I am a janitor."

He is not telling you the truth. Be careful, Timothy whispered.

Tracey laughed. "Not in that suit you're not."

"What is your name?"

"Tracey Masters."

"Masters? You are quite an observant young lady."

Tracey bit her lip. 'Young lady' didn't sound like a compliment the way he said it. "Who are you?"

"Your mayor."

Her face flushed. "Oh-em-gee. I should have known that, shouldn't I?"

He hummed. "Indeed." Tightening his grip around the door handle he gritted his teeth and pulled. The door creaked and swung open. The mayor ran his hands over his jacket to straighten it and tugged his tie back into place. Tracey spied a thick gold chain around the mayor's neck before the tie tug pulled his collar up over it. "Miss Masters, I do hope you will return another day and learn about your civic duties."

"Ah, sure." Tracey peeked around the edge of the open door. There was no sign of the fog. She put the snarky mayor out of her mind and jogged down the outside steps of the council building. She needed to find her mom and sister. *What was that weird fog about?* She recalled hearing laughter when she got splashed earlier and wondered if it had all been part of the same horrible prank.

The fog tried to grab her. She was sure of it. After a moment Tracey shook herself to get rid of the memory. *What a horrible morning.*

I do not think you should insist these tales are true.

6

Tracey bolted upright in bed, wondering what woke her. For a moment she sat still, holding her breath and listened to the silence. *Vrrrr Vrrr.* That was her cell phone vibrating on the charging pad outside her bedroom door. *Damian?* She jumped out of bed knowing she had to grab it before the sound woke her dad. Though he would be even madder if he knew she was about to bring her phone inside her bedroom. She cracked open her door, grabbed the noisy device and ducked back inside. Her hopes fell as she touched the display screen. *Jonny?* What was he doing calling at this time of night?

Jumping back onto her bed, she wrapped her comforter around her shoulders and tucked her feet under her butt. "Jonny, what's wrong? It's nearly midnight. We have school in the morning," she said.

"Hello, Tracey."

The words and the tone alerted her to who was *actually* calling. "Millicent?"

"Yes."

"Why are you calling me so late?"

"You have it, don't you?"

Tracey's heart gave off a weird *thump thump*. "I don't ... what are you talking about?"

"I know you have it."

"Have what?" Tracey stared at the darkened walls of her bedroom. *How can she possibly know?*

"He is dangerous, Tracey. You must not listen to him."

"Millicent, I —" Somehow the spirit inside the Crow's Heart knew Tracey held the Serpent's Kiss. She tried playing dumb. "Who?"

The snark in Millicent's voice said she failed. "He will try to twist your mind, Tracey. You must get rid of it."

Don't listen to her, Timothy whispered.

Tracey rubbed her forehead feeling a headache blooming behind her eyes. "I can't take it off," she reminded the other woman, then bit her tongue. Fruit tingles. Her words confirmed Millicent was right.

"He knows the location of the other stones."

That is not true, Tracey, Timothy said into her ear. *I want to help you find them.*

Tracey ignored him and spoke to Millicent. "How do you know?"

"You must stop him from finding them."

This was maddening. Why couldn't Millicent just tell Tracey what she knew and not be so darned cryptic about everything? "How do you know?" she repeated.

"I have Seen it."

Tracey swallowed hard, her throat closed up. "Am I going to die?"

"To stop what is coming you must learn about the Dreaming."

Dreaming again. "How do I do that? Dreamers are a myth. A story told to children to make them think they are all special."

"Learn about the Dreaming, Tracey. Find him."

"Find who?"

Millicent's voice faded. "The Trickster." The call disconnected.

"Millicent? Jonny?" Tracey stared at the dark cell phone. *Who the heck is the Trickster?*

I am afraid they will only publish them as a fantastical tale of fiction.

7

Returning to school was a little like that part in a video game where the player is forced to wait for the next scene to load and plays a scene that could not be skipped. She had to be patient and let it play. The first day at school after their holiday — which did not feel at all like a holiday — was like stepping back in time. A long, boring day of teachers, schoolwork, and tests. She had wanted to speak to Damian and find out why he was ghosting her, but she didn't see him. The only highlight was lunchtime.

Tracey and her friends huddled around their usual table whispering guesses and suggestions about the remaining stones. Around them the usual noises of the lunchroom ebbed and flowed as students came and went. Meatball Monday was always a wild affair.

Jonny seemed unaware of his nocturnal call to Tracey. He yawned throughout their conversation and she felt bad not telling him what had happened. If he knew Millicent possessed him at night, he would freak out. It was better that he didn't know. That way if Millicent needed to talk to Tracey again, she could. It was only a little secret she was keeping. Jonny ducked his head as a meatball splattered the wall behind him and the room erupted in laughter.

Tracey groaned loudly. "Oh, here we go." They all ducked under the table to avoid the worst of the coming splatter. Jonny cradled his bowler hat close to his purple shirt.

"I swear if they hit me someone is going to die." Laura promised. "This shirt is new." Tracey told Laura when she saw her that morning how gorgeous the fuchsia and sunshine yellow tie-dyed shirt looked with her white jeans. Tony's blue polo and Tracey's multi-sided dice gray shirt wouldn't look good with meatball stains either. Shouts and squeals filled the air. Carla screamed. A chant began — *"Meatball Monday madness!"* — as projectiles went flying. The food fight halted as quickly as it began with the sudden appearance of three teachers. Dave One was marched from the hall to the sound of jeers and loud clapping. They climbed out from under the table, moaning aggressively.

"Ugh meatheads," Tony said.

"Ha!" Jonny high-fived Tony, who reluctantly gave up his hand.

"Does anyone else feel that being in London was nothing more than a weird dream?" Laura asked changing the subject.

Tracey agreed. "School seems more unreal than running from mumbles or finding Millicent's body in a garden maze." Someone chuckled close by. Tracey peered around trying to spot who was listening in to their conversation but couldn't see anyone.

"Tracey?" Laura asked. Her gaze was fixed on Tracey's face. She peered in the same direction as Tracey as if trying to see what caught her attention. Meena held court at her table near the door and Carla cackled like the mad witch she was beside her. Meena's sharp, knowing gaze caught Tracey watching and she scowled. Tracey turned away.

"A laugh," Tracey mumbled.

Laura's nose crinkled. "Carla?"

"No. A boy. I've heard it before," Tracey insisted. The bell rang dragging a groan out of them all. "Let's go," Tracey said to her friends. As she stepped from the hall she shot one last look around. The meat-sauce-stained hall emptied quickly. She didn't hear the laugh again.

Tracey got home from school tired and grumpy. As she walked in through the front door her shoulders relaxed and she tossed her school bag into the entry hall. "Mom?" The hairs on her skin stood straight up. She froze and opened her core, throwing out her search spell. It buzzed wildly. Whatever set off her magic radar, it was coming from the next room.

"In the kitchen, honey," Grandma called.

Even though Grandma sounded calm, Tracey drew more of her magic from her imaginary closet and expanded a bubble around her body as a shield before she stepped cautiously in through the doorway. A strange woman sat at the table talking to Grandma. Prince Henry stood at the bench and turned, smiling at her entrance. "Tracey."

"Prince Henry?" Tracey dropped her bubble shield as a grin spread across her lips.

"I'm here a little sooner than I expected. Apologies for the lack of notice but I wanted to introduce you to my friend as soon as possible." His face was wrinkle-free and the shadows under his eyes were lighter than the last time she saw him. Not gone, but less inky and puffy. The gray suit and emerald button-down fit him like a glove. He looked as handsome as ever. Tracey's cheeks pinked. *Ha! Yeah, as if Prince Henry would ever be seen pale and dressed in ill-fitting clothing unless it was on purpose for an acting role.*

Tracey turned her attention to the unknown woman at the table who stood up at Tracey's entrance. Her body was a boxy shape with short, slightly wavy auburn hair and a great big warm smile. Her outfit was classy and rich looking, silky and shiny; a flowing, flower-printed, wide-sleeved shirt, and fitted blue trousers with green trainers. Tracey bit back a smile at the youthful footwear. This must be the new agent.

"Hello, Tracey. As usual, Hank is not exactly a gentleman when it comes to introductions. My name is Lucinda Epworth, but you can call me Loo Loo."

Tracey grinned. Loo Loo? She had a feeling she was going to like this new agent. "Sure."

Prince Henry laughed. "Loo, I was getting to it."

"And as always you take too long, you stuffy royal git. Now, get off with you and let me chat with Tracey here." She waved her arms widely as if shooing him away.

Prince Henry threw up his hands. "Okay, okay. I know when I'm not wanted. Tracey, Loo Loo will take good care of you. I trust her completely. But if you need to, you can call me anytime. Do you understand?"

Tracey nodded. "Sure."

With a final wave, Prince Henry left and Tracey turned her full attention to Agent Loo Loo.

"Hank has briefed me on everything that has happened and of course I've requested Malden's case files. They'll arrive in a day or two. But Tracey, I'd really like your view on it all. So, if you have time, please tell me everything you can about the Stones of Power and your investigation to date."

Tracey raised her eyebrows. "Everything?"

"Everything."

It took almost two hours. Tracey spoke fast, pausing to suck in great gulps of air every time she had to backtrack when she remembered events she had forgotten. Agent Loo Loo didn't interrupt once. She drank her tea and then the coffee Grandma made. She snacked on all the cookies Tracey's mom put down in front of them and let Tracey blurt out her story. Grandma stayed quiet, cradling her tea cup when it was empty. Mom stood next to the bench. Tracey wondered why her mom wouldn't sit down. Agent Loo Loo hummed whenever Tracey apologized for forgetting the order of things, and just waited for her to start again. She nodded in all the right places and in general let Tracey talk. Tracey explained the whole story, from the search for the missing necklace and Miss Tearning's death through to finding the Butterfly Stone and the Tiger's Eye.

Tracey told Loo Loo about fighting off Timothy's various attacks and of Agent Malden's betrayal. Mom brought Tracey a soda and a glass of water as she kept talking, providing more cookies, then a slice of cake for Grandma and Agent Loo Loo. Tracey told Agent Loo Loo everything except for finding the Serpent's Kiss. That was one secret she planned to keep to herself. Prince Henry might trust Agent Loo Loo, but Tracey didn't. Not yet, anyway. Agent Malden's betrayal was still too fresh in her mind. For now, she also decided to keep the Crow's Heart a secret.

When she stopped talking, Agent Loo Loo smacked her lips together. "Well, that is a lot to digest. You are certainly a brave young lady. You *and* all of your friends. I'm impressed, and I'm not easily impressed. Hank told me his version of this story and I didn't see how he could possibly be right about you. I see he was holding back."

"What happens now?" Tracey asked.

"I need to think about that. You have just given me a lot of information, and I need to analyze it and work out what our next steps should be."

"Can I ask you about Agent Malden?"

"Tracey!" Mom said. Grandma shook her head but remained silent.

Agent Loo Loo lowered her empty teacup and leaned back in her chair. "What about him, dear?"

"What happened to him?"

Agent Loo Loo sucked in a slow breath. "I understand why you are asking, Tracey. But I'm afraid I can't tell you anything. I've been kept out of the loop on his questioning. I don't even think Hank knows anything."

"Did you know Agent Malden?"

The agent pursed her lips. She had nibbled off most of her lipstick along with all of the cookies. "I met him once or twice. I didn't know him very well. Certainly, you know him better than I do."

"I don't know him at all," Tracey denied. "He lied to me and tried to hurt my friends. I just want to know what's going to happen to him. If you hear anything, are you allowed to tell me?" Grandma's soft-skinned hand covered Tracey's fingers and she squeezed.

"Unless it's classified, yes of course. In fact, I'll ask my boss to keep me apprised of his case, all right?"

"Will that be all for today, agent?" Mom asked. She still stood behind the kitchen bench watching them all like a hungry wolf. "It's getting late and I'd like to get dinner started for the kids."

"Where is everyone? It's way too quiet in here," Tracey said. There was no sign or sound of her brothers or Sarah in the house.

"Dad took them to the park."

"I'm going to take a nap," Grandma said standing slowly. "My whole body is falling asleep." She grumbled a little more as she stood still for a moment, gripping the table top tightly, before she shuffled out. "Wake me for dinner."

"We're done for now." Agent Loo Loo pushed to her feet. She shook her legs to straighten her trousers. "I'd like to catch up with you in a few days at my office, Tracey. Well, when I say office, it's not set up yet. I only arrived a few days ago before I was briefed by Hank and, oh listen to me, prattling on. I'll head off now and message you in a few days." She handed Tracey a business card. It was simple white card stock with basic black lettering. On it was a cell phone number and an email address. "Call me whenever you need to, or just to talk. I'm a great listener."

Tracey nodded. "What about the next stone?"

"Do you have any clues about where the next one might be hiding? Somewhere we can start?"

Tracey shook her head. When she stood up, she realized she was only a little shorter than the agent.

"It's a shame you didn't find the one Hank was so sure was in the UK."

Tracey examined her shoes, not wanting Agent Loo Loo to see the guilt written on her face. "Yeah. Bummer."

"Still, I do think we have something. Let me gather my thoughts and what data I have. We'll have a big team meeting next week, how does that sound to you? Do you think your friends will want to join us?"

"They can?" Tracey blurted, her eyes darting up to look onto the agent's knowing gaze. A weight lifted off her shoulders.

"Of course they can. I'm sure they have all sorts of ideas and thoughts. We must use all of our resources, Tracey. That's always been my motto." She smiled broadly.

Be careful with her, Tracey. She is not a genial as she comes across. I can teach you a spell to prevent her from slipping into your mind. You may need it.

Tracey ignored Timothy's whisper. "What about my uncle?" she asked.

"Oh, Tracey." Mom sighed loudly.

Agent Loo Loo glanced at Tracey's mom, a questioning expression on her face. "He's a detective, isn't he? I'd be glad of his help."

"He'll be thrilled," Mom said dryly.

Agent Loo Loo shot Tracey a one-raised-eyebrow look. Tracey snorted. "I'll tell him."

"Great." Agent Loo Loo clapped her hands together. "I'll head off then. It's been a pleasure, Mrs. Masters. I'll see myself out." Agent Loo Loo headed back through the house toward the front door, her trainers squeaking loudly against the kitchen tiles.

Mom held her hand up until she heard the front door close with a loud click. "Well, honey. What do you think?"

"I like her," Tracey said helping her Mom clear the table.

"You liked Agent Malden too." Mom pulled the plates for dinner out of the cupboard and started the stove to boil a pot of water.

Tracey's phone beeped. "Sarah says Dad's stopping for ice-cream," she read out. "Awww. I want ice-cream."

Mom ruffled Tracey's hair. She spun around and turned off the stove. "Come on then. Let's join them. Just be careful, hon. Agent Epworth's charming folksy chatter could be just how she operates to get under your radar. An act to make people think she's lovely and nice so they open up to her. It could be a ruse, hiding the bear beneath. Remember, she *is* an M-force agent."

As I said, Timothy muttered.

Jonathan, perhaps, if you were to advise them of such, they would look at the pages again?

Sarah waved and walked off toward the lower school, her bag bouncing on her back with every step. Tracey waited, scuffing her feet, for her friends at the side gate entrance off Elm. Jonny appeared first, riding his electric bicycle. Today he wore loose, baggy, gray cargo pants and left his button down shirt open over a black tank top. The shirt was a fiery-red color, the same color as the band around his bowler hat. He coasted to a stop next to Tracey and dragged off his gold-rimmed glasses to rub his eyes, yawning loudly. "Hey, Tracey."

"Hi, Jonny. Did you forget to sleep last night? You look like a zombie."

"I dunno. I went to bed early and everything. I just don't feel like I'm getting any sleep." He put his glasses back on and pushed them higher up his nose to stare at her.

Tracey knew Millicent was behind Jonny's lack of sleep. *I should tell him.* "Is anything off about your room? Like stuff that's moved around and so on? Maybe you're sleep walking?"

"Ha! I'd love it if I could sleep-homework."

Tracey snorted. *Just tell him.* She bit her bottom lip and remained silent. At the bottom of the hill Tracey spotted Jilly and Laura crossing the road, heading toward them. That tiny, twingey ache in her stomach still wondered if Laura and Jilly were talking about her behind her back. She huffed. *Stop it, Tracey. They're your friends.* Tony's mom's car pulled up to the curb behind Laura. Tony climbed out with an overly stuffed schoolbag.

"Hey Tony," Tracey said when they were all close enough to hear her properly. "Hey Laura. Hey Jilly."

"Hey Trace." Tony groaned and hiked his bag higher up on his back.

"What have you got there, Tony?" Laura asked, pointing to his overflowing bag. A corner of a binder stuck out preventing him from zipping it closed. Laura upended the remainder of her coffee into her mouth in one long gulp then sadly shook the empty reusable cup.

"Research, my laptop, and a few print outs."

"A few?" Laura laughed at Jonny's groan.

Jilly slipped her hand inside Jonny's as they leaned over Tony's bag to investigate. "I made a folder for everyone," Tony said, removing five green binders from his bag and passing them out.

"You're giving us homework now?" Jonny whined.

"Cool colors," Laura interrupted before Jonny could rant further. She pushed Jonny's shoulder, reminding him to be nice.

"Aw, man," he muttered softly.

"So, Tracey. Have you heard from Damian?" Laura asked.

Tracey shrugged. "I messaged but he hasn't replied."

"I'm sure it's nothing."

"Yeah," Tracey sighed. His silence hurt her heart. She turned back to Tony. "Can't you just tell us what you found?"

She flicked through the file. A heap of reading was definitely in her future.

"I want you to read it for yourselves and tell me what you think. I need to know if what I think I'm seeing is something that is actually there or not."

"That is good reasoning, Tony." Jilly shot them all a quelling look. It was like she knew exactly what Tracey and Jonny were thinking.

Jonny sighed epically loud and dragged his bag off his shoulder. He stuffed the folder inside.

"Where did you find all of this stuff?" Laura asked.

"A lot of it came from Noel."

Laura's lips pursed. She pressed her face close to Tracey's and they both cooed. "Oh, is he still emailing you?"

"Yeah." Tony's cheeks pinked at their collective *ooos* and *ahhhs*. "He's been searching through books from the archive and the ones in his dad's office."

"What did he find?" Tracey asked. She lifted the folder lid like she was about to unearth a spider and eyed the mountain of pages clipped inside. *Ugh.* She did not want to read all of this. Why weren't there Cliff's Notes?

Tony pointed to the binder. Tracey groaned, echoing Jonny.

"What about you, Tracey? Did you find anything else in Millicent's secret diary?" Tony asked.

She glanced away. "I haven't finished it yet." Disappointed looks surrounded her. "Fine, I'll read more tonight." At the knowing looks she whined. "I will."

"Have you done the stone search spell yet?" Jonny asked.

"Oh, I'm an idiot. I should have tried that as soon as I got home." She peered around suspiciously. "We don't have time to do it now and it's too out in the open here. I'll do it tonight. Besides, I have other things to tell you. I was chased by evil green fog yesterday." That got a loud reaction from her friends. "Before you ask —" she jumped in "— I have no idea what it was, or what it wanted."

"The Butterfly Stone, obviously," Jonny said.

"So, what happened, Trace?" Laura asked.

Tracey zipped her bag closed. "I ran away from it and hid in the council building — the one attached to the library."

"Aren't we going there next week with our civics class?" Jonny asked. He hefted his bag onto his shoulder and moaned dramatically at the additional weight.

"Oh, yeah. Ugh. Great. I hope we don't see the mayor. I don't think he likes me," Tracey told them.

"What happened with the fog?" Tony asked. He zipped his bag back up and threw its much lighter weight over his shoulders.

"It just went away. It was probably nothing," she said. In the distance, the school bell rang. "Oh crumbs," Jonny shouted. Tracey shouldered her schoolbag and ran after her friends toward the closest school building. Halfway down the hill she tripped and hit the ground hard.

Laura waited as she climbed to her feet. "What did you trip over?"

There was nothing on the path. "My own feet?" she offered.

A hideous laugh reached Tracey's ears. She peered around searching for it, but there was no one there.

"Come on, Trace. We're going to be late."

"Coming," she called and raced Laura the rest of the way to school.

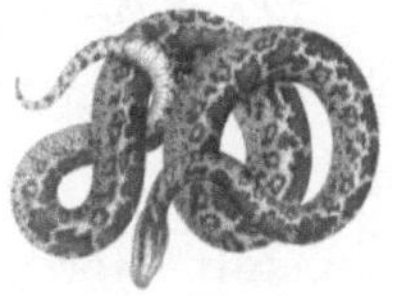

Tracey laughed when Tony slipped Dave his binder. The look on his face as they entered Mr. Rachette's classroom sustained her all the way through the morning. If there was anyone who hated homework more than herself and Jonny, it was Dave. He looked at Tony like he was reevaluating all of his life choices up until now.

Damian sat on the opposite side of the room. Tracey brightened at the sight of his cute face. At least she could ask him what was going on. All the seats around Damian were full. She sank down at an empty seat up the front and peered back. Damian wouldn't look at Tracey or otherwise acknowledge her, no matter how obvious she made her attempt at getting his attention. Mr. Rachette announced a pop quiz, sending up a range of moans. She didn't get a chance to go over to Damian and ask him what was wrong.

Tracey tapped her pen on the printout text page. Why had Damian sat there? He never sat on that side of the room. He must be angry about what happened in the UK. Wasn't he happy she saved his sister by removing the Serpent's Kiss? Perhaps it was his mom's influence? Mrs. Carter sure didn't like Tracey or her friends. She must have got into Damian's ear on the earlier plane trip home. Now that Tracey thought about it, Damian hadn't texted her back at all. *I really need to talk to him.* She pictured catching him at lunchtime and pulling him away from the door. *I'll ask what's wrong then I'll say I'm not mad his mom said he couldn't talk to me.*

A rotten egg smell drifted over the front desks. *OMG!* Tracey pulled her T-shirt neck up over her nose. Someone behind her snickered. A soft snort sounded and another student groaned. Which led to suppressed laughter. "Get on with the test," Mr. Rachette snapped silencing the room. After a moment Tracey peered over her shoulder. It had probably been Dave One. She searched for a red face, a dead giveaway to the culprit. She caught Meena's eye instead. The mean girl stared straight at her. Tracey met the look and held it. After everything she had gone through lately it was impossible to feel threatened by the fifteen-year old's glare. The proud and popular girl raised her chin, long black hair shining under the classroom lights.

Meena's lips twitched. *Ha! She flinched first.* Feeling vindicated, Tracey faced the front of the room again. *Wait. Had that been … a smile? From Meena?* Clearly since Tracey went to the UK the world had reversed direction or slipped into a mirror dimension or something. *Super weird.* A cold finger of worry slipped down Tracey's spine a moment later. *Oh. She's done something and is waiting for it to metaphorically explode. Told a story or taken a photo. Something she's going to share that will make me look stupid.* Tracey sighed and slumped in her chair. No doubt whatever little problem Meena schemed up would be exposed at lunchtime or after school or later in the week. Eventually, Tracey would discover what it was. There was no point stressing about it. She clenched her fingers around her test paper, crinkling the edges and told herself to get on with it.

She finished the quiz and knew she tanked it. Instead of reading over her answers, she stared off into the distance, eyes blurring the electronic whiteboard at the front of the room. Time seemed to stretch into forever, as it always did when she had better things to do. Her gaze was drawn time and again toward the door, mainly because she was trying *not* to look at Damian. She focused her thoughts on the binder in her bag. They drifted to the Crow's Heart around Jonny's neck and the Serpent's Kiss around her own. *Why is the Butterfly Stone so quiet?* Sneaky thoughts of Damian slunk into her mind while she was trying hard not to think about his soft lips or his deep brown eyes. Why was he sitting on the opposite side of the room? She forced her gaze to her test. Her mind wouldn't stop whirring. It was a relief when the bell rang.

Tracey plonked her lunch down on their usual table in the lunchroom and listened as Laura and Jonny speculated about the stones. Her mind and gaze drifted to the lone table at the back of the lunchroom where Damian sat on his own. *Why is he sitting all the way over there alone? Should I go over?*

Now that she could stare at him more freely, she realized his eyes were shadowed in a face paler than it used to be. She wondered if he was having problems sleeping, then wondered if thoughts of her had kept him awake, then wondered if that was a good thing or not. Even looking tired the handsome boy drew her gaze like no other. He might not want company. *I want to go over.* Tracey's head tilted as she stared at him and let out a soft soundless sigh.

"Tracey?"

"What?" she startled, head jerking at the tug to her sleeve. Laura grinned as her eyes flicked to Damian and back. Tracey's face burned. "Sorry? What did you say?"

"I asked if you had any ideas, but I don't think you were listening to us."

"Sorry." She sighed louder this time and more obviously. Laura looked like she wanted to ask questions, but Tracey didn't want to talk about it. She shook her head. Laura shrugged an "okay" but her eyes screwed up with her "we will talk about this later" look.

Tracey nodded.

"Sooooo," Jonny drawled, picking up on their silent conversation. "The fog?"

Tracey began again. "It was probably —"

"If you say nothing again I'm gonna shout at you. It's not normal. Getting chased by fog. It's gotta be about the stones," Jonny said.

"Yeah, I know but … there was this weird laugh," she said instead.

"Laugh?" Tony queried, wiping his hands after finishing his sandwich.

"Yes. Right after I stepped in that puddle."

"Only you, Tracey." Laura said hiding her smile behind the remains of her sandwich.

After peering around to check that all of the teachers had left. Jonny pushed his chair up onto its back legs. "Are you sure it wasn't just in your head?"

"Yes, I'm sure. I don't laugh inside my head without knowing about it," she snapped.

Tony pursed his lips. "But you do hear voices. Like Stephanie. Was it her?"

"No," Tracey didn't hesitate to say. "I heard it again this morning. Right after I tripped over …"

"Tripped?" Tony asked.

Laura waggled her fingers. "Over nothing."

Tracey had a sudden thought. Had it been Timothy laughing at her?

It wasn't, he said into her ear. The softness of his voice sent a shiver down her spine.

So, who was it? she asked silently. Timothy didn't answer. She imagined she could hear the laugh even now.

Wait.

She *could* hear it. "There it is again."

"What?" Jonny and Laura asked in unison.

"Tracey?" Tony asked.

Ignoring him, Tracey stood and spun around. The laughter grew louder. "Can't you hear that?"

"Is it Carla and Meena? Maybe they're up to something," Tony said, standing up and looking around too.

"They're not even here," Laura pointed out.

"I don't think —" Fruit juice splashed all over Tracey's head and neck. "What the —" she screeched, spinning around to get the culprit. Her hands rose, magic flooding out of her inner closet.

Tony slammed his fingers down on hers, pushing them away. "Trace, no."

A boy Tracey vaguely knew straightened his lunch tray. "Oh, I'm sorry. I tripped." His face was bright pink and he couldn't look her in the eyes.

Tracey stood in the middle of the lunchroom dripping red liquid. "Ewww," she grumbled and flicked her hands, now magicless, at her sides.

"What a horrible accident," Laura said, stifling a laugh. "Come on, Tracey. We'll dry you out in the bathroom. You'll need to wring out your shirt."

The boy scrambled away. Tracey couldn't see anything on the ground that could have caused his clumsiness. Unless it was his own feet. Steam built in her chest, her t-shirt neck grew too tight. Her eyes snapped to Meena's giant grin and then to Dave One. He pointed at her and he and his friends brayed like donkeys. The heat in Tracey's skin bloomed all the way down her back. If they had anything to do with this, she'd totally lose it. She slopped after Laura, doing her hardest to ignore the laughter of the teens in the lunchroom. Every stare and pointed finger prickled her skin. Inside her head, the wicked laugh faded.

Early one morning, a family
gathered in a field of giant stones.
The youngest daughter, Jane,
stood in the middle of the circle.

9

Racing to Uncle Donny's office after school, Tracey hoped he would be distracted so she could make a start on Tony's folder of information. *Come on, be honest. You're really just gonna sit there and stress about why Damian avoided you all day.* How could she ask Damian what was wrong if he stayed on the other side of the room and didn't reply to any of her messages?

When she pulled Tony's ginormous binder out of her bag, it was so heavy it thumped onto the desk and all of the pens in the cup rattled. Ignoring it for a moment, she logged into her computer and sent her uncle a text message to let him know she had arrived. She opened the binder. Ever organized, Tony's hand-decorated dividers split the insides into sections. There were photocopies of book pages under the first tab labeled *Unexplained Mage-kind Mysteries*. That sounded interesting. A fictional book or a collection of real stories? The second section looked like printed emails with Noel's email header. The third section was a bunch of official looking documents, old ones typed on an ancient typewriter — like the one Grandma kept in her tiny office at home. Tracey flicked past that section quickly — what little she read was a bunch of legal words and she bet the topics would be super boring. The last section were print outs from various websites. From the Norm internet browser, not the Mage-kind one. She could tell by the lack of an *M* watermark on the backgrounds or in the web address. There were a few copies of old newspaper articles too.

The phone on her desk trilled loudly, pulling her head up out of the folder.

Tracey answered it, her gaze springing to Uncle Donny's closed door. "Donald Masters' Detective Agency. How can I help you?"

"Tracey Masters?" The voice was that of a young man. He had a thick British accent, like the northern one her mom's favorite pair of television presenters spoke, only this guy spoke in a low rasp like he was trying to disguise his voice.

"Yes, who is this please?"

"I know what you have."

Tracey's eyes popped wide and she gripped the desk phone handset tight against her ear. "Excuse me?"

"Do yourself a favor. Get rid of it."

"Get rid of what?" Her gaze flicked to the app icon on her desktop computer, the one her uncle put there to record incoming calls. She pulled her hand from her chest where she covered the necklaces and reached for the mouse. She double clicked the app to start recording and grabbed her cell phone, typing out a quick message to her uncle.

`Creepy call. I'm recording it. Where are you?`

He replied quickly. `Be there soon, kiddo. Lock the doors.`

`Already done.`

While she was texting, the young man breathed heavily into the phone line. "I know you have it," he said at last, the words exploding out of him as if he had been fighting not to say anything at all.

"Have what?"

"It is nearly time."

Tracey's blood ran cold. "Time for what? I don't know what you're talking about. Who are you?"

"We'll meet soon, Tracey."

The call ended. *That was super creepy.* She was cold all over and shivered slightly in the overly warm office. She saved the file and emailed a copy to Tony. Her left hand still held the beeping handset. With a startled blink, she set the handset down in the cradle. Uncle Donny always said, "First impressions, kiddo. Get 'em down on paper as soon as you can." She grabbed the notepad from beside the phone and started writing. *Young, male, whispering — why? Scared or trying to disguise his voice?* With that accent it was practically impossible. Maybe he was making sure he couldn't be overheard by someone nearby?

He knew my name.

She underlined that twice and tapped the pen against her lips. He said, "I know you have it."

The stone? *But which one does he think I have?* Her fingers brushed over the stone necklaces under her shirt. She lifted the Butterfly Stone free of the fabric and wrapped her hand around it. "Stephanie?"

In a blink she was in the black place. Timothy stood opposite her in a spotlight of light, oozing charm and a faint reddish glow. "Hello, Tracey."

"Where's … I called for the Butterfly Stone. Why am I here?"

"You cannot contact it."

"Why?" she asked.

"Because I am here."

That was not good.

"What is it you wanted to ask?" he prompted.

Should she tell him about the unknown caller? Timothy said he would never lie to her, but he was the bad guy. Lying was what he did. It didn't matter how much of her life was he aware of, even if he listened in all the time, he would never tell her the truth about it. Despite telling her he would always tell her the truth. *Yeah, right.* He's the bad guy. Bag guys lie. "Someone knows about the stones. Someone I don't know," she said at last.

"Has it become common knowledge that you possess my stone?"

"A few people know about the Butterfly Stone and well, M-force, and the council do too, but no one knows about the Serpent's Kiss."

"Sounds like a lot of people know a little about something. Do they all have your confidence?"

She squinted. "What do you mean?"

"Do you trust your friends to keep your secret?"

Of course. "Um."

"Is anyone in your friend group likely to expose your secret? Perhaps someone you do not fully trust."

"I trust all my friends." *Well, there is Dave but he's proven to be trustworthy. Same with Noel.*

"What about the boy?"

"What boy — which one?"

"Your romantic crush."

Damian? "Oh, he won't —" Would he? No. Surely not but … he wasn't talking to her, and he *was* actively avoiding her. His mom knew about the stones, and she definitely hated Tracey. She dobbed them in to the council before. Who else would she be willing to tell?

"You must limit the number of people who know, Tracey."

She threw her hands up into the air. "Yeah, I get it. I didn't recognize the voice. It could have been anyone." She wished she could pace or even sit down. It was awful being stuck here in the black place. She couldn't see anything or walk around.

His lips quirked.

"Can you discover anything more about this boy?"

"Maybe," she muttered tapping her lips.

"Are you concerned?"

"Yeah, obviously. Some creepy guy names me directly and says he knows stuff about me? That's super freaky."

Timothy's head tilted. "Do you have personal protections in place?"

"Personal protections?"

"Spells. To prevent attacks and to call for help."

"Oh, yeah. I have an alert bracelet and my cell phone."

His chin pressed to his chest as he peered down his nose at her. "What about your mind, Tracey?"

"My mind?"

"Do you have protections in place to prevent a mind attack?" His words were slow, as if talking to a toddler.

"Do you think I should have?"

"I contact you — without encountering a barrier. You should consider erecting one."

That was actually a good idea. She knew how to push Stephanie from her mind now through trial and error, but it was difficult. She remembered Agent Striker forcing herself into Tracey's mind and that time she had seen Timothy's magic control Stephanie in that very first memory Vision Grandma showed her. Timothy was saying there was a way to block it out. "Show me."

"Use an actual image of the human brain. Your brain. Imagine you can see it inside your skull."

Tracey pictured a whole pink squishy floating brain.

"Raise your shield around it. Just like you do around your body during an attack."

Tracey raised her hands picturing her protective bubble around the imaginary brain. "Did it work?"

"Can you maintain it?"

"You're still here, shouldn't you disappear or something?" she asked.

"We are not inside your head, Tracey. You cannot block me when we are together in this place."

"Oh." She thought about what he said. "Holding my shield bubble up all the time is draining. I don't think I can keep a brain bubble up all the time too."

"You will have to practice. Thin it down so that it is transparent. You do not require a lot of energy to do this.

"Like this?" She thinned the bubble by imagining it as a soap bubble, thin and flimsy but shining with a rainbow of light.

"Very good." Timothy smiled as if he was proud of her achievement. Her stomach flip-flopped at the thought.

Tracey jerked back into reality, with familiar hands shaking her shoulders. "Tracey?"

Today would be the day she became
a witch — as powerful and as strong
as the rest of her family.

10

She peered up into her uncle's worried eyes and then around the empty office. "I'm back," she said, dizzy from the abrupt mental movement.

"I really hate it when you do that." He released her shoulders and slumped onto the faded ruby sofa, running his fingers through his wild curls. "What did Stephanie want?"

"Ah, nothing really," she said, tucking the Butterfly Stone away. "Are you okay?"

"Am I okay? Tracey, you took the call. Tell me about it. How are you feeling? What did the caller say, exactly?"

"I'm a bit shaky still. Hang on, I recorded it. Listen." She replayed the audio file.

Uncle Donny sat forward, arms braced on his knees, listening intently. When the call ended, he pressed back into the sofa. "That's certainly curious."

"He knew my name."

"Yes. And where you would be after school."

"I hadn't thought of that." Tracey clenched her fingers together and squeezed. The thought sent a crawling sensation over her skin. She shook her arms and legs to shake it off. "Bleh."

"I'll run a search to track the caller," Uncle Donny said and headed for his office.

"Oh, before you do, I was going to do the stone spell when I got here, but I was distracted."

Uncle Donny's steps froze. He spun on the spot, eyes lighting up. "Can I help?"

"Sure." She nearly laughed at how eager he was. Grinning, she opened the spell Tony emailed her weeks ago on her phone and got Uncle Donny to trace a salt circle in the middle of the office. He ran to flip the open sign to closed on the door. She grabbed a bottle of water from the fridge and the little container of dirt and candles from the storage cupboard. Uncle Donny pulled the blinds while Tracey plonked herself down in the middle of the circle and lit the fat, gold-decorated candle. She opened the water and the dirt container, and under her uncle's watch, she read out the spell. Colored lines sprouted from the stones on her chest. Red, green, blue, gold, black, and silver. The black and silver lines wrapped tight around her own body. She glanced up at Uncle Donny. *Fruit tingles.* "Can you see the lines?"

The black thread gave away that she wore the Serpent's Kiss. To her relief he shook his head.

"I can see threads," she said. "But …" Her voice trailed away as she followed the last two colors. The green and red threads — very thin and wispy — swirled in circles and then faded into nothing. The hopeful feeling warming Tracey's chest faded. She wanted to tear her hair out or blast something with her magic. *So annoying.* "It's got to be because we don't know anything about them yet, but the green and the red — oh um and the black one — just fade away." The circling threads were new, but she had no idea what that meant. "It's not working," she said deflating into her chair like a leaking balloon.

Uncle Donny frowned. "Right."

They cleaned up the spell makings. "Come on in here, kiddo. Let me show you what I've been working on." He paused to stare at her. "You are okay, aren't you?"

"Oh yeah. I'm fine," she insisted. She wasn't entirely sure that she was though. The unknown caller knew her name and where she worked. "What have you done?" she asked following him into his private office. Every empty space was taken up with large whiteboards. "Whoa!"

Notes covered most surfaces, written in her uncle's messy script. At the top of each whiteboard, he had written the stone name — if they knew it — and listed down all the details they knew about that stone. The whiteboard about the Butterfly Stone had the most written on it. Then the one on the Tiger's Eye. The information was divided into three segments. On the right-hand side of each whiteboard was a description of the stone, appearance, color, and so on. The middle section was all that they knew about the stone creator. On the left was how they found the stone and what clues they followed to get there. He included a description of who held it now, though Tracey noticed no names were written down. Obviously, her uncle didn't want to name them in case someone caught a glimpse of the whiteboards. She moved closer to read about the Crow's Heart. The first two segments of the Crow's Heart board was filled with text — the right side conspicuously blank.

The other two boards were blank though the segment lines were drawn. On each whiteboard was the name of

Stephanie's friends with a question mark and beneath that name the few points polka dotted down the board with what they knew about each person. Tracey went over to read them. "You found something?"

"A little. Some are details Hank found and some … came from Agent Malden, before he went all evil on us. Matthew was a Norm, so I don't believe he is one of the Six. We have a missing name."

"What have you got on Charles?"

"He is an interesting one. Charles Smith. A political wannabe."

"Politics?"

"He wanted to be Ellisborough's mayor. Of course, that dream fell apart when the Mage-kind uprising occurred."

"He didn't want to be known as Mage-kind?"

"Absolutely not."

He did. It was all his idea, Timothy whispered.

"It's an interesting story, actually," Uncle Donny went on, unaware of Timothy's commentary.

"Oh yeah?" Tracey sat on the chair jammed in amongst the boards. Uncle Donny picked up a whiteboard marker to use as a pointer.

"From what I've learned, Charles came from a fairly prominent family. His father was elected the previous mayor, and *his* father before that. It was assumed Charles would step into that role within the year. What worked against him was that he remained unmarried. With no wife and children, he was seen by the townsfolk as a young man with little direction or commitment."

"Stupid," Tracey said. "Wait, I've read letters written by the mayor in my English class. His name was different. Ah, it was … Mayor Jeffers. Bertrum Jeffers."

"Yes, well Jeffers lost his job after the *rebellion*," Uncle Donny said.

"Did Charles get the job then?"

"No — once he was outed as Mage-kind the entire family was ostracized."

"Why the whole family?"

"Not a lot of study had been done into the Mage-kind node — even by Mage-kind themselves. It was assumed that if there was one Mage-kind in the family, then the whole family must be Mage-kind."

Tracey stayed silent.

Uncle Donny shook his head. "Yes well, it was a different time and all that. Prior to the uprising, the family possessed a lot of money and a lot of land. From what I've pieced together, his servants did not think well of him. He was rude, aggressive, and a bit of a cards man. He was in a lot of debt. I actually wonder if he wanted to be mayor at all."

Oh, he wanted it, Timothy whispered.

The moment Tracey focused on his voice she was yanked forward and into the black place. Timothy was waiting for her. "Hello again, Tracey."

This uncontrolled flinging back and forth from reality into the stone and back was getting tiresome.

She would be taught
to heal the town's sick,
how to make the fields fertile,
and how to keep the livestock plentiful.

11

hat do you want?" she demanded. "Send me back!" The black room crept closer as Tracey's spotlight of yellow light shrank.

"To help you. You seem to be gathering information. I have answers. You need only ask me for them."

"Like I'm going to believe anything you tell me. And hey, stop listening in." She had forgotten to raise her brain protection spell after the excitement of casting the stone search spell. From now on she would have to remember to keep it activated.

Timothy smiled. "Would you ignore the information I can provide? I've already told you I will not lie to you."

"Fine. What do you know?"

"Not so fast. You should be more careful with the questions you ask. What is it you really want to know?"

Ugh, so much like Stephanie. He never answered any questions, only asked more. Who cared what type of questions she asked? "What do you know about Charles?"

"Come now, Tracey. I know you are smarter than this."

"I am smart," she snapped.

He sighed and rubbed his nose. It was a funny action given he was a spirit stuck inside a magic stone. He acted as though he possessed a real body, one that could express physical stress and frustration. Stephanie did it too. "Charles was determined to be mayor. He did everything possible to ensure it happened." He stared at Tracey, as if expecting her to ask what Charles did that was so bad.

She didn't care about Charles' dream of becoming mayor. She asked something else. "What do you know about Charles' stone?"

"At last. A good question. Alas, I know very little. They were kept secret."

"Whose idea was that? It makes searching for them so hard."

"With that much power, Tracey, do you think we would make it easy to take them from us?"

At first, she thought he meant keeping them from Norms, then the truth occurred to her. "You didn't trust each other, did you?"

He smiled. "As I have said you would be wise to question everything and trust no one."

Tracey nodded. "So, you didn't trust Charles? What was he like as a person?"

"He was an ass."

Tracey snorted.

"Old money," Timothy continued, tilting his head as he thought it through. "Arrogant. We met at school. He came from a rather influential family and thought that meant his opinions were worth more than of those around him."

"And you weren't from an important family?"

"Please, I was from a far more influential family than his could ever be. Charles believed himself above everyone and everything. He had many disagreements with Stephanie. He was a sad, pathetic little man wanting attention."

"What did they argue about?"

"It didn't matter."

"Because she was a girl?"

Timothy raised an eyebrow. "Gender has no bearing on magic. He couldn't see her true potential. He underestimated her. Always."

"What animal did he favor? If the animal reflects the person or their personality traits then what would you guess it was?"

"It would be a predator. He believed himself above all others. Stronger, better, no one was his equal. I do not know the type of stone he chose."

"So, he thought he was smarter than everyone else. Did that include you?"

Timothy sucked in his lips as if there was a bitter taste on his tongue. "I'm certain of it."

"Did he have any other friends?"

"Friends? I do not believe Charles had any."

"But —"

"Tracey?"

She blinked back to reality and focused on Uncle Donny's blurry, worried face. The sucking sensation that grabbed her body during her transition faded quickly. "What happened? What did Stephanie tell you? Any clues about the stone?" Questions popped out of him like popcorn kernels heating in a microwave bag.

"A little about Charles."

"What did she say?"

"Charles was proud and mean. Old money. Very arrogant."

"Hmmmm." Uncle Donny wrote that down on the whiteboard.

"I don't think we can fully trust what he — she says, though," Tracey suggested.

Her uncle spun around and his eyes narrowed on her. "Really, why?"

"They didn't trust each other not to steal the stones for themselves. I think we need to research them all separately." She thought of what Timothy told her. "Even Stephanie. She might not tell me everything, you know? Or tell me the whole truth."

"That's always a good idea. Did she say anything else?"

"Charles was desperate to be the town's mayor and would have done anything to get the role."

"Interesting. If Stephanie gives you anything else, let me know. I'll look into the political records of the time. Genealogies too. Might find something interesting. Look, the reason I pulled you out of your internal conversation is because your dad is here to take you home."

"Thanks, Dad!" she shouted through the open doorway. "Uncle Donny, is it okay if everyone comes over tomorrow after school?"

"You bet."

Dad patted Tracey's shoulder as she reached his side. "We're picking up takeaway for dinner. Let's go."

After dinner, Grandma gave her that look. The one that dipped her chin as she stared over her glasses; the one that told Tracey it was time to share another memory Vision of Stephanie's past.

Grandma followed Tracey into her bedroom. Tracey plopped down onto her bed and held out her hands. Grandma gripped Tracey's cold fingers tight. Tracey shut her eyes and breathed in Grandma's warm, sugar cookie smell. When she opened her eyes, she was in the gray world of Stephanie's memories. She hated the cold empty feeling of losing her magic, but at least she knew it was only temporary. As soon as she witnessed what she was supposed to see, she would wake up and her magic would be back.

She peered around, wondering where she was today. She stood in a long, wide, weirdly familiar room. It took a moment to realize she recognized the hallway as the one she walked in a few weeks ago. It was the manor house's third floor hallway leading to the ballroom. Tracey's ancestor Stephanie stood in the middle of the room, one hand pressed to her head. Her hair stuck to her face in sweaty tendrils and her long lacy dress seemed windblown and ruffled. Millicent lay crumpled at her feet and four men lay face down on the carpet spaced out in a wide circle. Tracey recognized the closest man as Jing Cho, Jilly's ancestor. Stephanie blinked rapidly as if just coming inside after staring directly into the sun. "What … what happened?" she muttered to herself.

Tracey examined the fallen people and the room more closely. The furniture was pushed back and tipped over like it had been blown back by an explosion. The darker stains on the carpet and walls told Tracey the same thing. She remembered white-painted walls and a thick rich carpet as she fought the mumble trying to kidnap Kylie. But of course, the modern hallway no longer looked like it had back in Stephanie's time.

Tracey's gaze slipped back to Stephanie, who was still rambling. "What has happened here?"

Millicent grimaced and moaned softly, rolling and twitching. Stephanie didn't even look at her friend or move to check on her. The black stains beneath them could have been anything. It was hard to tell in this gray place. Millicent rolled over and pushed to her hands and knees. "What …?"

Stephanie peered down at her. "You, girl. What has happened here?" she demanded, grabbing Millicent's arm and dragging her to her feet.

"What …?" Millicent had a dark wet substance on the side of her face. She wiped it away. "Blood?" She pulled from the other's claw-like grip. "Who? Who are you?" Millicent said. Her breathing became jerky, panicked and she pressed her free hand to her chest as if it ached.

Stephanie scowled. "That is what I am asking you."

"I do not know you," Millicent said.

"It appears as though we have the same thoughts. I do not know who you are either."

They stared blankly at each other as Millicent wiped her wet hands on her skirt. "I am injured."

"As are the others."

"Others?" Millicent stumbled to one of the fallen figures, knelt down and turned one face. It was Jing Cho. "Do you recognize him?"

"I do not."

"Neither do I."

Tracey blinked as the memory Vision faded. She stared at her grandma's pink curls and sweaty face. "What happened?"

"You know I cannot see what you see. Oh, I'm a little dizzy."

Tracey helped her grandma lay down on the bed. "Just rest, Grandma." She hesitated in the hall after closing the bedroom door. Stephanie and Millicent — the very best of friends — hadn't recognized each other. Tracey must have just seen the aftermath of the memory curse. They — presumably the men were part of the Sect too — all lay unconscious on the floor. No one else stood in the hallway. So who cast the curse? And what happened next?

She recalled Timothy questioning the truth of her own memories. If the curse affected all of the Sect, if Stephanie and Millicent couldn't remember each other, then how did Stephanie remember Millicent in her dreams? What if the memory Visions were wrong? Programmed somehow? Everything Tracey knew about Stephanie and Millicent, their behavior and mannerisms, made her wonder. She had read Millicent's secret journal, had even spoken to her. She knew Millicent had reservations about the stones spell and that she had been afraid. Stephanie's memory Vision — the first one Tracey was shown — was of Millicent trying to convince Stephanie to do a spell and Stephanie being worried about it … What if Timothy was right? What if Stephanie had convinced herself somehow that it was the other way around? What if — originally — it was Millicent who had warned Stephanie about the spell and Stephanie the one to convince Millicent to do it? Had Stephanie flipped the memory around like a mirror, switching their places? If that was true … what about the other memory Visions Tracey witnessed? What about the one of Timothy tangling Stephanie in red threads of magic?

What if …?

What if Timothy was right and Stephanie purposefully altered her memory to believe something happened differently. Was that why she passed her memories down through the family line? To convince herself that she was the innocent party. So much so that she had changed her memories to support the delusion?

Was Stephanie the bad guy and the one behind it all?

Oh.

Tracey sat down on the carpet outside her bedroom door as her wild thoughts overwhelmed her. Her stomach swirled and her skin turned icy cold.

Am I wrong about everything?

For that is what they did.
The family loved their little
town of Delmore and the people
of Delmore loved them in return

12

Tracey bolted upright breathing hard, covered in icy sweat. More nightmares. She was not surprised.

She stretched toward her side table, searching for her notebook to jot down what she could remember before it disappeared. Stephanie, Millicent, and Timothy all told her Dreaming was a power, not a myth. Clues often came to her about the stones via her nightmares. All she remembered this time was a feeling of fear. She was afraid and running. Always running. Tracey tapped the center of her forehead rapidly, trying to recall further details. There was a high-pitched yipping and a deep grunt and a hissing sound. And laughter.

Tracey glanced at her alarm clock. She had hours to go before morning. She smooshed her face into her pillow, knowing that when it did go off, she'd have to get dressed and head to school. She didn't want to go.

Damian totally blanked her yesterday. The squinchy feeling in the tummy grew as she thought about it. She desperately wanted to talk to him. Well, he would have to talk to her today because their joint assignment was due next week. *Does he still like me?* Thinking about the cute boy brought a clammy heat to her skin and she pushed down her blankets, huffing out a long breath. In all the time she had known

Damian — basically since the day he arrived at school — she'd been the tornado eye. The center of the pain whirling around him and his family, sucking his sister into the maelstrom. And his mom *hated* Tracey. She really couldn't blame him if he wanted to be left alone for a while. Maybe … maybe he would be better off if she never became his friend?

She liked him. Enough to want him to be happy.

Would he be happier without her?

That might be what he was brooding about, why he sat on his own. Maybe she should agree if he told her he wanted to break up. Tears prickled her suddenly hot eyes. *I don't want to.* She sniffed hard and rolled onto her back. It would be for the best though, wouldn't it? A tear broke free and ran over her cheek, down her neck and into her pillow. *It's not fair.*

Perhaps they should go back to being friends? She didn't want to be just friends, though; if it stopped her from losing him altogether then that would be okay, wouldn't it? She didn't want him hurting anymore and this way she wouldn't completely lose him. He would still be her friend.

Her hand drifted over the stones tucked under her pajama top. While she held the Serpent's Kiss, she didn't know what would happen, but it made her a target. Damian would be safer if they were only friends. Maybe, after she broke the spell on the stones, she could be his girlfriend again. *I just have to keep him as a friend for now.*

So, that was her plan. Until she was able to bring all of the stones together and break the spell on them, she would just keep her distance. *I should do that with Laura, Jonny, and Tony too.* Her heart clenched at the thought, screaming no, she couldn't send her friends away. She needed them. Jonny was already caught up in the stones drama, but she could try to protect Laura and Tony better. *Ugh.* Her thoughts circled back to Damian. She remembered the time he got angry with her for keeping silent. Laura had been mad too, when Tracey kept the truth from her. Maybe, rather than decide for Damian or for Laura and Tony, she should ask them if they wanted to stay friends. Laura and Tony would demand to be included, she knew that, but she should still ask.

One of the stones pulsed against her skin. She didn't look to see which one was trying to get her attention. She forced her thoughts back to the bad dream that woke her. Tracey's dreams about Nana and the attacking tigers or the empty stage with the swooping birds were clear. She couldn't forget them if she tried. That probably meant today's nightmare was just that. A normal nightmare. Tracey pushed her pen off the edge of her bed along with her notebook and clicked off the lamp.

She closed her eyes. After a while, she opened them again and stared up at the dark ceiling. Yep. Sleep was not happening. She switched the lamp on again and leaned over the side of her bed to tug Tony's binder from her bag, flicking through the pages mindlessly. She didn't reading anything in particular, she just needed something to do. That was when she spotted the anonymous letter written in familiar handwriting. Tracey dove back over her bed to yank Millicent's diary out of her school bag. The handwriting was familiar because it was Millicent's handwriting! And though the letter was unsigned, Tracey knew it was Millicent who wrote it.

My Dearest Friend,

I appreciate you allowing me to read the excerpt of your manuscript. It is very good. You simply must go ahead with your publishing dreams. I am astonished at the wild and extraordinary characters you have described. Oh, how I wish I were a Dreamer. Your creation of these fantastical myths and the tales contained therein of extraordinary abilities are as entertaining as they are exciting. I do hope your manuscript will be a success.

I hesitate to write the advice I now offer as I am unsure of how you will take it. I do not think you should insist these tales are true. I am afraid they will only publish them as a fantastical tale of fiction. Jonathan, perhaps, if you were to advise them of such, they would look at the pages again?

Aha! She knew it. She knew Dreamers were not real! *It is just a fairy tale.* She lowered the page and slipped it back into the binder, searching through the rest for any letters written in the same handwriting. She found a letter — dated a few days after the first. Not in Millicent's script but addressed to her, written in thick blocky handwriting.

My dear Millicent,

I shall remember our constitutionals through the garden until the end of my days. Your faith in my studies and my work heartens me indeed. I will continue to insist my work is studied research rather than fiction but perhaps I can be persuaded to embellish the author as a fiction, to lend a more fantastical air to the tale.

I pray that my research has given you hope. It is not a curse and you are not alone. One day soon I believe we will be known and accepted by more than merely our peers. When that day comes, I know you will be as revered as I for your good works and knowledge of our arts.

Tracey grabbed her phone and typed out a text to Tony before she remembered it was the middle of the night. She stared at the screen. *I have to put this back outside.* Oh well, as long as she did it before her dad woke up. *More secrets.* Tracey told her inner Mom-sounding voice to shush. She glanced at the binder again. Where did Tony find these letters?

Millicent never mentioned a "writer" friend in her diary. She complained about being alone, despite the presence of her friend Stephanie. *I need to know more.* What was this book they were talking about? Did it ever get published? Was it truly fact, or fiction as Millicent seemed to believe? *Jonathan.* Who was he? She needed the full author's name so she could find the book. And she had to finish reading Millicent's diary to see if the "friend" was ever mentioned. Tracey flopped back onto her bed. "I'll never sleep now," she whispered into the night. She switched the bedside lamp off again. Millicent and this man spent time walking in a garden. No wonder Millicent loved gardens. Had this writer friend known about the maze? Tracey's mind whirred with the possibilities. Poor Tony. She would bombard him with questions when she saw him later today. They had to find this book about Dreamers.

Tracey tugged the Butterfly Stone out from beneath her pajama top and stared at the painted wings. "Stephanie?"

She closed her hand around the stone and shut her eyes as that roller coaster feeling overtook her. *Ugh! Why here again?* She stared bitterly at the black place. The black was too black, like black hole black. It seemed to suck up all of the light from the spotlights, making them strain harder to light her and the other faintly red glowing figure. "Timothy?"

"Back again?"

"Why do I keep coming back here?" This was not good. She couldn't reach the Butterfly Stone at all.

Timothy remained silent.

"Um. Ah, do you know about a Dreamer book? It might have been published as a fantasy or as a horror story. Ugh, I don't know how fiction was put out in your time. A ghost story? Gothic speculation? It was written by a man named Jonathan. Does anything like sound familiar?"

Timothy pursed his lips and tapped his fingers together. "How odd of you to bring that up."

"So you do know a book like that?"

"Jonathan often wrote long boring research papers on magic. They were kept locked away of course."

Tracey bounced up and down on her toes. "That's it. That's the one. Jonathan was a member of the Sect, wasn't he?" *At last. A clue!*

"He was with us, yes."

"What was his last name?"

Timothy shook his head. "Strange, I … I cannot quite put my finger on it."

"Ugh, that's the curse talking. You can only confirm something after I find out about it. I know Jonathan's name now, but not his surname so you can't tell me what it is. Well, what can you tell me about Jonathan? How did you meet?"

Timothy smiled. It changed his whole face, making it softer somehow. "In school. He was, well, he was a good man, if completely naïve."

"Jonathan researched Dreamers, didn't he? What do you remember about his novel?" *This is great, another clue to a stone!*

"A scandalous tale did appear in print shortly before we fought for our independence. Why would you ask about it?"

"So it was published?" Tracey asked instead of answering. A trick she had learned from both Stephanie and Timothy and it gave her joy to use it against him in turn.

"It was. However, I believe it was destroyed once Magekind became known to the world."

"So no copies exist?"

"It is possible the first part survived as it was distributed before the fighting began, though I believe the sensational nature of the tale meant only a few read it."

"Scandalous?"

"Indeed. The protagonist was a woman. He didn't use the Mage descriptor, but described magic as illusions cast by magicians in confidence games rather than inherent internal magic. Literacy rates were not high, Tracey. I doubt it was seen by many."

"Did you read it?"

"Of course not. What did I have a need of to read about magic? I lived it."

"What was the book called?" Maybe it still for sale somewhere?

"*A Circle of Mystical Illusion.*"

Tracey blinked herself out of the black place. *I know a name now. Jonathan! I need Tony and I need to find that book.*

Her last thought before she fell back asleep was to wonder why she wasn't able to contact Stephanie.

What Jane and her family did not know was that the farmers from Hamsted, the next town over and not as prosperous as Delmore, were on their way to the circle, angry at the witches and determined to stop them.

13

With a heavy heart and feet that felt weighed down like the stones around her neck were boulders, Tracey plodded to the Carter's front door. Her buzz from learning the name of the last sect member had faded by the time her alarm went off and her chosen mission drew near. It was cold out, as if the very weather reflected her mood back at her. She puffed into her fingers to warm them. The dark, wood-stained door wouldn't answer any of her questions. She knocked and hoped Damian's mom would not answer. She practiced a story about schoolwork just in case and nearly blurted it all out when the door swung open. Instead, Tracey came face-to-face with Damian and quickly stepped back, heat rising in her cheeks. "Oh, hey."

The smile on his lips faded. Her heart plummeted at the sight. "Hey." He didn't invite her in.

"Um." She shifted her weight from foot to foot. "How are you?"

"Fine."

"How's Kylie?" she asked.

"She's all right."

It was like pulling a decision about which take out to order from her brothers. "Sarah says Kylie has been avoiding her at school."

"Is she? I didn't know that."

Why wasn't he inviting her inside? "You … um, you haven't spoken to me since we got back from London. Are you avoiding me?" Whoops, she hadn't meant to blurt it out like that. Lack of sleep and all the questions spinning around inside her brain clearly disconnected her mind from her mouth. Still, the decision she made that morning stayed at the forefront. She wanted to get it over with, but now that she was here didn't know how to start.

Damian sighed and tugged her inside.

"Is your mom at work?"

"Yeah."

"Where's Kylie?" she asked when he remained silent. It was awkward standing there in the entry hall with nothing to hold or fiddle with. Damian was dressed for school in torn jeans and a lime polo, and his hair was damp from his shower. He smelled soooo good. Crisp and clean. She tried to breathe it in subtly. He shot her a side-eyed squint as if wondering what she was doing.

"Already gone to school," he said.

Tracey let the door shut behind her and scuffed her feet against the entry hall tiles. She had to ask it. "Why haven't you spoken to me or replied to any of my texts?"

"Look, Tracey. It was a lot. That trip. The clay monsters. Agent Malden." He scrubbed a hand over his head, messing up his hair. "Kylie's life is finally back to normal. I just want her to be safe. To be a kid, you know?" He wouldn't meet her gaze.

Tracey shoved her hands into her pockets and pulled them out again. She didn't know what to do with them, but they felt in the way somehow. "Sarah misses Kylie. They were friends." Why was she even talking about her sister? She really wanted to know why Damian was being so weird with her. *Come on, Tracey. You know why. More importantly, do the thing you came here to do.*

"Yeah, no. I know that. Just, Sarah shouldn't push her."

Is he saying I should do that? That I shouldn't push? "I'll tell her." He fell silent again.

Urgh! She had to know. "I didn't get to talk to you because your mom moved you to that earlier flight, and um, we still have that assignment to do, but are we still friends?"

"I want things to go back to normal."

Tracey hung her head. She wanted, hoped, they could still be friends, but the implication in his words was like a twisting knife. "And I'm not normal. Is that what you mean?"

"No. No, that's wrong. No." His eyes sprang wide, looking like a surprised emoji. "I just — you're just — it's all drama. With you and your friends and those stones. You're always investigating something and chasing after things and getting into danger and I just want to play football and get passing grades. Can you understand? I am your friend. I'm still your friend, but until you finish this thing with the stones, I can't be more … I'm so sorry. You get it, don't you?"

Tracey swallowed hard and nodded. She had come here to do this very thing, but now that it was happening her heart was screaming *nooooo!* He wanted to stay friends. It was what she wanted too. A lump formed in her stomach. "It's funny. That's what I came over here to say."

His mouth dropped open. "You did?"

"I don't want to hurt you, Damian. And …" She swallowed. "You're right. My life is completely *blurgh* at the moment."

"Oh." He glanced down at his feet and then back up at her. "But you do want to stay friends? I was worried you'd be mad at me."

Tracey's eyes burned but her skin felt like she'd plummeted off a cliff-face into an icy ocean. "Oh yes. Totally okay." *No, no it's not. It's so unfair.* The stones around her neck grew heavier, pulling her head even lower. She was keeping so many secrets, what was one more? Even though the ache in her chest hurt, now that it was actually said and done she found she could breathe a little easier. She forced herself to stare up into his beautiful brown eyes. They shimmered under rapid blinks. Tracey cleared her throat.

This was what you wanted. Don't get upset. "After the stones …?" She let the question dangle, hoping he would jump in and answer it in a positive way.

"I … I can't promise anything. I just don't know. Tracey, I really like you. You are an amazing person and I don't want to lose that, or you. It's just all a bit much right now."

"Yeah." She forced a laugh. "So, our assignment?"

"We're good. We're still partners." He scrubbed a hand through his hair, messing it up further. His straight, tense stance relaxed and he slouched, rolling his shoulders. *So cute. Ugh, stop it, Trace.* "I'm sorry for not talking to you at school. I won't blank you again. I wasn't dealing with everything very well and I didn't know how to say what I wanted. I didn't want you to hate me."

"I think you did okay."

"Only because you're braver than me," he said, shooting her a smile. "I knew I had to say something, because it was eating me up inside, but I was afraid of losing everything and I … I chickened out. I should have just been honest. I don't want to lie to you and not tell you things."

Tracey's hand brushed over the stones. She cleared her throat again, her voice tight and a bit wobbly. "Yeah. Me neither." She spun around and tugged the front door open, unable to keep looking him in the eyes. "What should we tell everyone?"

"We're still friends, so … the truth I guess."

She nodded. "I'd better go. You probably don't want to walk to school with me, right?"

"Yeah, ah … I've got to get some things still."

"Oh yeah, sure." *He hates me. I knew it. He can't wait for me to leave.* She stared at the closed door before turning around. With slow steps she thumped off the porch down to the street. Damian's sad, beautiful eyes haunting her the whole way to school.

It's what you wanted. The lecture repeated itself over and over inside her head. A few tears leaked out anyway, but by the time she got to school her cheeks were dry. She sniffed and blew her nose into a damp tissue. *I don't even know why I'm upset. I already decided to break up with him. He agreed it was the right thing to do.* She searched the path ahead for Laura or Tony. There was no sign of either friend. "It's for the best," she muttered and paced back and forth in their meeting spot. "This way he won't find out the truth."

"What truth?"

Tracey turned. Meena stood right behind her, head tilted as if worried Tracey was nuts, what with her muttering to the trees. The mean girl was without her usual support flunkies and it was wrong to see her on her own.

"Nothing. I'm just talking to myself." Tracey waited for Meena to fling her hair and flounce off toward school.

Strangely, she didn't move. Her stare locked onto Tracey like a heat-seeking missile. "Have you been crying?"

"No, I have hay fever."

Meena moved closer. Tracey stumbled back and then planted her feet. She wasn't afraid of Meena.

Much.

"You look upset."

"I'm fine. Why don't you go find your friends."

Meena's back straightened, and she raised her chin. "What's going on with you?"

"Nothing. Are you looking for goss to use against me?"

The mean girl peered around. Whatever she was searching for she didn't find it. She glanced back at Tracey. "I was just asking."

"Well, I'm fine." Tracey spotted Laura in the distance. *Oh, thank goodness.*

"Whatever." Meena did spin around then, her hair flaring out behind her like a cape as she stomped away. Her backpack bounced angrily against her rigid spine. Tracey stared after her. *What the ...?*

"What did she want?" Laura asked as she drew closer.

"Dunno." Tracey stared curiously after the departing girl. *What was that all about?*

It was a twenty-minute walk to the town center from school. Every teen resented the trip mightily, whining and complaining as they marched along the sidewalk. Still, the bus would have been so much worse and that they all agreed on. Tracey plodded beside Tony and Damian. Meena and Carla were at the back of the excursion group and well behind Tracey and her friends. Yet Tracey could still feel the girls' glares on the back of her neck. She kept glancing up at Damian, wanting to speak, but when he looked at her she darted her gaze away. He smelled of the donuts she spied him and Dave eating at the first break. Her stomach grumbled every time she thought of it and his sugary lips. *Those soft warm lips I'll never get to kiss again.*

"They are in a particularly bad mood today," Tony griped.

"Meena and Carla? Tell me about it. It's like I've done something wrong but I have no idea what, so I can't even apologize for it."

"It wouldn't matter," Damian said. "They're like a twister of despair and aggression. You can't do or say anything they won't react to. You could say the sky was blue and they'd argue about it and make you sound like the stupid one. It's just the game they play. You can't ever win it."

Tracey sighed loudly. Inwardly, she was happy Damian was even walking with them. He had kept his promise. He was still talking to her. "I know. I just wish I knew what set Meena off this time. She's been really odd lately." Tracey tore her gaze from his perfect eyes again. *I'm flushed from the walk, that's all.* She kept her hands in her pockets so she couldn't accidentally brush her fingers against his.

"Can you believe we actually have to *tour* a building. I mean, it's a building."

"It's the council building, Trace," Tony said. "It's a civics thing."

"Soooooooooooo boring," Tracey continued. "Do you think he'll be there?"

"Who, the mayor? Probably."

"Ugh."

"What's up?" Damian asked.

She just loved his *I'm confused* face. "You said you wanted to be left out of um … stuff."

He rolled his eyes. "Just say it."

"There was an evil fog and the mayor thinks I'm bonkers."

Damian stared at her.

"You really think he'll say something to you?" Tony asked.

"I hope not. I hope he's forgotten all about me."

"Good luck with that." Dave's head appeared in between Tracey and Damian making them both jump. Tony cackled at their reaction.

"Rude," Tracey told him.

The council building loomed in the distance like a creepy castle in a video game, growing larger with each step they took. The three-story white monstrosity used to be one of Tracey's favorite buildings. Well, not the council part but the adjoining library, which was only accessible from the council building's entrance. She had loved the library as a kid. There were so many bright, colorful picture books to read and the librarian at the time was a master of different voices. The children's book club was one of Tracey's most favored memories. Of course, things changed when Tracey's family got the Xbox for Christmas. After that, she didn't go to the library anywhere near as much. Games were awesome! It was how she became friends with Jonny. He spotted her playing on her handheld at school and came over. They ended up late for class because they were too busy talking fast and frantically trying to tell each other every thought about their favorite games.

After her run in with the mayor, she was freaking out about going inside the council building. Her feet slowed as they approached. Tony hung back to walk with her. "Come on," he urged. The library was still his favorite place to go.

Mr. Rachette hurried them on with a shout. Tracey was the last one inside the ornate double doors and saw him immediately. The mayor waited at the top of the stairs, standing high above the gathered teens. He had already started his welcome speech. Tracey tried not to interrupt as she snuck in, her small stature helping her to disappear in the gathered group of teens. There was not a single murmur or mutter around her. She understood why. It was just something the mayor gave off. A *don't-mess-with-me* vibe.

"Now, children. Can you tell me when this building was built?" The mayor stared at Tracey like she was the only one he was addressing. The weight of his stare burrowed into her skin making her twitchy.

Grumbles started up around the group. No one answered the mayor's question. Not even Tony, who usually knew all the answers. The mayor let out a huff and gave a long speech about how it was built as a symbol of democracy and how it was the most important building in the town.

Tony let out a soft snort. "The most important building is the library. That's the only place that actually helps people."

Tracey snickered. Of course Tony would feel that way.

"Miss Masters, do you have something to add to the conversation?"

Fruit tingles. Tracey dragged her gaze up to find the mayor's stare fixed on her face. "Ah, no sir." She knew he would find a way to call her out. This was exactly why it didn't pay to be known by people like the mayor. Her classmates didn't try very hard to stifle their chuckles, and even Damian shook his head in amusement. Tracey rolled her eyes at him and shrugged. It was not her fault she was always getting picked on.

The mayor wore a black suit and a red tie. There was a smidge of something green at the tie's triangle base. Tracey wondered if Tony could see what it was from where he stood. She bet it was something that stroked his ego, like a lion or a dragon or something equally prideful. It was doubtful it would be something fun like a cartoon character or a movie reference. The mayor finally moved on, directing the teens to travel as a group down the hall. "And this is the Miltern Falls Council Chamber."

The mumbling around Tracey stayed soft as her schoolmates spread out around the new room. There was a long heavy looking wooden table at the end and movable chairs placed in rows. The chamber looked like a classroom.

"Miss Masters, why don't you come up here and join me at the head table."

Why me? She slunk to the front of the room.

"What sort of decisions do you think would be made from up here?" he asked in a voice loud enough for everyone to hear.

Tracey wanted the morning to be over. "I don't know. Telling people what they're allowed and not allowed to do?"

The mayor laughed. "If only it was that simple." He gestured for her to sit at the head seat right in the center of the long table. "It is mostly paperwork and issuing licenses."

"Then why would anyone want to be mayor?" she asked.

He raised his chin and looked down his nose at her. "Power."

"Sounds super boring," Dave One called from the floor. The teens laughed loudly.

Tracey's gaze caught on the mayor's knowing eyes. "Indeed." He leaned closer, making Tracey slide out of the head chair to get away from him. He followed, lowering his voice so no one else could hear him. "I understand your uncle is a detective?"

"What? Ah, I mean, why do you ask?" She stopped moving.

His smile grew teeth.

"Where does this door lead?" Dave One shouted, pointing to a locked door at the very front of the room. He tugged on the handle but it wouldn't turn.

"Nowhere important," the mayor said, raising his voice again. "Just the basement where the archives are kept. We call it the dungeon, haha. Unless you would like to help with the filing, young man? We have plenty of work around here that needs doing."

Tracey took advantage of the mayor's distraction and raced back to her friends. The mayor was super creepy. For a change, she couldn't wait to go back to school.

The family were afraid when they saw the farmers approaching with their flaming torches. They hid behind one of the stones, for there was nowhere else to hide.

14

Tracey grabbed Tony's arm, stopping him on the concrete path leading toward the lunch hall. A quick check around made sure no one was close enough to hear their conversation. She asked, "Where did you get the letters from?"

"What letters?"

"The ones in the binder."

"Oh." Tony paused and then grinned. "Noel found those. I'm not sure where he got them. He scanned a heap of documents for us —"

"I need more information on the fantasy book."

His eyes narrowed. "Did you have a Dream?"

"No, no, nothing like that. No, but I think the woman he was writing to was Millicent. I matched her handwriting to one of the letters."

"Seriously?"

"Yes. I need more on this Jonathan guy. I think he might be the last member of the Sect. So, who was he? How much did he know about Millicent? Did he know about the stones? What happened to him in the end?"

"Can't Jonny just ask Millicent for us?"

"As soon as I see him, I'll ask. But he said she doesn't talk to him." Tracey debated telling Tony that Millicent spoke to her while Jonny was asleep. She wasn't sure what Tony would think about that. He was so angry when Tracey used magic on him, he probably wouldn't be happy to hear Millicent could just take over Jonny's body without asking.

"You have learned something," Tracey spun around at the sound of Jilly's question. She stood next to Jonny, body tense like she was preparing for battle. "You have that look."

"Something. Maybe," Tracey answered then skewered Jonny with a sharp look. "Can you speak to Millicent yet?"

He shook his head. "I got nothing. I keep trying, but I dunno, I'm tired all the time. I figure it's gotta be connected to the stone, right? Who knows. She's been quiet."

Tracey groaned. She could talk to Millicent if Jonny just went to sleep. He did look exhausted. It had to be because Millicent was taking over at night, and if she was taking over, what else was she doing without Jonny's knowledge? Tracey pondered that as they stood in line for their lunch. She was particularly ravenous and devoured her meal as soon as they sat down. Eventually, she lifted her head to focus on Tony. "So those letters?"

"Yeah?"

"They mention a fantasy story about Dreamers." Tracey grinned. "Can you ask Noel to look for it, when he's next searching around his dad's office? I think it's important." She watched Tony's skin turn pink and shared a grin with Laura. "Is Noel being careful? If he gets caught, the council might find out, and they can't know we're still looking for the stones."

"I'll ask."

"Find out if we can get a copy of the book too."

He nodded.

"You said you might have something?" Jilly interrupted. "Is it this book we're talking about?"

"I spoke to, uh —" Tracey lowered her voice "— the stone and he-she said that Charles Smith, one of the Six, wanted political power and would have done anything to get it."

"How is that 'something'?" Jonny asked.

Jilly answered for Tracey. "Because we cannot enter a political field. Mage-kind are not permitted."

"That's so dumb. I can't see why not. You can be anything you want to be," Jonny said.

Jilly smiled at him softly. "If only that were true, Jonny."

"We'll make it true. You'd be an amazing president."

"Oh, that would be awesome," Laura added. "I can just see it now." She spread her hands wide. "Jilly Cho for President. Mage-kind genius, and a total boss. I'll be your campaign manager. Jonny can talk to the media."

"Wait … it's not entirely true that we can't get into politics. Remember our mayor? He's Mage-kind." Tracey blurted.

"How do you know that?" Tony grabbed his phone and started typing.

"I saw his identification bracelet."

"He must have gotten special permission from the government," Jilly said.

"See. So, it is possible. Jilly Cho for President," Jonny said, making them all laugh.

"What does your uncle say we should do now?" Laura asked, popping the last bite of her sandwich into her mouth. The football team thundered into the lunch hall, shouting and jeering at top volume. Tony and Jonny leaned in to listen over the sudden rise of noise.

"He said we have to treat it like a cold case," Tracey said.

"Like in those TV shows that investigate unsolved murders?" Laura asked.

"Exactly." Tracey played with her apple. "He's brought a bunch of whiteboards for the office and has written down everything we know about each stone."

"There's no current case to get in the way?" Jonny asked.

"You know Uncle Donny," Tracey said. "What's important is that he said you can all come over after school to help."

"What, seriously?" Laura said. She let out a little "whoop!" as the boys high-fived.

"Yeah. So you'll come?" Tracey asked.

Jonny held up his phone. "Texting my moms, right now."

Tracey raised her eyebrows at Tony. Laura and Jilly grabbed their phones and were doing the same as Jonny, but Tony hadn't moved. "What?" Tony quirked an eye-brow. "I just assumed we'd be talking about the binders so I already told my dad I'd be at your uncle's place."

Tracey grinned.

"What about Dave Two?" Tony asked.

Tracey glanced over at where the boy sat with the rest of the football team. He sat angled so he could look at Tracey and her friends but spent most of his time laughing at his best friend Dave One. At school it was just easier to call them Dave One and Dave Two. "We should include him, shouldn't we?" She pulled out her phone and texted him. It was safer than going over there and making her the focus of Dave One's attention. No one ever wanted that. Even though Dave

One knew Dave Two hung out with them after school, nobody spoke about it openly. A message popped up in her notifications from an anonymous number.

I know who you are.

Whoa. That didn't sound like the average spam text. It was way creepier. Probably a new form of phishing, someone trying to get her to reply and steal her details. She thought about the caller and that weird message at Uncle Donny's and wondered if it was the same person. She deleted the message and blocked the phone number before typing out her invitation to Dave Two.

That afternoon Tracey led her friends into Uncle Donny's office and discovered a feast laid out for them. There were sandwiches and cut up pieces of fruit, along with bottles of juice and clean coffee mugs. "Hey kids, come on in. Eat up because you all need fully functioning thinking processes. We have a lot to go through," Uncle Donny said.

"Why does this suddenly feel like school?" Dave Two asked, walking in behind them. They devoured the food and Uncle Donny coerced Jonny and Dave into dragging the whiteboards from his office out into the main room. They pushed them around to block the windows and the door. Tony pulled an extra binder out of his bag and passed it to Tracey's uncle. His eyes bulged as he flipped through the information inside. "Right, right. Let me read through this tonight. In the meantime, let's start by writing things up. Great work, Tony."

"Kiss ass," Dave muttered around his sandwich. Tony ignored him, shoving an entire orange quarter into his mouth. He grinned around the peel.

"How *is* Noel?" Laura asked.

Tony swallowed and pulled the orange peel out of his mouth. "He's good. He's back at school too, but he's been snooping — ahem — volunteering at the archive. Filing and coding and well, when he finds links to interesting manor house articles, he copies the details down for us and forwards them onto me."

"So you talk every night?" Jonny asked.

"Nearly."

"Aha!"

Their heads snapped up at Uncle Donny's shout. They found him on his feet staring at the binder in his hands.

"Uncle Donny?" Tracey called.

"I found a clue," he said, his eyes alight with glee.

Tracey loved the way her uncle looked when they caught a break in a case. His whole body became a bouncing ball of happy. "Really?" she asked.

"You see, we know to look for clues about the stones in the people around them and in the animal traits they imbue. Of course, we know the time frame for when the stones were created, but we haven't yet worked the 'after' angle."

"*After* angle?" Tracey hadn't heard her uncle talk about this before. She settled in, wiping her fingers on a napkin and took a sip of her drink. Uncle Donny turned to the whiteboards and spun the closest one around so that he had a blank board to write on. Tracey's friends sat down around her, recognizing the beginnings of a lecture.

"See, it *is* like school," Dave muttered before Laura shushed him.

"Right, so the usual steps with an investigation are to —"

Tracey cut in "— confirm the facts, investigate the crime scene or scenes, talk to witnesses, establish the truth, and find the evidence."

"Exactly. Historic investigations are a little trickier because, depending on the age of the case, you cannot talk to witnesses directly or establish and contain the crime scene, let alone study the physical evidence left behind or review the crime scene in situ —"

Dave waved his hand around. "What does that mean?"

"In situ? It means 'in the original place.' We would want to review the crime scene exactly as it was found, with nothing moved or cleaned up. What you *can* do with historical investigations is interrogate the reports and the behavior of the people around the original crime. You can analyze their behavior in the years after the crime took place."

"Behavior?" Jonny asked.

Tracey noticed Tony was taking notes on his phone.

"How can we investigate the crime scene — we're not in the UK, and it was hundreds of years ago," Dave complained.

"Too right!" Uncle Donny pointed at him. "But look here." He gestured to a series of drawings and the floor plan of the manor in Tony's folder. They reached for their own folders and with the loud snapping of turning pages found the ones Uncle Donny referred to. "What do you see?"

Tracey examined the drawings intently and the floor plans. "There are too many windows."

Her friends made *"Oooing"* sounds. "These drawings must have been done after the fire, not before it — after it was rebuilt," Laura said. "Wait. Look." She held up an old newspaper clipping with a grainy drawing photocopied onto a white page. "This is dated from before the fire. It's not just one window. The whole wing of the manor house looks smaller. When it was rebuilt they must have extended it on that side."

"What does that all mean?" Jonny asked.

Tony stared at Uncle Donny, dropping his phone to his lap. "The reports from the council, the ones Agent Malden and Prince Henry got from the archives, were wrong. They said the manor was rebuilt exactly."

Uncle Donny clicked his tongue and formed a gun shape with his fingers. "Which means what?"

"They're hiding something," Tracey said.

"They lied," Tony said straight after Tracey spoke.

"Yes," Uncle Donny said.

"What does the house size matter to the investigation?" Dave asked.

"It tells us they know more than they're telling. And if they're hiding something —"

"What else are they hiding?" Tracey interrupted.

"Yeah but —" Dave started.

"It gives us somewhere to begin," Jilly said to Dave.

"But," Dave mumbled. "I still don't get it."

"We start by petitioning the council to see the full archive," Uncle Donny announced.

Everyone spoke at once, creating a mess of sound that no one could understand.

"Quiet!" Jilly held up her hands. Everyone fell silent. "Sir, if you do that, the council will know we are looking into them."

"Not if we're smart about it," he told her. "I'll speak to your new agent, Tracey."

"So we don't have to do anything right now. We just wait for you?" Dave confirmed. He leaned back on his hands. "Good. I hate homework."

"Perhaps, I could speak with my mother," Jilly offered. Her face flushed under their sudden scrutiny. "She is petitioning to become a member of the council now that we are able to be remembered. She wishes to become more active in the Mage-kind community. She could request to see the archive as a part of the petition and take me with her."

"Thank you, Jilly. That is very generous," Uncle Donny said. "And a good idea. I'll speak to Prince Henry and Agent Loo Lou Epworth too. See if we can get them to seek access to the archive as well."

"What about Agent Malden?" Tracey asked quietly. Everyone turned to stare at her and she felt her face heat the way Jilly's had at the sudden attention. "I just thought … he might know something."

"Tracey, he's the bad guy," Jonny reminded her.

"And he's in prison," Tony added.

Dave looked at her as if she was loony. "You can't be serious."

"What? He knows people. He might still —" she tried.

"— help us? I don't think that's a good idea," Laura said, a frown marring her face.

"But would it hurt?" Tracey asked.

"Yes. He did hurt us, remember?" Dave snapped. "Giant clay monsters smashing up a movie studio? Ring any bells?"

"I know. I can't forget," Tracey snapped back. Kylie's pale face and temporarily dead body popped into her mind. She blinked the memory away quickly.

"Right kids, it's getting a little hot in here. Let's park that discussion," Uncle Donny said. "And focus on what we know. Let's make sure we're all on the same page, then we'll go home and read what's in these binders, all right?"

They made various sounds of agreement. Tony tapped Tracey's hand which was clenched around her t-shirt and the stones beneath it. "You good?"

She forced her hand to relax and opened her fingers. "Yeah. Just quick to anger these days. Dave doesn't help." Laura pressed closer to her knee and leaned against Tracey's leg. The teens spent the next thirty minutes discussing the Butterfly Stone, the Tiger's Eye, and the Crow's Heart, brainstorming and listing additions to the whiteboards.

"I wonder who her parents were?" Tony mused.

"Millicent's? She was an orphan, she didn't know. It's a shame we can't ask her," Laura said, twisting to give Jonny side eye.

He shrugged. "She's said nothing to me."

"Uncle Donny, what about the orphanage's records? Can we get them from the time Millicent was left there?" Tracey asked.

"I'm working on that actually — or well, Prince Henry is on our behalf."

They added everything they could think of to the white-boards. "There's no wrong answers, nothing is too crazy. You think of it, we add it," Uncle Donny told them. When there were only blank looks in reply and a lot of shrugs he said, "Okay, I think we're done for today. Head home. We'll —"

The ringing office phone cut him off. Uncle Donny answered it and waved for them to head out. Tracey shut the door behind them softly, blocking out her uncle discussing his late water bill with the provider and ushered her friends from the wider office. She flipped the closed sign and locked the door behind them.

"What now?" Laura asked.

"Home, eat, bed," Tracey muttered.

They laughed and separated. Tracey and Dave headed to the bus stop. Jonny and Jilly walked toward Jonny's house a few blocks away and Laura and Tony climbed into their parents' cars, waiting patiently outside. At her stop, Tracey jumped off the bus and walked home. Her brain overflowed with everything they had been talking about. It felt as though they had done a heap of work but gained very little new information. It was all a bit hopeless. How could they possibly find the last two stones when they could be anywhere in the entire world? It was improbable they would ever find them, even with all the clues they possessed. She peered up into the gloomy sky. It was getting dark. She quickened her steps on the footpath.

"Oh, Miss Masters?"

Tracey spun around. There was no one behind her. Laughter echoed down the street. "Who's there?" she called.

All she could see were encroaching shadows. A dog yipped somewhere close by, high-pitched and excited. Another dog joined in and the yips became a shared high-pitch howl. *Go home, Tracey.* Her eyes darted in all directions as she searched the darkness for whoever called her name. Memories hit her of the Shadowman chasing her down the dark street and she shivered in the cool evening air, pulling her hands from her pockets in case she needed quick use of her magic.

By the time she reached the bottom of her driveway she was spooked enough to run all the way to her front door. With light pouring in from the entry and her brothers' voices carrying into the front yard, Tracey felt brave enough to stand on the porch and stare out at the night. There was no one out there. She closed the door on the faint sound of laughter. "Who is that?" she whispered.

Jane remained standing in the circle. "I am not afraid," she told them, and she was not. For she had felt the power of the circle and the power that lay inside her.

15

Tracey stared around the warm, wood-paneled room. The flooring was old and stained beneath her dirty trainers, like that of a two-hundred-year-old church or a school room. She did not recognize where she was. There was no scent or sound in the air to help her identify her location. She did know that she was dreaming. She knew it in that way when things were not right but felt completely normal.

"Tracey?"

She turned. Behind her stood Jing Cho. He wore a comfortable red outfit and soft, black shoes. "Is this a dream?" she asked.

"It is."

"Why am I here? Where even *is* here?"

"This is a place of protection. A place where you can come to think."

"About what?"

"It is your head, Tracey. Your dream. You tell me."

"I — uh — what?"

"You are starting to question the truth," he said.

"What do you mean?"

"Talk through what you know."

"About the stones?" she asked.

"No."

"The laughing boy? Why was he laughing at me?"

"Not that either."

"Then tell me."

His head tilted and his lips quirked. "Tracey, this is your dream."

She squinted at him. "Who are you, really?"

Jing Cho's face blurred and Tracey stumbled back, recognizing that round face and tinted glasses. He wore the same clothes she had seen him in at the university. "Doctor Chan?"

"We must speak."

"Are you real?"

"You must find me. Come to me. I can help you."

"Help me with what?" Tracey demanded. "No, you're trying to trick me. What game are you playing? Is the laughing boy you or one of your minions?"

"I can help you save your friends," he said grabbing her arms and squeezing with icy fingers.

"My friends? What did you do to them?"

"Find me, Tracey."

Reluctance slowed every step Tracey took toward school the next morning. Sarah was three paces ahead and pretending she was walking alone. "Sars?" Tracey called.

"What?"

Ignoring her sister's snappy response through long practice, Tracey let air seep from her lips and asked the question buzzing around inside her brain. "Has Kylie said anything to you lately?"

Sarah walked backward staring at Tracey in surprise. She twisted her bracelets around her wrist. "She's avoiding me. Did Damian say why?"

"Damian's not, uh, not really talking to me either."

"That will make it weird on your next date," Sarah snickered.

"Not gonna be a problem anymore."

"Oh wait, what?" Sarah's suddenly concerned eyes locked onto Tracey's face. When Tracey nodded, Sarah sighed and stopped walking, letting Tracey catch up. "Are you okay?" They walked slowly toward school together.

"Yeah." Tracey's throat tightened when she squeezed the words out. "It was my decision, well, both of our decisions actually. We're still friends."

"Oh." Sarah was quiet for a moment and then asked. "Does that mean I can't be friends with Kylie anymore?"

Tracey grabbed Sarah's arm, stopping her in place. "Of course not. You can be friends with anyone. I wouldn't get in the way of that."

"If Kylie even wants to be friends with me," Sarah said. An epic frown took over her face.

"Yeah."

Both girls sighed and continued walking.

"Where were you last night?" Sarah asked.

Tracey stared off into the distance, hoping she wasn't about to start another fight. "Uncle Donny's."

"Are you trying to find the next, uh, thing?" Sarah whispered, glancing over her shoulder to see if anyone close enough to hear.

"Just a lot of talking and writing. We've got stuff to read too."

"Sounds like homework."

Tracey laughed. Sarah grinned at her. They separated when they got to school and while Tracey waited for her friends, Sarah continued off to the lower campus. Tracey's hand slipped to the Butterfly Stone. "Stephanie?"

She opened her eyes on the black space of the Serpent's Kiss and sighed.

"Hello, Tracey." Timothy withstood her examination silently. "What do you need?"

"I wanted to speak with Stephanie. So, why do I keep coming here?"

"I did not bring you here."

Why would Tracey come to the black place when she didn't want to? She stood silently, face scrunched as she tried to figure out if she had anything to ask the annoying man. She heard a voice inside her head laughing. "Can I track someone who is pranking me?"

"Pranking?"

"Playing dumb tricks — magic ones."

"Perhaps. Why are they bothering you?"

"I wish I knew," she grumbled. Now that she was here, she should continue investigating the stones and see if Timothy let any new information slip. "Jonathan and Charles. What can you tell me about them?"

"Jonathan?" He looked confused. "Why would you ask about Jonathan? Is it not Charles you are after?"

"Jonathan was a member of your super secret club too, wasn't he?" Timothy's confusion unsettled Tracey. Ugh, stupid curse locking the information on the stones to those who already knew about them. "You said you'd never lie to me."

"I did."

She recalled what he first told her. "How do you know when you're remembering something correctly?" she asked thinking of her Nana's lost memories and then of Stephanie's memory Visions.

His mouth dropped open. "What?"

"If you don't remember something, how would you know you'd forgotten it? I mean. How do you know there's not something that you have forgotten?"

His thin lips pursed. "Why are you asking this?"

"Why can't you tell me about Jonathan?"

"I'm … I don't understand."

"Stephanie, Jing, Millicent … They were all cursed and their curses affect their memories."

He crossed his arms. "And you think I have been affected too."

"Who cursed you?"

"An interesting question." He hummed. "You almost act as if you care."

"What? No. No I don't care about you," she said.

"If I am cursed, doesn't that make me a victim too?"

"You're not a victim. You're evil."

He smiled. "A compelling argument." His laughter made her angry.

She forced her lips together and snorted out through her nose. "Tell me about the Sect? Why did you form it?"

"From my point of view?"

"Obviously."

"So you accept that anything I tell you was experienced through my eyes and not that of your ancestor, and therefore could be different than what she might tell you about the same event?"

"You could lie."

"And Stephanie only ever tells you the complete truth, doesn't she?"

Tracey fell silent.

Timothy's smile twisted to one side. "Obviously." He nodded. "But it would also be from her point of view, wouldn't it?"

"Well, yes. But —"

"Perhaps her view is not as truthful as she tells it. What does she want you to think and why does she want you to think it?"

"I don't understand."

He spread his arms in a wide bow. "Permit me to show you." He kept one hand outstretched and moved it in her direction. "You have seen the memories she saved for you?"

"Some of them."

"Hmmmm. Why not all of them?"

"I was told I'm not ready." *Which is so annoying.* She could tell Timothy knew exactly what she thought about that. His eyebrows rose and his lips pressed together tightly. He hummed again.

"Do you feel ready?" he asked.

Tracey examined his face. And the hand he held out. "You can show me memories too?"

"If you are willing to see them."

"How can you show me? I can only see Stephanie's memories via my grandma."

"Allow me to access —"

She pulled her hand back. "No. You are not allowed in my mind. I told you that!"

His sideways smile returned. "You will. When you are ready. For now, all I want is for you to allow yourself to see — through me. I know you have seen Visions before. I can give you access to *my* mind, to *my* memories."

"Is it dangerous?"

"Would you believe my answer?"

"Nope."

He laughed and wiggled the fingers of his outstretched hand. "Let me show you."

Tracey's hand trembled but she gripped his cold fingers and in less than a blink he stood beside her. Shadows engulfed her as if she had slipped her head underwater. The same wave swept her away and she found herself in a familiar building. The manor house. Tracey stood in the hallway. The black and white nature of a memory Vision was at once familiar and unfamiliar. She jolted when she realized Timothy was still standing beside her. "What are you doing here?"

"It is my memory is it not?"

"Yeah, but Stephanie is never with me in her memories."

"Did you ask her why?"

"No."

His head tilted. "Hmmmm." She still held Timothy's hand and it squicked her out holding onto his clammy fingers. Tracey followed the direction he indicated and gasped when she realized six people stood within a rune-decorated circle drawn on the floor. They chanted softly but Tracey didn't recognize any of the words. All wore dark, shaded robes over their everyday clothing. *The Sect of Six!*

A light shone from each chest, glowing so brightly Tracey couldn't see what generated it. Then it came to her. *The stones.* She was watching the Sect perform a spell. An intricate spell if the language spoken and the signs etched onto the floor beneath their feet implied. She didn't know where to look first and tried to creep closer, but found she couldn't move. Her gaze darted to Timothy. He still gripped her hand. "If I let go the Vision ends," he warned her.

"What are they doing?"

"You know what they're doing."

This was it? *The* spell? The one that started everything? Her mouth dropped open and her gaze snapped back to the circle. *The spell?* If she could have felt anything at all in this place her hairs would be standing on end, and not just from the immense magic flooding the room. *This is it. The Spell.* Her eyes burned at how wide open she pressed them. She had to remember everything she saw.

Timothy wouldn't elaborate, just held a finger to his lips and pointed to the circle. Millicent stared at Stephanie, standing across from her on the circle's edge. Her familiar soft and sad face was twisted tight, unhappy. Jing's eyes were peacefully closed. Timothy — the one standing on the circle — also stared at Stephanie, a small tilt of his lips and shining eyes showing awe and triumph. Stephanie's face glowed. An enormous grin splitting her features, lighting her eyes as she stared up at the ceiling. Two figures stood with their backs to Tracey. A mid-sized white man, smaller than Timothy but taller than Jing, with brown wavy hair that touched his collar.

The other man's face was side on to Tracey. She had seen him in one of Stephanie's memories. That was Charles. A thin white man with sharp features, a cold face, and long bony hands. His small, mean looking eyes glared across the circle at Stephanie as if wishing her harm.

The light inside the circle grew brighter. Stephanie laughed, glowing with magic — they all were — and with a flash like sunlight reflecting off a mirror the spell took hold. Tracey caught sight of an echoing glint from the unknown man's hand. She twisted, trying to see what he held, but from this angle it was impossible to get a good look at it.

There was a crack and a thwack. Stephanie fell silent, her eyes widening further and her mouth dropped open in surprise. Jing and Millicent kept chanting, only their words were different to the ones the rest spoke and to each other. Stephanie gasped and bowed forward. Charles snarled and tried to pull his hand away from the man beside him. He couldn't escape the shackle-like grip. The unknown man laughed softly. Tracey's skin crawled to hear it. She knew that laugh. A glass vial shattered by his feet, releasing a puff of red powder.

Stephanie gasped. "No." She tore her stare from the unknown man and turned it on Timothy. "What are you doing?"

Tracey couldn't see that the Timothy in the circle was doing anything. She glanced up at the silent duplicate beside her. Was he hiding something from Tracey in this Vision, blocking her from seeing the truth of what happened? Millicent and Jing chanted on. The glowing light at each of their chests turned from bright sunshine into dirty yellow before shifting to brown. The color bled into the stones and into the Vision, staining them all. Pressure built. Growing faster, higher. A scream tore from their throats, forcing their heads back from the force of it. Tracey tried to cover her ears to block out the horrifying sound but she couldn't move. The scream grew until the circle could no longer contain it. Concussive force exploded outward, throwing each figure into the wall behind them. Everything turned black. Tracey found herself shaking, wobbling in place suddenly back inside the black place staring across the void at Timothy.

"What happened?" she demanded.

"Everything. Nothing. I don't know. I blacked out."

"What happened after you woke up?"

He hummed. "Disaster. Destruction. Death."

"What do you mean?"

Timothy blinked as if realizing what he was doing. "Enough." He flung out a hand and Tracey fell to her knees. She dug her hands into hard dirt and scratchy sharp grass, back in the real world and nearly puked from her abrupt ejection. Nausea rolled inside her stomach like ocean waves crashing upon a pebbly shore and she let out a distressed moan.

What the …? She knelt on the path leading to school and could hear the bell ringing in the distance. Tracey fumbled for her cell phone. The clock said she was late. *Fruit tingles.* She pushed to her feet and nearly fell, catching her balance just in time. Ugh.

As soon as her equilibrium returned enough to walk without falling, she stumbled toward the distant buildings.

Mr. Michaels read something out loud but Tracey's mind kept replaying what she had seen inside Timothy's memory Vision. Was that the spell creating the Stones of Power? Or had it been the failure of a different spell, one the Sect were supposed to be united in casting? It seemed to Tracey every member acted separately, conducting a separate variation that led to a massive explosion. She wondered if the broken spell was what caused the memory curse. Unless it was done on purpose? No, it had appeared as though they were acting against one another. Perhaps, if only one person had altered the spell it might have been okay. But five acting against it?

"Miss Masters!"

"What?" Tracey's head snapped up to find the whole class staring at her. "Um, yes, sir?"

Mr. Michaels sighed loudly. "Well?"

Fruit tingles. "I'm sorry, sir. Can you repeat the question?" She sank low in her seat and hid her face with her hair.

Laughter filled the classroom and beneath it she could hear Carla snickering. When Tracey glanced over her shoulder, she spotted Carla's venomous smile. Next to the blond girl, Meena's dark eyes were narrowed in a squint, as if she was trying to burrow into Tracey's head. *Creepy.* Damian wouldn't look at Tracey at all. His teeth were clenched, his shoulders tense and straight as he stared intently at his tablet.

"Your assignment?" Mr. Michaels snapped.

"I don't have it," she whispered. It was at home, on her desk in her bedroom. That was why Damian looked so mad. *Ugh. Could I possibly make things any worse between us?*

"Miss Masters, you are aware that you are dragging Mr. Carter's scores down with you, aren't you? Are you proud of that?"

"No, sir."

"Mr. Carter are you happy with that?"

"No, sir," Damian croaked.

"It's my fault, not his. I'm sorry, sir."

"Not acceptable, Miss Masters. You will return after class today and write an apology to me and to your work partner."

"Yes, sir."

When Mr. Michaels turned away to focus his ire on the two Daves, Tracey dropped her head into her hands. *Fruit tingles.*

"You are bad people and are frightening my family. Please leave us alone," she said as they drew near.

16

The rest of Tracey's day became one long continual nightmare. Everything that could go wrong, did go wrong. Uncle Donny would say it must be a full moon.

Everywhere Tracey turned, teens glared at her. Like someone had said something about her — and everyone knew what it was *but* her. The focus on Tracey was so intense it was giving her hives. Lunchtime break provided no respite from the judgmental looks. If anything, they grew worse.

"What did you do, Trace?" Jonny asked, pushing his chair up and onto its back legs. He rested his knees on the edge of the table and rocked shallowly back and forth.

She shrugged. "I don't know."

"No one is talking about what it is, but everyone seems peeved at you for something," Tony muttered, glancing up from his phone.

"Do you think they know about Damian?" Tracey asked.

Laura screwed up her nose, lips twisting in thought. "I don't think he'd tell anyone about what happened in London."

"No, not that. We, um, we broke up."

"What?" Laura dropped her sandwich. Jonny's chair thumped to all fours and they stared, their mouths hanging open in exaggerated pictures of shock.

Tracey quickly told them what happened.

"Why didn't you say anything?" Laura said, her hand pressed to Tracey's arm in support.

She almost shrugged off Laura's comfort before she realized she really wanted it. "I didn't want to talk about it, I guess."

"I'm so sorry, Tracey," Tony offered.

"It was both of our decisions. Maybe Damian was more hurt than he let on and told people?"

"What a jerk," Jonny snorted. "Trying to get people on his side. It explains the looks, don't it?"

"He seemed okay with it though, and he said he wanted to stay friends. I just hope whatever it is people are talking about, it's not something I've done."

"Magic related, maybe?" Tony sighed. "Eventually we'll know if it's him or someone else."

Tracey shoved her sandwich into her mouth and glanced around the room. Her skin prickled at all the dark looks shot her way.

"Any ideas about finding the next stone?" Tony asked, putting his cell phone face up on the table.

No one said anything.

Dave Two plopped down into the empty chair at Tracey's left. "What did you do?"

"Nothing," Tracey snapped. "What are they saying?"

"Aren't you worried about sitting with us?" Jonny asked waving his hands over the entire table.

Dave shook his head. "Nah, told 'em they have to deal. We're friends, whatever, right?"

"Right," Tony echoed, raising his eyebrows. "We are? Officially? That's brave of you."

Tracey glanced past Tony's head and caught sight of students staring their way and breaking into frantic whispers.

"They know what I am." Dave shook his wrist and the Mage-kind identification bracelet. "Not like I can hide this."

Tracey noticed Tony gripping his wrist where his bracelet was. "What are they saying about me?" she tried again when she realized Dave hadn't answered her question.

"That you've been using magic to get passing grades."

Voices rose around the table.

"What?" she gasped. "But they know Mr. Michaels hates me. And Mr. Rachette. My grades totally suck! They can see for themselves when they get posted."

"Who said it?" Jonny demanded, leaning forward. He shoved his empty tray into the center of the table. It clanged into Tracey's tray.

"Is someone making it up to get Tracey in trouble?" Laura asked.

"I don't know." Dave shook his head. "I dunno who started it."

"Well I know it wasn't Damian." Tracey said. "He's getting the same bad mark as me. It's the same assignment." Her stomach twisted sharply at the thought of someone telling such dangerous lies. If the school thought she cheated with magic then every Mage-kind student would be put through hell proving that they didn't. Sarah and Kylie, Tracey's brother, Tony, Jilly and all the other Mage-kind juniors. They'd be forever under suspicion. She peered at the table where Damian was sitting alone. He stared down at his food. Tracey's brow furrowed. He wouldn't do that. Not to his sister.

"Like you said. He wouldn't." Tony assured her.

"He might, if he was angry enough," Laura said in a whisper so no one outside of their table could hear.

Tracey buried her head in her hands. She heard soft feet approaching. She didn't raise her head recognizing Jilly's voice as she sat down. "They're all idiots."

"Who is?" Tracey mumbled.

"I assume you asked who, though I can barely hear you," Jilly said. "Carla and Dave One."

"So it was them? They are the ones spreading lies about Tracey?" Jonny snapped.

"Meena too?" Tracey asked.

"Odd, but no."

"Why?" Tracey mumbled. She lifted her head.

Jilly shrugged. Tracey speared a dark look at Dave Two.

"What? I'm not a part of it."

"Did you say anything to Meena?" she asked.

"No."

Laura pointed an accusatory finger at Tracey. "Why are you asking about Meena? It's Dave One and Carla we have to plot against. They are going down for this. I promise."

"Meena has been … weird," Tracey explained Meena's strange interactions. The looks, the squinting stares. The *not* saying anything.

They all glanced toward the girl in question, who — like Damian — was oddly sitting on her own.

"Should I go talk to her?" Tracey asked.

"No!" Laura, Tony, and Jonny said together.

Dave finished his lunch and stood up. "I'm out."

They said goodbye and Dave walked off. Tracey turned back to her friends. "Was that also weird?"

"Yes," Tony said immediately.

"Totes weird. Is that a thing now? Is Dave gonna sit with us from now on?" Jonny asked.

"I'm not sure how I feel about that," Laura said and sipped her juice.

"Weird," Tracey echoed. "Right, so plotting to get Dave One and Carla. Jonny? Any ideas?" She started stacking the empty trays on top of each other.

As she marched into Mr. Michaels room for detention, Tracey found Meena already seated at the back of the room, staring out through the window. Tracey didn't say anything. She just stood in the doorway and waited for Mr. Michaels to acknowledge her. It took a while. She tried not to fidget. *I've faced off with mumbles, a Shadowman, and a Dust Devil. I can handle Mr. Michaels.*

"Phone off," he ordered and pointed to the plastic tub on his desk. She complied, and he handed her a pencil and lined paper. "Write. Apology to me and Mr. Carter."

When she finished, she folded the paper and put her hands on the table. She could feel Meena's stare digging into her back and wondered if her skin would catch fire from the strength of the glare. *Why is she even here?*

Tracey rubbed her fingers against the desktop. She wanted to tap but knew that would annoy Mr. Michaels and probably end with an extension to her punishment.

It didn't make sense to just sit here and not do anything. Wouldn't it have been better to spend the time writing her assignment? Instead, she got to watch Mr. Michaels play with his phone. With his attention distracted she risked a glance over her shoulder. Yep. Her back itch was right. Meena *was* glaring at her.

"What?" Trace mouthed at her.

Meena sniffed and returned her gaze to the window.

What was *that* about?

A few minutes later Meena cleared her throat loudly. "Sir?"

"I said to remain silent, Miss Gulpta."

"Sir, Carla and Dave One, uh — Dave Stanley — have been telling kids that Tracey used magic in school."

Tracey's mouth dropped open. Meena was tattling? Tracey and her friends wouldn't need plan *bullies-going-down* after all. Jonny would be disappointed about not using the water bombs. So would Tony for not getting to use his hacking skills.

"Is that right, Miss Gulpta? They obviously haven't seen Miss Masters' scores. It's clear she is doing nothing to help her grades. Not even cheating."

"Sir!" Tracey said to put up a token complaint. He wasn't wrong.

"Very well, Miss Gulpta. I will take care of the rumors. Now. I said silence, girls."

After what felt like hours but was only thirty-three minutes, Mr. Michaels told them to get lost. Tracey grabbed her phone and switched it on, staring impatiently at the screen as she walked out of the classroom, plotting her text to Jonny to tell him the plan was off.

"Tracey?"

Lowering the phone, she peered back at Meena's uncertain call. "Why did you help me?" she asked.

Meena shrugged. "It's not just you who will be hurt by that story. I told them it was going too far."

"Well, thank you. I guess." Tracey turned away.

"Are you … um … okay?" Meena called after her.

"What?" Tracey spun around in surprise. Meena was acting so different. Almost … nice. Meena held her gaze though her face flushed. "What do you care?" Tracey asked, her voice losing its sharp edge with her confusion.

"I —"

"Just thanks for telling Mr. Michaels. I wish you didn't have too. I want them to just leave me alone." The stones beneath her shirt heated in heartbeat pulses against her chest, growing hotter, echoing Tracey's anger.

Meena's gaze zeroed in on Tracey's neck, flicking to her wrist before coming back up to her face. She stepped back and held up both hands. "I … never mind." Meena's hair swished in a wide curtain behind her as she stormed off.

Tracey stared after the rapidly disappearing girl. *Why is everyone acting so abnormal today?* Her phone beeped drawing her attention down as the screen lit up with a text message from her uncle.

Hey kiddo, get over here quick. I need your help with a case. A new one.

"New case?" she muttered. "But what about the stones?"

A short time later Tracey pushed open the door to Uncle Donny's private investigators office sending the little bell above the door tinkling wildly.

"At last. You're late." Her uncle was a flurry of activity, pushing whiteboards across the room to stack against the wall beside Tracey's desk. A large piece of brown paper taped to the front board hid the writing beneath from prying eyes.

"Had detention," she moaned.

Uncle Donny froze for a second and peered over at her. "What?" His eyes had that wild look that lit them when he was thinking about an investigation. His suit trousers and white shirt were wrinkled and his hair was a tangled mess. *What has he been up to?*

She waved his question off. "What's going on?"

"We have a job!" He ran into his private office and before she could blink returned with his notepad.

"What about the stones? We have to find the next one."

"It's a cold case, kiddo. What we've got here is a hot one and we need to catch it before it cools."

"But, Uncle Donny — ?"

"Money, kiddo. We still need to eat, and I've got bills to pay. Solving a case right now would really help me do that. I need your help."

Tracey sighed. "Of course. What's the case?"

"A local family has asked me to find their missing nephew — a young boy around your age."

"A missing boy? I haven't seen any alerts online."

"Apparently, he has a habit of running away. His parents travel a great deal for work and whenever they leave, the young lad is sent to his uncle who lives here in Miltern Falls. By the sound of it, he doesn't even run away for long. He always returns by the time his parents come home."

"So, where does he go?"

"No one knows. That's what they want us to find out. You're his age. I'm hoping you'll have some ideas about where a boy his age might go?"

"What's his name?"

"Sebastian Sawyer."

"What's he look like?"

Uncle Donny handed her a faded photograph. "He looks about eight in this," she complained.

"He doesn't like cameras. Refuses to let anyone take his picture."

"Hmmm." Tracey examined the photo. It was a candid shot of the side of a young boy's face. White skin, dark brown wavy hair, and bright blue eyes. In the photo he wore skinny jeans and a basketball jersey. His hair was long — about chin length — and his hand was in the process of pushing wispy strands behind his ear and out of his eyes. He was looking past the camera at something. His eyes seemed sad. "Did you try a search spell?"

"That's why I've been waiting for you. Come on."

He waved her into his private office. The chairs in front of his desk were gone and he had pushed the desk closer to the wall. It left a wide space on the floor free for the chalk circle drawn on the old worn carpet. Inside the circle was a piece of blue cloth. "Torn off his shirt by the pet dog," he said.

Tracey stood behind her uncle and rested her hand on his forearm. "Ready?"

"Do it."

Tracey drew a little magic from her core and imagined it zooming around her body in silvery glowing ribbons. She directed the ribbons down her arm and into her uncle. He straightened, sucking in a deep breath as the flood of magic filled his body. "Find Sebastian Sawyer," he whispered, lighting the circle with his magic. The spell was different to Tracey's search spell. Hers worked by searching for a token or a magically infused Object of Power, like the stones. Uncle Donny's spell searched for the echo that belonged to the object inside the circle.

The light filling the circle turned faintly yellow and began to pulse. The pulsing grew faster and when it became a steady tone it swirled up into three spinning hoop-like shapes moving faster and faster until they collapsed over the blue cloth. Tracey expected to see her uncle's balloon lift up from the hoops and float off in Sebastian's direction. Instead, the light grew brighter and larger, first the size of a baseball then a basketball then a beach ball, growing larger and brighter until it exploded with a loud bang, rattling the windows and knocking both Tracey and her uncle onto their butts. Tracey just got her shield up in time to protect them from the blast of hot air that bloomed over her protection bubble. When the light faded, the cloth and the circle were gone. A cloying smell of burnt rubber filled the office. They both scrunched their noses as Tracey lowered her shield bubble. She turned on her uncle, her fists clenched, her shoulders high around her ears. "Sebastian is Mage-kind?"

"Didn't I mention that?"

Tracey huffed. "No. You forgot that bit." They stared at the singed carpet. "Now what?" she asked.

He scratched the back of his neck. "Back to the drawing board."

"I'll keep an eye out for Sebastian after school and at the mall. You never know, he might be hiding in plain sight, blending in with other kids."

"Good thinking. I'll contact the uncle for another piece of clothing. We'll have to try a different tracking spell."

Tracey didn't think finding Sebastian was going to be that easy. The search spell blew back on them, which meant Sebastian didn't want to be found. He had put up a magic block. "Is there anything else you know about him?"

"He likes writing, reading, soccer and theatre, rock albums and musicals. Bit of a musician himself, he plays and sings in a band."

"Anything else?" Such an eclectic list would make finding Sebastian pretty hard.

"He's a good kid by all accounts. Bit of a joker though."

"I'm not sure that helps, but okay. Can I keep the photo to show the kids at school?"

"Great thinking. I've made copies." He passed her one and waved as she headed for the door.

She stopped just inside the door frame. "What about the stones?"

"We'll keep searching. Don't worry, kiddo. I've not forgotten."

Tracey eyed the stacked whiteboards and the hope inside her chest drained from her body. He didn't sound too convinced. "Sure." She headed outside and made her way to the bus stop. Standing near the sign, she tugged her phone from her back pocket and scrolled through her social media feeds. She pulled her earbuds from her front pocket and poked them into her ears turning the music up higher than she usually set it. *I wonder what Sebastian's band is called?* She could hunt around online for his band page. A laugh sounded right in her ears. She turned in place and tugged her earbuds from her ears to listen better. She didn't hear the laugh again. She put one earbud back in and replayed the song. There was no laugh on the track.

In the silence before the next song started, she heard it again. A strong pulse of air scorched her ankles. She screeched and jumped back as the grass in front of her feet burst into flames. She raised her shield bubble instinctively and stomped the fire out, searching the distance for the culprit. She was completely alone. *How on earth did the grass catch alight?*

She turned a few circles. Nothing looked out of place or overtly suspicious. The laugh in her head faded.

"You have made your crops prosper
and made ours fail!" he cried.

17

Tracey marched straight up to Mr. Michaels as she entered class the next day and presented her assignment with a flourish. He didn't thank her. She slipped into the empty seat beside Damian, who finally offered her a tiny smile. Several times she opened her mouth to say something and each time she closed it again, unsure of how to start. Her skin itched. She glanced over her shoulder and discovered Meena was staring again. Sheesh, was that yesterday's glare still? The girl needed some new facial expressions.

Peering the other way Tracey caught Jonny also watching her. He shrugged and shot her a quirk of his lips. Tony's attention was already absorbed in reading on his tablet.

"— work together."

She tuned into Mr. Michaels' voice as his instructions ended. *Oh rats.* She touched her tablet open when the class turned to chat with the person beside them and sheepishly smiled at Damian. "Hey."

"You didn't hear what he said, did you?" He gave a tiny shake of his head. He wore his leather jacket today and it made his arm muscles bulge.

Tracey tore her gaze away, bit her lips and muttered, "No. Can you …"

"Page eighty."

"Thanks."

"We have to discuss it before and then again after we read it."

"Before?" She glanced up into his dreamy eyes and swayed closer to his side, inhaling deeply. He smelled so good.

"Yeah, he said it's a social media article about Prince Henry and whether or not he was right to keep his Mage-kind identity secret — so um, what do you think?"

Tracey snapped straighter and grabbed her tablet. "Of course he was right to keep it secret. He wouldn't have been hired in all those cool movies if people knew. That's a good reason to keep it a secret." Did Mr. Michaels know Tracey was keeping a ton of secrets? He couldn't possibly know but somehow it felt like epic trolling on behalf of the teacher. She flicked her eyes at Damian to find he was watching her. "Um, what do *you* think?"

Damian shrugged. "I guess. He was lying to his fans though."

"Fans he never would have had if he'd told them who he really was. And *we* know he kept it secret because he's also an undercover M-force agent. Besides, keeping his status secret didn't hurt anyone."

"It would matter if the secret hurt someone?"

"Well, yeah. Isn't that why people keep secrets? To stop other people from getting hurt. Like if you were keeping a secret to protect someone. That's a good thing." It was why she kept the Serpent's Kiss secret from everyone. It protected them and her. If no one knew she wore it then no one would try and take it from her. She couldn't trust anyone with the truth.

"I was thinking it was the other way around actually." His chin dipped closer to his chest, his eyes shadowed as he thought. "What if exposing a secret saved someone's life, you know, like a drug addict."

Tracey blinked. "Oh, I guess. But what if —"

"If you don't want to tell, you shouldn't have to," Meena shouted. The whole class fell silent, their heads snapping up as they stared over at the fuming girl at the desk near the window. Meena's lips were almost white they were pressed together so tightly.

Beside her, Carla gave her friend a pointed eye roll. "Whatever."

"Get back to reading," Mr. Michaels ordered.

Tracey began to read. As she got to the second paragraph her phone vibrated in her pocket. She glanced up at Mr. Michaels. He didn't react to the slight buzzing. Soft chatter filled the room as the teens discussed what they were reading. It seemed to prevent Mr. Michaels narrowing in on the sound of her phone.

Damian squinted in her direction. "Was that you?" he whispered, glancing up to check where Mr. Michaels' attention lay.

"Yep."

He raised the tablet in front of his chest and angled it to cover Tracey's actions. "Put your tablet up too."

"Thanks." She slipped her phone from her pocket. Hidden by the two tablets she glanced at the text message. "It's from Prince Henry," she whispered. "Freaky timing."

"Do you need to answer it?"

"I can reply later." Tracey offered Damian a soft smile. He must have seen something in her face. His neck reddened and he scratched his collar. She wished she could touch his hand or press her shoulder against his arm. At least they were talking. That was better than nothing.

"We have to talk about the chapter. Read it quick," he said.

She skimmed over the black and white words though their meaning escaped her as Prince Henry's message flared bright in her mind.

`Have a clue. Call me back.`

What clue? What could the agent prince possibly have found? He wasn't supposed to be working the case anymore; he was supposed to be at his mother's. If he had been permitted back at work, his mom couldn't be as angry as Hank thought she'd be with the world learning he was Mage-kind. At least, that's what Tracey hoped. Rubbing her eyes and scratching the sand out of the corners, Tracey forced her attention back on the text, hoping she wouldn't be asked to speak to the class about it. "So, what do you think?"

"I think he was right not to tell the truth. But the second time I read it, I think it's more a story about making the wrong choice and being stuck with that choice for the rest of your life. It's not so much about the secret but the choice," Damian said.

Tracey's eyebrows sprang up. "I didn't think that at all. I thought he was right not to tell the secret because he knew it would ruin everything if he did."

"You don't think that's sad? And lonely?" he mused.

Tracey frowned as a faint male laugh reached her ears. "Do you hear that?"

"Hear what?" Damian's face took on that adorably confused look again as he raised his head and peered around the room. "Is Meena going to explode again or is it something the Daves are doing?"

"That laugh."

"What laugh?"

The sound cut off as the fire alarm screeched above the heads. They all chorused a groan. None louder than Mr. Michaels. "Right. Leave your bags here — single file. Let's go." As the class reached the corridor, Tracey heard Mr. Michaels complaining to Mr. Rachette. "They usually give us a heads up. What the hell? This drill will cut into my marking time."

"Not a drill," Mr. Rachette said glancing at his phone.

The alarmed look Mr. Michaels shot him sent a shiver down Tracey's spine. Mr. Michaels glanced at his own phone. "Right." With a wave he hustled the line to move faster.

Tracey shared a worried look with Damian and Tony. She searched the crowd for Jonny. "A real fire? Where is it? Can you smell any smoke?" The whole line of teens peered around, anxiety levels rising upon seeing the teachers' stony expressions. Tracey texted Laura and Jilly as they walked. The laugh in her head grew louder. Her right eye twitched. She stopped walking and almost caused a stampede as the teens behind her were forced to dart left and right to get around her, swearing and berating her sudden stop. Tendrils of smoke and an acrid smell seeped into the corridor. A few kids screamed. The chatter grew thunderous. Every adult face was pinched with worry. "Move!"

"Tracey?" Tony waded back through the crowded corridor to reach her side.

"I think someone lit the fire on purpose. If it is a real fire," she said. Damian stopped at her side. His hand brushed her arm. Normally she would enjoy the tingles at his touch. Now, she barely felt them. The laughter grew into a bellow. "Ow! So loud. Shut up!" She moaned, slapping her hands over her ears.

"Fake? Who would do that?" Tony asked.

"I don't know. Ugh, can't you hear that?"

"Hear what?" Damian twisted and tilted his head but seemed unable to hear what she could hear.

"The laughter."

Tony's mouth pinched. He stared at the ground as he focused his hearing on the corridor. Feet in squeaky trainers, teens calling for each other, shouting teachers, it was all a nightmare of clashing and mangled sounds. "Where do you think it is coming from?"

"I can't tell." Tracey head ached from the noise.

"Keep moving you three. Hustle." Mr. Michaels' voice jerked all three of them into moving. They quick-marched down the hall to join their classmates.

"Tony, I think I can find it if I Listen. You know?" she said stopping again.

"It's a fire," he reminded her. "At least let's get outside."

"Right yes, I know. It's just … what if it's not a fire?"

"Not a fire?"

"Yeah."

"I can smell smoke," Damian said.

"But where is it coming from? Where did it start? How did it start?"

"Move it, kids," Mr. Rachette shouted, catching sight of them dawdling.

They sped up and were the last to exit the building. As she stepped onto the concrete path, Tracey heard her name whispered on the breeze. She turned left and was yanked back by Damian. "It's okay," she told him. His fingers were warm and soft around hers. Reluctantly she tugged loose from his grip. "Can you and Tony cover for me? I need to find out who it is. I think … I think … they're doing it to get my attention."

"Doesn't seem like good attention," Damian said. His gaze darted over the crowd searching for any teachers who might catch them loitering near the door. The alarms were still blaring and the scent of smoke was stronger out here. "Be careful."

Tracey smiled at his worried expression. "I will." She focused on letting her magic out of her inner imaginary closet. She pressed it up to her ear in a silvery blur and mag-icked her hearing. Every sound became louder, sharper, clearer. She moaned at the increased pounding in her temples. The noise hurt her brain. Students loudly speculated about the fire and if it was a drill or not. Teachers stressed about where the fire was. In the distance she caught the sound of approaching sirens. Three fire trucks. And then she Listened.

"I'm waiting for you."

Her eyes sprang open. It was a boy's voice. Tracey fol-lowed it, spurred on by her own curiosity and annoyance. She wanted the laughter to stop. And she also needed to know what the boy was laughing about. Something she did, or because he knew something she should know?

She found him sitting on the wall just outside the school gate. Normally, she would not get this far without being spotted and called back by a teacher, but with the confusion of the evacuation no one even looked their way. The boy was her age and had dark brown wavy hair that came down to his ears. He wore a sky-blue polo shirt that made his eyes glow like sapphires. She didn't recognize him. He must go to a different school. Unless he was new? He wore a Mage-kind identification bracelet around his left wrist.

She yelled at him as she drew close. "What are you doing?"

He grinned. "Waiting."

"For what?"

"For you."

"Who are you?" She swallowed down her anger and lowered her voice, but it was hard to do. Her head still throbbed and her ears ached.

His grin grew broader. Tracey's heart twitched at the sight. He was cute — super cute — but she was mad, so she refused to notice. Much. "Who are you?" he countered. His lips widened as his smile deepened.

Her tummy flipped. *Wow.* She shook her dazed head clear. *Stay mad.* "You said you were waiting for me. You already know who I am."

"Who are any of us? Are we just meat dolls given a soul? What is life? Or living for that matter? Do we exist? Are we even real?" With the longer speech she could hear his northern English accent. *Oh, I love that accent!* It curled inside her ears and sent tingles over her skin. Then she focused on his words.

This cute boy was clearly crazy.

Her voice lowered further, deepening with the fury she forced into it. "So, who am I?" she demanded, stepping closer.

"I know who you are."

Her growled groan made her sound like a frustrated pirate. She stared up into the blue sky. "Then why did you —"

"I want to know who you are. Are you Tracey Masters, or are you the magic stone?"

Her head snapped down at that. *How does he know about that?*

"You know the answer to that already," he said, answering her unasked question. "I don't have to tell you. I'm just here to make sure you decide."

"Decide what?"

"You'll know when the time comes," he said and smiled again.

Her breath caught at the sight. *Ugh, do not fall for the crazy kid, Trace!* "I don't understand."

"You will."

Tracey's skin heated in anger or embarrassment or possibly — *definitely* — annoyance. Her hand rose to wrap around the Butterfly Stone. "I'll show you who I am."

The boy leaped off the fence and brushed his hands over the seat of his skinny jeans. Her hands followed the motion. *Oh boy!* She looked up and got caught in his stare again. He was way taller than her and looked down on her with a tilt of his head. "Don't touch it, please."

"How do you know about the Butterfly Stone?" she demanded.

"That's not the stone I'm talking about."

Tracey's thrumming blood turned to ice. She stepped back. "What?" It sounded like he knew about the Serpent's Kiss. *How?* "Who are you?"

"Look, I can be a friend, or I can be an enemy. It's up to you."

"I don't even know who you are. How do I know I can trust you? I don't know what your game is. What do you want from me?"

His lips twisted as if he knew she knew he wouldn't answer and that she shouldn't have asked in the first place. Liked he believed she should be smarter than that.

"Did you set fire to the school?" she accused instead.

"Of course not."

As she expected. "Smoke bomb?"

"Smoke illusion actually. It's a pretty cool spell."

It was the sort of spell Jonny would have loved to learn if he had any magic. "Well, you got me out here to talk alone. What do you want to tell me?'

"I just wanted to meet you properly."

"Why?"

"To see if I can trust you."

"Look," she said, imagining she was breathing out dragon smoke. "I'm not going to play these games with you. I don't care how cute you are. If you won't tell me anything, go away and leave me alone."

His eyes twinkled. "You think I'm cute?"

Her skin flamed. *Oh. My. God.* "That's not … ugh!"

"I'll think about it, Tracey Masters." He walked away down the street, whistling. His voice drifted back to her. "I'll see you around."

Tracey stared after him, her mouth hanging open.

What. The. Heck?

"So, who was he?" Laura asked.

"I have no freaking idea." Tracey leaned forward and propped her elbows up on her desk resting her chin in her hands. Laura was the only one able to come to Uncle Donny's with her after school and as soon as they sat down Tracey blurted the whole thing out to her friend. Laura leaned back in the client chair in front of Tracey's desk and blew lightly on her hot chocolate. Her white jacket was new and her dark hair gleamed against it where it lay over her shoulders. "What did he look like?"

"Cute. Though I'm too annoyed to want to think of him like that. Wavy dark brown hair — like my brothers though not quite as curly — and a pokey nose."

"Pokey?"

"You know," Tracey waved her hands in front of her face. "Pokey. Not too huge but not tiny, just …"

"Pokey?"

"Exactly!" Tracey slumped in her chair. "I mean, he's super cute if you like that sort of thing."

Laura grinned. "You said that already."

"He's sad though. Like, I dunno, his face has only ever made sad expressions so it's kinda stuck that way. Northern English accent. I think it's called Geordie? I looked it up."

Laura squinted over her hot chocolate mug. "Eyes?"

Dreamy. Knowing. Intelligent. "Blue. I don't know, Laura. I wasn't paying that much attention." *Liar. Liar, pants on fire.*

"And you haven't seen him around before?" Laura's lips quirked as if she knew exactly what Tracey was thinking.

"No." Tracey's skin heated.

"And he didn't say how he knew you?"

"Annoying right? He clearly knew who I was, and he knew about the Butterfly Stone. I know he's Mage-kind, but like, who is he? He didn't even tell me his name."

"We need to put Tony on it. Get him to do some research."

"Yep."

Laura pursed her lips and put her mug on the desk. Tracey rubbed at the dirt stain on her jeans. *How long has that been there?* She leapt to her feet and twisted around staring down at her legs and pulled her sci-fi shirt out at the bottom searching for more stains. She was covered in wrinkles. "Oh my God, look at me. I look hideous." Her skin was on fire.

Laura burst out laughing. "You look fine. Besides, you said he was annoying."

"Yeah, well, yeah. Shut up." Tracey slumped back into her chair and huffed.

"So what about Damian?"

"What about him?"

"You seem to be getting on better at school."

"Yeah, so."

"New cute boy distraction," Laura picked up her mug again.

Tracey moaned. She pointed sharply at her grinning friend. "Don't start!" Tracey glanced at the time on her desktop display. "Prince Henry should be calling any minute now."

"He didn't say what he wanted to tell you?"

"No. He only sent that second message to say he'd call at this time."

"Where's your uncle?" Laura slurped her hot chocolate; the sound made them both laugh.

She shrugged as the laughter died down. Uncle Donny was often out when Tracey arrived. She pushed the unknown *cute* boy out of her brain. "What do you think is going on with Meena?"

Laura put her mug down on Tracey's desk and leaned back in her chair. "She has been a bit odd, hasn't she? I noticed that too."

"No gossip you've heard?"

"Nothing. But we're not the only ones who have noticed."

Tracey leaned forward. "Do you think — ?" The ring tone of her cell phone cut her off. She poked the speaker button as soon as she answered so Laura could hear too. "Hi, Hank." Laura smirked at the casual greeting. "Laura's with me. Is that okay?"

"Hi, ladies. I have some information from the archives."

Straight into it today, no small talk. He must be in a hurry. "What did you find?" she asked.

"You were right about the curse's characteristics. Once information is known about a stone you can dig up more information on it. Your uncle got in touch with me and told me what you learned about the Crow's Heart."

Tracey sighed. She had been right not to tell her uncle about the Serpent's Kiss. He was such a blabber mouth. She formed a grumbly face at Laura who shrugged in a *'are-you-surprised'* look.

"Because we know the Crow's Heart hasn't been held by anyone since Millicent's death, I've been able to look into her disappearance and the fire a little more closely. I have to say the information I've found is a little hinky."

"Hinky?"

"Not right, but I'm not sure in what way. The files from the council archive are contradictory at best."

"Which means what?"

"I don't trust it. I'm seeking the source documents which is taking some time."

Tracey knew Millicent had not died in the fire. She'd died afterwards, in the maze. Alone. She explained all of that to Prince Henry.

"Interesting. It was reported publicly that she set the fire and disappeared. Since her body was never found it was speculated that she lit the fire on purpose and escaped. The fire was deemed to be arson."

"They blamed her?"

"That's what was locally believed at the time, yes."

"Anything else?"

"We know Stephanie survived, because you wouldn't be here otherwise. Obviously. There were other bodies found but … well, science and technology back then were not as sophisticated as they are today. They believed they had the Sect members and closed the case."

"But you don't think that's who they were?"

He hummed.

"What did Stephanie do after the fire?" Laura asked.

"She sold the estate. Moved south where she and Matthew were married. They migrated to your country shortly after, to a little town called Falter Hills. Agent Epworth is there now, looking through the local council and library records to locate their arrival details and what they did next."

"So you don't think Matthew was a member of the Sect?"

"He was a Norm," Prince Henry reminded her. She knew that. Besides, she was sure the other member was Jonathan. "You think none of the stone Protectors died in the fire?"

"Possibly."

"Possibly? What do you mean? Did you find something?"

Prince Henry laughed. "You're quick. I'll give you that. You take after your uncle. Possibly. As I said three male bodies were found. We cannot be absolutely certain that Charles Smith, Timothy Hart, and our mysterious third stone Protector died in or due to the fire."

Tracey sat back in her chair feeling a weight settle over her chest. "So, we have less than nothing."

"Don't be too dejected, Tracey. We have more than we did before."

"If Timothy got away, the others might have too. We have no idea what they did next or where they went then."

"True."

"So, the last two stones could be anywhere in the world."

"Well … yes. But we know more about them, Tracey. We are making progress every day. Stay positive. Since you found the Crow's Heart, we'll learn more. Have you tried your tracking spell now that you have three stones?"

"Yeah. The remaining threads just kept circling in place. I think the curse is blocking them. We need to know more about the other stones before my spell will work."

"Darn. That's bad luck."

"I might have something though. You've been investigating Charles and Timothy. Did they know a man named Jonathan?"

"Jonathan what?"

"I don't know. That's the problem."

"Hmmm. Let me look into it. A clue from Stephanie, huh?"

"Ah, yeah. Ha ha. Obviously."

"Right, I'll add the name to my list. Oh, wait. So that's why Tony asked me to search for a book called '*A Circle of Mystical Illusion?*' That's what I'm calling to tell you about. I found it. And interesting coincidence, though I think you're about to tell me it is not a coincidence at all, the man who wrote it is named Jonathan."

"Your animals are fat and your people are healthy. Ours are thin and full of sickness. You have cursed us," he cried.

18

Tracey's eyes popped wide. "You found it?"

"Yes. So, I know a little about the author already. Jonathan Bennett. You think Jonathan Bennett is the last member of the Sect?"

"I think he knew Millicent and went to school with Timothy."

"That's great intel, Tracey. I'll get right on to it. In the meantime, I'll scan a copy of the book and send it through to you. It's a fairy tale about Mage-kind. I've not read it before. It is certainly interesting."

"Was it the only book he wrote?"

"Sadly yes. All of the contracts were canceled when the Mage-kind rebellion happened. Good hunting, Tracey. I hope this book gives you more clues."

Her chest buzzed at the thought of reading the book. "Great, thank you. Terrific work, Prince Henry."

He laughed. "I appreciate the encouragement. I'll email you the scanned copy shortly. And of course, Tracey, if you have anything else to tell me, anything at all, you can tell me. I hope you know that."

Laura's hand movements grew wilder.

"Ah, nope nothing else. All good here."

There was a long pause. Tracey had the feeling he didn't believe her. She pulled an *eeeep* face at Laura; wide popped-out eyes, her lips pulled back showing her teeth in a grimace.

"Thanks for the update," she shouted and closed the call. "Oh, fruit tingles. I just hung up on Prince Henry."

"You hung up on Prince Henry?" Laura whispered, her fingers hiding her mouth.

"I did. I hung up on Prince Henry!"

They burst out laughing. Uncle Donny poked his head in through the doorway, saw them laughing and stopped for a second before entering and tossing his rumpled suit jacket onto the sofa. He yanked off his tie. "Having fun, girls?"

Tracey cleared her throat. "Brainstorming ideas about the stones."

"Anything new?" he asked. He bounced his weight between his left and right foot. Tracey squinted at him. He caught her look and grinned. His hair was wilder than usual, like he had been running his fingers through it and his shirt and trousers were as rumpled as his jacket. *He slept in them?*

"What have you been doing?"

"You know that new case? The one about the missing boy. I've been on a stakeout."

"Did you find him?"

"No, but I have a clue and I think it will help us find him. I need your help. Hello, Laura, do you want to help too?"

"Oh, yes please," she said sitting up straighter.

At the same time Tracey asked, "Why us?"

"There's a teen party at the bowling alley. I'll stick out like a crocodile at an alligator party if I try to sneak in."

"You think he's at the party?" Tracey asked.

"Good intel says yes. So yes. Will you go in for me?"

"Do you have a current picture of him yet?"

"Yes." He held out a folded piece of paper.

Tracey unfolded it, examined the face, and passed it to Laura, widening her eyes at her best friend. "Kinda cute, huh? Pokey nose."

Laura's eyes snapped up and she locked eyes with Tracey. Her mouth dropped open at Tracey's enormous eyes and bouncing eyebrows. "Ah yeah. Super cute. Why … um … why are you looking for him, Mr. Masters?"

The boy her uncle was looking for was the same Magekind teen who had been annoying Tracey! Sebastian Sawyer. *Oh, but that's such a sweet name.*

"The mayor is his uncle. He's worried the boy has run off."

"The mayor?" Tracey's mouth dropped open further. "You said Sebastian was missing," Tracey said. "But why is he missing? Did he have a fight with the mayor?" Now she knew why the mayor asked about her uncle. She pictured the creepy man and figured she knew exactly why Sebastian had run off. The mayor gave Tracey the willies.

"Let's talk on the way, girls." Uncle Donny ushered them from the office and locked the door behind them. Tracey's mind whirred. Oh yeah. Tracey would help her uncle find Sebastian Sawyer. And not just to solve the case, but to demand answers of her own: Why was he pranking her? Until she found out, she wouldn't tell her uncle she knew him.

Tracey led the way to her uncle's old compact and climbed into the front seat after swiping all the crushed takeaway food bags and crumbs onto the floor.

Laura slipped into the back seat and buckled up, shifting shopping bags and empty clothes hangers to the seat beside her. "What makes you think he's at this party?"

"I've been interrogating his school friends," Uncle Donny said.

"Interrogating?" Tracey asked buckling up.

"Well, questioning. He likes to sneak into birthday parties, especially big ones like sixteenth and eighteenth birthdays. And he loves bowling."

"Yeah, but why does he like sneaking in?" Tracey asked.

Uncle Donny hummed. "For the thrill of it? The risk of getting caught?"

That sounded like the same boy.

"It's possible he's there then," Laura said from the back seat. She held onto her seat belt strap as Uncle Donny took the next turn too quickly. Tracey rocked side to side and scowled at her uncle.

"If he's there, don't approach him. Just come out and get me," Uncle Donny said.

"What if he talks to us?" Tracey asked. "We could casually ask him where he's staying?"

"I don't want you two putting yourselves in any danger but yes, any intel you can gather would be a great help to the case."

"Why would it be dangerous, Mr. Masters?" Laura asked. Tracey knew what her uncle was going to say before he said it.

"Because he's Mage-kind."

"Yeah, but Tracey is Mage-kind. So are you. Why does that automatically mean this kid is dangerous?"

"You just don't know, Laura. Teens and emotions are never an easy mix. Throw in a party — that he snuck into, so he knows he can't get caught — and the fact that he's a runaway? Just be careful. Please. Both of you." Uncle Donny's eyes flicked to Tracey and then over his shoulder so he could include Laura in the lecture.

"We will," Tracey promised.

They pulled into a car space in the underground mall car park and Uncle Donny speared them with another long sharp look. "Be careful. If you can find out where he is staying, great. If not, then find out where he frequents. No magic." He pointed at Tracey as he said it.

"I know. I won't."

"Text me or call. I'll wait here. No —" he turned off the car motor "— I'll loiter one floor down. In the food court. That way I'll be close by if there's any trouble. When you get him out of the party, call me and I'll come running."

Tracey nodded and slammed the car door shut. She and Laura walked toward the southern mall entrance, making straight for the escalators. There were people everywhere. Shoppers juggling over-stuffed bags, and people chatting loudly on phones held up in front of their faces. Tracey ducked around several kids in basketball uniforms sucking on large icy drinks. Loud music blared from another person's cell phone. Level four held the cinema and bowling alley, as well as two restaurants. Level three was the food court and most of the teen shops. The department stores and sports stores were all located on the ground level. As soon as they were out of Uncle Donny's earshot they whispered frantically to each other, voices high-pitched and overlapping.

"It's the same guy?"

"The same guy." Tracey peered over her shoulder and glared at the woman one step behind. She stood far too close to Tracey for her liking. The woman's Mage-kind bracelet jangled as she hiked her handbag strap higher up on her shoulder. Tracey turned back to Laura. "Uncle Donny said his name is Sebastian. You know, he's been a pain in my butt, but I almost don't want to help Uncle Donny find him. The mayor is a major creep." Two kids Sarah's age pushed past them on the escalator, laughing loudly. They didn't even say sorry, too focused on their video call or live story streaming or whatever it was they were doing.

"Yeah, but this Sebastian guy's been harassing you."

"More like pranking me, but sure."

"Even though he's cute it's no excuse, Tracey. The guy's a troll."

"I know."

"And you've already met him. He *knows* who you are. As soon as he sees you coming, he'll take off. How are we going to stop him?"

"I think he'll talk to me when he sees me."

"Or he'll run."

"Let's hope he doesn't. I *need* to talk to him first and find out how he knows about the Butterfly Stone. Besides, you're with me."

"What do you mean?" They got to the top of the escalator, turned, and headed up again.

"You're cute too … he might stay and talk to you."

Laura's face flushed. She hit Tracey on the arm. "Are you kidding me?"

"Sorry." Tracey giggled.

"I'm not even Mage-kind."

"What does that matter? You're fascinating."

Laura shook her head at Tracey's fangirling. "Stop it."

"Excuse me," interrupted a man in a navy suit carrying far too many shopping bags. Both girls squished closer to the handrail as he pushed past.

"Besides, Sebastian better hang around," Tracey continued. "I want to talk to him."

"We'll go after him if he runs."

Tracey nodded. "You bet we will."

"Glad I'm wearing my trainers," Laura added softly.

Tracey laughed. She only ever wore trainers. They were easier to run in. And no matter how much she hated running, somehow she always ended up running somewhere.

"So, what's the plan?" Laura asked tugging her long tresses up and into a ponytail she tied with the elastic bard from around her wrist.

"We let ourselves be seen. If he's here, I think he'll want to know what we're doing. He'll be curious. That's how we get him," Tracey said.

"Who is he anyway?"

"I have no idea. But he knows about the stones and that makes him dangerous." Tracey's phone pinged with an email notification. She got off the escalator at the third floor to check it. Laura trailed after her as she shifted from the path of the shoppers continuing onto level four. "Prince Henry just sent through the book."

"Do you think it will have any clues?"

Tracey moaned, her finger swiping down her phone screen as she scrolled through the email. "It's like a hundred pages!" She locked eyes with her friend. "We have to read it. Jonathan wrote it and he knew Stephanie and Millicent and T — probably Timothy and Charles too."

The girls made the quick trip to the fourth floor. Once they stepped off the escalator they headed left, passing the entrance to the cinemas. Tracey stared over the line of patrons that stretched down the corridor. Fans mingled in the foyer dressed in colorful costumes. "Ah, I wanna see that one."

"Of course you do." Laura's smirk grew wider at Tracey's moan.

Loud crashing pins scattering across multiple wooden lanes and hard balls hitting wooden surfaces directed them to the bowling alley. "I haven't been here for years," Laura muttered. Loud electronic music thumped from overhead speakers making it difficult to hear each other even standing outside the alley.

"We should book a lane soon," Tracey told her. It looked like the birthday party had booked out the whole place. Teens and balloons were scattered all over the alley. Flashing in time with the loud music, red, green, and blue fluorescent lighting strips broke up the murkiness of the alleys. Tracey eyed the lone security guard standing outside the entrance. "Damn. How do we get in?"

"I got this." Laura stomped straight up to him. "Hey," she shouted above the pounding bass line. The guard straightened and eyeballed her suspiciously. He ran a hand over his oily hair. He was older than Tracey's oldest brother, but not by much. His wrinkled shirt collar had a food stain right beneath his chin. "My twin is in there," Laura shouted. "My mom said he couldn't come to this party. He did anyway and my mom's super pissed. Can you go get him? Dark hair. Eyes like mine? His name's Sean."

"What?" The security guard squinted at Laura and then peered over his shoulder at the party inside. His pale face was riddled with angry red pimples.

"My brother. He has to come home. Now. My mom's gonna call the cops."

Tracey stretched her eyes to fake a scared look, but mainly to stop herself from laughing at Laura's snobby tone.

"I can't leave this spot, kid."

"Dude, listen. My mom is losing her mind. If Sean doesn't come out right now —"

"Can't you just go in and get him?" the guard said.

Laura sighed epically. "How am I supposed to find him in the dark? Don't you have like a PA system so we can call him —"

"Listen, kid. Just go in. Both of you. Be quick, okay?"

"Fine!" Laura grabbed Tracey's hand and dragged her past the guard.

"Man, your mom is scary," Tracey said loudly, throwing a quiver into her voice. "Sean's going to wet himself."

"She's so piss — right, I don't think he can hear us anymore."

Tracey pulled Laura to a stop. "That was awesome."

"What can I say, I do cranky better than anyone. Besides, people never want more work. I figured it was a fifty-fifty shot he'd let us through."

"What if he'd said no?"

"He didn't. Come on. Let's find Sebastian. He'd better be here after all that."

"Split up," Tracey suggested. "You try the arcade and the restaurant, I'll check the lanes."

"Meet back here?"

"Yep."

Laura disappeared into the noise and flashing lights of the arcade while Tracey headed for the first lane to examine the gathered teens near the ball return chute. All were dressed in jeans of some sort; black, blue, or white and a bowling shirt with "Terence Mason is No. 1" written on it in rainbow colors. Sebastian was going to be tricky to spot amongst this crowd. Terence Mason sure had a lot of friends. A sixteen-year-old would be in the year above her at school, but she didn't recognize any of the bowlers. They must go to Miltern South.

"What are you looking at?" One tall boy with a head of red curls stood next to the ball rack. "Who are you?"

Tracey offered a big smile. Was it that obvious she wasn't a part of the party? "I'm looking for Sebastian?"

"You a friend?"

"Yeah. Is he here?"

The boy looked up and down the lanes. "Lane eight."

"Thanks." Tracey smiled and moved off, hoping the boy would forget his question about who she was. She zeroed-in on lane eight. There were two teams of six sitting and stand-ing around waiting to bowl. They talked and laughed loudly, shouting over each other to be heard. Tracey moved closer. One boy had his back to her. He seemed to sense her stare and his head rose, peering around suspiciously. He spotted Tracey and launched to his feet, eyes wide.

"Hey Seb, it's your turn." A pretty girl stopped his escape by grabbing his arm. Her blue-sprayed hair was tied up in a high ponytail and it swished dramatically as she spun around.

Sebastian looked torn. He stepped forward then back when the girl didn't let go of his arm. "Ugh …"

Tracey stopped at the arc of seats. "Go ahead. I can wait," she called, wriggling her fingers at him in a wave.

The two boys on either side of Sebastian laughed and pushed his shoulder, glancing from Tracey to Sebastian and back again.

"Ooooo." The blue haired girl whistled. "Go, Sebby."

"Aw shut it, all of you."

"Your go!" Another girl ordered. "Bowl then flirt." She grinned at Tracey and wiggled her own fingers in a cute wave.

Tracey hoped her face was not as red as Sebastian's. The wanted boy threw up his hands and groaned loudly. "Let me do this first." He picked up his ball.

"What's your name?" the blue-haired girl asked, leaning over the back of her seat. "I haven't seen you around here before. How do you know Terry? I used to do karate with him."

"I'm Tracey," she answered, watching Sebastian swing into a fluid, four-step movement. He released the ball and watched it zoom down the lane toward the ten pins at the end. Tracey's mouth dropped open as she felt magic zipping after the ball, nudging it straighter. All ten pins flew apart with a sharp crack.

"You have beaten your animals. You have not tended to your lands and your people are mean and full of hate. You have caused your own misfortune," Jane told him.

19

You cheated!" They sat at the table behind lane eight so Sebastian could see when it was his turn to bowl again. With all the noise in the bowling alley and the pumping music, Tracey had no fear they would be overheard. The tables around them were empty anyway while the games were being played.

Sebastian held her gaze, piercing blue eyes locked onto hers and her skin erupted in goose pimples. "I don't know what you're talking about," he said.

Tracey rolled her eyes at the obvious lie.

"How did you find me?" he asked.

"I'm a detective."

"No, you work for your uncle during the school holidays. He's the detective."

Sebastian had done his homework. It was a little creepy — *a lot creepy* — knowing he had looked into her. "And yet, here I am."

"I found you first," he reminded her. His stare wouldn't leave her face. She wondered what he could see, what he was looking for. She became self-conscious of her face. Were her eyes squinting? Was her nose red? Did she have something stuck between her teeth? She pressed her lips together hard and his eyes darted down and back up.

"Found me first?" she repeated hoping her face wasn't as fiery as it felt. "It's not a competition."

"Isn't it?" His teeth flashed. He didn't seem panicked or upset that she found him. He didn't seem super annoyed or angry either. His reaction confused her. It was like he was searching for something, something he expected to find in her face or in her words but he couldn't locate it. A flicker of disappointment darted across his face before his skin smoothed out again.

"You're my current case. At least you're my uncle's current case. Your family is worried about you."

His eyes widened. "My family?"

"Yes. Why did you run away?"

"I didn't — okay, listen. He's not my family. Not my real family. You need to convince your uncle to tell his client you can't find me."

"Why should I help you?"

"Because you want me in your debt."

"Hey, Seb. It's your turn." The girl with the blue hair shouted, startling them out of their intense conversation. "Come on!"

He pressed his hands to the tabletop and pushed to his feet, though his eyes remained locked on Tracey. "Watch out for the Crocodile Man. I can help you, but I need you to help me too." He jogged to the lane and picked up his bowling ball. Tracey's brow furrowed as she watched him bowl another strike. *Crocodile Man?*

"Hey Trace, what's going on? Why are you just sitting here?"

She glanced up at Laura and waved her over. "I found him."

"Where?" Laura searched the lanes, turning in a semi-circle.

"Just there, he's bowling and —" Tracey rubbed her eyes. *I'm going crazy.* "He was right there. Bowling." With a loud clang his red ball appeared from the chute. "That's his ball in the thing." There was no sign of the tall annoying boy. Tracey abandoned her table and ran up to the girl lining up for her turn. "Where'd he go?"

Blue hair swished as she turned, eyes sparkling. "Who?"

"Sebastian."

"Who?"

"The boy I was talking to earlier. The one with the brown wavy hair and blue eyes."

"You mean Stevie?" She pointed to a short, slight boy with long arms. He looked nothing like Sebastian.

"No, a different guy. Sebastian."

The girl shrugged and turned to bowl.

Tracey waved the rest of the bowling team over and asked the same question. Laura looked on as if Tracey had lost her mind. The teens shrugged. Tracey turned her shocked gaze to Laura. "He's gone."

After twenty minutes they gave up the search and walked out of the bowling alley. They had checked every lane, the arcade, the eating area, and the bathrooms. *Well, the girls' bathroom, though we did stand outside the boys for a while and asked anyone coming out if Sebastian was inside.* There was no sign of the Mage-kind boy anywhere and no one had any idea who they were talking about.

"It has to be a spell," Laura said.

Tracey shrugged. She had not felt any magic other than when Sebastian cheated his two strikes, but that didn't mean the boy hadn't cast some sort of concealment spell. For the Mage-kind to know a spell of that sort meant he was practiced at using magic outside the home. Which fit with his pranking her at school. *Did I imagine talking to him?* "I heard his ball land. It hit the lane hard and he got two strikes. You saw his ball reappear. The red one."

"I did see a red ball." Laura pursed her lips. "So what are you thinking?"

"I'll sound bonkers."

"Tell me anyway."

"What if he is a ... a ... ghost. Or he's invisible or something."

"Can ghosts move stuff around? You said that girl and the other teens spoke to him. He must have been there."

"But she said she didn't know who I was talking about."

"Isn't it simpler that he did a disappearing spell like the memory curse that was on Jilly? You forgot her every time she left the room."

"He's our age. He shouldn't be using magic outside the home."

"You do."

"Yeah, but I have *reasons.*"

"Maybe he does too," Laura said. They stepped onto the downward escalator.

Tracey pondered that. "He said not his real family and his face was all pinched. You know, like he ate a lemon. I actually believe him. Uncle Donny said the mayor hired him to find his nephew. So if the mayor is not his real uncle, what's the mayor's deal? Why does he want to find Sebastian so badly?"

"That's a good question." Laura peered over the side of the escalator. "Now what?"

"Now, we find Uncle Donny and go home. I'm tired," Tracey said around a giant yawn.

Uncle Donny pressed Tracey for further details about Sebastian after they dropped Laura off at home. She told him the missing boy did a runner as soon as he spotted them prowling through the bowling alley. It was close enough to the truth. Sebastian had slipped their net — *a very holey net given it was only me and Laura inside.* Uncle Donny gave up when all of Tracey's answers were a shrug or an, "I don't know." He told Tracey he would focus on finding the next party Sebastian might sneak into.

Tracey waved as he drove away from her house. She was soooo tired. Even her bones were tired. Her shoulders slumped and her spine bent forward. Sebastian was nothing more than a distraction keeping Uncle Donny busy and away from looking for more stones. She just wished she didn't get body tingles every time she thought of Sebastian's incredible eyes.

A voice whispered her name in the dark, snapping her head up. Her first thought was that it was Sebastian again and that he followed her home. Then her name was whispered again and she recognized the voice.

"Nope," she said to Timothy. "I am not in the mood."

The Serpent's Kiss heated against her skin as her name was said again — right into her ear. She threw up her hands and growled. "Stop it."

That boy is not who you think he is.

Tracey's feet froze. It was a little like her shoes had stepped into glue. She couldn't lift her feet. She tilted her head instead. "Who is he then?"

Timothy hummed.

"I'm not coming back into the black place. So either tell me or leave me alone."

Do not trust that boy.

"I don't trust you. Maybe I should trust Sebastian simply because you don't."

So contrary, Tracey. I am trying to help you.

"Sure. Sure." She huffed out a breath and imagined a thin transparent bubble around her brain, shoving his voice out. As soon as she did, she was able to move again and pushed open the front door. The TV volume blasted her eardrums as she entered. The twins were playing their football game on the big TV, the one with all the chanting and cheering. Tracey's oldest brother, Peter, sat in the dining room plucking on his guitar. Sarah was on a stool at the kitchen bench next to Mom gesturing wildly, telling Dad a school story. Dad hummed at Sarah as he pulled a steaming dish from the microwave, a tray from the oven and shook the basket of the air fryer with all the grace of a restaurant chef.

"Good timing, kiddo," Dad called catching sight of Tracey standing in the entrance hall.

Tracey wished she could go upstairs and fall into bed, instead she diverted into the dining room and plonked down at the table next to Peter. "Hey."

"Hey Trace, what's up?" His hand moved up and down the fretboard as he formed chord shapes with his fingers.

"Nothing."

He held his fingers and the strings still and squinted at her. "Sure."

When she didn't say anything else his fingers slid over the frets again and he plucked out an unfamiliar tune. "What are you playing?" she asked.

"Trying something new. What do you think?" He played a rhythm she didn't recognize. She liked the way the notes were soft but seemed joyous, not sad.

"Sounds good."

He grinned and stopped playing, hugging the guitar to his chest. "You look tired."

"I could sleep for a week, I think."

"How's school?"

"Fine. Mr. Michaels is being a total pain."

"He hasn't changed."

"There's this girl at school. Meena. I dunno. She's like the world's worst bully but lately she's been — different, I guess. Staring and such. I know she doesn't like me. She doesn't like anyone Mage-kind, but usually she's a lot more verbal, you know? It makes me uncomfortable."

"That she's not bullying you?"

Tracey snorted. "No, that's not it."

"Has anything happened with her?"

"Not with Meena specifically. Well not lately." Tracey thought about mentioning Damian and how they were "just friends" now. She couldn't imagine that would affect Meena though. Then again, Damian showed an interest in Meena first. At least, according to Meena he had. Could that be it? The real reason behind Meena's current weirdness? Tracey didn't want to tell all of that to Peter though — especially when Mom and Sarah could hear her if they focused hard enough. She shrugged instead. Peter hummed.

Cheering erupted from the front room.

Mom's voice rose up over all the noise. "Boys! Pack it up. Dinner's ready."

Peter placed his guitar on the stand near the wall as the twins, Sarah and Dad flew into the dining room. Sarah plonked down on Tracey's left which meant Grandma ended up sitting opposite Tracey. Her brow furrowed as her stare ran over Tracey's body. "Are you feeling okay, Tracey?"

"I'm just tired," she mumbled, taking the warm plate Mom passed over. Chatter flew over her head as she focused on eating her lasagna and vegetables. She didn't even complain about the pumpkin on her plate like she would normally. Her head was blessedly silent of voices and her thoughts were blank. Dad was listening to the kick-by-kick replay of the boys' video game and Grandma talked softly to Tracey's mom. No one even looked at Tracey or paid her any attention until Sarah knocked against Tracey's shoulder with her own. "What?"

"What's wrong?" Sarah asked.

Tracey shook her head flicking the fuzziness out of her mind or at least sending it bouncing to the other side of the empty abyss inside her head. "What? Sorry. I'm super tired. I'm not paying attention."

Sarah's sour expression softened. "I asked how's Damian?"

Tracey choked on the green bean she was chewing. She coughed it up and gulped from her water glass to clear her throat. "Why ask me?"

"Just something Kylie said. I mean, she asked me and like, that's weird because he's her brother, not mine. Why didn't she ask him herself?"

"What did she say?"

"That Damian was all sad and stuff. Mopey. He keeps telling her he's fine. She was just … maybe something happened at school? Is Meena and Dave One picking on him or something?"

"No, I — uh — I don't think so, but I guess I haven't really noticed." Because every time she saw him she couldn't think for a few minutes, she just lost herself in his dreamy gaze and muscly shoulders. She shoved away the sudden memory of Sebastian's cute smirk and gorgeous blue eyes. "I could ask him if you want?"

"Kylie's worried."

"How is Kylie?"

Sarah grinned and relaxed back in her chair, sipping from her water glass. "Great actually. She's not as angry as she used to be. I don't know if that's because Timothy's gone or if it's because she can use her magic again but she seems to be … I dunno … peaceful."

"Does she remember anything from when Timothy was in control? Like, what he was doing or thinking? Did she overhear any of his plans?"

"I can ask. She doesn't really talk about it. We just chat about camp and training and magic and boys."

"Oh yeah?" Tracey laughed. "Wait, what boys?"

Sarah's cheeks bloomed red and she shoved a forkful of lasagna into her mouth, making Tracey laugh. "I used to do that with Laura. Still do actually. If you get the chance could you ask Kylie if she remembers Timothy whispering or incessantly chatting to her and boring her to death?"

Oh, well excuse me, Timothy grumped.

Tracey strengthened her flickering brain bubble and pushed him out again. Sarah tilted her head. "Shhhhure."

Gulping her own water, Tracey emptied the glass and forced a bright smile. "Great. Thanks. It might give us clues. About him. About Timothy, I mean, and maybe the other stone holders. The more details we can get the better, you know? Does, uh, does Kylie say if Damian ever mentions me?"

Sarah smirked. "Seriously?"

"You know what, shut up. I don't care."

"Shhhhure," Sarah sang again.

Tracey shoveled down the rest of her dinner and ignored her sister's soft laugh.

"Tracey, what's the hurry?" Dad asked, chuckling at the picture she made.

"I'm just tired. I have a lot of homework to do before I go to bed. Can I be excused?" she asked standing up and lifting her plate to clear her place.

"Don't you want any desert?" Mom asked.

"It's chocolate cake," the twins chorused.

Tracey dropped back down into her chair. "I could stay a bit longer," she said. The whole family laughed and this time Tracey joined in.

"You are an evil witch. Your existence
means Hamsted is not as bountiful as
Delmore and that is unfair.
We will drive you away," he said.

20

In the dark, whispers crept around Tracey. There were no words she could make out. It was just a buzz that filled the air and raised the hair on her arms. A negative, aggressive hiss of noise. A grunt startled her backward.

Laughter exploded out of the black — coming from right in front of her. Running feet pounded the ground, sending Tracey's head snapping left and right to track it. She narrowed her gaze to see what was there, but it was too dark. She could see nothing. The feet sounds were strange. Odd. Softer than shoes. More like … paws. Sweat broke out across Tracey's body. Her mind created a picture of Jilly's tiger on the prowl.

Oh.

It's a dream.

This is a dream.

And she knew that laugh.

The running footsteps — animal paws — slowed.

Another set of paws joined the first. Soon all she could hear were panting animals surrounding her, paws landing, coming closer and darting away. Circling her.

Within one heartbeat and the next all the sounds stopped. The whispers, the padding feet, the laughter.

In the silence she heard her own heartbeat.

The sound was cut off by a sharp snapping sound.

Tracey screamed.

And woke up, panting like she had run three miles.

Jane's magic rose up in response to his anger and filled the circle.

21

Tracey stared up at her bedroom ceiling. For a moment her vision blurred and she had no idea what day it was. *Friday?* No, it was not a school day. *Saturday.* No school. *Oh thank goodness.* She squeezed her eyes shut and willed her brain to go back to sleep.

After a few minutes spent desperately wishing her mind would just listen to her body for once, she sighed and shoved away her bedding. Another long sigh forced her to her feet. She shook her pajamas legs down her calves and grabbed her dressing gown. Sliding on her slippers she bent down just outside her bedroom door to grab her phone off the charger board where it sat next to her siblings' phones.

Scrolling through her notifications she headed downstairs. Grandma sat at the kitchen table, drinking a cup of tea. "Morning," Tracey mumbled.

"I'm over here, Tracey. Not on your phone," Grandma corrected.

Tracey head flew up. *Whoops.* She put her phone into her dressing gown pocket. "Sorry, Grandma."

The older woman smiled. "Good morning. How did you sleep?"

"I had a nightmare," she admitted. Grandma didn't say anything, only patted Tracey's hand with her knotty fingers. "I think it was another stone dream. Maybe. I don't know. Nana wasn't in it, but there was laughter and an animal and whispers. I couldn't see anything." Tracey rubbed her face with her fingers, scratching the grit out of the corners of her eyes.

"What kind of animal?"

She shrugged. "Four feet? A snappy sound? I heard grunting too."

"Hmmmm. What kind of feet. Hoofs, claws, or pads?"

"Paws. I think. It moved fast and um, there was more than one. They were circling me. Maybe it's a dog?"

"Hmmm. Could be. Or perhaps feline? Not an insect or bird. That's good. We can rule some animals out."

"I suppose. Or not. Could be a monkey? Or a lizard? Or a wombat? Bears even? And there are hundreds of dogs and cats."

"Still, it does limit your possibilities somewhat."

"Yeah, I guess." Tracey dragged herself to her feet and grabbed a bowl and the cereal box off the bench. As she sat down she asked, "Do you have any more memory Visions you can share with me?"

"You know I can't control when it happens."

"Stupid rules."

"Indeed." Grandma grinned at Tracey's pout.

Mom bustled in dressed in sweatpants and a wrinkled T-shirt, carrying an overloaded laundry basket that she dropped with a dull *thunk* on the floor. "Morning you two. Looking forward to today?"

"What's today?" Tracey asked.

"It's your Nana's birthday. We're going to Tavel House to visit her. We have cake. Remember?"

"Oh yeah." Tracey eyed her Grandma, who stared into her empty coffee cup as if willing it to magically refill. Tracey wondered if her Grandma actually could magically refill it and asked.

"You cannot make something from nothing, Tracey. As you well know. It would need to be already made somewhere. Besides, it never tastes as good."

"Are you coming to the party with us?"

"Yes. So remember to wear your nice clothes please," Grandma said.

Tracey let out a grumble and shoveled another spoonful of cereal and milk into her mouth.

They gathered in the large pale pink dining room at Tavel House because there were too many people to fit into Nana's small bedroom. Several of the elderly residents were seated on the sidelines so they could join in the festivities. The old men licked their lips as Mom brought in the massive cream cake. She lowered it carefully onto the table in the center of the room and it seemed no one could tear their eyes away from it. She bet they were all hoping to score a second piece. Mom made it big so the other residents and some of the nursing staff could have a piece if they wanted.

Tracey waved at Shirley, Olive, Margaret, Leslie, and Janet who sat close to Nana's table. They all wore party hats and held streamers, ribbons, and hooters in their gnarled hands. Nana's friends — when Nana remembered them. They usually sat at the same table in the dining room together and were all terribly competitive at cards and at bingo. Given the prizes were little chocolate bars Tracey could totally understand wanting to win all the games.

Nana sat at the head of the table with a red party hat on and stared at the cake. "Is this for me?"

"Of course, Mom." Tracey's mother handed over a paper plate. Nana took it with trembling hands. "It's your birthday."

"Is it?" Nana laughed. "Perhaps if I tell you later that I've forgotten about it we can have cake again tomorrow?" Everyone who heard the comment laughed. Tracey spied a few old men asking each other what was said because they couldn't hear. It set up a weird echo of every conversation.

Simon and Sarah sat on either side of Nana, their eyes glued to the cake as well. Tracey stood at the back of the room, watching everyone laugh and talk at top volume. She felt weirdly excluded, even though no one said anything specific to her or pointedly ignored her. The day wasn't about her. It was about their nana. Still, no one reached out to include Tracey in their conversation and she didn't feel like initiating any of her own. She played photographer instead and took a few photos of the party on her phone.

Tracey sang when everyone sang, and cheered loudly. She ate her slice of cake which was really yummy but didn't try for a second piece like her brothers. Finally, she wriggled close enough to the head of the table to sit down next to Nana.

"How are you, dear?" Nana's eyes didn't focus on Tracey at all. She stared into the distance, as if she could see straight through the walls. Tracey touched Nana lightly on the wrist. The old woman startled, blinked, and focused through her smudgy eyeglasses. "Do I know you, dear?"

Tracey's mouth dropped open. She snapped her mouth closed and wet her lips with a swipe of her tongue. "I'm Tracey."

"Tracey who?"

"Your granddaughter."

"Sarah is over there." Nana pointed, her hand trembling in the air.

Tracey clasped Nana's fingers. "It's me. Tracey. I'm one of your granddaughters."

"I don't think so."

Tears welled in Tracey's eyes. "I don't —" She loved her nana but this was making her a little angry and a little afraid. Nana's next statement made Tracey drop her fingers and grip the arms of her plastic chair tightly.

"I see leathery claws. Snap snap." She focused suddenly. "You shouldn't be here. You're evil. I know who you are."

Tracey swallowed hard. "Nana?"

"You get out of that girl. She is *not* yours."

"Nana?"

"Mom, stop that. That's Tracey. You be nice to her." Tracey's mom pulled Tracey out of the chair and tucked her behind her body, scowling down at the older woman and wagging her finger. "We are having a nice day. Breathe and focus." Tracey's mom picked up Nana's hand and squeezed her fingers.

When Tracey looked around she found everyone was staring.

"I … uh …" The prickle of every judgmental eye jabbed at Tracey's skin. Her hands dampened with sweat. She squeezed her fingers into fists. "It's not …"

Nana's mouth twisted into a nasty sneer. "You get away from me, you monster. I'll kill you if you come any closer."

Tears filled Tracey's eyes blurring every face. Dad tugged on her shoulder and pulled her out of the room. "Hon, your nana doesn't know what she's saying. She's not well, remember?"

Tracey had seen that look in Nana's eyes before and felt the power of her glare. Nana meant every word. Tracey pulled away from her dad and buried her head in her hands to hide her tears.

"She doesn't know who you are, hon. It's the dementia. She still loves you."

"She … she …" Tracey's mind was thick, numb. She couldn't feel anything. Dad pulled her into a big hug.

"It's okay, honey. It's okay to be upset. Come on. Let's pop outside for a breather," Tracey took her dad's hand and clenched hard around his thick fingers as they walked outside.

If Nana couldn't see Tracey, then who *had* she seen?

Silence lay heavy over every member of the family on the ride home. Simon kept shooting Tracey sad looks, leaning past Sarah to see her and then leaning back pretending he wasn't looking. Sarah was squished between them in the middle seat, and stared out through Simon's window. Tracey pushed closer to her own window in response. Grandma sat in the front passenger seat. Dad was driving. Mom drove the car behind them with Charlie and Peter.

"Enough silence," Grandma said suddenly. "Magic practice in the backyard. All the kids."

Simon sighed loudly.

"That includes you, Simon."

He gasped and leaned forward, stretching his seat belt. "Grandma, I'm a Norm. I can't —"

"Simon, I want your help. Magic or not, you are joining us."

Tracey exchanged a look with Sarah and giggled at Simon's open mouth. They were all getting a distraction this afternoon it seemed. Tracey's dark mood shifted with Grandma's announcement. As they pulled into the driveway her stomach swirled with anticipation and she leaped from the vehicle, racing her sister into the backyard. Grandma rounded up Peter and Charlie as they climbed from Mom's car.

"Tracey, you need an outlet for your emotions and we are going to provide it. Raise your shield."

How did Grandma know she was feeling stuck inside her own skin, like it was too tight and she could not get out. The not-knowing-what-was-coming weighed on her, making her heart throb and her chest hurt. Grandma said the feeling was called anxiety. Tracey didn't like it. It made her nose itch and her left eye twitch. On top of the stones, Sebastian, Damian, and Timothy, was Nana's accusation. Her voice played like a metronome inside Tracey's head.

Tick tick tick.

I know who you are. Evil. Monster.

Did she know Tracey's secret?

Did she know about the Serpent's Kiss?

Did she think Timothy had control?

He didn't.

But he *was* in her head whispering, urging, making her see things from a different point of view. Sometimes she didn't know what was real anymore.

Like Stephanie.

Stephanie, who had been strangely silent all this time.

Why?

"Ready?" Grandma called.

Tracey nodded. Her siblings were scattered around the garden in a wide circle. Tracey raised her shield bubble around her body and focused on Simon, the only non-Mage-kind in the group. He was the most dangerous one out here because he was the only one she couldn't sense. Just like how she had used Jonny and Laura against Timothy.

A clever ruse, Timothy whispered. *You used my ego and bias against me. I'm impressed, Tracey.*

She snorted and forced the whisper out of her right ear, strengthening her brain bubble against him.

"I'm ready!" she called.

Pin needle sharp magical blasts came from everywhere all at once. The bombardment slammed against her shield forcing her total focus into holding it still. Zaps even came from Grandma and Mom, who had joined them in the garden.

A heavier series of thuds came from Simon's direction — a baseball, a tennis ball, another baseball.

"A baseball? Come on!" Tracey whined. Real balls were way more dangerous than the magic bursting into stardust against her shield. If she wavered even slightly Simon's throws would get through, and they would hurt if they hit.

A basketball came next. She saw it coming, squealed and pushed her shield in that direction. A football came flying at the side of her face. *Ugh!* She stepped back with her left foot, reinforcing her stance the way Prince Henry and Jilly had shown her. "Not fair!" she shouted.

"Focus, Tracey. Push everything out of your mind. There is only the here and now," Grandma ordered. The pounding was relentless. Unending. Tracey couldn't hear a sound over it. Her mind focused tightly on her shield bubble and the colorful starbursts of magic rippling over her barrier. She could only hold out for so long and her family knew it. Tracey could either let herself be worn down and overcome or she could take the attack back to her family and force them to focus on their own protection.

Let me help. Timothy's voice curled around her thoughts. Her focus trembled as she shifted to block him out. Her shield wobbled.

"No! I won't let you have control."

You will.

"Never."

You can beat them, Tracey. I sense your determination. With a little guidance —

"Ugh!" Tracey spat the sound out like a bullet. "Shut up!"

The whispers continued, urging, cajoling, hinting, offering. She shut her mind to them all by thickening her brain bubble like a brick wall. It taxed her to the point where she almost lost her outer shield entirely.

She crouched, making the area she had to protect so much smaller. Her whole body shook as exhaustion made itself known in her cramping muscles. She shrunk her shield bubble to lay just above her skin and gathered what she could of her magic. Her *own* magic. The magic that lurked deep inside her core and from nowhere else. Breathing deep she launched her gathered magic into the air, throwing her arms out wide. "Enough!" Her magic turned her shield bubble into a mirror and reflected every blast back upon its creator.

Screams filled the garden as Tracey fell to her knees.

"If you had come with kindness and simply asked for help, your town would be plentiful and fertile also."

22

Simon let out an "oof" as a football slammed into his belly, knocking him onto his butt. When the magic cleared, Tracey found her family flat on the ground around her, moaning and groaning. She sucked in great gulps of air and when she had enough oxygen she shouted, "Sorry!"

Grandma rolled onto her belly and pushed up onto her hands and knees. Tracey ran to help her up. Dad — who sat out of the session watching the whole thing — helped Mom to her feet. Charlie and Sarah stayed on the ground.

"Cripes, Tracey. What the heck?" Charlie moaned.

Tracey laughed. It was as though the bowling ball of stress she had been carrying had dissolved into ash and drifted away from her shoulders. True, the magic practice hadn't exactly solved any of her problems, but her limbs were softer now, her muscles looser, and the tension that filled her body was gone. "Thanks. That actually did help."

"Now help me," Simon moaned. "I'm not Mage-kind. That football hurt!"

"Gotta be quicker to duck, Simon," Tracey said, letting loose another laugh. Her family gathered, praising her strength and quick thinking to reverse their zaps with a mirror spell. She took the compliments happily, her grin broad enough to hurt her face.

"What spell was that? I don't know that I've ever seen it before," Charlie said.

Tracey shrugged. "Not really a spell, I guess. I just kinda pushed everyone back."

"Not a spell?" Sarah asked, her eyes wide.

Tracey caught Mom and Dad's knowing look to Grandma. "What? What was that? What Grandma?" Tracey asked.

"Nothing, dear."

"Grandma, what is it?"

"Hmmmm? Well —"

Tracey's phone trilled. She fished it out of her pocket. Reading Jilly's message turned her blood to ice. "Jilly and Jonny have been attacked," she said. "A magic attack."

Mom drove madly toward Jessie Park, bobbing and weaving in and out of traffic. Grandma sat silently in the passenger seat, her hand gripping the overhead handle tightly. Tracey stared through the window but didn't see anything, her mind was racing with questions and fears. Who attacked her friends and why? Had someone discovered Jonny held a Stone of Power? Thank goodness Jilly was with him. Jonny had no way to protect himself. By letting him hold onto the Crow's Heart, Tracey had put her friend in danger.

"Do you know what happened?" Mom asked beeping her horn at the car turning in front of her.

"No. Only that first message from Jilly. I called, but she didn't answer. I tried Jonny too. I'm really worried."

Tracey's blood pounded. Still, her mind was weirdly blank. She tried calling for Jilly in her head. There was no response.

"We have no idea what we are driving into," Grandma said softly. "Beth, we must be cautious."

"Should I message Agent Loo Loo?" Tracey asked.

"Good idea, hon. Yes," Mom said.

Tracey did so and then plastered her face to the window as the car screeched around the final corner bringing the park into view. Trees were beginning to change color and families, people with dogs, runners, and teens filming themselves on their phones were spread out across the grass. She hunted for any sign of magic. The park seemed peaceful. No flashes of errant magic or police, M-force, or screaming and evacuating park goers anywhere to be seen.

"Looks quiet," Mom said, slowing the car for the tight turn into the car park.

"Look, what's that?" Tracey pointed but her mom and grandma could already see it. A strange, low-lying, green fog rolled and swelled at knee height down one end of the park.

"You said they were attacked magically?" Grandma asked.

"That's what the message said," Tracey mumbled. "That fog ... I've seen it before."

"What?" Two voices snapped.

"Yeah, a few days ago. On Main Street."

"You were attacked and you didn't say anything?" Mom asked, her voice sharp. She twisted in her seat to stare at Tracey.

"I wasn't really attacked. But it did, kinda, come after me. I thought it was a prank. It didn't touch me."

"How did you get away?" Mom demanded.

"Ran into the council building."

"A safe place for sure," Grandma said. Tracey hummed. It hadn't felt safe at the time. Her thoughts flew to Sebastian. Was this another one of his pranks? Jilly's message sounded scared and she wasn't the type to get scared easily. Tracey pushed Sebastian's cute face out of her mind. Who else could be behind the fog? She wore Timothy's stone, so not him, and Doctor Chan was in prison, as was Agent Malden. Who was left to dare attack Tracey's friends?

The council.

Mom parked the car and Tracey jumped out immediately throwing up her search net to find her friends. The fog reflected her magic back at her and left an acidic taste in the back of her throat. The buzz of Jilly's magic rose up in a cloud burst from the picnic area. Tracey ran, leaving her mom and grandma to follow along behind. The wall of green fog flattened out and hugged the grass exposing Jilly and Jonny standing as still as statues, staring off into the distance. Jilly's phone was gripped tightly in her hand, her index finger frozen above the touchpad. *Why aren't they moving?*

"Jilly! Jonny!" Tracey shouted. They didn't turn at her cry. She knew the park's walking paths like the back of her hand, but could not see the trails ahead. The fog drifted menacingly around Jilly and Jonny's feet. Tracey couldn't reach them without walking through it. Her instincts screamed at her not to let the fog touch her and skidded to a halt. "Jilly, Jonny?"

Not an eye-lid twitched. Not a mouth opened. They seemed completely frozen. Like living statues. At least she hoped they were living. Tracey reached out with her mind. *"Jilly? Jonny?"* She got no answer. She crept closer and stopped right at the fog's edge. Mom appeared at Tracey's side. Grandma was way behind her, still on her way though, she just moved a lot slower. "Do you feel it?" Tracey whispered.

"Dark intent. Don't touch that fog. We have to remove it somehow." Mom uttered a spell beneath her breath and a gust of wind blew up behind Tracey. It pushed the fog away. Unfortunately, straight toward the children's play equipment.

"Mom!" Tracey gasped, pointing to the kids climbing all over the equipment in the distance.

Grandma twisted and headed toward the playground instead.

Tracey's mom raced after Grandma. As soon as the fog left her friends' feet Tracey inched forward and gently touched Jilly's arm. She pushed a little magic into her friend. It bounced back like Tracey had pushed two magnets together, repelling her push. It wasn't a shield bubble or a wall, she just couldn't magically touch Jilly. She pulled back on her magic, and lowered her hand, until her fingers made contact with Jilly's arm. Icy cold radiated up from Jilly's skin. "Oh no."

Tracey touched Jonny's neck. His skin was ice cold too. She couldn't find his pulse and panicked. "No. No," she muttered pressing harder and shifting her fingers around until she located a slow thump.

Her sigh of relief was so epic she nearly fell over from the force of it. *What do I do now?* Both of her friends wore a Stone of Power. Perhaps she could access the stone's magic and unfreeze them. She stretched for the Tiger's Eye around Jilly's neck. Her hand bounced back. "Ugh." She tried the Crow's Heart around Jonny's neck and the same thing happened. "Fruit tingles."

At least that meant whoever did this to her friends hadn't got stones either. Or they hadn't wanted them. But if they weren't after the stones, then why attack her friends? "Timothy?"

Tracey? His voice curled around her ears.

"What's wrong with my friends?"

Hmmmm. You'd best be careful. This is a powerful spell. Let me in. I can help.

"No way." Tracey pushed the voice away.

"Tracey?"

She spun around to lock her horrified stare on her mother. "They're not moving."

Mom walked a slow circle around the frozen teens. Tracey felt her mother's magic flow out to surround them. Tracey held her breath, but nothing happened.

"Mom?"

Her mother reached out and pressed her fingers to Jilly's wrist. "Alive."

Tracey peered around, searching for Grandma. "What happened?"

"Your grandmother is holding the fog at the rear of the park where no one is around."

"She couldn't stop it?"

"No. At least your friends are both alive," Mom confirmed after checking Jonny's pulse too.

"I could try that wake-up spell I used in London? The one that woke you up after Agent Malden spelled you all asleep?"

"Before you try to break it, reach out with your magic and see if you can track the origin of the spell. You should always check to see if there are any snares or traps that could go off if you try to break it."

Fruit tingles. She hadn't thought of that. It was one of the first steps in investigating magic or Mage-kind crime scenes. She had learned that not from her uncle but from the numerous M-force crime shows her mom and dad loved to watch. Before a spell was broken — if it could be broken — M-force always traced the spell back to its caster. Of course, this was real life and not a scripted drama. Magic worked differently than it did in fictional shows. Everything depended on the skill level of the caster and how old the spell was. Tracey's abilities could break old spells but it took time. This spell was fresh.

Grandma was rated Significant — the highest official level of Mage-kind magic. If anyone could break the spell, it was her, but they would have to wait for her to come back. Tracey wondered if Mom was asking Tracey to track the spell back to the caster to save Grandma time? It was probably easier to break a spell if the original caster could be found. "I'll try."

Mom went to get Grandma. Tracey blew out her breath until it felt like she had no oxygen left in her lungs. Sucking in a cleansing gulp of cool air she centered her thoughts on her core. The little closet door — the one she used to keep locked shut — sprang open. Tracey drew her magic into her body and prepared her search spell. Before she threw it out, she needed to link it to the spell wrapped around Jilly and Jonny. She pushed her magic out to flow over their bodies, not touching them with her magic knowing it would just bounce off again. Jonny's eyes closed. Tracey lost her grip on her magic and her search net fell apart. For a second she thought she had broken the spell that froze him into a statue but no other part of Jonny moved. His eyes popped open again, glowing faintly blue. Tracey stumbled back in shock.

"Tracey?"

She recognized that soft flowing voice. "Millicent?"

"Yes. What has happened to the boy?"

"A spell. It's frozen Jonny and Jilly into statues."

"A spell?"

"Yes. I'm trying to track it back to the caster."

"Did you attempt to access the stones' power?"

"I can't touch them."

Millicent flicked Jonny's eyes. It was as clear as a head move would have been. "Don't. It would distract from your spell. Too many voices. You need silence."

"Silence?"

"Search for the vibration that surrounds your friends. It will be as unique as a fingerprint." Jonny's eyes flicked side to side again. "The spell is powerful. But Tracey, so are you. Be careful." Jonny's eyes blanked as Millicent's presence faded.

"Tracey?" Grandma puffed slightly as she approached, holding tight to Tracey's mom's arm. Poor Grandma, she had traveled a long distance today.

"They were hit by a spell. A strong one. It wasn't an accident. They were attacked, but —" Tracey dropped her voice to a whisper "— they, uh, Jilly still has her stone. So, whoever attacked her didn't try and take it."

"Or they tried and did not succeed," Grandma said. "Very well. What have you attempted?"

"I was going to try my wake-up spell, but Mom wants me to track the caster first."

"I've called your uncle and placed another call to Agent Epworth," Mom said. "We need additional help to break the spell on your friends. M-force are on their way to lock down the park and get everyone out of danger. Be careful tracking the spell and don't confront anyone. Not on your own."

"Yes, Mom."

"We'll stay with your friends. Find who did this, Tracey."

Tracey closed her eyes and exactly as Millicent said to do, she locked down the Butterfly Stone and the Serpent's Kiss. Once more, she drew magic from her core and readied her search spell. She held her hand above Jilly and Jonny's arms and Looked for the vibration. It manifested as a sick green colored gas cloud floating around her friends — a lot like the spell that trapped them in the first place. She focused on the gas. The color made her queasy to look at, and there was a faint metallic taste in the back of her throat. It was the same as the one she had noticed earlier. As she pushed her senses wide open the scent taste in the back of her throat grew stronger, like she had licked the top of a battery. With the scent, taste and sight of the attacking spell filling her senses she threw up her search net again, wider, and higher than she'd ever thrown it before. It fell over the park like a giant blanket, spread cling-wrap thin to cover everything. The faint, icky green glow surrounding her friends twisted off into a thin thread and headed toward town. "Gotcha."

"Be careful," Grandma said and kissed Tracey on the forehead.

Tracey bolted after the thread, following it through the park onto the bitumen walking trail and then onto the side-walk. She ran toward town.

"Now we will not help you."

23

Tracey sprinted along Main Street following the green line of magic residue, doing her best to not look like she was using magic by keeping her hands at her sides. Only her fingers twitched and she mumbled under her breath. Every few minutes she stopped in place and flicked her fingers, throwing her search spell in a net over the street. Fortunately, her Mage-kind identification bracelet still shone with its bright emerald light, hiding her use of magic. It was harder to hide her odd, meandering path. She crossed the road several times, heading up and down alleys and side streets. If anyone paid close attention, they would think she was not in her right mind. Especially as she was sweaty and her face held that heat that made her aware of how red her cheeks must be. *Where is it going?*

If anyone actually stopped her, she would claim she was searching for a lost cat. So far, she had received only a few raised eyebrows but that would change if they realized she was using magic.

In case there were any Mage-kind walking past she kept her shield bubble raised, cracked only to pick up the direction of the green thread. It was a lot of sneaky magic and a headache bloomed behind her eyes from the strain. Still, she did get the occasional squinted stare from a pedestrian with their wrist covered. She stared blankly back, keeping her ID bracelet on full display, green light shining. *See, no magic use here.*

Awareness seeped into her slowly. The green thread was like following the stones' threads. Which made her wonder if the caster held one of the stones too. Her feet jerked to a stop, almost throwing her into the fruit stand outside the local market. No, the green thread couldn't belong to a stone. Tracey could only cast that search spell after she knew about the stone itself. And she didn't know anything about the last two stones. Not yet.

This green thread had to mean something else — it certainly connected the caster of the statue spell and the evil fog. Whoever he was, Tracey was going to find him and stop him. He dared to attack her friends. She wouldn't let that stand.

The thread was slightly brighter now. She must be getting close. In the distance she could see the mall, the train station, and the council buildings including the library. The caster must be hiding in one of these places.

The green line gave a pop like a balloon exploding and disappeared. Tracey spun around. *What happened? Where'd it go?*

Fog tendrils were drifting along a side street toward her, raising alarm as voices exclaimed at the oddity. Fortunately, the fog swirled and looped around anyone walking past. *Oh, that's disturbing.* "Stay away from it!" she shouted. The fog touched one man who stepped purposefully into its path. As soon as people saw him freeze, panic set in. Movement filled the area as the street self-evacuated. Tracey was the only one who didn't move. The spell caster must be trying to disrupt her tracking spell.

Now alone, she threw up a new search blanket, raising her arms high and hoped no one was filming her on their phone. Approaching sirens, that odd, uneven *whoo-whee* that was M-force, sounded louder. Tracey hunted for the elusive taste of metal. She couldn't find it. The fog flattened and billowed across the now empty Main Street. The chill touch of a breeze picking up snatched at the fog and blew it away. Tracey spun in a tight circle. *Fruit tingles*. The thread was completely gone. Sirens grew louder, forcing Tracey to take off. She couldn't get caught out in the open after weird magic infected the area and scared off the locals.

Tracey recognized Jonny's mom's car parked in their driveway as she ran up over the front yard. There was an unrecognizable car next to it — one of those fancy electric cars. The red paint gleamed in the sunlight. She assumed her mom called Jonny and Jilly's families to tell them what happened as soon as she got home. Or M-force did. Tracey's chest ached from her run but also from imagining all the sad faces, tears, and anger bubbling up inside the house. She didn't want to admit to them she failed to find the spell caster. M-force couldn't break the statue spell without the caster. As Tracey reached the front door, a black 4WD pulled into the driveway. Agent Loo Loo climbed out and waved. Tracey waited for the agent on the top of the porch steps.

"Main Street, Tracey? Using magic in a public setting?"

"People were in danger," Tracey tried to explain.

"I've seen the CCTV footage, Tracey. That was reckless."

Tracey gulped. "I'm-I'm sorry."

"I've intercepted the order to find you. Said it was authorized use but you cannot keep doing this. Let's get inside where you can tell me what happened."

Tracey held the door open for the M-force agent. She stared at her feet, feeling the dampness of her clothing from her sweaty run grow chilly from the cold look of disappointment on Agent Loo Loo's face. Once inside, they found a strange silent tableau. Jilly and Jonny stood frozen in the middle of the room. Their bodies in the exact same poses they were found in at the park. Jilly's mom stood beside her daughter whispering softly into her ear. A low buzz of magic surrounded the two females. Jonny's mom, Martha, sat on the sofa, staring up at Jonny. Her mascara was smudged and it left long lines down her cheeks from her tears. Her eyes were dry now, though. Her hands were clasped together and she kept rubbing her palms with her thumbs like she could not stop herself from doing it. One of her stick-on nails had come off and lay on the carpet between her feet. Tracey didn't think she even knew it was missing. She didn't look up as Tracey came inside.

"Any luck?" Mom asked, catching sight of Tracey hovering just outside the living room door.

Tracey shook her head. "I lost him. I'm so sorry. How did you get Jonny and Jilly back here?"

"Your Grandma and M-force. M-force sent a van."

Tracey wanted more details but her mom just stared. Jonny's mom launched to her feet. "Tracey, what happened?"

She couldn't hold Martha's gaze. "I'm sorry. I lost the thread." Martha slumped back onto the sofa with a loud sigh.

Agent Loo Loo held a hushed conversation in the corner with Jilly's mom. Mrs. Cho seemed reluctant to leave her daughter's side. Tracey felt the moment Mrs. Cho's magic faded as she forced herself to walk away. They went into the kitchen with Tracey's mom. Tracey sat down beside Martha on the sofa and peered up at Jilly and Jonny. Martha dropped her hand over Tracey's. Her fingers were chilly but they warmed up quickly. "Do you want to come and hear what happened?" Tracey asked.

"I can't do anything to help, Tracey. I'll just be in the way."

Tracey clenched her fingers around Martha's. "You'd never be in the way."

Martha's sniff was a bit wobbly. "You're sweet, hon. Go and talk to them. I'll watch over Jonny and Jilly."

"All right," Tracey agreed. "I will help them. I promise."

"I know, hon."

Tracey peered back when she got to the kitchen doorway. Martha dabbed her eyes with a tissue but otherwise didn't make a sound.

"Explain it to me. Everything that has happened," Agent Loo Loo ordered. Tracey handed over her phone to show her Jilly's text message. "Jilly messaged that she and Jonny were under attack. Mom drove me and Grandma to the park but by the time we got there they were —" Tracey pointed back toward the living room "— like that."

Agent Loo Loo examined Tracey's face carefully. "Did you notice anything when you arrived? Anything unusual?"

Mom rolled her wrist for Tracey to speak first. "There was a fog all over the park. Kinda greenish. The closer we got to it the more it creeped me out. Like, I knew we couldn't let it touch us. It was — I felt icky. I'm sure that's what made Jilly and Jonny —" she looked to the living room again "— like that. Mom said she'd stay with my friends and I went after the spell caster."

"Dangerous," Agent Loo Loo commented.

"I promised Mom I wouldn't get close. Only find out where he was hiding."

"How?"

"I, uh, I know I'm not supposed to use magic —"

"Just tell me what happened," Agent Loo Loo said and offered a soft smile.

"I used my search spell and picked up the vibration of the statue curse around Jilly and Jonny — it was a sick greenish thread. I followed it into town, but the fog appeared. I thought it was going to attack me. I ran, and I — uh — I lost the trail."

"You lost the trail in Main Street?" Agent Loo Loo confirmed.

"Yeah, near the main council building. Um. I should tell you that the fog has attacked me there before."

"What?" Agent Loo Loo's head snapped up at that.

Mom scowled.

"It's fine. I escaped then, but —"

"— obviously the caster is staying locally. I'll send a team out. We'll scour Main Street. If the caster is anywhere nearby, we'll find him," Agent Loo Loo promised.

"I don't think they'll be able to. It completely disappeared. The fog too," Tracey said.

"We have more resources and spells than you have, Tracey. We'll find him."

"So what caused it?" Martha asked from the doorway. "What froze my boy? How will you fix him?"

Mrs. Cho turned her head from where she stared out through the back window. She stood so still and quiet Tracey had forgotten she was there. "It is strong magic. We can break the curse, but it will take work. It would be better to have the caster in custody. I can sense the spell surrounding my daughter. It is growing stronger."

Martha rubbed the skin of her face. "I've called Tsee. She's coming straight from work but she's still over an hour away. Will my Jonny be okay? He is not Mage-kind."

"I know," Mrs. Cho answered. Her lips stayed in a straight line. "We must hurry. The longer they stay like this, the harder it will be to get them back unharmed."

"Oh Lord," Martha muttered. "Tracey?"

"We'll help him," Tracey promised again. She hoped desperately it was true.

Grandma glanced at Mrs. Cho. "You are rated Significant?"

"I am."

The old woman stood and slapped her hands on her thighs. "Then we can initiate a holding spell. Agent Epworth you must find the caster quickly and break the curse."

Agent Loo Loo stood as well and gestured to Tracey. "Take me to the spot where you found your friends. I must examine the scene. We'll go forward from there."

"Okay." Finally, she would get to see what Agent Loo Loo could do. "Should I call Laura and Tony? They'll want to help."

"Better that you should warn them to watch their backs. We are not sure why your friends were attacked. We have to assume it's about the stones."

"You think they're in danger?"

"Best to warn them to keep an eye out," Agent Loo Loo said.

Tracey's stomach churned. She grabbed her cell phone and immediately messaged her friends as she followed Agent Loo Loo to her 4WD. From the passenger seat Tracey directed the agent toward Jessie Park. "What can we really do? What are we going to find at the park now? Jilly and Jonny aren't even there anymore and I know the fog was coming from Main Street. Wouldn't it be faster to go straight there?"

Agent Loo Loo's fingers tightened on the steering wheel. "There may be clues you and your family missed in your panic over your friends' frozen state. We need clear heads here, Tracey. Uncontrolled or extreme emotions cloud your magic. Perhaps that is why you were unable to pick up on the caster's presence."

Your anger will help you, Timothy whispered. *Let it out. Take control!*

Tracey ignored him, staring up at the agent's solemn profile. "So, how do we find the bad guy?"

"There is a standard search procedure for M-force agents. A special tracking spell." Agent Loo Loo grinned, a smudge of her hot pink lipstick stained her front teeth. "Let me teach it to you."

With her mind she extinguished their torches and turned their pitchforks into snakes.

24

They drove along Main Street and Tracey pointed out where the thread disappeared. Agent Loo Loo swore they would come back this way to examine the scene in greater detail. Tracey spied several M-force vehicles blocking off Main Street.

"How's Hank? Have you heard from him?" Agent Loo Loo asked after they drove past.

Tracey lowered the cell phone she was fiddling with, wishing desperately for Laura or Tony to text back. "Yeah, but he had nothing new to report. They haven't found Timothy's stone." She assumed Prince Henry already told all of this to Agent Loo Loo. *Is this a test? Is she testing me?*

"I see." Agent Loo Loo opened her mouth and closed it again. After a moment she opened it again. A small sound popped from her throat. Tracey watched on in amusement.

"Agent?"

"Hmmm?"

"Do you want to tell me something?"

Agent Loo Loo raised an eyebrow. "Tell you what?"

"You're twitching. Swallowing funny. Breathing in deep and then opening your mouth. They're all tells that you want to say something but you don't know if you should."

"You're very observant, Tracey."

"My uncle has a body language book in his office. When it's not busy I get bored; I should do my homework but …"

Agent Loo Loo laughed. "You read instead. I get it. The park is just up here?" she asked, pointing ahead.

"Yes. So, what did you want to tell me?"

"I really shouldn't say."

Tracey examined Agent Loo Loo's face. She was biting her lips and it was eating away more of her lipstick. "Tell me what?"

"Trent Malden wants to speak to you."

Tracey's hands fell to her lap. "What? But isn't Agent Malden in jail?"

"That's why I wasn't sure if I should say anything."

"What does he want to tell me?"

"He won't say. Not to me. He says he'll only speak directly with you. You don't have to agree to speak with him, Tracey. You don't even have to see him —"

"I'll go." Tracey swallowed hard and cleared her throat. "After Jilly and Jonny are safe."

"Malden's case files arrived last night, maybe I'll find something in them and we won't need to talk to him at all." Agent Loo Loo parked in the car park and popped her seat belt open. "Right. Let's focus on the now and come back to this discussion later. Take me to where you found your friends."

Tracey led Agent Loo Loo to the exact spot and gasped. "Look at the grass." A large yellow circle stained the spot where Jonny and Jilly once stood. "It wasn't like that before."

Tracey looked closer. The grass was dry and crackled under her feet.

"Hmmm. You mentioned a magic fog?" Agent Loo Loo pursed her lips and walked to the edge of the yellow grass. It crunched loudly as she stepped onto it. She knelt down, touching it carefully.

"Is it dead?"

"Frostbite."

"Frost? Like ice? But the fog wasn't cold," Tracey said.

"It wasn't?"

"No. It was warm. Like in the desert. The fog was creepy, but it wasn't cold."

Agent Loo Loo inhaled deeply through her nose. "An intriguing aspect of the spell." She pulled a little black device from her jacket pocket. It was the size of a pen. When she placed it on the ground two little wings popped up out of the back of it. It looked like a dragonfly. "This drone will search out the spell caster. We just need to give it a taste of the spell."

"How does it work?" Tracey caught the salt bag Agent Loo Loo tossed over. "You want me to do the circle?" she asked.

"If you would."

Tracey made a crooked shape out of her mouth. "My circles can be a bit wonky."

"All the more reason to practice them. Close the circle with some of your magic."

Tracey poked a small hole in the salt bag and followed the edge of the brown deadened grass. As she joined the edges of the circle together, she drew some magic from her core and touched her fingers to the salt. The circle snapped closed with a buzz. The drone's motor revved and it trembled as it rose up and hovered at waist height in front of them.

Agent Loo Loo traced several symbols Tracey didn't recognize onto the grass outside the circle, explaining they were runes to hold the spell firm at a distance. Tracey watched, curious, as Agent Loo Loo touched each symbol in what looked like a random order though it obviously wasn't. The agent whispered something in another language. "Locus Findan Oriri. Old English," she said at Tracey's raised eyebrows. "It's a simplified spell that's been refined over time."

The jittering drone shot up into the sky like a ride in a theme park and zipped off toward the town center.

"How did you do that?" Tracey asked. "Mom uses long, song-like sentence spells."

"It's an agency spell. Often more precise. M-force like to make things quick and brutal."

"Where's it going?"

Agent Loo Loo held up her phone. The app she opened showed a 3D map of Miltern Falls. The little drone hovered over parts of the town, blinking in and out of sight so fast she lost it several times. "Let's follow the path you took this morning. We'll check if your path matches this one and search for clues along the way."

Tracey led the agent through the park along the worn path in the grass she had followed earlier that day, moving past the children's playground and onto the sidewalk. She kept glancing at Agent Loo Loo as they walked. The agent's eyes darted from her phone to the path ahead and over the grass to either side. She also examined the road.

"If we don't break the spell on Jonny and Jilly quickly, what will happen to them?"

"Don't concern yourself over that, Tracey. Focus on the now. That is what we *can* do."

"It's not brown," Tracey said, pointing to the grass along the side of the road.

"What?"

"The fog completely covered this area. But look, it didn't kill the grass."

"Well spotted. You're right. I believe your friends may have walked into or been directed into a trap set for them."

Tracey frowned. They followed the sidewalk toward the town center. It was a lovely sunny day and Tracey's pullover was thick, trapping heat close to her skin. She yanked it off and tied it around her waist. The smell of a BBQ rose up in the distance making her stomach rumble.

"But why? Who would attack Jonny and Jilly like that? Why freeze them? They — uh — Jilly has a stone. The bad guy, whoever did it, didn't try to remove it. So, if he didn't want the stone why did he attack them?"

Agent Loo Loo's lips twisted while she thought. "Perhaps you and your family arrived too quickly and scared him away?"

"You think they might have been attacked for a different reason?" Tracey asked.

"Why attack *your* friends?" The agent asked. She stopped walking. Tracey only realized it after she walked a few more steps. She traveled back to the agent.

"I don't know. Uncle Donny says sometimes the reason that's obvious is not always the reason a crime is committed. Sometimes, it's happenstance — uh — crime of convenience."

"If so, then we should locate the caster relatively quickly. For now, let's go with Occam's Razor."

"What's that?" Tracey asked.

"It's a theory that states the simplest, most obvious solution is usually the truth. The stones are a great power. Any Mage-kind who knows about them will be after them."

"Like Doctor Chan?"

"Exactly." The agent started walking. Tracey stared after her.

"Who else wants the stones?"

"We have a very large file."

Tracey ran after the agent. "Can I see it?"

"Tracey, it is an M-force —"

"Uncle Donny is a detective. We can help," she said ignoring the agent's shaking head. "Sometimes he sees things others miss."

Agent Loo Loo narrowed her eyes at Tracey. "You mean you do."

"Would it hurt to let me see the file? Is it really that classified? I mean, if it's about the stones then I should know everything you know. Especially if me and my friends are in danger."

The agent pressed her lips together. "I'll see what I can do." She held up her phone, checking on the drone's progress.

Tracey stopped again. "Um —"

"Yes, Tracey."

"Never mind." They turned the corner onto Main Street. Tracey thought about throwing up her search net again but Agent Loo Loo told her not to use her magic so obviously in public. She *was* with an M-force agent. Surely that would be okay?

Agent Loo Loo's lips quirked. "Didn't you tell me earlier there are certain tells a person gives off when they really want to say something?"

"Busted." Tracey snorted. "If we go to see Agent Malden, I'm — can you — I want to see Doctor Chan too."

"Tracey?"

"He might know something."

"Tracey."

"Please."

"I don't think that is a good idea."

"You can organize it though. Can't you?"

"I can, but …" Agent Loo Loo shut her eyes on Tracey's pleading look. "I'll see what I can do," she said again with a long groan.

"And don't tell my mom."

"Now, Tracey —"

"You said you might not even be able to organize it. Right? So just don't mention it to her yet. Please?"

Agent Loo Loo pursed her lips, eventually she nodded.

Tracey's phone rang. The ringtone was familiar. She answered it quickly. "Mom?"

"Your sister has been attacked."

Tracey and Agent Loo Loo ran in through the front door and found Tracey's mom and dad standing in front of Sarah's frozen form. M-force officers filled the house, black suited figures holding buzzing boxes and looked like they were scanning the statues of her friends. Other officers walked around each room holding up beeping devices. They all froze when Tracey entered, staring at her intently. Tracey almost shouted. "I didn't do it."

Agent Loo Loo went straight over and spoke with the agents.

Sarah stood frozen beside Jilly and Jonny. Both of Sarah's hands were up as if caught by surprise. Her eyes were wide and her mouth hung open.

"What happened?" Tracey demanded, waving her hand in front of her sister's face. Sarah didn't blink or twitch at all. Martha's head poked in from the kitchen doorway and watched everyone. Her eyes were still red, though she had fixed her make-up. Jilly's mom stared out through the window again.

"Kylie called. She and Sarah were walking home from the mall. They were hunted by a weird fog. Both girls ran, separating in the hope they could get away. Kylie lost sight of Sarah and when she found her, she was like this.

"Is Kylie okay?"

"Unharmed, thankfully. Agents are at her house now. They'll watch over her until we sort all this out."

Tracey held her hand above Sarah's cold arm and searched for her sister's mind with her own. *"Sarah?"* There was no reply. She couldn't sense Sarah's magic either. "Sarah doesn't wear a stone," Tracey mumbled. She caught Agent

Loo Loo's sharp look, but when the agent said nothing more Tracey didn't explain. Thoughts flew madly around inside her mind. Jonny, Jilly, and now Sarah.

"How do we fix this?" Martha asked, her voice soft.

Agent Loo Loo shook her head. "I've called in M-force's immediate incident medical team. They should arrive this afternoon. We will fix this, ma'am, I promise you that."

Tracey's eyebrows rose. When did Agent Loo Loo make that call?

Mrs. Cho came to life as she spun sharply around. "Without the spell caster, there is nothing that can be done," she snarled. It made her eyes burn and her nostrils flare. Like a dragon about to spew a fireball.

"They are all linked to me. Agent Loo Loo, we *have* to warn Tony and Laura. If Sarah and Jonny were attacked — then Tony and Laura could be at risk too." *How did Kylie escape?*

"You are a target as well, Tracey." Agent Loo Loo turned to Tracey's mom and dad. "I'm going to suggest putting all of you in protective custody."

"What? Why?" Voices rose throughout the house.

"It will be safer," Agent Loo Loo argued.

"I can't," Tracey said raising her voice to be heard over everyone.

Agent Loo Loo turned to face her. "Why not?"

"I have to find the other stones." Voices rose again but Tracey waved their arguments away. "The stones can fix this. If we have them all then we can use the magic to break the frozen curse."

"That will take too long," Dad argued.

Mom's voice was louder. "We have to do something now!" Martha agreed, moving closer to Tracey's mom. She kept giving the emotionless agents in the rest of the house side-eye.

Agent Loo Loo raised her hands calling for quiet. Tracey's parents and Jilly's mom rounded on the agent. Martha kept close to Tracey's mom, nodding at her every word. Grandma shifted quickly to stand between them all. "This curse is the focus for now," she reminded them.

"I'll organize something and come back to you," Agent Loo Loo said.

"What about the stones?" Tracey asked. No one listened to her. "What about the stones?" she said louder. Mom hugged Dad and listened to Jilly's mom, Grandma, and Agent Loo Loo argue about the curse and the types of spells they could use to try and break it. Martha just stood there looking lost. Her eyes kept darting to Jonny. Tracey had to warn Laura and Tony before they were attacked. They weren't replying to her text messages. She would have to go in person. She ran toward the door.

"Tracey!" Mom shouted.

She couldn't stop. She couldn't listen. They'd prevent her from leaving if she gave them the chance. She had to find Tony and Laura and she had to find them now.

She sent them back to their own town with a single thought.

25

Tracey's phone buzzed incessantly. She turned it off and shoved it deep into her pocket, not wanting the distraction. Mom's constant calling wasn't helping her own panicked state.

She tried Laura's house first. No one was home. It took another twenty minutes to run to Tony's house. She was gasping for breath by the time she reached his driveway. Feeling like she was going to vomit, she threw out her magic search blanket as she stomped up the steps to his front porch. The buzz from inside told her someone was home. Tracey pounded on white-painted door, bending over to suck in a deep breath, and groaned softly. *Ugh.* Why did it always have to be running? She couldn't wait until she was older and had a car license. Driving would be so much quicker.

The door opened, exposing the sour face of Tony's mom. She was in track pants and a sweaty gym shirt, her hair tied back in a ponytail. "Yes?"

Tracey gasped. "Is Tony here?"

"He is busy."

"Please, Mrs. O'Shae. I really need to talk to Tony."

"You should call your mother."

Tracey's stomach dropped to her knees. "My mom already called you?"

"She did."

"Please, I'll just stay a moment. Let me talk to him. For just a few minutes?"

"Is my son in danger?"

Tracey gulped. "Maybe."

Mrs. O'Shae nodded sharply. "Fine. You have five minutes. But he is *not* helping you, do you understand? Tony does not leave this house."

"Yes, ma'am." Tracey tried not to fidget under Mrs. O'Shae's unwavering stare. After a long moment she opened the door wider and Tracey brushed past, moving quickly through the crimson entryway, past the lamp filled living room and knocked on Tony's bedroom door. He opened it dressed in a pale blue polo and baggy black jeans. "Trace?" One ear was exposed beneath his noise canceling headphones. He pulled them all the way off. "What's up?"

Tracey pushed into his room. His game station was paused on the save game screen. "Jilly and Jonny were attacked at the park."

Tony plonked down on his messy bed, paused and leaped back up. "What?"

"Then Sarah was attacked."

"Oh my God, is she okay? Are they all okay? What happened?"

"They're frozen into statues. We haven't been able to break the curse. Kylie wasn't touched. She was with Sarah but —"

"That's … that's awful. What are you doing to help them? Do you need me to —"

"Sarah doesn't hold a stone. And —" she lowered her voice "— no one knows Jonny has a stone. Only us. The attacks aren't about the stone Protectors. It's all —"

"Us. You. We're connected to you. Crap. I'd better warn Mom and Dad."

"My mom already called them. I couldn't wait though. I had to come and warn you."

"What about Dave and Laura?"

Tracey rubbed her eyes. "Fruit tingles. I forgot about Dave."

"Again?"

She growled. "Shut up. Laura's not at home. We have to call Dave."

They dug out their cell phones. "No answer," Tracey said.

Tony texted and then looked up, shaking his head. "Nothing. What do we do now?"

"We have to find him. Warn him. His mom hates Magekind. She won't believe anything my mom says."

Tony burst into movement, flinging open his closet door. He rummaged around and yanked out a hoodie. He shoved his phone into his rear jeans pocket. "We have to go find him."

"What?"

"Football practice, Trace. That's where he'll be."

"Yes. Yes. Okay." She held out her hands stopping him from opening the door. "I'll go —"

Tony stepped back, frowning. "What about me?"

"Your mom won't let you come with me."

"Then I'll sneak out."

"You can't. Tony, your parents are mad enough. And you're in danger now too."

"Well, so are you."

"I can take care of myself."

"So can I. I'm coming, Tracey."

Her eyes narrowed on his. "Your parents will be pissed."

"Yep. So we'd better go quick." He ran to the window and popped it open. "Try to avoid landing on Mom's roses."

Tracey wriggled out through the window and jumped down into the garden wobbling on one foot as her shoes slipped on the wood chips. She flung out her hands for balance and came close to landing butt first in the blooming orange rose bush. Tony landed like a cat beside her and grabbed her arm. "Come on." They ducked low and ran along the edge of the perfectly pruned garden. Fortunately, the shrubs were bigger than they were so they were able to stay out of sight until they reached the footpath.

More running!

"Where are we going?" Tracey panted. She followed as Tony ducked down a worn path beside the neighbor's house.

"There's a trail just up here. It's a shortcut I take to school when I have to walk."

Tracey followed Tony into the gap in the fence and down a long walking trail through the housing estate. "What about Laura?" Tony asked.

"I think she's at her grandma's this weekend. It's her uncle's fortieth. They were having a big party." Tracey's T-shirt was soaked with sweat. *Why. Why does everything involve so much exercise?* At least Tony was panting as hard as she was.

They had to find Dave before the evil fog did. "We'll get Dave and stake out Laura's place until she gets home."

"Yeah," Tony sucked in a giant breath. "Slow down for a sec." He nodded when he got his breath back, "I can't believe you ran off after us."

Tracey's side ached with a stitch that wouldn't go away. She swiped at the sweat on her brow. Her calves ached. So did the soles of her feet. "You did too," she panted out. She checked her cell and cringed at the number of missed call notifications. She swiped them all away without reading them.

"I did. Oh God. I'm gonna be in so much trouble when I get home."

"Me too."

Now that she could see her fingers and the keypad on her phone — just — she tried Laura's cell again. There was still no answer. She sent another text message and moaned. "Okay, let's run."

School buildings came into view in the distance. "Why are they at practice today?" she asked panting hard.

"I dunno, it's football. They're all weird. I don't get it."

"Ha!" As they approached the ground where the boys were running drills Tracey's phone rang. She slowed. "Can you tell Dave —"

"Yep." Tony ran off toward the gathered players.

Tracey halted and answered the phone gasping for breath. "Laura."

"Why are you panting? What is it? There's like five missed calls on my phone and all these texts and none of them make any sense and —"

"Jonny and Jilly were attacked. Sarah too. Someone's coming after us. When do you get home?" She watched Tony in the distance reach the players. Dave ran straight to him, ignoring Coach's shouts to come back.

"Wait, what? What do you … attacked? What happened?" Laura's voice jumped high and accelerated. Tracey could hear fear in her questions.

"If you see a creepy green fog. Run. Don't let it touch you."

"What? Tracey, I don't —"

"Tell your dad to call my mom."

"You think I'm in danger?" Laura's voice rose even higher.

Tracey watched Tony stop Coach from following after them by shouting something. He then spoke rapidly. Coach's scowl deepened and his hands fell off his hips. "We all are. Tony and Dave are here but you need to get somewhere safe."

"If it's magic how do I stop it?"

"I dunno. When you come home from your grandma's tell your dad to bring you straight to my place. We can protect you."

"You said Sarah was attacked?"

"Yeah. Kylie was with her."

"Is Kylie okay?"

"She got away." Tracey's breathing at last normalized. She walked in a small circle as she talked but made sure to keep an eye on Dave and Tony. Coach shouted something and pushed past Tony like he wasn't there. Tony spun around and chased after him. "They're frozen. Like statues," she told Laura.

"That's awful. Can you unfreeze them?"

"Agent Loo Loo is here and M-force is working with Mom and Grandma to break the spell."

"Okay. I see my dad. I'll tell him to call your mom."

"Good. And if you see fog?"

"Run. I got it. Stay safe, Tracey."

"You too."

Tracey ended the call and headed down the hill to join Tony and Dave. They were still arguing with Coach. Tracey had always found him an intimidating man. He stood too close and shouted far too loud. Tony stood his ground against him though, chin thrust out, looking totally badass.

"I'm not stopping the drills. You kids need to go home," Coach shouted.

"Dave has to come with us. It's an emergency," she said reaching them.

Coach sneered at Tracey. "You *special* kids need to leave Dave alone." The way he said *"special"* made her skin quiver. Tony's face paled but he didn't step back.

"Excuse me?" Tracey said, straightening her shoulders. "Do you have a problem with Mage-kind?" She pushed up her sleeves so that her bracelet was on full display.

Dave yanked off his helmet and stalked toward the bench. Coach tailed after him still shouting. "Mr. Betts, don't even think about leaving. Back to the drills. All of you. Move!"

A strange vibration buzzed against Tracey's skin drawing her gaze toward the distant trees. They looked blurry. "Oh no." She pointed at the goal posts quickly disappearing under a thick green rolling fog.

"What the hell is going on?" Coach swore.

A buzzing noise seemed to come from the fog. It hurt Tracey's ears. The three teens bolted toward the street, ignoring Coach's screamed threats. Tracey glanced behind them. "It's following us."

"What the heck is going on?" Dave bellowed.

"Don't let the fog touch you. It froze Jonny, Jilly, and Sarah. It's after all of us," Tracey warned him.

"Stones?" Dave wasn't as out of breath as Tony or Tracey. "Is it Timothy?"

"Don't know."

She couldn't take the time to explain. Every time she glanced back her steps slowed. She couldn't stop herself. The fog was gaining on them. "It's gonna catch us," she shouted. "We have to do something."

"How do you stop fog?" Dave asked.

"Wait … fog … we uh … we need heat," Tony said.

"Heat?" Tracey sucked magic from her core, pulling it into her body to help her fitness levels and give her a burst of energy. It fizzled out. Her body's exhaustion left her brain unable to concentrate enough to do it successfully. "How do we do that?"

"I don't know!"

Tracey did her best to keep up but she was flagging. Her thighs, calves, and stomach muscles all ached and she was breathing so hard she was dizzy. She drew on her core again. Soft words curled inside her ears. *Fill your muscles with power. You must learn to use it instinctively. Magic is you and you are magic,* Timothy whispered. Tracey sucked in a deep breath and focused her thoughts on her core. As power seeped into her body, she imagined it shining inside her blood, moving through her veins with every frantic beat of her heart. Soon her whole body glowed with imagined silver light. Her muscles stopped aching and her head cleared.

As she came up alongside Tony, he shot her a wide-eyed look. "How are you doing that?"

"Magic."

"It's still gaining on us. We can't out run it," he told her. Sweat poured from his skin.

"We need to bait it!" Dave shouted. He peeled off to the right.

"No, Dave!" Tracey shouted after him. There was no way she could catch up to him, even with the help of her magic.

"You can't save us if you get caught!" he shouted back.

"Dave!"

Tony broke left. Tracey was so surprised she nearly stopped running. "Tony, what are you doing?"

"He's right. Find a way to save us, Tracey. Fog is just cold air. You need to burn it off with hot air."

"Tony, no!" Tracey glanced over her shoulder. The fog split in half, like torn Christmas paper, right down the middle. Half rolled after Dave and the other half zoomed after Tony. Tracey stopped running. The fog didn't come for her at all.

Why?

If it wasn't coming after her, then she *was* the only one who could stop it. She called on Stephanie and the Butterfly Stone and opened her eyes on the black place. "No! I don't want you. I need Stephanie!" she shouted at the man waiting for her.

Timothy examined her through sharp eyes. "I can help you. Let me in. Let me take control."

"No!" She shook her head. "I won't listen to anything you have to say."

"And put your friends at further risk? We have no time, Tracey. I know this spell. I can help you."

"Teach it to me." She glared him down. "Quick!"

Timothy squeezed his eyes shut and drew in a deep breath. She thought she heard him mutter, "So stubborn, like her." His eyes opened. "Call on the Serpent's Kiss. Bring its magic into yourself. Fill your senses with it. Just like you did with your core magic to strengthen your endurance. Use the fog against itself."

"That makes no sense."

"Tracey, your magic is different from any other. Your mind is stronger than I have ever seen. You can control the —"

She stumbled as someone yanked hard at her mind. The room she stood in changed, like she was zooming along a highway at high speed without a car. She staggered and blinked, finding herself surrounded by a pale red, almost a yellow-rose color. A dog howled somewhere close by. A high-pitched yipping howl that was echoed by more nearby. The invisible animals surrounded her with constant sound and movement.

"Don't listen to him." A familiar boy's figure appeared at the edge of the shadows.

Sebastian? "What are you doing? How am I here?" she asked. Inside her chest her heart thumped like a clock hand ticking. Time was running out. How could Sebastian be here, in this place that looked so much like a stone room? *Sebastian?* The fog was him! All this was a horrible, vicious prank on her, targeting all her friends. "Let me go!"

"I can't," he said. "I didn't call you here, young lady."

"Timothy was —"

Sebastian's face stayed smooth though his voice trembled and broke. His eyebrows met in the middle of his face. "Don't listen to him. You don't need him. You're better than that. Stronger than him. Draw on your magic. Draw on your stone, Tracey. Fight him."

"My friends are in danger."

"I can help. Let me help you. Take my hand and let me in."

Tracey jolted back. She had heard that before. "You're not the one doing this to me," she said.

The tilt of his head and his pained expression made her think she'd upset him. "What?"

"I know you've been playing tricks on me and my friends. Testing us."

"Testing you? You are mistaken. This is someone far more dangerous."

"Who?" she asked.

"The Hunter."

She cursed their land to never grow crops, for the people to always be sickly and for their animals to run away.

26

he Hunter?" Did he mean the Crocodile Man? Sebastian warned her about him before. So, why didn't he just call him that? The yellowy rose hue of the room felt cold somehow. Clingy. With all the howling animals circling her, she felt very unsafe. "Who is the Hunter?" Tracey demanded.

"That's what I call him." Sebastian said.

Tracey blinked, wishing she could step back. Stuck as she was in this room, she realized she couldn't move. *That's not what you called him before.* "You were attacked?" she asked.

He shook his head, his blue eyes wide. "Hunted. He's hunting me."

"Why?"

"He's been after me for as long as I can remember. He's after you now because you know me." Sebastian hung his head.

"I don't know you!" she screeched. His head snapped up at her reaction, his eyes wide. His lips pressed hard together. "It's my friends he's attacked. You have to tell me everything. Why is he after you?"

"You know why," he snapped. His voice turned so cold it crackled. "Don't play dumb. It does not flatter you."

She wished she could move away but this place wouldn't let her, she just wobbled in place. It was exactly like the white room and the black room. She knew this helpless feeling all too well. It was a stone room, which meant … "You have one too. A stone. Show me."

His hand went to his chest, fingers fluttering before he tugged a thick leather strap from beneath his shirt. He didn't lift the stone out to show her.

"You *are* a stone Protector," she accused. "You have a Stone of Power." The shape beneath his shirt buzzed with an icky, oily, emerald magic.

"Yes."

"And the Hunter wants it?" she clarified.

He nodded. "Yes."

"What's it called?"

"I can't tell you that. If the Hunter gets you he could pull the information from your mind and come after me." Sebastian's voice was cutting, his lips pulled back in anger. He had never sounded so mean before.

"Tell me where you are then," she tried, holding her hands out to placate him. "I can help you."

"You can't. Where are you? I'll come to you," he said instead. His eyes glittered.

The swirling in Tracey's belly grew faster. He was behaving so oddly. His voice and words unusually sharp and cruel. His adorable face was scrunched in a sneer. Sebastian was weird, sure, but this felt wrong. Previously, while he kept his secrets, he had listened to her. Now, it was like everything she said was wrong. Like she had suddenly grown stupid in his eyes. He made her doubt every word and she felt strangely afraid of him.

"Why am I here?" she asked. Her words flowed slower as her mind ticked over all the clues. He wasn't acting like Sebastian, he was acting like someone else, someone familiar … like … "My friends are in trouble. I should be out there helping them, not stuck in here getting distract —" she stopped. Her head tilted as she thought about Timothy and Stephanie. And Millicent. And then about Sebastian. She had been annoyed by the clever boy but she'd never felt this icky, horribly cloying magic around him. "Practical jokes," she mused.

Sebastian tilted his head the same direction as Tracey's. "What?"

"Your practical jokes didn't leak icky oily magic before. But the fog does. The statues do too. You … you're not Sebastian at all. *You're* the hunter. *You're* the Crocodile Man."

The figure she thought was Sebastian laughed. The room around her bled green until she was soaked in it. All shades, all tones of green; emerald, grassy green, lime green, olive, pine, pear. It was the same as the green glow coming from Fake-Sebastian's chest. The boy blurred and grew into a taller figure wearing a forest green cloak and a hood. She couldn't see his face. "I'm impressed and it is rather hard to impress me, young lady."

That should have been her first clue. Sebastian would never call her *young lady*. Tracey bristled. "Let me out of here."

"It is too late, Tracey. I needed to distract you long enough for my fog to capture your friends. And you. You are now one of my living statues. Mine to control." He held out his hand. "Tell me where the other stones are? The statues were taken from the park before I could get to them. I must collect them all. They hold the key to my future power."

"Never. You think I can't get out of this place?" Tracey snapped. "My family are working on a way to break the spell and when they do, I'll come after you for hurting my friends."

"There is no escape, Tracey. You are stuck in here. With me. Let me into your mind. Give me control of your stone and tell me where your friends are."

Tracey threw out her hands as if she could raise her bubble shield. In here she had no magic. She couldn't move. She *was* trapped. "No. You need my permission and I won't give it to you. I can block you."

"And yet, you have not woken up. I am in control here, Tracey. Where are the statues of your friends?"

She would be sweating if she could be. Her mind raced. She was trapped, stuck inside this stone room prison. But though she could not move, neither could he. The distance between them was locked.

The cloaked man's fists opened and clenched closed, exposing his frustration. "How did you remove Timothy's stone from your little girlfriend?"

How did he know about Kylie? Did that mean he knew Tracey held the Serpent's Kiss now? "I'm not telling you."

"You will. Where is Timothy's stone?"

He doesn't know. Thank goodness. "No idea. It was lost," Tracey blurted. "Are you afraid of Timothy?" When the hooded man said nothing more, Tracey forced a laugh. "You are. He's more dangerous than you are and you know it."

"Oh, child. You have no idea where the true danger lies. You will tell me. I have faith. I will return when you are a little more amenable to my wishes."

The cloaked man disappeared.

Remembering Millicent's instructions once upon a time that all she needed to do was will herself awake, she shut her eyes. "Wake up!" There was no sucking sensation or sliding movement. She reached for her core, searching for her magic and found nothing.

If she was frozen in the outside world, cursed into a living statue by the evil fog, then she was truly stuck. She couldn't move while she was trapped in here and she couldn't move out in the real world.

"What am I going to do?"

"How did you do that?"
Jane's mother asked.

27

Heart thudding painfully, Tracey realized she was alone and thoroughly trapped. *Don't freak out!* She was imprisoned in the green place. A stone room. The one that belonged to the Crocodile Man. He had tried to trick her with Sebastian's face and a different stone room, but it had been him all along.

Wait.

Why had he used Sebastian's image to trick her? Her hands flew to her mouth as realization dawned. Sebastian did have a stone! That was why the Crocodile Man was hunting him. Sebastian was a stone Protector and the Crocodile Man used Sebastian's image to try and trick Tracey into revealing her whereabouts to him. He must have seen Tracey talking with Sebastian at the bowling alley and that put him onto her trail. But what about her friends? How had the Crocodile Man known about Jilly and Jonny and that they each held a stone? Unless … unless the Crocodile Man had been watching her for a longer time. She wracked her brain — tapping against her skull with her fingertips — for any clue that she had been watched. Surely, she would have noticed someone unknown hanging around. The investigation into the Stones of Power meant she was always checking for someone listening into their conversations. She would have seen someone. *Right?*

The only new person in her life was Sebastian. He must have betrayed her. Timothy was right. She couldn't trust anyone.

If this was another prank, she would be furious. If the Crocodile Man was just a figment of Sebastian's imagination created to test or scare her, then he would find out how truly scary she could be when she was angry.

She stared around the green room. "How do I get out of here?"

If she *was* frozen, like her sister, Jilly, and Jonny, then she would only escape if Grandma and Agent Loo Loo broke the curse. She just had to wait.

But what if … What if they can't break it?

She would be stuck in here forever.

No, there has to be a way out.

Tracey stared around the green room searching for an exit. *I'm inside a stone.* The Crocodile Man — she had nothing else to call him for now so that would have to do — the Crocodile Man didn't know she held *two* stones. And all of the stones were linked. *Timothy? Stephanie?* She called inside her head. There was no sudden appearance or bleeding black or white color of any kind.

Jilly was frozen and she was Mage-kind, unlike Jonny, so Tracey's best chance would be to try to link to her. "Jilly? Can you hear me?" she called into the empty air. "Jing Cho?"

Nothing happened.

Jonny had no magic. The Crow's Heart was not linked to Jonny and therefore it wasn't linked to the frozen statue spell.

She closed her eyes. "Millicent, are you there? Can you hear me?"

Again, there was no response. Tracey stomped her feet. It made no sound. *Fine.* To speak with Stephanie, she needed to be in the white place. She was currently in the green place. Maybe she could communicate with the spirit held within the Crocodile Man's stone? The only question was, whose stone was it? There were only two men left. Charles and Jonathan. Only, she didn't know any further details about either of them. Perhaps, she could try calling out and see if they answered?

If the Crocodile Man was the current stone Protector then he could be in communication with the spirit inside the stone the same way she was. Instead of talking with the stone's creator she should try the stone's guardian instead. *Oh wait.* She needed the Butterfly Stone's guardian to communicate with the other stones' guardians. And she couldn't access the Butterfly Stone. Tracey sighed, slumping her shoulders. She could not move so she couldn't even sit down.

There was only one thing left to try. She really did not want to, but she had no other choice. Up until now she hadn't tried to contact the Serpent's Kiss guardian. She was too afraid it would be dark and evil just like Timothy. She met it only that one time, when she had first communicated with it and the Tiger's Eye guardian to lock the Serpent's Kiss's magic up so Timothy couldn't hurt Kylie.

She closed her eyes and called for the Serpent's Kiss's guardian.

A jerking sensation tugged her forward. Her eyes sprang open as the world around her changed. Black smoke filled the green room, staining the invisible walls, flowing faster and swirling around her until she was surrounded on all sides by a thick, impenetrable darkness. A shape formed out of the black, its colors sickly, like the light was tainted and it affected the entire color pallet. A purple circle undulating with a gray octagon. Its movements were jerky, jagged like it was trying to lunge forward but was restrained.

"What is it, child?"

Tracey cleared her throat. "You are the guardian of the Serpent's Kiss?"

"We are."

"I hold the Serpent's Kiss now and I need your help."

"Why should we help you?"

What was she supposed to say to that? Shouldn't they want to help her because she held the Serpent's Kiss?

"We cannot wake you," it said as if it knew what she was thinking.

"Why not?"

"We are currently locked to that kind of power — you are cursed in the waking world."

"Then please, I need to speak with the guardian of another stone." If she was able to speak to another stone's guardian then she could ask to speak with that stone's current Protector. The only one who could possibly help her was Sebastian — the real Sebastian. The only one not frozen by the Crocodile Man's fog curse. "I know you are linked to the other stones. I know you can put me in contact with them."

"What will you give us for helping you?"

Ugh. She knew it. The Serpent's Kiss guardian *was* like Timothy. All twisted and evil. It wouldn't help her. She had run out of options. The words dripped out of her as if they were dragged out against her will. "What do you want?"

"Break the curse on the stones. Separate us."

Wait.

What?

The Serpent's Kiss's guardian *wanted* her to break the curse on the stones? Tracey's stomach twisted sharply. That had been her plan all along, but why would the guardian want that? Wouldn't it lessen Timothy's power when he got all of the stones? It made no sense. "Then that's what I'll do. I agree. Now, I want to talk to the guardian of a stone I have no knowledge of, but I know its current Protector. A boy named Sebastian Sawyer. His stone is —" Oh, she didn't know what Sebastian's stone looked like or what it was called. Oh, this would never work. Her heart sank.

Another shape blurrily formed out of the black to her right. A triangle over a hexagon. Bright shining yellow and rose red. The shapes danced and undulated over and around each other rapidly — she'd almost say happily. *"Greetings, Tracey."*

She laughed out a sound of relief. *It worked.* "Greetings, Guardian." Why it had worked she had no idea but it had worked. Perhaps because she held two stones? "Guardian, I need your help. I need to speak with Sebastian Sawyer. The current holder — the current Protector — of your stone."

Yellow streaks burst through the blackness, bright and sparkling — so bright that she almost couldn't see.

"Tracey? What are you doing here?"

"Sebastian?"

The boy appeared in front of her dressed in tight black jeans and a red polo. His hair was a wavy mess about his head. She was so glad to see him she wanted to grab his hand. She actually reached out to try, but he was too far away.

"How can you be here?" he asked.

"The guardian brought me."

"What guardian?"

"The — oh never mind. The Crocodile Man caught me. I'm trapped in his stone room. He's frozen me and —"

"What?" Sebastian's whole body deflated in an instant. "Then it's over. Wait," His head snapped up. "If you are trapped in *his* stone room — how are you here in mine?"

"Oh, well. The guardian —"

"No, don't you get it? If you're here … then you escaped. You escaped the Crocodile Man's spell. No one has done before that. You *are* strong enough." His eyes took on a pleading shape as his hands reached for her in return. "You *can* help me. I need —"

He was right. She was out. Inside her head, Tracey called for the stones around her neck.

With a hard yanking sensation that hurt her ribs and her lungs, Tracey was swept into a maelstrom of magical energy, like the worst kind of showground ride. It surrounded her completely, lifted her up into the air, and flung her around. She let out a cry and everything went black.

"I was angry at the farmers
for scaring you."

28

W ell, that was exceedingly unpleasant."

Tracey opened her eyes in the black place and found Timothy standing in front of her. *Oh thank goodness.* "What happened?" she demanded.

"I was about to ask you the same question."

"How am I here?" She couldn't tell Timothy she was in communication with the other stones. It felt as though all she was doing these days was keeping secrets. If only she knew how much Timothy could hear and understand what was happening to her.

She remembered being trapped in a nowhere place when Stephanie took control of her body. Back then, she had no idea what was happening in the outside world. She could only see and hear when she'd been strong enough to force herself forward. Timothy was so much stronger than Tracey. He could know everything and be lying to her about what he knew. All she could do was operate as if he didn't know. Eventually, he would betray himself. Tracey was currently stuck, bouncing between one stone and the next. *I need to wake up from this horrible nightmare.*

Millicent's voice returned to her from long ago. *"Just will yourself to wake up."* Tracey had tried that. Hadn't she?

But that was when she had been trapped inside the Crocodile Man's stone room — the green place. She'd escaped that mind trap now. She was back in Timothy's realm, which meant she was inside her own stone. Maybe, just maybe, she could get out now.

She closed her eyes.

"Tracey, what is going on?" Timothy demanded.

She ignored him. *Get out, wake up. Tracey, wake up!*

Her mind slammed into her physical body like a train emerging from a tunnel. Sight, sound, smell, and magic returned all at once. Her mind screamed. She fell to her knees and scrunched her fingers into the soft grass and dirt. Her fingers released a loamy fragrance that swam up her nose. A tree root stabbed into her left knee. Everything was too bright, too colorful. Her brain was overwhelmed trying to process it all. *My magic is back.* "Whoa!"

"Take it easy, Tracey."

Hands gripped her shoulders and kept her from face planting right there in the middle of her backyard. "What am I doing outside?" she asked, blinking away the bright sunlight spearing into her eyes. Heat from above warmed her chilly skin. "I was in the park with —" *Fruit tingles.* Her frantic gaze darted around the backyard searching for her friends. She found them all — all except Jonny and Jilly. A diorama of statues stood frozen in all sorts of weird and terrified shapes. Hands were raised, mouths hung open screaming silently inside their prisons. All of her friends had been caught. Tony, Dave, and Sarah had been moved to stand inside a large salt circle poured over the grass. Then Tracey's horror became a true nightmare. "No!" The sound tore from her throat as she saw more statues. Her mom and dad, her brothers, and Grandma all stood frozen inside the circle too.

Mr. and Mrs. O'Shae — Tony's mom and dad — stood outside the circle next to Mrs. Cho. They stared at Tracey in surprise and moved at once to her side. "Tracey, you're back!"

"What happened?" Tracey gasped. "Are you performing a spell? Is that what got me out? What happened to my family? Where are Jonny and Jilly?"

"We haven't started the spell yet." Agent Loo Loo was the one holding onto Tracey's shoulders. She knelt in front of Tracey, holding her upright as Tracey wobbled and nearly fell over. "You woke up before we could start."

"What happened?"

"We are not sure. Mrs. Cho and I found you and your friends standing frozen in the school sport's field. Coach called us. When we returned here with you, we found … your family, Jonny's mother, and the remaining agents … I'm so sorry, Tracey, Jilly and Jonny have been taken."

Tracey couldn't tear her eyes from her mom and dad's frozen forms. "How did you wake me up?"

"We didn't," Agent Loo Loo said. "You woke up on your own." The agent's clothing was wrinkled and the three adults looked awfully pale. Each had dark shadows under their eyes and the creases around their eyes and mouths were more pronounced. They seemed as tired as Tracey felt.

"I don't feel so good." She moaned as her head wobbled.

Mrs. O'Shae helped Tracey stand up. "I'll take her inside. Keep going," she urged the agent.

"No, first she must tell us how she escaped the mind lock," Mr. O'Shae demanded, getting right up into Tracey's face.

She leaned back to get away from him but Mrs. O'Shae held her tightly in place. "Mind lock?" Tracey repeated.

"We've discovered what the statue curse is. It is very old magic," Mrs. O'Shae said. "We have found a spell we hope will break it."

"I know who attacked us," Tracey said. She again attempted to escape Mrs. O'Shae's tight grip, glancing back at Agent Loo Loo and Mrs. Cho. "Will it help if you know who cast it? It's the Crocodile Man."

"Who?" Mrs. Cho asked.

"He's another stone Protector."

Questions and grunts of confusion surrounded Tracey.

"How did you escape the mind lock?" Mr. O'Shae demanded again, his voice was louder this time, determined to get answers. He yanked Tracey from his wife's tight grip by the arm. Tracey shoved him away.

"I don't know. I — it was the stones — they — I convinced — well, I didn't, but I linked to the Ser — Butterfly Stone. It broke through the mind lock somehow. Jilly might be able to break out in time but Tony and Dave and my family? They don't have a stone, I'm so sorry. I don't know how to get them out."

"Always with these stones. They take and take. Save my son," Mr. O'Shae growled.

"I will," Tracey told him. "Can I help with the spell?" she asked.

Agent Loo Loo shook her head. "You should go and rest, Tracey. While you can."

Mrs. O'Shae led Tracey inside. "Come on, hon."

Tracey managed to get upstairs with Mrs. O'Shae's assistance and flopped onto her bed. She pulled the covers up over her trembling body. "I feel kinda spacey."

"You've been frozen for several days."

"Days?" Tracey tried to sit up, but Mrs. O'Shae pushed her down into her pillow. Tracey's brain was thick, her thoughts slower than usual. *How could I have been frozen for days? It was only minutes.*

"Rest."

"It can't have been days," she repeated. "How did Agent Loo Loo find me?" Tracey asked.

"Via your phone."

"Tony and Dave?"

"They weren't far from you."

"I … I'm sorry about Tony. You said he couldn't come. If he'd stayed home … he would be safe."

Mrs. O'Shae scowled. "I know." Tracey flinched and tore her gaze away from the angry woman. Tracey couldn't even blame her. If only Tracey had done what she had been told.

"It's my fault."

Mrs. O'Shae touched Tracey's arm with gentle fingers. "I am angry, but I know my boy. He would have found a way out regardless. You are not entirely to blame."

Tracey stroked her palm over the face of the brightly smiling cartoon Lego character on her bed cover. "But now Jonny and Jilly have been taken. How do we find them? I shouldn't have run off. If I'd been here, I could have stopped this."

"You would not have been able to prevent what happened. I am glad you're awake. Once you've rested, you can help us wake my son and your family."

"Are you going back down there to help?" Tracey asked.

"Yes."

As soon as Mrs. O'Shae shut the door, Tracey pulled the Butterfly Stone out from under her shirt. "Stephanie?"

The Serpent's Kiss buzzed violently against her skin sending an icy tingle down her spine. She hadn't been able to talk to Stephanie since she put on the Serpent's Kiss. Timothy's presence must be stopping her from reaching her ancestor. Maybe the power of one stone canceled out the other. Tracey closed her eyes and opened her core. Her magic fluttered. As weakened and tired as she was, even the trickle of her own magic was like chocolate fudge on ice-cream. Everything was instantly better. She took hold of the Serpent's Kiss and the Butterfly Stone and called, "Sebastian?"

With a jolt she was thrown forward into a bright place. Not the white room but a place that was warmer, glowier; yellow and red rose mixed together in great swirls that blended and stretched in long wild waves around her. The colors didn't clash. Rather, they felt surprisingly peaceful. Though she'd seen the room before, now she could *feel* it.

"How did you get back here?" Sebastian stood before her in the same skinny black jeans and ruby-red polo. He wrung his hands together. "You *have* to leave."

"I need to ask about your stone."

"You can't be here."

"Seb —"

"He'll find you. He'll track you and then he'll find me." Though Sebastian was taller than Tracey, he looked smaller when he hunched in on himself. In this brilliantly happy place, he seemed so sad. His bright blue eyes were dull and lifeless.

"No, it's okay. I escaped. I'm not frozen anymore," she told him.

"You escaped? Completely?" His back straightened as his lips twitched. "You are so powerful."

"Sebastian, tell me about your stone."

His gaze sharpened. "No. You're not coming after me too."

"Don't be crazy. I don't want your stone. The Crocodile Man attacked my family and my friends. I'm going after him. And if you help me catch him, you'll be safe from him forever. He can't hurt you if we catch him first."

"You should stay away, Tracey. Your family are not the first he has attacked." Sebastian's expression soured as his face paled. "My family are gone now. I hoped you could help. I tested you to see if you were strong enough, but my tricks were harmless." He shook his head. The loss of his gaze was like turning off a light, everything around her dimmed. "I'm so sorry he came after the people you love. It's better if you just stay away from me. Stay safe, Tracey."

"Sebastian?"

He thrust out a hand and she went flying from the warm yellow-red swirly room. She thunked back into her body with a jolt, panting slightly.

"Fruit tingles."

Tracey spent a while worrying about Sebastian. Where was he? How was he surviving on his own? The stress and mental exhaustion she felt finally sucked her under regardless of how hard she fought it. She dragged herself out of bed a few hours later. Surprised because, firstly, she slept at all knowing her family and friends were in danger and, secondly, that no one woke her when they broke the curse. Heading downstairs Tracey discovered why no one came to get her. Her family and friends were still statues. "It didn't work?" she asked, her voice falling flat when she caught sight of them. The statues had been moved back into the living room. They crowded the space like a creepy wax museum. Tracey inched past each frozen form, ducking and weaving around outstretched arms to reach the M-force agent.

Agent Loo Loo sat bent over on the sofa, her elbows propped up on her knees. Her chin rested on her hands. She shook her head sadly. "No."

"Did you move them in here?" Tracey asked.

"Yes," she said. "Not without some difficulty."

"Where are Tony's parents?"

"Mr. and Mrs. O'Shae have gone to talk with their Mage-kind contacts. Mrs. Cho is still here. She's in the kitchen speaking with the council on her cell." Agent Loo Loo pushed wearily to her feet.

"What do we do now?" Tracey followed the agent out of the living room and into the kitchen. It was so dreary in the usually bright and bustling room. Mom should be racing around cleaning, her brothers playing their video games or eating. Sarah would talk everyone's ears off and Dad would be cooking. Now, it was as silent as a graveyard. It gave her the willies. Catching sight of them, Mrs. Cho put down her phone and lowered herself into a chair. "What about Uncle Donny?" Tracey asked. "He can help, right?"

Agent Loo Loo shook her head, her lips twisting, but she didn't speak.

Tracey's heart clenched. "Not him too?" She sank into a chair at the table beside Mrs. Cho.

"I have agents bringing his frozen body here."

Everyone she knew was being taken away from her. Tracey planted her hands onto the tabletop and pressed her forehead onto her fingers. Her stomach rumbled. She opened her mouth to shout for permission to get a snack and groaned softly. *No Mom and Dad. No one.* This had to be how Sebastian felt all the time. *It's awful.* She pushed to her feet and stepped toward the pantry then stopped and spun back. "What about my friend Damian and his sister? Kylie is Mage-kind. She wore the … Timothy's stone for a while. Can you send someone to check on them?"

Agent Loo Loo nodded. "I've had agents watching over them since Kylie's escape when Sarah was caught."

Tracey fetched a glass and swung the refrigerator door open to yank out the OJ. She poured herself a glass and drank it quickly, then scooped up the cookie tin and brought it back to the table. "What did the council say?" She grabbed a chocolate chip cookie out of the tin and offered the rest around. No one took anything.

"I'm waiting for them to call me back," Mrs. Cho said softly. Fury flashed in her eyes. "Apparently, they are rather busy at the moment."

"How are you feeling, Tracey?" Agent Loo Loo asked joining them at the table.

"Still tired. I have a headache. So, the spell didn't work?" Tracey ate another cookie. Crumbs fell to the table in front of her and she swiped them onto the floor. Mom would kill her when she saw them. She glanced toward the living room. *Oh.* Tracey's shoulders drooped.

"Frustratingly, it did not," Agent Loo Loo said. "I have other ideas though. All is not lost."

"Can I help with any of them?" Tracey asked. "We have to find Jonny and Jilly. Who took them? Do you have any leads?"

Mrs. Cho stood up and her chair screeched across the tiles. She stalked to the window and stared out over the garden. Her lips curled. "They do not have long, frozen like this."

Tracey's chest tightened. "How long do they have?"

"Days at most. Whatever we do, we must do it soon."

Tracey sprang to her feet. "So, what do we do? Agent? We have to do something."

Agent Loo Loo cleared her throat. "Do you remember what we were talking about when we were investigating the spell site at the park?

"Ah, about …" Tracey glanced at Mrs. Cho, not sure if she was supposed to speak about it in front of the other woman.

"I've already told her," Agent Lo Loo confirmed.

"You said Agent Malden wanted to speak to me."

"Yes. Well …"

"My brother, Steven Cho, who you know as Doctor Chan —" Mrs. Cho's voice sliced through Agent Loo Loo's hesitation. "— is held at the same facility as Trent Malden. If you are going to see him then I'm coming with you."

Agent Loo Loo's face paled. "That is not going to happen."

"He has studied the stones. He may know how to break this statue curse."

"You want to see him for yourself," Agent Loo Lo accused. "I know you've been petitioning to see him."

"I have and I will continue to do so. I will come with you when you take Tracey to see Malden."

"I'm not —"

"Steven has information. It is imperative that we learn what he knows. We must interrogate him."

"Professionals have —"

"They are not us. They are not me." The venom in Mrs. Cho's voice scared Tracey.

"I should probably talk to him too," Tracey said. She really didn't want to but if it helped save her family and friends then she'd talk to anyone. "Remember, I said I wanted to? Mrs. Cho is right. He might know something."

"This is not a good idea," Agent Loo Loo insisted.

"What else can I do? I want to help."

"We must see Steven." Mrs. Cho's face was set. They would not dissuade her.

"If I'm going to see Agent Malden, I'll be there anyway," Tracey argued.

"Chan will attempt to get into your head." Agent Loo Loo's lips made a cat's bum shape — like she had tasted something really sour.

"You will be there, and so will Mrs. Cho. I'll be perfectly safe. If Agent — ex-agent Malden or Doctor Chan can help us unfreeze everyone, then we have to try. What other options do we have?"

Mrs. Cho had a tiny smile in her eyes though nothing showed on her face. Agent Loo Loo stood and nodded sharply. "Fine. Let's do it."

"So I imagined everything they accused me of doing would come true for them," Jane said.

29

They arrived late in the afternoon. The sun speared into their eyes as they emerged from the 4WD. Tracey's hand rose to shade her face and stared at the single-story red brick motel stretched out like a Lego block in front of them. Doors were spaced along the outside and the gardens to either side were overgrown. They could hear heavy traffic roaring along the nearby highway. On the long drive, Agent Loo Loo told them they would have to overnight in a motel. "I could only get permission to visit the prison early tomorrow morning."

"But what will happen if my family and friends stay frozen? They can't sleep, they can't eat, they can't even drink!"

Agent Loo Loo assured Tracey that her family and friends would be fine for a short time and reminded her there were agents at the house with medics to monitor them. Mrs. Cho stayed horribly silent in the front passenger seat. "Why can't we go today?" Tracey complained again.

Agent Loo Loo sighed. "We can only go in with permission. Tomorrow morning was the earliest visitation time I could get approval for."

"But Mrs. Cho said we don't have much time."

"I know, Tracey. But this is a federal prison. We just can't storm in."

Mrs. Cho got a room of her own. Tracey had to share a twin bedroom with Agent Loo Loo. "It's only for the night." The agent took the bed closest to the door. She put her handbag and small suitcase beside the bed and went back outside.

Their room was exactly as Tracey imagined a budget motel room would look like. Everything was dressed in shades of brown. Curtains, carpet, even the bedspread. *Bleh.* Agent Loo Loo nudged the door open with her foot. She held a heavy archive box in her hands. "There's three more in the car," she said.

"Do you really need to bring them all inside?" Tracey asked. She paced the length of the room, seven steps back and forth. "I feel like we should be out there doing something."

"Grab a box, Tracey. We'll keep busy."

"Research now? Really?"

Agent Loo Loo shot Tracey a long look. Tracey slumped down onto the bed sending a puff of stale musty air up into her nostrils. "Ugh."

"Okay, let's at least do something about the smell in here before we deal with the files I haven't read yet."

"Magic?"

"Yep. Watch carefully. To purify or cleanse the air I'm going to push my magic out of my core and fill the room." She did exactly what she said and Tracey's skin buzzed like humming birds sat on her arms, their wings beating so fast she couldn't see them only feel the moving air quiver the hairs.

"Cool."

"Now, I'm going to target the musty odor clinging to the air. I'm actually targeting moisture in the air. That's what tends to hold the bad odor you can smell. Obviously, this would be easier in a smokey room because the particulate matter bouncing off the oxygen molecules are heavier thus easier to grasp, though carbon dioxide can be trickier to detect." She muttered under her breath, "Clear and Cleanse."

Tracey's eyes popped wide. "Oh!" A light tugging sensation pulled at the exposed skin of her arms like standing on the shore as the tide sucked sand from beneath her toes. "Oh."

"Do you feel that? I'm creating an electric static charge to separate them."

It was a little bit similar to the tiny bits of electricity Tracey pulled from her brain. In her mind Tracey mirrored the spell, doing her best to remember it. Hopefully she could add this to her list of spells, though when she would ever use it she had no idea.

Tracey sniffed deeply as the flare of magic faded. The dead smell was gone. "Cool."

"Now," Agent Loo Loo pointed to the archive boxes. "I've not had a chance to read through these in great detail. Too much has happened in too short a time. I don't know where it will take us, but it will keep us moving forward. I know you're frustrated and scared. I am too." The agent sat on the other bed and bounced a little. "What would your uncle say to do?"

"Keep working the problem."

"Right. Well, we have these files and books of Malden's. That is what we can do. I'll grab the other boxes, and we'll order pizza and work the problem. I'll even show you a little more magic. The boxes are spelled so no one can open them but me. We'll add you to the spell, all right?"

Tracey sighed but nodded her agreement. Learning more magic could be fun. *Better than studying.* Agent Loo Loo headed back outside. Tracey stood up again and paced to the wall. She was itching to get moving. It was like a bug crawling under her skin. "Timothy? Why can't you help?"

If you gave me control—

"Not happening."

Then I cannot help. His annoying voice fell silent. A low hum came from the light bulb above Tracey's head and the soft plinking of dripping water came from the adjoining open bathroom door. She bet Timothy *could* help. If only she had a way to force the ghostly presence to assist.

The next time Agent Loo Loo came inside the archive box she carried didn't seem quite as heavy. Tracey clambered off the bed as she lowered it onto the first box. "What's in this one?"

"Books and other things."

"Books? Like from the council archive? Should you even have those out here?"

"It's just some bedtime reading."

Tracey rolled her eyes at that. *Just like Tony!* Agent Loo Loo laughed. "I've got this. How about you get yourself ready for bed. Fancy a quick shower? It's all yours. I'll order the pizza and then we'll do a little more magic, hmmm?"

She acquiesced and checked her phone before taking her pajamas into the bathroom. At first, she was surprised to find no messages then her shoulders sagged. Of course she didn't have any messages. All her friends were frozen. She sent a text to Damian to check in on him and Kylie. When she came out of the bathroom in her pajamas, she found Agent Loo Loo already sitting on the other bed with her legs outstretched, reading a heavy green-covered book and eating a slice of pizza.

"That was fast. Should I get Mrs. Cho?" Tracey asked.

"She ordered something else. Come and eat."

Tracey's gaze strayed over the four archive boxes. She recognized the book Agent Loo Loo was reading as one she had seen Agent Malden carrying around. Was this all that was left of Agent Malden's working life, or were there more boxes packed away in storage somewhere, locked up the same way he was? It seemed really sad. Four boxes was not a lot for a whole career. She grabbed a slice and checked her cell as she climbed onto her bed. Damian's reply must have come through while she was in the shower.

Mom's pissed. There are agents here. But we're okay. Are you okay? What about the others?

She typed quickly. They're okay. That's what Agent Loo Loo keeps telling me.

Then they'll be okay. Hang in there, Tracey. I know you'll find a way to save everyone.

Thanks, she typed, her cheeks heating. She only hoped that what Damian said was true. In reality she felt completely useless. Just stuck waiting for things to happen.

"Here." Agent Loo Loo threw a book onto the bed. "Since you can't settle, read this." Tracey sighed and bit into her cooling slice of pepperoni. Lifting the hard book cover, she coughed at the dust that sprinkled the bed cover beneath it. Soon she would rescue her friends and family. She flipped through the crinkled, well-thumbed pages. *Soon.*

The trip to the Mage-kind prison the next morning passed in a blur. For a start, it was way too early in the morning for anyone to be awake. Tracey didn't eat breakfast. All she could think about were her friends and family. Did it hurt to be frozen in one body position for so long? Agent Loo Loo said no, but Tracey figured she might be lying to make her feel better.

It was still dark outside. They breathed out white foggy breaths as they moved from the 4WD to the prison entrance. It reminded her of visiting Nana in Tavel House. She felt eyes burrowing into her back and the sensation of crawling feet all over her skin. Looking up, she spied dark plastic-covered cameras in the ceiling and peered over her shoulder expecting to see armed guards standing at every corridor junction, staring at her intently. There were guards, but their sharp suspicious stares were locked on Agent Loo Loo and Mrs. Cho, not on the teenage girl standing between them.

Every wall held strict signs repeating the rules of how to behave so as not to agitate the inmates. Tracey's crawling skin prickled worse, like her skin was trying to peel itself off so it could run away. There was a funny hospital chemical smell in the air around her. The guards reminded her of the nurses at

Tavel House, the ones who looked at her with suspicion and annoyance for altering their daily routine.

The guard in front of them processed their visitor registrations painfully slowly. His shirt had crisp creases at the shoulders that ran down his long sleeves, mirrored by the creases in his trousers. His pale, watery eyes narrowed as his gaze dropped to Tracey. "Do not put your hands near the inmate. Do not pass the inmate any object. If the inmate stands up, we will sound an alert. If the inmate does not immediately retake his seat, we will enter to subdue him. If this occurs, move directly to the wall and remain silent. Do you understand these rules as I have given them to you?"

Tracey nodded, her skin quivering. *This is horrible.* Somewhere inside this cold, concrete prison Agent Malden was locked away serving time because he was a bad guy.

"Do not use magic near the inmate or you will be immediately escorted from the premises. Put all jewelry, phone, identification, and sharp objects into the tray provided. Do not talk about magic. Do not imply or infer magic. Before you enter the cell, you must lock down your core. Do you understand?"

Tracey nodded again and placed her phone into the gray plastic tray. She didn't touch her neck. If the guard demanded she take off her necklaces she couldn't comply. Suddenly worried, she peered up at Agent Loo Loo. The M-force agent remained silent. Sweat broke out across Tracey's skin. She glanced at Mrs. Cho.

The powerful woman was filling her tray with items from her pockets. It redirected the guard's full attention. Computer chips and flash drives, three blue pens. A short, sharpened pencil. Her wallet and a fold-out batten. Three gold rings and one silver one. A leather neck tie with a little silver star. Four bangles and a charm bracelet. Hair ties and clips. Two cell phones and a nail file. A giggle welled up in Tracey's throat as Mrs. Cho kept going. A red piece of Lego. A blue string. A ribbon with Hello Kitty images on it. A little computer in the shape of a dog. A key chain. More hair ties. Sealed sticking plasters, a wooden nail file, a tube of lip gloss and little tin of lip balm. A gold lipstick case and a cracked eyeshadow container. A plastic straw and another pen — a fountain pen.

By the time Mrs. Cho stopped emptying her pockets and handed her overloaded tray to the guard he looked exhausted.

"What about our Mage-kind bracelets?" Tracey asked holding up her hand.

"You're cleared for those." His gaze dropped to her neck. "And I have a form clearing your necklace." The guard waved them toward the elevator doors at the end of the corridor. They had to pass through a people-sized scanner. When nothing beeped, Agent Loo Loo led Tracey forward and pressed the basement level *B3* button. No one spoke as they descended. The elevator doors opened with a bright sounding ping.

They stood at the mouth of a long concrete corridor. The smell of chemical cleaners was stronger down here. The floor was polished concrete gray with several colored lines painted on it. Again, Tracey was uncomfortably reminded of Tavel House. The similarities were eerie enough to be extremely disturbing. Agent Loo Loo followed the green line. Tracey and Mrs. Cho trailed after her. Tracey wondered what the woman was thinking about. Voices cried out around them as they passed, making Tracey jump and flinch.

The sickness in her belly grew sharper as she made out their words and whispered intentions. She crossed her arms, hugging herself for comfort. "I don't like it here." Not having access to her magic at least meant she couldn't feel the waves of hatred drifting off the inmates. It didn't block her ears though.

"Just look forward. Don't listen," Agent Loo Loo said.

Yeah right. At least with her power locked away Timothy couldn't pop into her head and cause any mischief.

They turned right, then left, and then right again past several thick, locked doors. At last, they stopped in front of a gray faceless door. Someone shouted and the door gave a loud *thunk* before sliding open with a rattling squeal. Agent Loo Loo led them into a small room.

The door shut behind them with a clunk that sent a shiver down Tracey's spine. The room was divided in half by a barred wall. Behind the bars, Agent Malden sat on a finger-thin bed. He had lost more weight. His arms were pale beneath his white T-shirt sleeves and his bare feet stuck out like twigs from soft, blue, pajama-style trousers. Tracey wondered if he was cold.

He looked up when the outer door clanked shut. "Agent Epworth, what are you doing here?" His eyes widened further when Tracey stepped out from behind Loo Loo. He launched to his feet. "Tracey."

A loud buzzer sounded. Agent Loo Loo held up her hand. "Sit down, Trent."

He sat and glanced warily up at the camera in the corner. Tracey examined his bare cell. There was a notebook and some crayons on a little shelf stuck to the wall and a metal toilet in the corner. An empty food tray lay on the floor. "A spell was cast on my family and friends," Tracey blurted. She wasn't sure how to address him anymore, so she didn't try.

He worked his jaw for a moment then got out, "What?"

"My family and friends are frozen into statues. We don't know how to break the spell."

"M-force —"

"Nothing has worked," Tracey said.

"You studied the stones," Agent Loo Loo stepped forward, drawing Malden's attention to her.

"What makes you think this attack is connected to the stones?" Malden asked.

Tracey grunted. His gaze swung back to her face. "Only my friends and family were attacked."

"You suspect Timothy is behind it?"

"Who else could it be?" Agent Loo Loo asked.

"The Crocodile Man," Tracey said.

Malden, Agent Loo Loo, and Mrs. Cho all stared at her. "The who?" Malden asked.

"Another stone Protector."

"Timothy's stone?"

"No, I think the Crocodile Man has a different stone."

"He attacked Tracey," Agent Loo Loo offered.

Malden's mouth closed with a clack. He swiped his tongue over dry lips. "How did you get away, Tracey?"

She touched her neckline. He nodded, understanding. He would think she had used the Butterfly Stone. She didn't correct him.

"Then you should be able to wake your friends the same way."

"Nothing has worked," she snapped and stomped up to the bars. "Tell me what I can do. There must be something. Anything!"

He didn't act upset or annoyed by her anger. "The archive has several books that I studied during my research on the stones. From when I was …" He fell silent. Tracey was able to fill in what he couldn't voice. From when he studied the Stones of Power to use them to fuel his spell to return his love — Agent Striker — to life. Tracey managed to stop him and by defeating his plans he ended up here. *She'd* put him here. Her skin crawled, imagining being stuck behind these bars for days on end, with no phone and no friends. No escape. "I assume my office was packed up."

Agent Loo Loo nodded. "I have your files. You think something in your notes will help?"

"Possibly. You should call in the council to assist."

Tracey's blood boiled over. "No!" She stepped closer to Malden's cell forcing her anger down low in her belly as she focused on the sad man in front of her. "What did you want to tell me, Agent Malden? Oh, that's right, you're not an agent anymore."

He winced at her words. "Yes, I —" He spied Mrs. Cho behind Agent Loo Loo and his head rose. His stare sharpened. Mrs. Cho stared at him without speaking, lifting her chin.

Malden's gaze flicked back to Agent Loo Loo. "I take it I can't speak to Tracey alone?"

"What do you think?" she snapped back.

He sighed. Tracey pushed closer to the bars. The magical buzz against her skin grew stronger.

"Be careful, Tracey. The anti-magic wards are painful if you touch them," Agent Loo Loo warned. Tracey's gaze fell to Malden's Mage-kind identification bracelet. He wore a plain prison bangle with a light in the center. The light was a familiar horrid blue. Tracey knew what that meant. Malden's magic had been locked away, deep inside his core where he couldn't access it. She remembered how dreadful that felt, being so cold and empty all the time, like her own skin didn't fit right. She wouldn't wish that punishment on anyone.

"Has Timothy's stone been found?" Malden asked.

Tracey shook her head. She didn't want to lie but she couldn't tell him the truth either. "Prince Henry hasn't found it yet," she said. It was true. He couldn't find it. It was around Tracey's neck.

She twitched as Agent Loo Loo gripped her shoulder. "You wanted to speak to Tracey. Get on with it or I am taking this young woman out of here."

"No, wait. Of course, yes." He straightened. "Tracey, before the … before I did what I … what I shouldn't have done, I located a book in the archives I believe may help you with destroying the stones."

"Will it unfreeze my family? My friends? That's the only reason we're here." Movement behind Tracey caught her attention. Mrs. Cho leaned back against the rear wall. There was a tiny vibration of air against Tracey's skin. She squinted at Mrs. Cho. Their magic was supposed to be locked down so Malden couldn't feel its presence and lose his mind or whatever it was the guards thought he would do if he could sense magic. Tracey knew from experience he wouldn't be able to feel their magic at all, even if it was blazing right in front of him.

"A book that details a way to break the curse that links the stones together."

"What?" Tracey shouted. "Forget about the stones. How do I unfreeze my family and friends?"

"Tracey. If you break the curse on the stones, Timothy and this Crocodile Man won't be able to find the others. Ever. You can hide them away and everyone will be safe."

For half a second Tracey thought it was a good idea. Then she realized the curse at least meant she could track down the other stones and communicate with them. If the Crocodile Man was able to get the stone off Jilly or Jonny then Tracey could still find it. "We can't do that," Tracey said. "We need *all* of the stones to destroy them." She shook her head. "My friends —"

"If you break the link between the stones then they can never be used together. There would be no way for Timothy to use their magic," Malden insisted.

"Why are you telling me this? Why now?"

"I couldn't before. I wanted to use that link to increase their power —"

"I stopped you."

"You did and I am thankful for it." He smiled but she couldn't match it.

"Even if we break the link between the stones," Agent Loo Loo said, "they will still retain their individual power. If the wrong person gets hold of one, they can still use the magic stored within it."

"But Timothy could never return," Malden insisted.

Agent Loo Loo shook her head. "This was what you couldn't tell me? You could only tell this to Tracey? Really?"

"I can tell you where to find the book —"

"Stop it," Tracey shouted. "We're here to help —" A blaring alarm speared into their soft chatter. "What's that?" Tracey asked. Worry crossed Agent Loo Loo's face. The alarm grew steadily louder. In the corridor outside, heavily booted feet ran past and raised voices echoed, their shouting filled with fear.

Agent Loo Loo moved to the door and listened carefully. The door gave a loud *thunk* and unlocked. Tracey felt a surge of magic but didn't know if it came from Agent Loo Loo or Mrs. Cho. Mrs. Cho pressed a hand to the agent's shoulder and slipped past her into the corridor beyond. Agent Loo Loo pointed at Tracey. "Stay here. We'll find out what's going on." She stepped into the corridor after Mrs. Cho and the door clanged shut behind them.

"What's happening?" Tracey asked turning back to Malden. She suddenly realized she was all alone in the room with the man who had betrayed her.

"That is a hard lesson to learn,"
Jane's father said.

30

Malden leapt to his feet and stood as close as he could to the bars of his cell. "You're not supposed to stand up," Tracey reminded him. His sharp stare was fixed on her face. This close she could see the redness of his eyeballs and the creases between his brows.

"You are being watched."

"I'm being watched by everyone. Agent Loo Loo is my handler." Two booming bongs sounded from somewhere down the corridor outside. The ongoing blaring of the alarm did nothing to help Tracey's fear levels. She stared over her shoulder at the sealed door.

"You have been isolated from your friends and family. I was forbidden from calling you directly. Loo Loo refused to bring you here."

"You think she's working with the Crocodile Man?" Tracey shook her head again and waved her hands around. Faint shouting traveled down the corridor outside. Thudding feet grew louder then softer. "Agent Loo Loo is not bad. Not like you. She'd never try to hurt me. She told me you wanted to speak to me."

"You don't know her," he said.

"Neither do you!"

"Hank trusted me."

She growled. "You're trying to get in my head and confuse me."

"Can't you see they're here to take the stones. You must break the link between them so the others can never be found." Another boom echoed. This one sounded further away.

"I will, when I destroy them all," she said.

The outer door sprang open. Mrs. Cho grabbed Tracey's arm. "Come with me."

"Tracey — !" Malden shouted.

Mrs. Cho pulled Tracey out of the room and the door clanged shut, cutting off Malden's shouts. "What did he tell you?"

"That someone is trying to isolate me."

"Who?"

"He didn't say." Mrs. Cho pulled Tracey by her wrist down the corridor in the opposite direction to the elevators. "Where are we going?" Above their heads she could make out the rapid calling of anxious and terrified voices and more running feet. The alarm was giving her a headache.

"Stay quiet. Do not draw attention to us. We must move quickly."

Tracey ran in Mrs. Cho's shadow. She didn't have much choice. The woman gripped her arm with sharp nails and wouldn't let go. "Ouch, you're hurting me. Where's Agent Loo Loo?"

"Upstairs."

"What's happening?"

"The prison is under attack."

"By who?" Tracey gasped.

"I don't know." They ran into an open elevator, but instead of going up — the way Tracey expected — they went down. Realization hit Tracey like a truck. "You're taking me to see Doctor Chan?"

"Stay silent. We must be quick. Do you understand?"

"Do you think this attack is to free him?"

"We cannot allow him to escape. Unleash your core and prepare to use your magic."

Tracey swallowed hard. She threw open her core and drew out her magic, imbuing it with her internal storage of electricity the way Noel taught her back when she was fighting the mumbles. Her magic crackled like live wires. *What is happening?* Timothy's voice slammed into Tracey's head. With access to her magic, the spirit had returned.

Mrs. Cho shot Tracey a shocked look at the crackle surrounding her. Tracey didn't explain. She was afraid of Doctor Chan and planned to use all of her magic to defend against him if he attacked. When the elevator doors sprang open, the sound of popping filled their ears. The shouting voices were louder out here but she couldn't make out what they were saying. All she got was the impression of panic. Tracey followed Jilly's mom down a long dark corridor. "What happened to the lights?" Another echoing boom rocked the walls. "We have to get out of here."

"Shhhh. Stay silent now."

Tracey followed Mrs. Cho through two open doors. The cold corridors were identical and Tracey was quickly lost. The scattering pops grew more frantic. Someone screamed and her stress levels ratcheted higher.

Stop. Timothy's voice froze Tracey's feet. Mrs. Cho jerked back when Tracey refused to move. *Do you sense that? Magic.* The flare came from her right. The lights above them flickered off and came back on again. She heard another scream and more popping.

"What is it?" Mrs. Cho whispered.

"Magic," Tracey said, keeping her own voice hushed. Mrs. Cho's eyes glowed brightly, her teeth baring in a sharp grin.

"Well done, Tracey. You have found him." Mrs. Cho sent a spear of magic right into the wall and an invisible door slid open.

A familiar, evil voice called out. "Hello, Tracey."

Jane nodded. "If the people of Hamsted wish to move to another town they may. They may even come to Delmore."

31

You do not speak to her. You speak to me." Mrs. Cho came forward and slammed her hand against the thick bars that separated her from her brother.

"Xing, what are you doing here?" Doctor Chan's face paled at the sight of his sister. Tracey wondered if he would faint right there in front of them. The thought made her smile. Another loud boom echoed from somewhere above them. It sounded closer. The smile fell off her face.

Doctor Chan didn't look well. It was the first thing Tracey noticed. His hands trembled. The sheen on his face was oil, not sweat, and his greasy hair hung in limp clumps around his face. His cheek bones were sharper, making his cheeks thinner, like he hadn't been eating. He pushed to his feet and stepped close to the bars. No alert sounded above the still-screaming alarm. His eyeglasses were held together with scotch tape, and his prison wristband emitted the same blue glow as the one Malden wore. Doctor Chan's stare fixed on Tracey and the only word she could use to describe it was hunger. He looked at her as if she were a takeaway meal he wanted to devour. With the door to the corridor behind them shut, a lot of the battle sounds faded. Tracey could still make out the occasional explosion over the alarm.

Mrs. Cho bared her teeth. "I have much to say to you."

"You cannot be here. I ordered you not be permitted to see me," he shouted.

"Ordered? Who are you to order *me*?"

"What is Tracey doing here? You cannot have received permission to bring her here."

Tracey stepped forward, not wanting to be pushed aside in Mrs. Cho's quest for … whatever it was she came here to do. "Tell me about the stone Protectors."

He laughed. "I will tell you nothing."

I know all about his quest for power, Tracey. He is a sad, pathetic, needy little man desperate for attention, and power. Timothy whispered into her mind. *Ask me for leverage.* Doctor Chan had been his servant. If she used information only Timothy knew then Doctor Chan would know she'd found the Serpent's Kiss. He might tell Mrs. Cho. But … but … Timothy did know a lot about Doctor Chan. Indecision froze her voice. She shoved Timothy back. "Tell me," she ordered.

"No."

Tracey let magic fill her body. Her hands glowed brightly. "I'll make you."

"Enough. Where is the book, Steven?"

Doctor Chan smirked at his sister. "Where you will never find it."

"Book, what book?" Tracey asked.

"It belongs to me," Mrs. Cho shouted ignoring Tracey's question. "Where is it?"

Doctor Chan lowered himself to his bunk, eyes narrowed on the angry Mage-kind. Another boom sounded overhead, so much louder and closer. Tracey's worried glance darted to the ceiling. When she looked back, a tiny smile played upon Doctor Chan's lips. "He has come for me."

More magic filled Tracey's hands, crackling loudly with her stored electricity. She wanted him afraid of her power, afraid of her.

His eyes widened.

It pleased her immensely. "Not him. The Crocodile Man," she stated.

Doctor Chan stood up again. His hands clenched into fists. "What? You've met him?"

Not *how do you know him?* or *how did you find out about him?* Interesting. "Yes."

"You survived?"

"Obviously."

"You still have the Butterfly Stone?"

"Yes."

He wet his dry lips. "What did he say to you?"

Tracey smiled, showing teeth, the way she had seen Mrs. Cho do. She felt powerful and scary. She liked the feeling. She used what Timothy told her against him. "That he's more dangerous than you. That you were a sad and pathetic little man wanting attention. I thought that was a bit rude. Then I figured he'd clearly met you." Doctor Chan wouldn't know it was Timothy who told her that and not the Crocodile Man. The booming sounds were speeding up, growing closer together. They really needed to get out of here. *Where's Agent Loo Loo?*

"We have met," Doctor Chan confirmed and sat down on his flat bed.

"You're scared of him," Mrs. Cho accused.

"You should be too."

"Why?"

"He is the reason Timothy must return."

"What?"

"Timothy is the only one who can fight … that man."

Tracey tilted her head. "You were bringing Timothy back to fight the Crocodile Man?"

"You have no idea how dangerous he is, Tracey. Only Timothy at full strength can stop him."

How flattering.

Tracey's fingers fluttered near her chest. "Stop him from doing what?"

An explosion rattled the concrete walls around her. Tracey's stare snapped to the other door. "What the …?"

Mrs. Cho's lips pressed tightly together. Her hands clenched into fists. "Stay here," she ordered and swept from the room leaving Tracey alone with Doctor Chan. *Why does everyone leave me alone with these men?*

"— possessing everyone."

"What?" She stepped closer to the bars.

"The Crocodile Man wants total control." Doctor Chan said staring at his chipped fingernails.

"But he doesn't have the Butterfly Stone or, uh, any of the other stones."

"He doesn't need them."

"Then why did he attack my friends?"

Doctor Chan launched to his feet again moving so fast Tracey jumped back despite the bars between them. "What happened to your friends? Oh. He froze them, didn't he?" He pursed his lips. "And you."

"Yes."

"How did you escape?"

"The stone," she admitted.

Doctor Chan hummed loudly. "So it is true."

"What is?"

"About you and your connection to the stones."

"What are you talking about?"

He lowered his body back down on the camp-cot like bed. It didn't look any more comfortable than Malden's had seemed. "You have not yet realized, have you?"

"Realized what?" she snapped. The prison was under attack and he was just stalling. "How do I unfreeze my family?"

Doctor Chan tilted his head down until he could stare at her over his eyeglasses. "Realized what you are."

Come, Tracey. You have suspected the truth. Why you can do things other Mage-kind your age cannot. How you can connect to the power of the stones so readily. Why your magic seems to activate without your conscious control, Timothy whispered.

Inside her head bloomed a word she had heard several times.

In Millicent's voice.

In Nana's voice.

Dreamer.

"That can't be true," she muttered.

"You know it is."

She shook her head. "Dreamers are a myth. A legend told in children's stories. Dreamers are not real."

"You are real."

"You're saying I'm a … a … Dreamer?" Millicent told her that too. Tracey hadn't believed her.

"Yes," Doctor Chan confirmed.

"So how do I control it?"

"That is something I can help you with."

"How? You're a prisoner. Besides, I don't trust you."

"You must gather the stones and bring Timothy back. He is the only one who can stop the Crocodile Man."

"If I'm a Dreamer then I can stop the Crocodile Man myself."

The door behind her groaned open. Mrs. Cho stood there, magic crackling in a fury around her. "What did you do?" she screamed at Doctor Chan.

"I did nothing."

"They are here for you."

Doctor Chan's face reddened. "If it is the Crocodile Man, then he is here to kill me." He turned back to Tracey. "You must get me out of here. I can save your friends and family."

Yes, excellent idea. Release him, Tracey. He can help your friends. Timothy's voice curled around her mind.

"Ignore him," Mrs. Cho said. "He is attempting to manipulate you."

"But, if he can help …?"

"We will find another way," Mrs. Cho insisted. She took Tracey's arm and tugged her toward the door.

"Wait. You wanted a book from Doctor Chan? That's why you came here."

"It is no longer important. He is impotent, trapped, and now a target. It is a just punishment. I will find the book on my own. It is too dangerous for us to remain here."

"You must get me out of here, Tracey. They will kill me if I stay. This is him. The Crocodile Man. This attack is by him. I am the only one who can help you defeat him and he knows it. That's why he's here to kill me."

Tracey's blood ran cold. "I can't help you escape."

You can. Timothy whispered. *He can save your family, Tracey. The risk is worth it.*

"Of course you cannot." Mrs. Cho pulled Tracey toward the door.

"I'll stay with you," Doctor Chan begged. "You are the only one who can protect me."

"This is ridiculous. Tracey, we must leave," Mrs. Cho urged.

Doctor Chan's voice rose as if he couldn't believe Tracey would just walk away. "He'll kill me."

"Good." The woman hissed at her brother. "It will be what you deserve."

Tracey yanked her hand from Mrs. Cho's grip. She didn't like the look in the other woman's eyes. "Mrs. Cho. That's not … you can't say that. Even if it's what he deserves, you can't *say* that."

"I can," she countered. "He bought this upon himself."

"Tracey," Doctor Chan tried again. "I can help your friends. Together we can stop the Crocodile Man. You must take me with you." He pressed as close to the cell door as he could, smooshing his face against the bars. Tracey's skin tingled as the magically infused barrier tried to push him back.

Let him out, Tracey. Your enemy will kill him, and then who will be left to help your family? Timothy said.

"We can't let him die," Tracey said to Mrs. Cho. She turned back to the cell. "But … I can't let you out. It's against the law."

"I can't help you if I die," he said softly.

Tracey shook her head. She couldn't do this. The floor trembled beneath her feet and the walls shook again. She peered up, worried the roof would cave in.

"If you let him out, I will kill him," Mrs. Cho told Tracey. "Stay here until I return. The attack is coming closer. I will find us a safe way out."

Tracey watched the door clank shut behind Mrs. Cho again. She glanced at Doctor Chan. *What do I do now?* The walls trembled with such violence bits fell off and the corridor outside rattled with pounding boots. Tracey threw out her hands for balance but one sharp wobble dashed her to the floor. When she looked up, Doctor Chan's barred door had cracked right down the frame. It gave off sparks of orange magic before there was a sudden bright flash and the sparking stopped. Doctor Chan pushed on the door and it swung open. Tracey raised her shield against him. He held up his wrist and its blue light, reminding her that the lock on his magic was still active.

Tentatively, she lowered her shield bubble. When nothing pushed against her, she let it fall. "What are you doing?" she demanded as he pushed past and pressed the hidden lever Mrs. Cho used to activate the sliding corridor door.

"Getting out of here." He slowed his movements and peered back over his shoulder at her. "I am leaving, Tracey. Will you let me get away?"

Perhaps you should keep an eye on him. Ensure he doesn't escape, hmmm? Timothy suggested.

Tracey raised her hands and readied her magic. "I'll stop you."

Doctor Chan ducked out through the doorway. Tracey waited for the voices in her head to tell her what to do. For once, the voices were silent.

Tracey raced after Doctor Chan.

"As long as they do not blame other people for their own failures they will prosper," she promised.

32

The corridor was full of gray smoke. Coughing hard, Tracey covered her mouth with her hand to block out the acrid smell. "What's going on?" she shouted.

"The cameras are out." Doctor Chan held a hand over his mouth and pointed up with the other. The red lights on the ceiling cameras were dark, the lenses no longer swiveling. "We have to get out of this smoke."

Tracey threw up her bubble shield and expanded it over the magic-less man. With a burst of silver magic she used the "clear and cleanse" spell Agent Loo Loo taught her. She thinned her magic until it drifted inside the air they breathed and filled their lungs. She then clung to the smoke molecules and pulled back on her magic, sucking the smoke from their lungs like she did when she drew magic out of people's cores. Tracey squinted through the hazy air. The heavy prison doors at the end of the corridor yawned wide open. Doctor Chan ran forward forcing Tracey to keep up. She couldn't let him get away — not when he said he could help her family. Besides, he couldn't use his magic, which meant she had control of the situation. *Kind of.*

They found a guard slumped against the wall, head leaning against the frame of the open door. Doctor Chan checked his pulse.

"Alive," he said, wiping the guards' blood from his fingers onto the guard's own shirt.

Screams erupted up ahead. Those rapid popping sounds filled the air and then … there was silence.

They ran to the corner. Tracey gasped. "No!" In front of her stood Agent Loo Loo and Mrs. Cho; both frozen, hands held out in front of them as if about to or in the process of blasting magic at someone. Tracey bent over, hands on her knees, and inhaled sharply. *What do I do now?*

"Tracey, we must go," Doctor Chan urged.

I'm all alone. It was just as Malden had said. She had been isolated from everyone who could help her. She jolted at the press of a hot hand on her shoulder. "We must go," Doctor Chan repeated. Thundering footsteps ran out in corridors to either side of them. Loud clanging signaled heavy doors sliding shut one after the other.

Tracey followed Doctor Chan into the open elevator. He pressed the button for the ground floor. She sprang forward, swiftly hitting the button for B3 instead. Before Doctor Chan could demand to know what she was doing, the elevator doors sprang open.

She cut off his complaints with a look and a raised finger. "I'm getting us help." Inside her chest she threw her inner door wide open yanking out the store of electrified magic she kept at the ready and brought it down into her hands. She ran straight to Malden's cell.

What are you doing, Tracey? Timothy asked.

Trent Malden stood close to the barred door, clenching and unclenching his hands around the bars. His eyes widened when Tracey ran in and grew enormous when he spied Doctor Chan behind her. "Tracey, what is going on? What is that man doing with you?" His eyes dropped to her glowing hands.

"Agent Loo Loo and Mrs. Cho are frozen. I need your help."

"Contain him with your magic. Put him in a cell and call the guards. You cannot let him escape," Malden ordered.

She shook her head. "He said he can help my family and friends."

"Tracey, no."

"Tracey, yes," she countered. She slammed both electrified hands onto the bars and shoved every bit of magic she had into the cell door's lock. *Damn it, just open. I need him. Open!* Magic poured from her core, more than she should have access to without the stones and the magical barrier sparked wildly. Malden stumbled back as the flashes flared, humming excruciatingly loud and then with a last epic squeal popped like a light bulb filament. The latches inside dissolved and the spell on the door pulsed. The barred door gave off a loud thunk and creaked open. "There's no one left to help me, so you have to."

"Tracey." Malden backed toward the bed and away from the door. In the corridor they could hear terrified shouting growing louder, wilder. Another person screamed.

"You have to help me, and to watch him. Make sure he doesn't hurt anyone. Please, Agent Malden. I need you."

"Not an agent anymore," Malden reminded her.

"Please?" she begged.

"Tracey, this will be considered a prison escape. You'll ruin your future."

She stared at him. "I can't do this by myself."

He shook his head sharply. Tracey said nothing more. She did not know what she would do if he didn't come out. He sighed and his chin dropped to his chest as he rubbed the skin between his eyes. His head rose. He took a deep breath and stepped out of the cell. "If only to stop you from making an even bigger mistake."

Tracey led the two prisoners into the suddenly silent corridor. "What happened?" Tracey whispered.

"Shhhh!" Doctor Chan's eyes widened. He was covered in sweat.

"The Shadowman?" Malden queried, pointing ahead.

Tracey stared at the drifting green-white clouds of fog that floated over the corridor floor ahead. She bit her lip, her heart racing. *He's here.* "It's the Crocodile Man." Both prisoners stared at her. "If the fog touches us, we'll be trapped as statues. Alive, but prisoners. No different from you being stuck behind those bars in those cells."

"We cannot help you or your family if we're caught in that," Malden said.

"It will be worse than that. We will be unable to communicate. Frozen in time. A living statue," Doctor Chan told him.

"How do we get past it? There's no other way out," Tracey said. The smell of the fog, that icky oily metal smell, flooded her senses and pushed her fear higher and higher.

"We have no magic —" Malden waved the arm with his bracelet "— and no time to cast the spell to break the lock on our core."

"My shield doesn't stop the fog," Tracey muttered, staring at the slowly moving, green-white gaseous form. The buzzing against her skin warned of its proximity. She turned her thoughts to her magic. *If Doctor Chan is right, if I am a Dreamer, maybe I can just will the fog away.* She squatted down and touched the floor, filling her hands with magic.

"What are you doing?" Mr. Malden asked.

Ignoring him, she focused on the fog in the distance. She tried to push it away, watching intently for any movement. There was no reaction from the fog. It billowed like a vicious cloud at the end of the corridor, menacingly innocent but growing thicker as it waited for their move. She thought of various superheroes and blew out her magic in a long breath trying to blow the cloud of fog away. She tried waving it away and tried warming the ground. The fog — if any-thing — grew denser. *I'm making it worse.*

Tracey, let me in. I can help. Timothy's voice swept down her ear canal and wrapped around her brain. *Let me take control.*

The fog creeped closer.

"Are you talking to Stephanie?" Malden asked. "Can she help?"

Doctor Chan stared at Tracey's face, sending a ripple down her spine. It was like he knew, somehow, that she was talking to Timothy. "Shhhhh." She turned her thoughts inwards.

I only want to teach you, Tracey. To help you reach your full poten-tial. Together we can do anything.

He was lying. Telling her what she wanted to hear, exactly as Stephanie had done. The evil fog swirled closer. Tracey couldn't do it. Even if by doing it, it would save her life.

The Crocodile Man had come for them all.

"No," she said to Timothy. "I'll never choose you."

The farmers who stayed in Hamsted were miserable. They went to their graves cursing the witches for destroying their lives.

33

Instead of letting Timothy in, she called for the Serpent's Kiss's guardian. In a blink she was in the black place staring at the purple and gray shapes dancing in front of her. "Help me," she begged. "I need your magic to stop someone hurting a lot of people."

"What would you have us do?" The guardian's voice sent a shiver down Tracey's insubstantial back. Soft, whispered hisses — like snakes brought to life. It echoed like there was more than one thing speaking.

"Let me access the Butterfly Stone?" she begged.

"We cannot. That power is blocked to us."

"Then tell me how to defeat the poisonous fog?"

There was a tug against her core. She flexed her fingers and realized she was back in the corridor of the prison. Magic sprang into her hands, the glow surrounding them shining impossibly brighter. "Whoa." The magic tasted icky. Like ink, only greasy on her tongue.

"Your internal magic is ice, Tracey," the Serpent's Kiss's guardian told her. *"To defeat this toxic fog, you must use its natural enemy against it. You must be fast, hard and unflinching. Only fire can burn it away."*

"Tracey, what is happening?" Malden stepped back, raising his own hands though he had no magic to charge them. She didn't look up. It stopped her seeing the inevitably disappointed expression on his face. She let the magic tell her what to do and returned her hands to the concrete floor. Flames rose from her fingertips and zoomed down the corridors as if it were coated in gasoline. Fire filled the corridor, licking up over the walls and across the ceiling.

A scream erupted ahead of them.

The power in her hands didn't slow. She tried to pull it back, but it fought her grip. The flames burned brighter, hotter like a forest fire fanned by a wild wind.

The fog gathered itself up into a man-like shape at the very end of the corridor. It hissed angrily and withdrew, leaping up into the vents like it had been sucked into a hoover.

Malden clenched cold fingers around her upper arm, spinning her around. "Stop, Tracey. It's gone."

She laughed but wanted to scream and battled to push the oily Serpent's Kiss's magic back inside the stone. It resisted her efforts with a violent pull on her core. But fight all it might, the Serpent's Kiss couldn't resist her fear-fueled anger. Tracey let the anger take hold and did the only thing she knew how to do. She sucked the dark magic inside her own core and worked to slam her closet door over it. The door fought her too. Tracey drew her fear into anger and pushed harder. She had plenty of experience being angry and in forcibly containing her wayward magic. The door creaked in her imagination as she forced it shut with a furious grunt and an epic mental push.

She withdrew her shaking hands from the concrete and the flames died, leaving the corridor stained with smoke lines, still crackling and smelling of campfire smoke. "Let's get out of here." Her voice trembled. She coughed to hide it, leading the two prisoners down the corridor. They found a locked door at the end. *The way out at last?* Using her rumbling anger, she burst through the lock with an explosion of magic. The door shattered. Behind it, they found another corridor and all the Crocodile Man's victims. Every guard and security person trapped in a silent scream, their unnaturally still faces locked in a horror they could not escape.

"Does Stephanie know how to wake them?" Malden asked.

Thankfully the ex-agent had not realized it was Tracey in control this whole time. She played along. "No."

The dark curling fear-anger-joy inside her core told her the Serpent's Kiss knew her dilemma and enjoyed her mental squirming. She now needed a way to force the dark magic out of her body and back into the stone.

Doctor Chan nattered away beside her as they walked, suggesting ways to stop the Crocodile Man. They walked straight out of the prison, exiting through the imposing solid doors and down the concrete path to the outer security gate. No one stopped them. No one was awake to see them. The concrete building cast a long shadow over the outer wall and the gate at the end stood wide open. Surely the Crocodile Man hadn't got everyone. But it became evident that he had as they continued unhindered into the car park past frozen statues of guards, drivers and delivery people. "I don't have the car keys," Tracey said suddenly. "Agent Loo Loo put them into a tub in the prison reception storeroom."

"We'll have to walk," Doctor Chan muttered. "Our first move must be to break the spell on our bracelets. Then we must plan our attack on the Crocodile Man."

Malden *tsked* softly at Tracey's left shoulder. "That is what we shouldn't do. Tracey, we need somewhere to hide."

"Where are we going?" Tracey asked following Malden as he turned left at the end of the road and then a right at the first side street, taking them further from the prison. Tracey glanced around, wondering at the dried grass and cracked footpaths. The streets here were plain and empty. No cars passed. There were no buildings, or warehouses.

"We have to get off this road and out of sight," Malden muttered. "We are too exposed out here." Tracey pointed to a line of trees in the distance. They turned in that direction.

"We must unlock our magic," Doctor Chan said, holding up his wrist.

"That wasn't part of the plan." Tracey said. "You promised to save my friends and family and that's what we're going to do. You can just tell me how to do it and I'll use *my* magic."

"You will need our help. To do that, we need our magic back," Doctor Chan said slowly, talking to her like she was a toddler.

"Can't you just tell me how to break the curse on my family?"

"No."

"You said … You lied." She groaned. "Of course you lied."

"Did you expect anything else?" he asked, a smile coloring his voice.

Malden's face turned red. He stepped aggressively toward Doctor Chan stalling their escape yet again. Tracey sprang between them.

Let me teach you how to remove the magic lock on the bracelets, Timothy said. *You will need both Chan and Malden's strength to help you remain unseen until you confront your enemy. Take hold of Chan's wrist.* Tracey's hand closed over Doctor Chan's wrist before she could think through the consequences. He startled but didn't pull away.

"Tracey, what are you doing?" Malden asked.

Call on your magic. Fill the bracelet. Force it to overload like you did with the cell door.

A rush of power flooded down her arm.

Removēre. Unbidan. Frēo, Timothy told her. *Draw on the storage of power inside the Serpent's Kiss.*

She unlocked the closet door inside her chest and released the tainted magic. For the first time she felt how much darkness was stored with her own. It writhed and jumped free as soon as she relaxed her hold on her core. It was ravenous and there was so much of it. More than she had ever felt before, tinged with negative energy. It twisted inside her body like a leashed beast, desperate for freedom, and surged down her arms. She repeated the words. "Removēre. Unbidan. Frēo," Black stained silver magic surged through her fingers into the bracelet around Doctor Chan's wrist.

When she removed her hand, Doctor Chan's bracelet glowed with a red light rather than the sickly blue of locked magic. Doctor Chan stared at his wrist in surprise. "How ...?"

Malden stepped back. "Tracey, what have you done?"

Doctor Chan held up his hands. They glowed brightly golden as he filled them with magic.

She turned and held out her hand for Malden's wrist.

Doctor Chan ran.

Malden sprang after him, tripping the escaping man before he could take more than two steps. Doctor Chan landed with a thud. Malden kneeled on his back and pinned his wrists. "Contain him, Tracey," he ordered.

Take his air. He cannot run if he cannot breathe, Timothy ordered.

Tracey threw out her hands and surrounded Doctor Chan in a tight bubble of magic. She shrank the bubble until it lay just above his skin and hardened it into a shell. In seconds he stopped struggling, unable to breathe. She waited until he blacked out before she dropped the shield bubble and allowed oxygen back in. Malden hands dropped. He tilted his head and shook it sadly. "What?" she asked, catching sight of his reaction.

"That was rather brutal, wasn't it?"

"It was the quickest way to stop him." She stared down at the fallen man. Restoring his magic had been a terrible mistake.

"How do I lock his magic back up?" she asked.

Malden shook his head. "It's a M-force spell. I no longer have access to it."

"You must remember it? You're trained to contain uncontrolled magic."

He held up his wrist. "No power. I cannot help you help."

Tracey bit her lip. She sprang forward and wrapped her hand around Malden's wrist, covering his bracelet.

"Tracey?" He tried to yank his arm away, but she tightened her grip.

"Removēre. Unbidan. Frēo."

Oh very clever, Tracey, Timothy whispered. She grinned gleefully at the shadow in her mind.

Malden gasped. When Tracey removed her hand, the stone in his prison bangle shone bright green. "Tracey! You should not have done that."

"I need your help. With him," she said pointing at the unconscious man drooling on the grass.

"This is madness. We should return to the prison and hand ourselves in. If they discover you have aided in our escape, you'll be arrested."

"How do I know you'll go back?"

"It's the right thing to do." He stared down at the prone man. "I may have done the wrong thing before, but I am trying to atone for my actions. I was an agent. That part of me is still there. I will do what needs to be done."

She dug her upper teeth into her bottom lip. "I can't let you go back. I need your help to break the curse on my family. And I can't trust him."

"Tracey, it's over. Let me take him back and protect you."

"I can't drive!" she shouted. "My friends are frozen, my family are frozen, even Agent Loo Loo and Mrs. Cho. I don't know how to wake them. The Crocodile Man must be stopped. And I don't have enough magic or the battle skills to take him on by myself. Please Agent Malden — Mr. Malden — please. I need you."

"You should call the council."

"And what will they do? You just said they'll arrest me. We have to capture the Crocodile Man and make him undo the frozen spell. You have to help me."

"And him?" he pointed to the ground.

"Um, well." She scratched her ear as she thought about it. "We might need his magic."

"Tracey, I don't know how we can do this. How can we — the two of us — and him, do anything to stop this Crocodile Man and help your family? We don't know the full extent of his power."

"If we catch the Crocodile Man, he can reverse the frozen spell. Correct?" she asked.

"Technically, yes. But we must capture him first and then find a way to force him to undo the chaos he has caused. We can't trust him to do that."

"Well, you're M-force, or you used to be. Don't you know how to make people undo their spells?"

"Tracey, I can … maybe … but we will need help. Stronger help."

She stamped her foot in frustration. "He's taken everyone — oh wait, what about Prince Henry?"

Malden's eyes lit up. "Yes. Where is he? Hank can certainly help us."

"Right, so me, you, Prince Henry, and Doctor Chan. That's a lot of magic. Will it be enough?"

"I'm not sure —"

"She's a Dreamer," Doctor Chan said suddenly.

Tracey and Malden's eyes snapped down to the man spread out on the ground. He didn't move to stand up and she couldn't feel his magic gathering to use against her.

"What?" Malden asked.

"She's a Dreamer," Doctor Chan said again.

Malden's head snapped around to stare at Tracey. "That's not possible."

Tracey shrugged. "Apparently, I am."

The people who left their cursed town and moved to Delmore were happy and prospered.

34

Emerging from the trees, the three fugitives found themselves on the outskirts of a town. To remain unseen, Malden led them into an underground car park; the third one they investigated. "Stay quiet," he told them.

"Why here?" Tracey asked.

"It's an older build. See, no cameras."

Every sound they made echoed inside the rough concrete space. They kept their voices to a hushed whisper as they crouched behind a pillar near the rear wall. Malden and Doctor Chan angled themselves to see both the drive-in entrance and the door to the stairs. With the lack of people, murky light, and chilly underground air it was especially creepy. Doctor Chan handed Tracey a cell phone. "Where did you get this?"

"Off someone we passed," he said.

How did he do that? One moment his hand was empty and in the next, a cell phone appeared — unlocked. Luckily, she remembered Prince Henry's number.

The prince was suspicious. It did not help that he hadn't recognized the caller ID number and let it go to his message bank three times. Tracey left increasingly stressed messages, worried he wouldn't listen to any of them. At last, the cell phone in her hand rang. "We need your help. Can you come here, please?" she blurted as soon as she heard his voice.

"Why are you calling me from a new number? Did you lose your phone? Look, I'm already in the country. Loo called me in. Where is she? She's not answering her cell."

Tracey told him everything that had happened.

"You what …?" he repeated.

She winced, holding the cell phone tight to her ear to stop Malden and Doctor Chan from listening in. "It's a super long story. Agent Loo Loo is frozen and so are all my friends and family. I have no one else to ask."

"Don't do anything, I mean *anything*, until I get there. Do you understand?"

"Yes, sir."

"Christ." The swear was uttered under Prince Henry's breath. Tracey didn't think she was meant to hear it. His voice came back suddenly clearer. "Do you have somewhere safe to go until I get there?"

She glanced at the ex-prisoners waiting for her. "Um."

"It can't be anywhere anyone would think *you* would go. Or anywhere connected to those men. Do you hear me? No school. No friends. No police." There was anger in Prince Henry's voice. She didn't like hearing it directed at her. It wasn't as if she had a choice in all of this. It wasn't her fault. It just kinda happened; letting the prisoners out, running away with them, releasing their magic. Okay, she had purposely done that last one, but she needed them.

"Okay," she mumbled.

"I'll be in Miltern Falls by the end of the day. Get another phone. Call me from that number at exactly 6 p.m. your time. Got it?"

"Yes, but how do I do that?"

"Get Malden to do it," Prince Henry said.

Tracey peered at the man in question. Malden's sharp stare continuously darted from the concrete ramp entry way to the closed stairwell door, watching for anyone who might enter and see them. He didn't seem able to stay still. His hands twitched, he shifted his weight, he stretched his neck. In comparison, Doctor Chan was like a glassy lake surface. "We have to go back to Miltern Falls and trap the Crocodile Man. He's the only one who can reverse his spell. Oh, wait. Will M-force be waiting for us?" Tracey asked.

"Probably. You need to find a place to hide. I will come to you —"

"No, we have to come back. Agent Loo Loo couldn't break the spell. Not even Grandma or Mrs. Cho could do it and Mrs. Cho said the longer my family and friends stay frozen the harder it will be to save them. We don't have time to hide and wait. We have to break the spell. The Crocodile Man can do it, if we can make him do it."

Prince Henry was silent for a long time, then he groaned. She heard a slapping scrubbing sound like he was rubbing his face. "Fine. Get back to Miltern Falls carefully and stay out of sight. I'll meet you there." He hung up on her. She stared at the black screen of the phone.

"What did he say?" Malden asked, stepping closer.

Tracey sat down on a concrete parking stopper. Her whole body sagged as she hunched over and clasped her arms around her knees. The fluorescent light above their heads flashed at odd intervals bringing the shadows to life around them. It was cold and creepy down here and it smelled bad too — a lot like the stinky alley behind Uncle Donny's office.

"We can't stay here," Malden said. "M-force searchers will be tracking us. We need to keep moving."

"We have to go back to Miltern Falls to capture the Crocodile Man," Tracey said.

"Only if we stop M-force tracking us first," Doctor Chan muttered. "Otherwise we will just walk right into a trap and end up back in prison."

Malden shot him a sharp look.

"What?" Doctor Chan said. "It is no good returning to Miltern Falls if they follow us there."

Tracey sighed. "You know he's right."

Malden's hands rested on his hips. "Stephanie."

"What about Stephanie?"

"Does she currently control you?"

"No, of course not," Tracey said, maintaining eye contact with the ex-agent.

"It would be better to ask about her other occupant," Doctor Chan whispered.

Tracey's eyes popped wide. *No!* He couldn't tell Malden about Timothy. She straightened her shoulders and scowled at him, flexing her fingers, warning she would use magic if he betrayed her. The evil man grinned but nodded, accepting her silent demand. Malden's stare turned suspicious.

"Let us focus on what matters. Without Timothy to fight the Crocodile Man we are left with Tracey. She is a Dreamer,"

Doctor Chan said. "She has the power to do what needs to be done but is without the knowledge or the experience."

"And Dreamer means what, exactly?" she snapped at him. "People keep saying that's what I am but no one actually tells me what it means!"

Doctor Chan exhaled. "I see we will need a history lesson."

"Let's get moving," Malden said, his nostrils flaring. "If we are heading back to Miltern Falls we'll need a car."

"Prince Henry said you need to get another phone too," she told him.

He nodded but didn't explain how he would do that. She didn't ask. She figured the less she knew the better. "How can M-force track us? Is there a way we can hide from them?"

Malden raised his wrist with the bracelet. "Prison bracelet. Also a tracking device in the event of an escape."

Tracey's eyes bulged as she eyed the bangle. She raised her own wrist. "So, not mine?" He shook his head. The pressure squeezing her chest didn't seem as suddenly tight. "So we have to get your bracelets off."

"No prison bracelet. No tracking." Malden paused, tilted his head and clarified, "Well, that's not entirely true. But they would need a powerful spell caster and access to our — or well — your DNA via hair or a blood sample or by using an Object of Power tied only to you. There *are* ways, Tracey. We must stay on the move if we are to keep you and us ahead of them."

"Then we get the bracelets off," she said. "Do you know how?"

"I will need one of my books," he admitted softly.

"All of your stuff was confiscated by M-force," she reminded him.

He nodded. "They would have been placed in storage, controlled by M-force. There is such a facility here in the city. Perhaps it is still —"

"Oh, wait. Agent Loo Loo requested your files so she could go over all the evidence, in case you — um — failed to report something," Tracey blurted, excitement and urgency coloring her voice. "We stayed at a motel last night before traveling to the prison super early this morning. She had archive boxes of your files and books. We were reading them last night, looking for clues. They're still at the motel. We were going to go back and get our stuff and check out after the prison trip."

"They won't expect us to head toward M-force," Malden said. "We need that book."

Tracey pointed up the ramp toward the street.

Malden shook his head. "We must stay off the main roads." He gestured to the stairwell door. "Let's go."

The trip took longer because they had to travel through back alleys, car parks, and side streets, but eventually they reached the motel.

"Room ten," Tracey said, pointing to the stained door of the single-story motel room.

"They certainly don't pay you agents enough," Doctor Chan said.

Malden snorted. "We have to move fast. They'll figure out where we are quickly. Are probably already on their way here."

Tracey stood back and waited for the two men to run to the motel. They didn't move from where they all crouched behind a silver 4WD in the car park. "Well?"

Malden winced. "You should go in without us."

"What?"

"Our mugshots will have been released to the media by now. You might still remain unknown. See there, and there. Surveillance cameras."

"I don't know what book you need though. Can't you just disguise yourselves with magic?"

"Tracey, that's illegal."

Both Tracey and Doctor Chan stared at him. "Bit late for rules," Doctor Chan said.

Malden dropped his chin to his chest. "Tracey, you might still be able to get out of this —"

"She released two prisoners. She's stuck with us." Doctor Chan raised his hand at the cameras. Tracey felt the burst of magic shoot from his fingers and they all heard the loud pop as the cameras exploded with a poof of smoke and fire. "They're off. Let's go." He ran to the door, pressed his hand to the knob and broke the lock with another spurt of magic.

Tracey shrugged at Malden. "I have to save my family and friends. He's trying to help."

She ran for the door and slipped inside after Doctor Chan. Malden ducked in behind her and closed the door carefully. "Security spells," he warned.

"The agent wasn't here long enough," Doctor Chan replied.

Tracey knew how dangerous Mage-kind home security spells could be. But motels and hotels weren't technically a home, so magic rarely seeped into them to the extent that an automatic protection spell kicked in. That only happened in long stay locations — like the room Doctor Chan once hid in back in Miltern Falls. Tracey rubbed her shoulder, remembering being flung hard into the wall. Without Agent Loo Loo here to set off a protection spell, it was just an empty motel room. Tracey peered around, wondering if she should pack up her bag and spare clothes. When she grabbed her duffle bag Malden shook his head. "Leave everything as it is."

"If I leave my stuff here, they can use it to track us though. You said DNA or our belongings, right Mr. Malden?"

Malden's lips screwed up as he thought about it. "Leave it. This will be one of the first places they search. If it looks like you have been here, they will wonder why and what else you took. This will only delay them for a little while but every second we have will help. In fact, we really must hurry."

"But — ?" She sighed and moved to the archive boxes.

Magic flowed around Malden, vibrating against Tracey's skin. A bright yellow light bloomed from his hands. As it reached the boxes it bounced off. "Protection spell, damn."

"Hardly surprising," Doctor Chan muttered. As usual he went for brute force, throwing his magic at the archive boxes like a series of bricks. They reflected off, dissolving into a spray of pink glittery shards. "We don't have time for this," he complained.

Tracey pushed both men out of the way. "Let me do it. Agent Loo Loo altered the spell last night so that I can touch them. What does the book look like?"

"Hardcover. Emerald green with a gold line border."

Tracey searched through the top archive box moving the next box when she didn't find it. "This one is full of knick-knacks. I don't even know why she has this one." She opened the third box. "Is this it?"

Malden didn't answer. He was watching Doctor Chan. The evil man stared hungrily at the box of knick-knacks.

"Doctor Chan?"

"That box. Show me what is inside. I sense a familiar magic."

"It's just desk drawer stuff I think," she lifted the lid briefly. "See."

"Mine," he hissed. "I recognize —"

Tracey waved her hands at him, forcing him to step back. "That's not important. The book, Mr. Malden. Is this it?"

"What? Oh, yes that's it." He took the book from her hands and flipped through the pages until he landed on one in the middle. "We'll need supplies." They heard faint sirens and peered toward the window, listening to see if they were growing closer or moving away. The siren volume increased.

"We'd better go," Tracey said.

Doctor Chan pressed forward. "My things. We should find your spell ingredients in there."

She squinted at him. He was up to something but she wasn't sure what. *There is a reason you don't trust him.* Malden listed off what they needed. Doctor Chan pointed out the various items, and Tracey grabbed the ingredients, handing them to Malden one after the other. A black squishy bag filled with salt, a silk-wrapped fat half-burned yellow candle, a box of matches, and a Tupperware container of dirt with a green lid. "Can we go now?"

"Take that book too," Doctor Chan said. It had a hard cover and was bound in red leather. The Chinese characters on the cover were embossed in green. The book buzzed in Tracey's hands bringing warmth to her fingers.

Sirens outside grew even louder. Separating into numerous screeching wails.

"Right, let's get out of here," Malden said and herded them toward the door.

Jane and her family remained happy and content for the rest of their days.

35

Tracey's sides ached. Her legs trembled. "Stupid running," she complained. "This is rubbish. We need a car." The three fugitives made their way through town and into an industrial area of bridges, concrete pylons, and cracked, pot-holed streets. At each bridge Tracey peered over the side at the raging river below. Thoughts of her family and friends stuck as statues kept appearing in her mind. She imagined a clock ticking away the time they were wasting. Tears bubbled up. She blinked them back and forced herself to look ahead, focusing only on her next steps. She would do whatever it took to save her family and friends.

At the next bridge Doctor Chan led them down a set of concrete steps toward the river. "We're too exposed out here," Malden said, peering at the dirty water and the trash dumped along the river's edge.

"One of my previous, oh, ah … hideouts," Doctor Chan stammered, "well, places of research, is nearby. It is spelled. And it will scramble our signal. But even that won't last for long against M-force. We must hurry."

M-force sirens burst to life again in the distance. "They've found us," Tracey said. The three fugitives raced down the stairs. The river smelled of chemicals, gasoline, and a sour, bitter ickiness. The dirty water traveled quickly, lapping at the concrete edges. There were no animal sounds down here at all, no natural birdsong, no grass growing. It was like the whole area was slowly dying, or already dead.

"Under the bridge," Doctor Chan said.

Tracey was astonished to find a wooden door stuck onto the side of a bridge pylon. "Where does that go? Isn't that just stuck on solid concrete?"

Doctor Chan raised an eyebrow.

"Right, magic." Tracey imagined the door would act as a portal to somewhere else. She shook her head. Her life was not a superhero movie. Mage-kind couldn't portal! She would definitely know if they could do that. *Can we do that?*

The door swung open as Doctor Chan approached. He led them down a narrow staircase with a splintery guard rail stuck to the wall. "Won't we get trapped down here?" she asked, listening to the sirens growing louder above them. When Doctor Chan pulled the door shut, the sirens cut off.

"Not if we hurry."

Tracey held onto a cold metal rail as they descended. Icy gusts of air brushed her skin, coming from somewhere down below. All she could smell was stagnant sea water. At the bottom of the stairs a light snapped on. A single bulb dangled from a long cord and swung slowly back and forth, illuminating a room that was more shadows than open space. She had the sense that it was a vaguely circular shape, though that was more of a feeling than what she could actually see. Rotten crates and lopsided shelves ran along both sides of the walls making the room seem even smaller. "What is this place?"

"History. Living — or I guess past — history. Mage-kind history," Doctor Chan said. He pushed a chair and a red-stained desk with a hobbly leg aside to create an open space in the middle of the room. Malden leaped to assist.

Tracey's eyes boggled. "What was it used for?"

"To hide from Norms. There are places like this scattered all over the world."

"I had no idea," Malden murmured, shoving a large wood-paneled crate out of the way. "M-force are not aware of this."

"That you've been told," Doctor Chan snapped at him.

Tracey winced as Malden hunched his shoulders, seemingly embarrassed by his lack of knowledge. *Secrets upon secrets. Typical.* She bet the council knew all about the secret hiding places, even if M-force did not.

"I was hardly going to volunteer that information," Doctor Chan said in the following silence.

"Focus! Tracking spell, remember," she reminded them. "Prison bracelets first, shouting later."

Both men nodded. Doctor Chan rolled up an old blackened carpet covered in various dark stains and uncovered a painted circle on the concrete beneath. "Will this do?"

Malden nodded. He told Tracey to spread salt along the circle's edge, while he stood in the center and directed Doctor Chan to unpack the various boxes and items they took from Agent Loo Loo's motel room. Doctor Chan poured a little of the dirt from the green sealed tub into a pile to Tracey's left.

"Right. Stand here," Malden told Chan. He stood in the circle opposite Doctor Chan and held up the book. He began to read. The circle snapped closed with a crackle that raised the fine hairs on Tracey's arms. At their feet, the little black box with the powdered incense burst open and silver dust particles filled the air making them all cough. Tracey covered her mouth with her hands but the fine powder couldn't breach the spell's barrier.

She didn't recognize the language Malden was speaking. It sounded old. Old and dark, making her think of shadows crawling around the room. Then she realized the shadows outside the circle *were* moving, growing longer and closer and darker. The two stones under Tracey's shirt vibrated together making a click-clicking sound. She slammed a hand over them and blinked her eyes open on the black space that was Timothy's stone room.

"What is going on?" he demanded.

"We're doing a spell."

"To do what?"

"Remove their prison bracelets — the identification tags the government uses to track Mage-kind prisoners."

Timothy nodded. "A good idea. Who is casting the spell? The magic is familiar." His eyes sparkled as he worked it out. "Your agent friend. But Chan is here also. Good. Follow their directions but do not trust them. They will betray everyone at the first opportunity to save their own necks."

"I know Doctor Chan will. Malden is my friend, well, he was my friend." Tracey shook her head. Malden had betrayed her once. Perhaps she *should* watch him more carefully. "Once we get their bracelets off, how do we hunt down the Crocodile Man?" Her priority was to capture him and force him to release her family and friends. And take his stone, if she could manage it.

"As you know, the curse on the stones is powerful. Not even I — stuck in here as I am — know how to break it. Or even how it came about, as I have previously told you. I believe your magic is the key, Tracey."

"So how do I use it?"

"You have discovered the truth about yourself, have you not?"

She nodded.

"Then Chan will teach you how to harness it. You must discover how the curse came to lock the stones in the first place and then you must take the stones from your enemy. To break the curse on the stones you must hold them all."

"If I get them, you can use them to come back!"

"Is that what you think I want?"

"Isn't it?"

His face took on the same expression Tracey had seen on many of her teachers over the years. Disappointment.

"You do!" she shouted. "Stop trying to convince me otherwise."

"I'm only trying to help you."

Tracey's body jerked sideways. She held out her arms. Sebastian's yellow and rose room surrounded her. The boy in question stood right in front of her, stunning blue eyes wide, his long body trembling. "Where are you?" His voice cracked.

"What's wrong?" she asked.

"He's come for me. You have to help me. I need protection. If you help me, I'll tell you all about my stone and how I got it."

"I'm on my way — I promise but it will take a few hours. I have help though, where are you?"

"Shoot. I hoped you were close by. Never mind. I have to move. I can't stay here. Meet me at the Milton Falls cemetery at midnight." He frowned. "If I last that long."

Tracey fell out of Sebastian's room and to her knees on cold concrete, now back in Chan's secret bunker. Wild magic zoomed around her body, creating a whirlpool of bright orange light.

The magic barrier — the circle around Malden and Chan that was meant to contain and amplify their spell — was down and her wrist burned. She raised her hand. It looked perfectly normal, so it was not on actual fire, it only felt that way. Tears streamed down her face and she clutched her wrist to her chest, gasping against the waves of stinging pain. Her wrist was going to shatter. "Stop, stop!" she begged.

"Hold on!" Doctor Chan cried out. His face was twisted in pain. Red splotches covered his cheeks and his glasses were all steamed up. Malden stood motionless. The only sign that he felt any pain at all was in his wet face and clenched teeth. Tracey curled up on the floor, sobbing, as with one final sharp twisting sensation the Mage-kind identification bracelet around her wrist snapped open and fell to the floor.

The pain stopped.

The noise in Tracey's head calmed. Her hearing returned to normal as the magic buffeting her body faded. Malden's chant softened and fell away. Cold air brushed Tracey's damp cheeks. "What happened?" she asked staring at her bare wrist.

"Is everyone okay?" Malden's voice was unable to bury his lingering pain as it broke and crackled like he had a chesty cough.

"Yes." Tracey gasped, her own voice practically non-existence. "Ouch."

"It worked," Doctor Chan said. He stared at the bracelets on the floor, his eyes alight with a strange, greenish-yellow glow. "It's gone."

Tracey's gaze returned to Malden. His lips were pressed together tightly, his spine ramrod straight as he stared at the gleeful man. This must have been what Doctor Chan wanted all along. They had helped the criminal escape identification as a Mage-kind prisoner. *Oh, fruit tingles.*

"We should leave," Doctor Chan said extinguishing the candle flame. He seemed larger now, more sure of himself and his power. "No doubt M-force will have tracked our general location. Provided we are not spotted leaving here, they can no longer follow where we go next."

"How did the circle break?" Tracey asked. "Shouldn't that have wrecked the spell?" She spied the silk cloth from around the fat candle. It lay across the painted circle. "Oh," she pointed it out.

Malden cursed and took several steps back. He scraped his foot over the floor exposing another circular line. A metallic silver band pressed into the concrete. "This entire room is one large circle."

"You set us up. What else have you done?" Tracey glared at Doctor Chan.

He simply smiled in her direction. "Now you are free as well."

"What does that mean?"

The secretive man shook his head. "Come. We must return to Miltern Falls."

Tracey stood up and wobbled on unsteady legs. "Whoa!" Her head swam and she threw out her arms for balance as she tilted sideways.

"Don't move too quickly, Tracey." Malden clasped her shoulders gently. Tracey slammed her eyes shut and breathed in through her nose. It took a moment before she could stand on her own. She stepped back and opened her eyes.

"Wait." Doctor Chan ran to a nearby shelf and grabbed several books, quickly stacking them into his arms. She recognized one as the book he brought from the motel room.

"We can't carry all of that!" Tracey complained.

"They are books on Dreamers," he told her.

She immediately held out her arms. "I can take some." Malden took a few as well. "We have to capture the Crocodile Man now," she said. "And I know how to lure him to us." She just had to keep Sebastian safe when the Crocodile Man came for him.

"Let's go steal a car," Doctor Chan said.

Tracey and Doctor Chan hid amongst the crowds of passengers in the local train station while Malden procured them a car. The ex-agent said that blending in with the crowd would delay M-force since the only way they had of tracking them now was to use a DNA spell or work the Norm route by checking security cameras, which would take time. The more people around, the harder that would be, even harder if they avoided being seen by the security cameras. Tracey wore a green woolen beanie pulled low over her face. She had tucked her hair up under it. She also wore mirrored sunglasses. Doctor Chan swiped them from a kiosk on the level above using a spurt of magic and a flick of his fingers to knock over a card stand distracting everyone from seeing what he was doing. He also waved a hand at the security camera in the corner — she assumed to blank the footage or fritz the technology. He got changed in the men's room and now wore a stolen sky-blue jacket and tree-green cargo pants.

They sat down on a chipped, purple-painted metal bench. Her wrist was cold and weirdly light with her bracelet gone. She had noticed an immediate difference in the way strangers looked at her. The eyes drifting over her did not contain judging concern or hidden fear anymore. They just glanced at her and moved on. She even got an occasional smile.

Sighing softly, she leaned back and crossed her arms. Mom and Dad would be so angry when they found out what she had done. Breaking criminals out of prison, going on the run, removing her bracelet, and petty theft — not to mention the car Malden was "borrowing." Her whole life had been turned upside down by these stupid stones.

Ruined. Your life has been ruined by the stones.

Tears heated her eyes and she scrubbed a hand over her face to push them away. *I'll make it all right. I'll fix it.* Once they captured the Crocodile Man, they would force him to unfreeze her friends and family and then Doctor Chan and Malden could return to prison and everything could go back to normal.

Doctor Chan nudged her shoulder and pointed to the station entrance. Malden stepped into view. He wore a green jacket, slouchy blue jeans, and a baseball hat. He waved them over to join him. "Time to go to work," Doctor Chan told her.

The townspeople of Delmore knew never to blame another for their own choices and, if a stranger came into town, they spoke to them and became friends.

36

Malden drove a green hatchback. Tracey did not ask how he got it or where he got it from, and he didn't tell her. Doctor Chan gave the ex-agent a funny, knowing look but stayed quiet. Tracey kept the two men separated by sitting in the front passenger seat. It forced Doctor Chan to sit in the back.

"You said you knew how to draw out the Crocodile Man?" Malden asked. They traveled at a normal speed down the expressway. Malden explained that despite their urgency he had to drive sedately, with no passing or going too fast; nothing that would bring attention to their vehicle.

"The Miltern Falls cemetery," she said.

His brow furrowed. "Why there?"

"There's a boy the Crocodile Man wants. He will be there. The Crocodile Man is hunting him."

"Who is this boy?"

"Sebastian is a stone Protector. I don't know him. Not really. He's a pain actually, but he said the Crocodile Man is hunting him for the stone he carries. So we can't let him catch Sebastian and take his stone."

"If we locate this boy, we could lead the Crocodile Man straight to him, putting him in danger." Malden said.

"But the Crocodile Man will be there. And then we can catch him."

"You want to use this boy as bait."

She cringed and shuffled uncomfortably in her seat. "Not exactly. The Crocodile Man knows more about Sebastian than I do. He is still more likely to find him, but this way we can be there to catch him and save Sebastian. I figure if we find Sebastian first the Crocodile Man will come to us. Maybe. Probably. So, um, we should plan how to catch him."

"Tracey, by doing this we will be purposefully walking into danger. You are putting this boy at great risk. If we fail, this Crocodile Man will have him *and* you."

"I know." She examined Malden's face. He glanced at her and then back to the road. "Tell me about Dreamers," she asked.

For a moment both men were silent. Tracey sensed there was a conversation going on between them that she could not hear. Which was totally not fair. She wasn't a child. It was her power they were talking about and deciding whether or not to tell her about it wasn't their decision to make.

"Do we assume this Crocodile Man has been so named because it is his stone? A Crocodile Stone?" Malden asked, clearly trying to redirect the conversation back to the plan.

"I figured Sebastian must have worked that out and that's why he calls him that."

"What about the boy's stone?"

"I have no idea. He wouldn't tell me anything about it, but his stone room is yellow and rose. The Crocodile Man's room is green."

"Room?"

"It's a stone thing," she said not wanting to explain further.

Malden cleared his throat. Doctor Chan got in first. "You asked about Dreamers?"

"Yeah, how does the magic work and why does everyone think I am one?"

"Honestly, I'm not sure," Malden said.

Tracey peered at Doctor Chan. "Then why do *you* think I am one?"

How do you know you are not? Timothy whispered. *Your magic is rather unique, Tracey.*

"As I told you, and as you have told me, Dreamers are a myth. A story told through the generations of how and why we began," Doctor Chan leaned forward.

"We?"

"Mage-kind. Stories that were lost to us as politics and governments sought to control Mage-kind through technology and magic."

"The council." She grunted unhappily, remembering the chairman. Just thinking about him made goosepimples break out all over her skin.

"May I continue?" Doctor Chan said. There was a twinge of annoyance in his voice.

Tracey slumped down. It pulled her seat belt up under her chin. "Fine."

"It is said that Dreamers were the first Mage-kind. The leaders, the teachers, and the healers of the clans. They could see magic."

Tracey's mouth opened. *I see magic.* "What do you mean see it?" It wasn't — that didn't make sense. Didn't everyone see magic the way Tracey did? What did everyone see, if they didn't "see" magic? "Don't you see magic?"

"Not without a spell," Malden said.

Doctor Chan's silence hung in the air. Tracey twisted around to find the man skewering her with his sharp, knowing gaze. "You see magic, don't you, Tracey."

"I ...? What else do you know about Dreamers? How do they use their magic?" she said instead.

"The fact that they can 'see' magic means they — you — can alter it from the very basic blocks of existence. Dreamers *create* magic."

"What does *that* mean?"

He hummed. "I don't completely know."

"Helpful," she grumped. "So how do I use it?"

"Tracey —" Malden interrupted "— you have to understand, there are no Dreamers. They don't exist. It is just a story that someone made up long ago."

"How would you know, though? If you don't think they exist, then you don't go looking for them. How would you know you're a Dreamer if you didn't have any information to tell you that's what you are?" *Exactly like the curse on the stones.*

"That is what I believe the Sect of Six were doing," Doctor Chan said.

Tracey turned and gripped the back of the car seat. "What?"

"They were trying to understand Dreamers. Trying to turn themselves into Dreamers. That was the spell that created the stones."

Tracey slumped back into her chair in shock. "Whoa."

"It's complete nonsense," Malden said.

Doctor Chan leaned forward, gesturing between their seats with a pointing finger. "It is true."

"Did it work?" Tracey asked. "If I'm a Dreamer then it must have worked. They succeeded, didn't they? Only they didn't make themselves into Dreamers, they just made it so that Dreamers are possible."

"You are living proof."

"She's not," Malden argued. "We have no way of proving any of this. It is just a story. Tracey is a Significant. That is all. There are no mythical magic users."

"She *can* see magic. She *is* a Dreamer," Doctor Chan argued back. "Tell me, Tracey. What do you see when you look at magic?"

She didn't want to say. Malden looked curiously over his shoulder.

"Just colors and lines and stuff. I dunno." She turned to stare out of the passenger side window at the cars passing in the next lane.

"Fascinating."

Tracey groaned loudly to stop their argument before they got started. "How do I use it?"

"I don't know."

"Well, how am I supposed to prove if I am one or not?"

"I don't know," Doctor Chan echoed Mr. Malden's previous comment.

"You are all soooooooooo helpful," she complained. She pushed upright in her seat, dropping the seat belt back to its normal position. She included Timothy in her rebuke. For a change, he didn't respond. "So if you can't teach me how to use this Dreamer magic, then how do we capture the Crocodile Man?"

"Do you have any idea who he is?" Malden asked.

"No." She stared forward again watching the scenery change from the expressway to outer suburbia. What if the Six only *said* they created Dreamers? What if Dreamers didn't really exist? She touched the Butterfly Stone hanging around her neck. It had been silent for so long. She needed to talk to Stephanie, but couldn't and without Stephanie and the magic stored inside the stone, how could Tracey possibly hope to fight the Crocodile Man? She did not want to call on the tainted inky magic of the Serpent's Kiss or ask Timothy for help, but she had no idea how to use Dreamer magic — if that was even a thing. She needed concrete power and without her friends to help her only Stephanie and the Butterfly Stone could give her that. She refused to call on Timothy. Ever. It was not happening. No way.

You will.

Ugh. She shoved Timothy's presence out of her mind with her brain bubble. She couldn't even ask Grandma or Mom for help because they were frozen.

Oh.

"Wait. We have to go somewhere else first."

They never cast judgement on another or raised a hand against another again, and they never blamed anyone for the things they themselves had done.

37

She left Malden in the car to watch Doctor Chan and entered Tavel House on her own. Her heart beat so fast she could feel her pulse in her fingertips as she tapped lightly on Nana's bedroom door. If she was asleep, Tracey would not bother her, she'd just go without.

The door sprang open. "Can I help you?" Nana looked at Tracey with a polite smile but there was no recognition in her eyes. She wore the shirt Tracey's mom bought for her birthday and wrinkled brown slacks.

"Hi, Nana. It's me, Tracey."

"Who, dear?"

At least Nana didn't shout this time. Tracey's chest ached at the blank look on Nana's face. She forced a deep breath and straightened her shoulders. "Can I come in?"

"Are you a friend of Beth's, dear?" Nana widened the door to allow Tracey inside. Beth was Tracey's mom's name. Tracey blinked back tears and smiled. "Yes."

"Well, I don't get many visitors. Come on in. Would you like a cup of tea?"

"Love one, yeah thanks," Tracey knew she would forget to make it. The bed was messy and Nana's gray curls were sort of smooshed on one side as if she just woke up from a nap.

"What can I do for you, dear?"

"Do you know anything about Dreamers?" Tracey asked.

"Oh." Nana's eyes took on a far away look. "My grand-mama used to tell me a story about Dreamers when she put me to bed at night. It's a lovely fairy tale. There are a few actually. All are about impossible magic, impossible strength, and impossible adventure." Nana pulled a book from the shelf and passed it over to Tracey. She clutched it tight in surprise. *A Circle of Mystical Illusion,* by Jonathan Bennett.

Tracey sank into the chair beside the little round table pushed next to Nana's bed. This was the same book Prince Henry found in the UK and sent her the scanned copy to read. The book Jonathan Bennett wrote about Dreamers. Nana had a copy all along! The old woman took her little electric kettle into the attached bathroom and filled it with water. Tracey flicked through the book's pages, running her fingers along the cracked spine as Nana put the kettle onto the electrified base and flipped it on with a snap of the switch. Two mugs waited beside the kettle with teabags already inside. "Do you want to hear one of the stories, dear?"

"Yes, please." Tracey hoped Nana would continue without prompting. The water boiled but Nana didn't look up. Tracey sprang to her feet and poured the water. She dipped the peppermint tea bags a few times the way she knew Nana liked, breathing in the crisp welcoming scent and carefully carried both mugs to the table.

Nana blinked. "Oh, tea. Lovely. Thank you, dear."

Tracey suppressed a sigh. "You were going to tell me a story about Dreamers?"

"Oh yes. of course. This is the story of the first Dreamer as my grandmama told it to me.

"*Early one morning, a family gathered in a field of giant stones. The youngest daughter, Jane, stood in the middle of the circle. Today would be the day she became a witch — as powerful and as strong as the rest of her family. She would be taught to heal the town's sick, how to make the fields fertile, and how to keep the livestock plentiful. For that is what they did. The family loved their little town of Delmore and the people of Delmore loved them in return.*

"*What Jane and her family did not know was that the farmers from Hamsted, the next town over and not as prosperous as Delmore, were on their way to the circle, angry at the witches and determined to stop them.*

"*The family were afraid when they saw the farmers approaching with their flaming torches. They hid behind one of the stones, for there was nowhere else to hide. Jane remained standing in the circle. 'I am not afraid,' she told them, and she was not. For she had felt the power of the circle and the power that lay inside her. 'You are bad people and are frightening my family. Please leave us alone,' she said as they drew near.*

"*The angriest of the farmers strode forward and waved his flaming torch. 'Leave this place,' he demanded. 'You have made your crops prosper and made ours fail. Your animals are fat and your people are healthy. Ours are thin and full of sickness. You have cursed us,' he cried.*

"'*You have beaten your animals. You have not tended to your lands and your people are mean and full of hate. You have caused your own misfortune,' Jane told him.*

"'*You are an evil witch. Your existence means Hamsted is not as bountiful as Delmore and that is unfair. We will drive you away,' he said.*

"*Jane's magic rose up in response to his anger and filled the circle. 'If you had come with kindness and simply asked for help, your town would be plentiful and fertile also. Now we will not help you.' With her mind she extinguished their torches and turned their pitchforks into snakes. She sent them back to their own town with a single thought. She cursed their land to never grow crops, for the people to always be sickly and for their animals to run away.*

"How did you do that?' Jane's mother asked.

"I was angry at the farmers for scaring you. So I imagined everything they accused me of doing would come true for them,' Jane said.

"That is a hard lesson to learn,' Jane's father said.

"Jane nodded. 'If the people of Hamsted wish to move to another town they may. They may even come to Delmore. As long as they do not blame other people for their own failures they will prosper,' she promised.

"The farmers who stayed in Hamsted were miserable. They went to their graves cursing the witches for destroying their lives. The people who left their cursed town and moved to Delmore were happy and prospered.

"Jane and her family remained happy and content for the rest of their days. The townspeople of Delmore knew never to blame another for their own choices and, if a stranger came into town, they spoke to them and became friends. They never cast judgement on another or raised a hand against another again, and they never blamed anyone for the things they themselves had done. The town prospered and still prospers to this day.

"Jane's descendants were filled with the magic that would enable them to protect and serve their town. Magic that was equal and opposite to that driven by fear and misplaced accusation.

"So you can see, my dear. It runs in the family."

"What does?"

"Dreaming. My granddaughter is one." A soft smile tilted Nana's thin lips up at the corners.

"I am? I mean, she is?"

"Yes. Poor thing. I've been meaning to talk with her about it. I don't see her anymore though. She's gone now."

"I'm right here, Nana." Tracey's chest ached from the pain caused by the accusation. Gone where? Where would Tracey be but right here? *What's wrong with me?*

The old woman stared at her intently. "You're not Tracey. You have a darkness inside you. A serpent in disguise." Her voice was low and slow, almost hypnotic. It made Tracey's skin crawl to listen to it. "You must rid yourself of the stones. Accept your fate, child."

"What?"

Nana's smile was crooked. "Dreamers are creators, dear. They see the makings of the world," she whispered. "They can remake the world."

"How?"

Nana didn't reply. She glanced up at the wall above Tracey's head.

"Nana?" Tracey asked, hoping she would come back from where she had gone. Tracey flicked her gaze to the clock on the wall. It was getting late. She had to go.

After a moment Nana licked her lips and twisted. She leaned forward to look Tracey right in the eyes. "The story I was told as a child is that you will know how to use your power when the time comes. It cannot be taught. It is just understood. The stones are a false power. They were trying to create that which already existed. You must get rid of the stones. They taint your natural abilities. You cannot be strong while they weigh you down."

"I can't take them off," Tracey said. *At least, not without dying first.*

"You cannot win while you are trapped by them."

They were going in circles. "How do you know Dreamers are real?"

"How do you know they are not?"

Tracey sighed and rubbed her forehead. "How does Dreamer magic work?"

Nana shrugged. "How do you breathe? How do you scratch your nose? How do you blink? You just do it."

Tracey pulled Nana's deck of tarot cards from the center of the table and shuffled them. She chose three and flipped them over.

"Nightmare, collapse, and a choice," Nana muttered. "Help the boy."

"Sebastian?"

"He is the key. But he is also the trap. Don't trust him. And honey, watch out for the crocodile's claws. They are sharp." Nana smiled and it lit up her entire face.

Tracey smiled in return as she repeated the sentence in her head. *Crocodile's claws?*

The old woman stood up, her skin suddenly pale. She bared her teeth. "Who are you? Get out of my room."

"Nana?"

"Get out."

Tracey rose. "Thanks, Nana. I love you."

"Leave!"

Tracey slammed the door shut behind her and juggled the book in her hands to swipe away her blossoming tears.

Crocodile's claws?

What if the crocodile's claws wasn't just her nana rambling but a clue to the Crocodile Man? The image of a leathery dinosaur pattern floated into her mind. Where had she seen it before? The memory taunted her, but stayed just out of her reach.

Jane's descendants were filled with the magic that would enable them to protect and serve their town.

38

Night had fallen by the time they arrived at the cemetery, leaving the entrance in shadowy blackness. "Oh, the gate is closed," Tracey said, her heart sinking. Part of her was relieved. The thought of creeping around a cemetery at night filled her with killer bees buzzing in fury, desperate to break free of her chest.

Malden waved her forward. "I'm sure that's not a problem."

Tracey rolled her eyes. *Amazing.* He had become such a criminal in such a short space of time. Before his arrest he was such a stickler for the rules. She crept up to the gate behind the two men and marveled at how she had gotten to this point.

To change the direction of her thoughts, she went over the plan again. They had to find Sebastian, get him somewhere safe and then trick the Crocodile Man into falling for their trap. Her priority was to save her family and friends. Then she could destroy all of the stones. Peering over her shoulder she hoped to find Prince Henry arriving behind them in a blaze of light like a knight out of a fairy tale. So far, there was no sign of him.

Tracey's back itched with the creepy feeling of being watched. She recognized it from school whenever Meena, Carla, and Dave One were focused on her. It had to be Sebastian. He was probably hidden somewhere close by, staying just out of sight so the Crocodile Man wouldn't find him.

Hopefully.

Probably.

The cemetery was a well-tended, grassy expanse of land dotted with long pathways that arched around headstones and plaques. During the day, it was peaceful and picturesque. In the dark, everything took on a more sinister gloom. A dark place of trip hazards and ghosts. It reminded Tracey of her favorite video game. She almost expected a wraith to come screeching out of the star-filled sky heading straight toward them. That had to be the source of the creepy feeling flooding her mind. *Why did I agree to meet Sebastian here?*

If she let herself contemplate the reality of losing her family and friends and being on the run with two wanted criminals, she would break out in hives. *My life is over.* Even if she did save her friends and family, what good would it do? She could not go home.

Not now.

Maybe never again.

Before she totally spiraled, Malden popped the lock on the gate with his magic and led them into the spooky place of the dead. "Do you think there are ghosts here?" she whispered.

"Ghosts don't exist," Malden said.

Doctor Chan snorted. "They do. In a way."

Tracey stopped walking. "What?"

"You talk to your ancestor, do you not?"

"Oh, yeah." *I guess ghosts do exist. And they're not at all scary. More like super annoying.* Tracey's gaze traveled as far as the glow the streetlights allowed. When Malden deemed they were far enough out of sight of the main road, the three Mage-kind raised a glowing ball of light each. At last Tracey could see and the weird shadow shapes around her resolved into trees and bushes, headstones, and waist-high wire fences. The crisp air puffed from her mouth like a smokey jet trail.

"Where did this boy say to meet you?"

"He didn't. I think that means he'll find me."

"Hmmm," Malden mused. "He might not approach if he sees us with you."

"You're not leaving me alone," she snapped.

Doctor Chan shared a look with Malden. Honestly, it was disturbing how well they were working together. "We will not go far. Just out of sight." Doctor Chan pointed toward the distant gravestones. "Remember, you fought off Timothy and the Shadowman all by yourself."

"And Dust Devils and mumbles. You can successfully protect yourself in a variety of situations, Tracey. I believe in you. You will be fine," Malden added. He patted her on the shoulder. "Just shout and we'll come running."

She glared. "Sure." The two men extinguished their glowing lights and disappeared into the darkest of the shadows. And just like that the cemetery was even creepier. Tracey bounced in place to keep warm, burrowing her hands into the pockets of her oversized jacket. She kept the hood off. Sebastian needed to recognize her. Her ears were icy cold and the rest of her body was freezing. Honestly, who would want to hang out in a cemetery after dark? She turned to her left. Grandpa was buried over there somewhere. If it were not so dark and she wasn't so creeped out she would go over and say hello. She would never find the right plaque now.

Tracey sniffed and imagined she could smell dead things. All she could really smell were roses. A twig cracked somewhere to her left. She squinted in that direction.

"Tracey?"

"Sebastian?" She raised her glowing ball. The lean boy wore a black hoodie and black skinny jeans. All she could see were his bright blue eyes and a reddened nose.

"Are you alone?" he asked sniffing softly.

She made an exaggerated point of staring around without speaking. If she said anything, he would know she was lying. "Why did you want to meet here?"

"It's spooky? Who else would come here. We should go though, it's still too exposed out here."

"Where do you want to go?"

"We have to keep moving or he'll find us." Sebastian shuffled from foot to foot, searching the shadows for watching eyes.

"How is he tracking you?"

"I wish I knew."

"Who is the Crocodile Man?" she asked. "Is he M-force?"

"I don't know." Sebastian's eyes never stopped moving as he scanned the shadows around them. "I don't know how he found out about me. I told no one I had a stone."

"How did you get it?"

He tilted his head as he looked at her. "I'm not telling you that."

"He knows about me too," Tracey admitted softly. "He's always one step ahead of us."

"Then let's get out of here. He might have followed you."

"I — I can't. Not yet," she said, trying not to peer in the direction where she knew Malden and Doctor Chan were hiding. Was the Crocodile Man on his way yet?

Sebastian's eyes narrowed as his body tensed. "Why not … why …" He stepped back. "You're using me as bait to get him here. How could you do that to me?"

Tracey grabbed his wrist as he turned to run. Sebastian pulled away, his nostrils flaring.

She held up both hands, sorry she had touched him. "You've been playing tricks on me," she accused.

"I didn't put you in danger."

She snorted. "It was a fire, Sebastian."

"It was never a real fire."

"The grass fire was!" she snapped. Silence fell over the cemetery like a thick, crochet blanket. Anger heated her blood. She puffed out smoke. It wasn't from anger, it was cold and growing quickly colder. She realized her fiery mood had masked how cold it had suddenly grown. Her fingers were freezing.

"So what, you're punishing me?" he snapped.

Tracey peered around, distracted. An oily, sickly smell seeped into her nose. "What's that?"

"What?" Sebastian repeated. Her paranoia infected him and his head snapped around searching the dark too.

"Can you smell that?"

He squinted at her. "What?"

She shook her head. There was nothing out there. "What did you say before?"

"Are you punishing me?"

"No. Listen. The memory curse doesn't affect the Crocodile Man or his stone," she said watching the shadows for movement. "What makes him different? He keeps coming after you. He's attacked everyone I love. We have to stop him. We have to bring the battle to him. Help us." She couldn't confirm she only wanted him here to bring the Crocodile Man to them.

"Us?"

Avoiding Sebastian's accusing eyes, Tracey's gaze fell to her feet. "Fruit tingles." Foggy tendrils were winding stealthily along the path toward her feet. The Crocodile Man! She pointed and jogged backward. Sebastian threw out a bolt of fire, burning the fog right off the ground. They heard a gasp and a long groan as if the fog was in pain. Sebastian grabbed Tracey's hand. "Run."

"I have help," she shouted and tugged him toward the two men hiding in the darkness.

"You said you'd come alone."

"Well —"

"Tracey!"

Her name was echoed in the distance by Malden and Doctor Chan. Fire blasts scorched the ground at their hiding place. Tracey wracked her brain, trying to remember what the Serpent's Kiss did with the flames at the prison. She threw out her hands and a gust of wind flew from them. All it did was fan the fog, spreading it faster. *Ugh*. She couldn't concentrate. "How are you doing the fire thing?" she shouted.

"Come on!" Sebastian dragged her in the opposite direction. "If we stay to help your friends, he'll get us."

"But they can help us. They're stronger than we are."

"With the stones we're stronger and he'll still get us. We have to go. Now!"

Tracey's hesitation nearly got them frozen. The fog rose up out of the darkness and launched at them with long viney fingers.

Sebastian squeaked and jumped aside, throwing more fire. The vines burned and screamed, twisting sharply.

"Tell me how to do that. I can help!" she shouted. "I only know how to light little flames and candles."

"Point at it and use the stone's magic. Think inferno with your mind. Picture the word until that's all that's in your head," he panted. "Then shoot the magic in a really tight, tiny line. Fast and sharp, so it sets itself alight with friction from the air." He clearly did not like running any more than she did, but his legs were longer and she couldn't keep up. He tugged hard on her hand, and she stumbled along behind him.

"I can't focus!" she shouted. "Stop pulling me."

"You gotta find a way."

Let me help. Timothy said.

"No!" she snapped, unable to push the ghostly man from her mind with her full focus locked on outrunning the fog and keeping up with Sebastian.

Tracey!

"Shut up!" In moments the fog surrounded them. "If we get split up, go into your stone room and call for me. Try to find me."

"This way." Sebastian sent a spurt of fire to the right and they jumped over the burning fog vines, running for the pebbled walking path in the distance. They skidded to a stop. Right in the middle of the path stood a man-like shape of curling, undulating greenish fog.

"That's not good," Tracey said. How did you fight a floating insubstantial creature?

Oh.

She had done it before. When fighting the Shadowman. She had used light to disperse the shadow. Fire worked against fog. But Tracey's true strength lay in the ice magic belonging to her ancestor. Could she freeze the fog? Turn it into a solid? She drew on her core and on the stones she wore. The Serpent's Kiss responded, sending more twisting inky magic into her body, lighting her chest on fire. She gasped at the sharp cuts of power slashing in and out of her chest. It hurt so much. *I can control it. Let me take over!* Timothy shouted. Tracey forced her body to still and pulled magic from her core. It filled her veins and the sharp pain settled into an icy fire that flowed like liquid silver in her blood. Next to her, Sebastian let out another fire burst, protecting Tracey as much as he could, but their circle of safety was shrinking as the fog advanced. Sebastian spun, sending fire in long streams like a firehose but every time he turned the fog crept closer.

"Come on, hurry," he urged.

Tracey focused with all of her mind, throwing her magic ice out like snow to cover the entire area. The glowing ball of light she held above them popped, plunging them into pure blackness. Fear gripped Tracey's insides, turning her to jelly and she lost her focus. The icy magic glow lighting her hands disappeared with a pop. *Help!*

Something answered. Not Timothy, but something else. Tracey's eyes snapped open and this time the darkness was her friend.

Everything slowed, like time itself had slowed. She could see as if it was daylight. Magic exploded from her body in a massive, pink-tinted wave that spread out in front of her like ripples in a lake. The wave crested and crashed, flattening the fog where it stood. "Whoa!"

Sebastian stared at her in awe, the fire shooting from his hands dying away. "How did you do that?" he asked. "Did you — ? Was that the Butterfly stone? The fog just … disappeared."

"You didn't see the wave?"

"What wave?"

He couldn't see magic. Tracey shook her head. The word *Dreamer* thundered inside her mind, echoing like a meditation drum.

"I don't know how I did that," she muttered. She had been afraid and called for help. Fear filled her hands with magic and her body reacted as though it had known what to do. *Is this Dreamer magic?* "Let's get out of here." She spun around and lurched back immediately as a man loomed out of the darkness. The silk shirt. The embroidered green leather dinosaur-like pattern — crocodile skin — on a tie. A blurry image: A crocodile with its front foot clamped around its prey. The Crocodile's Claw. The clues came together in a waterfall of understanding. The figure had a familiar round shape, balding head, large nose, and reddish cheeks.

The mayor smiled a nasty, lip-curling smile. "Hello Tracey. I see you have found my prize for me. Thank you for that."

Tracey pushed Sebastian behind her, projecting her thoughts into the boy's head. *When the time comes, get out of here.*

"Are you talking to me? How are you inside my head? Wait, what? I'm not leaving you."

"When I say run, run," she ordered without looking at him. Aloud, she addressed the mayor. "So, you're the one behind the freeze fog. You're the Crocodile Man."

"The Crocodile Man? A rather childish moniker, but yes, I guess I am, and yes the fog is my creation. If you'll come with me, I will release your family."

"You really expect me to believe that?"

"My dear young lady, I expect you to do as you are told."

Oh, that's it. I'm not your dear *anything.* Tracey threw up her shield bubble, ensuring both herself and Sebastian were safely encased within it.

The mayor threw out his own hands.

They didn't stand a chance.

Tracey and Sebastian were lifted clear off the ground inside her bubble and thrown into an angel statue three arched footpaths away.

They hit the ground hard, skidding several feet, tearing up the grass and gravel beneath them. Tracey's head swam. Her body ached. She heard a moan roll out of Sebastian and flopped over to check if he was okay. "Are you …?"

He moaned his answer. "Ugh."

"Get up," she urged and pushed to her hands and knees. Every part of her hurt. "He's too strong."

"So are you." Sebastian rolled sideways. He staggered to his feet. "You can stop him."

Without warning they were hit again. The invisible pressure slammed the air out of her lungs and flung them both across the ground into another headstone.

Tracey moaned and rolled to examine what they had hit. It wasn't a headstone.

It was Malden and Doctor Chan. Their frozen bodies stood in the middle of the path, looking like every other statue in the cemetery. A pained groan erupted from Tracey's lips. Who was left to help them now? Tracey used Malden's jacket to pull her trembling body to her feet. Before she could get any further upright, she realized she was stuck halfway off the ground, held tight in a cling wrap net of magic. When she tried to shout her mouth gaped open, empty of sound, empty of air. It was like she had been laminated; it was exactly what she'd done to Doctor Chan to stop him from escaping earlier that day.

She couldn't breathe, her eyes bulged, and she turned to Sebastian for help. He gripped his throat with both hands, his lips fishing open for air. The Crocodile Man had caught them. Tracey croaked and fell sideways. Her vision went spotty then shrunk to pinpricks as she blacked out. The last thing she heard was a thump as Sebastian hit the ground beside her.

Magic that was equal and opposite
to that driven by fear
and misplaced accusation.

39

Tracey came to with a start and jerked forward — or tried to. When she leaned forward a heavy weight pulled her back. She was sitting on a wooden floor, her legs outstretched in front of her. Weirdly, her shoes were missing; her toes wriggled inside her green superhero socks, regaining some feeling. Behind her, a boy let out a moan. "Sebastian?" she queried.

"Yeah. What happened?"

Tracey tried to stand but the ropes tying her to the boy — back-to-back — would not let her move. Before she gave in to the panic welling inside her chest, she searched the room for a way out. There was a single bulb above their heads which let her see the room was the size of an average class-room, built with thick, mud-brick stones that were a grimy, aged-gray color. The ceiling was plastered, but the old and chipped paint speckled the wood floor in flakes of color. It made her think no one had been in this room for a very long time. Her eyes burned. She blinked hoping to clear her vision but everything stayed blurry and wobbly.

Checking her core, she breathed out a giant sigh when she realized she could still feel her magic. "Huh."

"What?" Sebastian groaned out the word.

"Can you feel your core?"

"Yeah."

"He didn't block us from using our magic."

"Why?"

It was a good question, and the possible answers were worrying. Panic simmered inside her chest but she had control of it for now. The faster she breathed the worse her head throbbed.

A thick silver-colored circle was printed on the wooden floorboards surrounding them, covered in chalk-drawn runes.

"Can you see anyone?" she asked. She felt a pull on the ropes tying them together and another grunted groan escaped the boy behind her.

"Two frozen people," he said. "Your friends maybe? An Asian girl with long dark hair and a black boy with a cool hat."

Tracey twisted side to side. "That's Jilly and Jonny. I can't see them." At least she knew where they were now. Her great plan to catch the Crocodile Man had misfired badly. She had gotten both Sebastian and herself caught too.

"We have to get out of here." Sebastian's pitch rose as panic took over. He pulled hard at the rope, his struggles jamming the unyielding fibers tighter into Tracey's stomach.

"Ouch."

"Sorry." The pull on the rope stopped.

"Don't panic," she said knowing that she needed to take her own advice.

"Don't panic? We're surrounded by the makings of a spell. On us. It's a spell on us."

"I wish I could say this is the first time this has happened to me."

"Oh?"

"Yeah."

"How did that work out?"

"Well, I'm here so …" She sat straighter, pulling the rope tighter.

"Ouch," he complained. It wasn't an angry tone. More resigned, like all his hope was gone.

"Sorry. I just realized something."

"What?"

Her heart rate shot into orbit. "The stones. He's got all of us." Her friends were in even more danger now. And so was she. Just because she had thought she could trick the Crocodile Man into coming here. She was such an idiot. He was too strong and now they would all fall. Swirls of guilt and fear filled her chest, fighting for supremacy. How had the mayor known Jonny carried a stone? Why hadn't he just pulled it from Jonny's neck and left him behind?

Tracey blinked rapidly as her brain turned the clues over in her mind. Maybe the mayor didn't know the stone curse acted differently because Jonny was a Norm? Which meant he didn't know everything. And that meant, she could still find a way out of this. Maybe.

"He's got all the stones," she muttered again, under her breath this time, hoping Sebastian would be the only one to hear.

Sebastian wriggled around, pressing his hot back against hers. With their hands tied behind them she scrabbled to grab his fingers. His hand twisted around hers and squeezed. "The mayor's spell isn't active yet. He'll need to be inside the circle himself to cast a spell using all the stones," he said.

That was true. His words gave her a little comfort. As did the warm fingers threaded between hers. She squeezed his hands. If the mayor entered the circle Tracey could potentially influence the spell. She had done that when Agent Malden cast his spell on Kylie, Jilly, and Tracey. She held two stones now, and that gave her more power than him, right? But the Butterfly Stone was still locked to her. Without its stored power, she had no hope of overpowering the Crocodile Man's spell, nor in stopping it. And she didn't know *how* to use her Dreamer power yet — if that was what she really held inside of her.

"Tracey?" Sebastian's voice sounded softer. "Are you okay?" His fingers squeezed hers again.

Timothy's voice snuck into her ear. *Let me help. Let me take control.*

No, she told him. *Stay silent.* She raised the brain bubble against Timothy and his presence disappeared from her mind. "We have to get out of here," she said aloud.

Sebastian snorted. "How? We're tied up and your friends are frozen."

"Then we unfreeze them."

Sebastian's voice sounded drier. "How?"

"I've done it before — on me. I mean, I unfroze myself."

"And?"

"Uh, I don't really know. Not for sure. I used the stones' guardians to communicate with the other stones."

"You've mentioned the guardians before. You mean Protectors, don't you? We're the Protectors. I don't understand how you can use us to communicate with the frozen ones."

"No, the stones have an actual guardian. I see them as colored shapes inside the stone room. They seem to have a power of their own. Separate to the Sect."

Sebastian's stunned silence broke as he murmured, "I had no idea. Well, what do the guardians do?"

"I think they're connected to the original spell that created the stones. So, you haven't spoken to your stone's guardian at all?"

"Never."

"What about Jonathan — the spirit inside your stone?"

"A few times. To be honest, he's not really that helpful."

"Tell me about it," she muttered. "Okay, we have to call on the stone's guardian, and um —"

"Wait you said all the stones. So I was right. You do have —" his voice dropped to a whisper so soft she barely heard it as he pressed closer against her back and tilted his chin down close to her ear. "— Timothy's stone."

"I do," she admitted just as softly.

His breath brushed her ear and her skin quivered. "Then he does have them all. You have to stop him."

This time it was her turn to ask. "How?"

Sebastian struggled with the rope again, pulling it tight around her chest again. "We have to get loose."

"Try your magic," she suggested, gasping for breath as the rope squeezed air out of her lungs.

"Sorry. Oh yeah, I forgot."

Tracey let her focus fall into the Serpent's Kiss and drew on its magic. She heard no whisper of a response from Timothy this time, but prepared to shut him down again if he tried to convince her to release control to him. She drew the tainted power into her chest and pushed it down her arms into her fingers. "What's that burn spell again?"

"*Inferno* and picture fire. Tight bursts."

"That's it?"

"Well that's how I do it." His voice took on that tone her brother Simon had when Charlie said something dumb.

"But you didn't do that at school?"

"No that was a smoke illusion."

"How did you do that?"

"Illusions are tough. You have to magic everyone in the room — all their senses — and convince them that it's real. The more people there are the harder it is to cast the illusion. A fire is easier — you can trick people with just the smell and their minds fill in the blanks."

"Yes, but how? What's the spell?"

"Do you know what fire smoke smells like?"

"Of course."

"Just focus on that smell. Like totally focus. So much so that you believe it yourself. Then inside a salt circle you cast the spell. I use the words *campfire, smoke, billowy, inhale, and scent*."

"So, it's a detailed spell?"

"Illusions are, yeah."

"But it didn't create a real fire."

"Weirdly, creating real fire is easier," he said.

She remembered sitting near the campfire deep in the forest on Mount Hawthy and Prince Henry showing her how to light it with her magic. Her head snapped up almost smashing against the back of Sebastian's skull. She felt the whisper touch against her hair. "Prince Henry," she blurted.

"What are you talking about?" Sebastian's head twisted, trying to look at her. She squeezed his hand to calm him.

"Prince Henry is coming. He'll help us."

"Prince He — are you crazy?"

"He's my friend. And an M-force agent."

"Seriously?" Sebastian fell silent. After a moment she heard a thoughtful growl and he asked, "But isn't he, like, overseas?"

"Nah, I called him."

"You called a prince?"

Tracey laughed. Sebastian sounded so much like Dave. Her chest tightened thinking of her friend. He and Tony had been caught up in the Crocodile Man's horrible plans. They did not deserve what happened to them. None of her friends and family did. She had to find a way to fix this.

As she focused on her friends, a voice drifted into her mind and for a moment she didn't recognize it, thinking it was her own inner voice. *"Tracey?"*

She let out a deep breath as she realized someone was talking to her inside her head and that she recognized the voice. *"Kylie?"*

"Yes."

"How can you — where are you?"

"I'm right outside."

"What? Outside where?"

"The council building."

Kylie was … Oh. "We're in the council building?"

"What?" Sebastian asked sounding confused. "How do you know that?"

She returned to the voice in her head. *"It's the mayor, Kylie. He's the bad guy."*

"We guessed. Prince Henry found me. He was looking for you. We tracked you down with a spell and one of your pullovers. Everyone else is frozen. They're all at your house. What the heck is going on?"

"The mayor has a stone."

"Ah poop."

"He's powerful and super dangerous. Where's Prince Henry?" Tracey tried to find his mind but came up blank. *"I can't reach him."*

"I don't know where he is. He told me to wait here. He was going to scout around the building. But it's been a while since he left and I'm worried."

Tracey tried to find him again. *"Prince Henry?"* There was no answer. *"Kylie, you need to get more help. He's got me, Sebastian, Jonny, and Jilly in here, and he's about to do a spell on the stones."*

"Who's Sebastian?" Kylie grunted. *"Forget that. It sounds like we need an army, and we don't have one. While you're in there you can be used as a hostage or something. That's what Prince Henry said. Can you get out? I'll go get more help."*

"We'll try," Tracey told the younger girl. Kylie's presence faded from Tracey's mind.

"What's happening?" Sebastian asked. "I felt magic. What were you doing?"

"We have to get untied. Help is coming but —" Heavy footfalls snapped her attention to the door. "Oh no."

"Don't say anything," Sebastian warned her.

"I'm blocked from using the Butterfly Stone," she muttered.

"Then unblock it. Fast."

"It's not that easy," she grumbled. She had to think of something else because she could not contact the Butterfly Stone anymore. The door flew open and the mayor stomped in. His face was a fiery red and he panted a little as he moved. "Problem?" Tracey asked sweetly.

"Nothing I can't handle. You have too many friends." His scowl darkened.

Tracey snorted. "They'll never stop coming."

The mayor's lips quirked. "You mean Prince Henry?"

A sudden bad feeling filled Tracey's chest. It made her ribs ache. The mayor waved a hand at the door and a wrapped, frozen statue floated into the room. Followed by two more.

Malden, Doctor Chan, and … Prince Henry.

Fruit tingles.

"I'm gathering quite the collection, young lady. I'm afraid you are losing teammates at an alarming rate. How many friends do you have left?"

She couldn't let him know about Kylie. She forced a sob from her throat. "Please, please let us go." Sebastian's fingers gripped hers tightly.

"Once I've cast the spell to find the Serpent's Kiss, I will have them all and we can finally begin."

He didn't know she had it! "You can't take them off. That's part of the curse," she reminded him.

The mayor smirked at her. "I am well aware of that, young lady. I need them to stay on. The only way I can use their magic is to have each Protector here. The stones must be kept separate. They are far too dangerous to be brought together. I need all of you here, inside my circle, so I can use their power together."

That was information Tracey had not heard before. It explained why she couldn't access the Butterfly Stone. It was blocked because she was holding the Serpent's Kiss. She knew two things the mayor didn't. She *did* have more friends coming and she *wore* the Serpent's Kiss and the Butterfly Stone. If the stones had to be around the neck of a separate Protector, then his spell — whatever he was planning — wouldn't work. Still, she was trapped in here and her powerful friends were incapacitated. The bad guy was stronger than her and there didn't seem to be any escape. Even if Kylie was able to bring more people, what could they possibly do? The mayor was too powerful. Her eyes filled with legitimate tears.

The only way out was to do something she swore she would never to do. She would give in. Like he told her she would. Like she had denied all this time. He was right.

She would let him in.

"Timothy, I say yes," she said.

At last.

My dear Millicent.

I shall remember our constitutionals through the garden until the end of my days.

40

She heard the mayor's exclamation of shock a split second before she lost all awareness of her body. Timothy's joy filled her as his laugh erupted from her mouth. Tracey pushed her way to the front of her mind to see what was happening and felt rather than heard Timothy's shock at her presence. Stephanie's takeover had taught Tracey a lot. Yes, Timothy needed her acceptance to take over but it was still *her* mind and she could force him out when she needed too. To prove it, she quirked her own lips. It exhausted her but she did it.

Timothy understood. She heard her own voice say. "I see. Very well, Tracey. We shall be in partnership."

Magic bloomed through Tracey's body, flooding her senses. Heat exploded out of her pores like she was a volcanic explosion. It was so unlike her own core magic. This was all Timothy and the fiery magic stored inside the Serpent's Kiss. It was brutally efficient. He blasted her inner closet door apart and forced her magic to meld with his. Unlike the icky, sickly feeling she got from the mayor's stone, this magic carried a heavy scent of smoke, ash, and rotten eggs. So much raw power. She had never pulled so much before, but for Timothy it seemed effortless. He blasted the mayor back with tight, laser-like magic bolts, forcing the man to raise a shield wall to defend against the fierce attack.

The ropes around Tracey's wrists and chest snapped as Timothy spared them a single glance. Words flowed from her mouth, spells she had never heard before, and the circle around her and her friends snapped closed, controlled by Timothy instead of the Crocodile Man. *Oh, clever,* she told him. His magic swirled and grew inside the circle. He used Tracey's ability to draw magic from those around her and pulled on Sebastian's core, augmenting his power even further. An *"oooomph"* pushed out of the magical boy as he folded over in pain. She tried to tell Sebastian she was sorry but she couldn't speak. Timothy attacked the mayor with a barrage of blasts. At the same time, he split part of his concentration off and focused on Tracey's frozen friends.

You need Jilly, Tracey told him.

He hummed. *I understand why you want your friends awake, and though I have a different reason, I do agree that is what we need.*

Silver-black magic swirled faster, rising up in Jilly like the Shadowman that once spewed out of Officer Jameson and Kylie. Timothy was using Tracey's Dreamer ability to unpick the spell around Jilly. The curse freezing her friend's body became clear to Tracey's eyes as a golden woven net stretched tight around her frame, holding her limbs still. Now that Tracey's could *see* the spell, she knew she could break it.

You see, Tracey. We can work together in harmonious equity.

The hairs all over Tracey's body quivered. She couldn't trust Timothy any more than she could trust Stephanie or Doctor Chan. Timothy would use her to stay in control and then he would start hurting people.

Timothy worked quickly to unpick the net around Jilly while fighting off the mayor. Timothy's concentration and control were astonishing. He held a barrier bubble around himself that the mayor seemed unable to break. The mayor blasted and drilled and exploded his magic against the impossible-to-pass barrier, growing more and more frustrated with every hit.

What about Jonny? We have to release him too.

"Jonny has no magic," Timothy explained. "There is no point in releasing him. The boy is completely useless to us."

Tracey bristled. Jonny was not useless. His very presence changed the course of many battles. Besides, he was her friend. Timothy could not help but show his true colors, and Tracey's resolve hardened. He could not be trusted. She would have to get rid of him as soon as his help was no longer required.

It was clear Timothy couldn't sense the direction of her thoughts as he didn't respond to her threat. She kept him out of her mind somehow. He might be in her head, but he could not control her thoughts.

In her spirit state Tracey was able to wrap herself in her core magic — it was everywhere after all — and the circle around them only strengthened her power. She let it seep into Timothy's mind. It was easier than she expected. Probably because he was still fighting off the mayor and focused on unpicking the spell around Jilly. Whatever he was doing was working. Tracey could see minute movements in Jilly's body now. A wriggle of a finger. A twitch of her nose. Eyelashes fluttering as her eyelids moved agonizingly slowly.

Keep going, she urged and let her mind find the edges of Timothy's shadowy thoughts. She found the brain bubble he held against her intrusion and duplicated the words that swelled inside her head.

She burrowed into Timothy's mind, found his memory center, and jumped.

Similar to how she experienced Stephanie's memory Visions, Tracey found Timothy's memory Vision world to be a black and white place full of shadows and blurred edges. She peered around curiously, wondering where she had ended up. She needed the truth about the stones and the curse that bound them. Specifically, Timothy's connection to the curse. From her own dreams and Visions, and from what Tracey had experienced with Stephanie's memories, she knew Visions were seldom linear and were often centered around heightened emotion.

She stood inside a pub built of wood with thick, dark roof beams. The wallboards were covered in framed paintings of landscapes, rivers, and open countryside with half-clothed women lounging beside the water. Tracey quickly turned away. *Ew.* The pub was only half full. Patrons in hats and suits pressed up against grime covered figures wearing rough, homespun fabric, and open collars. The floorboards were covered in dirt, crumbs, and something slimy giving it a perpetually damp look.

A man stood near the back, hidden in the darkness, dressed in a clean, well-tailored suit. He seemed lost in his thoughts. The beer stein he held in one hand was full of liquid.

It became apparent he was waiting for someone when another man appeared soundlessly at his elbow. His face was familiar, though it took Tracey a moment to figure out how she knew it. He was a figure from the photograph Tracey had seen in Doctor Chan's university office — a member of the Sect of Six.

"Charles," Timothy muttered, not turning to look at the man.

"Shall we?" With a wave of Charles' hand, a door appeared in the rear wall. A cleverly disguised illusion. Tracey followed the two men into what looked like a small inner office. A round table sat pride of place in the center, sur-rounded by four empty chairs. The walls were framed with bookshelves but, weirdly, the shelves were bare. There were no windows.

The two men sat on opposite sides of the table. For a moment, neither man spoke. They just stared as if expecting the other to start.

"You guarantee she has no idea?" Charles began, startling Tracey with his booming tone. She lingered near the now invisible door. Why was this memory so prominent in Timo-thy's mind? It was clearly important; it was the sharpest memory and she had found it so easily.

"None. She remains completely unaware that it is her magic we are after rather than the results of the experiment we officially undertake."

Charles tapped his fingers against the tabletop. "She must not discover our plan."

"Our plan?" Timothy leaned back in his chair until the wooden back creaked. "I believe you are the one here seeking political backing."

"That is where our future lies," Charles said licking his dry lips. "I will not deny that."

"She will not go along with bloodshed."

"Then you must help her to see reason. We will become a political force in our own right, which means presenting ourselves to the world on our terms. They must learn who and more importantly what we are."

"Our power is best served by remaining in the shadows. We can better control them without their knowledge," Timothy argued.

Charles shook his head. "True force comes from acknowledging our autonomy."

"Once they discover our existence, there will be no going back."

Tracey was surprised. She figured the two evil men would be in agreement. They were not. Each wanted power but in a different way. Timothy wanted to keep Mage-kind a secret. Charles wanted to tell the whole world.

"Yes." Charles sat back in his chair examining Timothy with an intense gaze.

"Why should you speak for all of us?"

"Why should you? My family —"

"— are of little concern," Timothy scoffed. "You seek to lose us any power we may gain from this experiment. Stephanie will see that."

"You speak as though she is the leader of our coven," Charles said.

Timothy pressed his hands to the tabletop and leaned forward. "You know her power exceeds our own."

"And you think you control her, do you?"

Timothy narrowed his eyes at the pompous man. "I have some influence, yes."

"As do I. I have been her companion over many long years. You know we schooled together. Well, magically speaking. The way these un-mage mortals control women is frankly disgusting. They are not breeding animals or children who cannot think for themselves, as you well know."

Ugh. Tracey groaned loudly, knowing the two men couldn't hear her.

Timothy leaned back in his chair again. "The world as it currently stands enables control —"

"You do not control her!" Charles pushed to his feet, the light above them flickering.

"Calm yourself, my friend."

"Once the stones are linked —"

"Your idea or hers?" Timothy's pointing finger seemed to irritate Charles.

"Hers, of course."

Timothy gestured to the empty chair. "Do sit down."

"You have no intention of taking hold of that shared power, do you?" Charles said, his grip on the chair back tightened, his knuckles cracking loudly.

"It will increase the strength of all the stones," Timothy said.

"If one could control that power …?" Charles pushed away from the chair he held. "Convince her," he ordered and stalked from the room.

"Convince her!" Timothy echoed, once Charles had gone. "Convince her! There is no telling Stephanie to do anything."

Tracey fumed. If she could have felt her own body, she knew everything would ache from how tightly she clenched her muscles. Her face would be red from the heat of the fire in her belly. These horrible men were speaking about control and power and hurting innocent people. They knew the announcement of Mage-kind existence would end in bloodshed and they didn't care.

A light tap against the hidden door signaled the appearance of another man. Jing Cho. He strode in and stopped beside the table, locking eyes with Timothy. "Well?" Jing asked.

"He will not yield. If I push him he will make the announcement regardless. He has plans in place. Even if we were to stop him directly —" Timothy raised an eyebrow. Jing nodded slowly. "— he would have yet another sleeve and another trick up it. We cannot afford to wait. Did you find it?"

"I did," Jing said. He stood beside the table, his hands disappearing into the sleeves of his red coat. "When Charles reveals all of his cards, we will take care of him. The spell is powerful enough to undo what he seeks to release."

"So if the un-mage mortals learn of our power …"

Jing nodded sharply. "We make them forget."

Timothy's lips quirked. "Excellent."

"But …"

"But?" Timothy's voice turned silky soft. It sent a shiver over Tracey's ghostly body.

"We will require power from all of the stones. If there is the slightest interference the spell could backfire or worse," Jing warned.

"Then we must ensure there is no interference."

Jing nodded and left the room in a flurry of robes. Timothy stroked his chin and leaned back once more. The wooden seat squealed sharply. "I must speak to Millicent and Jonathan." He lowered his head and stared at Tracey. "Get out of my head."

Tracey's mind was flung back, slamming into her own body though she was still locked out of control by Timothy's presence. She pushed forward to find out what was going on. The door to the room they were trapped in had been blown off its hinges. Wooden shards lay all over the floor. Tracey's shield bubble was raised against a shadowy figure standing in the doorway. Behind the shattered door was a stairwell leading up. *Oh, we're underground.*

The man swept his hood off his head with one hand.

It wasn't a man.

It was Kylie.

Timothy thrust out Tracey's hands and electrified magic shards flew at the younger girl. "Kylie!" Tracey screamed.

Your faith in my studies and my work heartens me indeed.

41

Tracey shoved Timothy out of her body in an instant, redirecting the magic flung at Kylie into the wall beside Kylie's head. Kylie screeched and dove aside. Tracey raised her hands — now in full control — but wobbled, dizzy from the mental movement. "It's me. It's Tracey. I'm back." Her stomach jerked and she swallowed the sudden moisture filling her mouth. *I'm gonna hurl.*

"Tracey?" Kylie lowered her hands and her own shield bubble flickered. There was a massive, mayor-sized hole in the wall to the left and a tunnel leading up. Timothy must have knocked the mayor right out of the building seconds before Kylie blasted her way inside.

"It's me, sorry I was … the stone was … you know."

"Stephanie?" Kylie nodded and released her magic. "But you're you again, right?"

Tracey nodded. Her eyes widened as Damian ran down the stairs behind Kylie. His beautiful, perfect face grinned at her. His arms rose as if he wanted to pull her into a giant hug and make sure she was safe. She jolted toward him, reaching out for the hug too before halting. Her gaze darted guiltily to Sebastian. His gorgeous blue eyes locked onto hers and she saw hurt in them at her reaction. *Oh, um.* Her face flamed. "What are you doing here?" she asked the Norm boy.

Damian helped Sebastian to his feet. "You needed help," he said. "I don't have magic but —"

"I do," Kylie interrupted.

"It's not just me either." Damian added. "Laura and the whole football team is outside."

"What?"

"Yeah, they're pissed about what happened to Dave. Laura figured we needed as much muscle as possible if we didn't have magic. So yeah. We're the muscle."

Tracey's gaze flew to the man-sized hole in the wall. How long did they have before the Crocodile Man came back? "We have to get everyone out of here," she said, twisting her head. "Including Jilly and Jonny." Jilly's body moved in jerky jilted twitches. Timothy hadn't finished unpicking the spell wrapped around her. Jonny was still frozen.

"Can you wake Jonny up?" Damian asked. "I don't think I can carry him without help."

Tracey vaguely remembered the words Timothy used while unpicking the spell around Jilly. She had to hurry. She pulled silvery magic from her core into her hands and wrapped them around Jilly to expose the spell weave to her eyes again. Many of the threads were frayed but too many were still intact.

"Didn't you wake everyone up after Agent Malden used that sleep spell?" Kylie asked. "Can't you use that?"

Tracey shook her head. "They're frozen, not asleep."

"When has being told you can't do something ever stopped you?" Damian asked.

Dreamer.

Tracey's face flamed again. "I can try."

"You can do it, Tracey," Sebastian said, coming to stand beside her. He took her hand. "I believe in you."

She stared up into his eyes. They shone back at her as if she was royalty. *Whoa.* Beside him, Damian's scowl grew.

Tracey returned to the spell weave. Timothy had been unpicking it thread by thread. Tracey knew how to do that and she had an idea how to unravel it a lot faster. She needed magic. A heap of it. She thought about the Dreamer story.

Tracey needed the Butterfly Stone. "Hang on." She recalled the pull on her muscles when Timothy drew on the Serpent's Kiss's storehouse of magic. There had been the briefest echo beside it. Faint, but there nonetheless. She might not be able to call on Stephanie or the Butterfly Stone, but she'd felt something. She pulled the Butterfly Stone out from beneath her shirt and using her own core power examined the stone for the color of the spell weave around it. She zoomed in on the thread's edge. Rather than pull, she exploded her mind against the weave.

It blew apart.

At last, the Butterfly Stone responded to her touch. Tracey drew on the storage of power inside the Butterfly Stone and felt the addictive rush of heat fill her limbs pushing out the smoky grittiness of the Serpent's Kiss. But no, she needed that too. Somehow, she had to link to two magics together and make them attract rather than repel, like flipping magnets so that the opposite ends could touch.

Ice and smoke. She couldn't harden the smoke but ice could become steam. And the two gases could then mingle and become one. She drew the ice magic out of her body, and put an imaginary flame under it, melting it into water then boiling it into steam. The visualization worked in seconds. She pulled smoke from the Serpent's Kiss and blew the two gases together. She then sucked it all back inside her core.

"What are you doing? What's happening?" Sebastian asked.

Tracey ignored him and glanced at Kylie and Damian.

"You're safe," Damian said.

"You've got this, Tracey." Kylie agreed, her eyes shining.

Damian's hot hands came to rest gently on her shoulders, grounding her. Sebastian reached forward to take both of her hands. She clenched fingers. "Help me."

Damian lifted his hands off her shoulders. She turned her head. "Stay." Damian's eyes were shadowed by his scowl but his hands returned.

Sebastian looked over her head and fixed his gaze on Damian. "She's amazing."

"She is."

"We have to protect her."

Tracey didn't hear them. She focused on the half-un-picked spell around Jilly and the fully formed woven net around Jonny. She let the infused smokey steam swirl around her body filling her senses until it made her dizzy. Heat poured from her skin, bringing beads of sweat to her upper lip, forehead and down her back. It soaked into her shirt and made her jeans stick to her legs.

She poured the steam into the salt circle around her friends and closed it again. She coated Jilly and Jonny in the magic. Tugging lightly, she pulled her hands from Sebastian's grip and turned, bringing her hands together in front of her chest. Ripping her hands apart, she shouted, *"Wake up!"* rupturing the weave of the frozen spell with an explosion of magic.

I will continue to insist my work is studied research rather than fiction but perhaps I can be persuaded to embellish the author as a fiction, to lend a more fantastical air to the tale.

42

Jilly and Jonny both moaned and fell to their knees, and then the room filled with noise.

Sebastian screeched as the Crocodile Man zoomed back in through the hole he had been blasted out of. "You," the mayor shouted and fired green shards of raw magic straight at them all.

"Jilly, shield!" Tracey shouted, throwing her own bubble shield up and over herself, Sebastian, and Damian. "Call on your stone," she ordered, grabbing Sebastian's arm and shaking it. "We need all of them to fight the mayor."

"Tracey?" Jonny shouted. "What do I do?" He crouched beneath Jilly's shield.

"Hang on," Tracey called. She turned to Kylie. "Take Damian and get out of here," she ordered.

"No, Tracey —" Damian grabbed her hand and squeezed her fingers.

Kylie ran over to cover Damian with her shield. Damian reluctantly released Tracey's hand and stepped back. Tracey tightened her shield until it covered only herself and Sebastian.

"Jilly, call on the stone," Tracey said.

"I can't. I must shield Jonny!" she shouted back.

Tracey fired several electrified blasts of colored magic at the mayor, forcing him to focus on blocking her blasts.

"I've got him!" Kylie shouted. Damian ran with his sister over to Jilly. Kylie extended her hands, and her shield bubble stretched out to cover Jonny.

Jilly lowered her arms. "Thank you." She ran to Tracey's side, her spear forming quickly in her hands. It flew impossibly fast and hard at the mayor.

"Is your shield up?" Tracey asked.

"I'm good," Jilly confirmed, forming another spear. "Sebastian?"

His own shield bubble rose around his body. "I'm sorted." Both Sebastian and Jilly separated, running to opposite corners of the room. Jilly's spear flew again toward the mayor. Sebastian fired his magic in jet flames like he did with his flame-thrower power earlier that day. The mayor roared and turned to fight them off.

Tracey ran to Kylie. The younger girl let Tracey through her shield bubble then thickened it over all of them, rocking back on her feet as the mayor alternated his shots between firing at her and at Jilly and Sebastian.

"Jonny." Tracey took his hands. "Let Millicent take control."

"What? Are you freaking kidding me? You said she couldn't do that."

"She needs you to let her," Tracey said. "We need her magic."

"How do I even do that?"

"Watch out!" Sebastian shouted. He dove one way, and Jilly dove the other, hitting the ground hard as an explosion of light and magic rattled the walls, reflecting and refracting over all of them. Tracey, Jonny, Kylie, and Damian ducked inside Kylie's bubble shield as hot air exploded against it. Kylie screeched. When the flare of power faded, they could see the mayor's protection shield — a giant circle of light — had withstood Sebastian's wild, magic-bomb explosion. *Bomb?* The Crocodile Man laughed madly like he was enjoying the battle. His hands circled and a massive ball of electrical power formed between them.

Tracey thought of the magic lesson her grandma gave her whole family after they got back from Nana's birthday. "Get down," Tracey shouted. Her friends hit the ground as Tracey erected a giant shield dome over them all and turned it into a mirror — drawing on both of her stones, the ice and fiery shadow magic — and reversed the arcing ball back at the man with a scream. It caught him full on, zooming through his body as if it were paper. He fell to the ground, shaking and jolting. Tracey let the dark magic of the Serpent's Kiss fill her body completely and with a scream she poured the Shadowman out of her throat.

The Shadowman reared up into the air above them, bellowing out its pleasure at its sudden release.

"Tracey?!" Her friends' exclamations of horror filled the air. Kylie cried out in shock, "No!"

Tracey couldn't answer them. She commanded the Shadowman to attack the mayor. The man managed to roll, evading the Shadowman's attack.

He stared up at the monstrous shape. "You have it. The snake. It was you all along."

In less than a heartbeat, his fog monster poured from his lips, rising up to take on the Shadowman, tangling and writing against it. Both creatures shrieked in fury as they whipped around trying, to tear the other's ghostly form apart.

"Tracey?"

"Jonny, now!" Tracey shouted. Jonny's eyes flared with violet light as Millicent took control. His shoulders straightened.

"Tracey!" Millicent shouted. "We must stop him. Now. While his power is split."

"Any idea how?" she shouted back.

Above their heads a chorus of wings fluttered, growing louder as the screeching of a hundred crows rose up loud enough to shatter their ear drums. The black cloud of wings slammed into the Shadowman and the gas monster, ripping them both apart.

"Oh!" Jilly exclaimed. She stared at the wild battle taking place above their heads. She clasped both hands around the Tiger's Eye and scrunched her eyes shut. A golden tiger shape sprang forth from Jilly's Stone of Power. It quivered, fighting to maintain its form, flashing in and out of sight. Jilly grunted and gripped her stone tighter, the effort turned her fingers white. "Jing, help me! Take control." Her eyes flashed red, and the tiger shape solidified. The tiger launched straight at the mayor as he struggled back to his feet.

The tiger's leap caught him as he turned but the evil man jerked back and got off one fierce energy bolt that threw Tracey, Jilly — no, *Jing* — and the tiger across the room. Yipping howls erupted from behind Tracey. Knee high canine-like creatures with high triangular ears appeared and disappeared around them, golden eyes flashing as they surrounded the mayor. The shapes disappeared but the howls and high-pitched growls remained. The invisible hunters were focused wholly on their prey. Sebastian stepped between the invisible animals, only Tracey realized that wasn't Sebastian. His eyes shone yellow-gold, and the fury he poured into the mayor was unlike Sebastian's trickster nature. Ball after ball of hot fiery magic pounded the man until he fell to his knees.

"All this boy's life. Hunting him. Chasing him. Terrifying him. You ruined his life!"

The mayor's eyes flashed green. "Jonathan, is that you?" As *Jonathan* stepped forward, Tracey snapped out a thin, ghostly hand and captured the mayor by one leg the way she'd contained the giant mumbles back in the UK. Jing, through Jilly's body, ensnared the mayor's right wrist. Millicent encircled his left wrist and yanked the writhing man to the floor. Jonathan directed Sebastian's body and grabbed the mayor's last flailing limb with his flesh and blood hand, pouring magic down the link between them, tearing into the man's mind.

Tracey reached out. "Jonathan, no!"

The furious man didn't hear her. Sebastian's beautiful blue eyes glowed yellow-gold, like the gleaming eyes of his surrounding pack. The Crocodile Man screamed.

"Sebastian! Ugh, Jonathan, stop. We have him," Tracey pleaded.

Jonathan pushed forward. His face molten lava red, his eyes burning with golden hatred.

"Jonathan," Tracey begged. "Don't do it." Jonathan's eyes were locked onto the mayor, his fury in total control.

The Crocodile Man laughed, teeth suddenly sharp.

Why is he laughing?

He stared up into Jonathan's eyes and Tracey saw the moment they flashed green. Tendrils of gas shot up into Sebastian's eyes, nose, ears, and mouth from the stone on the mayor's chest.

"No!" Tracey screamed. She felt the flow of magic suddenly reverse, dragging them all forward, sucking power from the stones on their chests. Tracey tore her gaze from the mayor to the floor. The runes drawn on the wood all glowed brightly emerald. The Crocodile Man had activated his spell.

The power from the stones was being drained from them.

And they couldn't stop it.

The mayor's laugh grew manic.

Tracey, Jilly, Sebastian, and Jonny collapsed, screaming as sharp knives of pain tore their chests open.

*I pray that my research has
given you hope. It is not a curse
and you are not alone.*

43

Tracey lay on her back, gasping as hot, sharp, tugging pains pulled the life from her chest. Sebastian lay beside her. Jonny and Jilly sprawled somewhere near her feet.

Kylie had a protection bubble raised over her brother. Damian shouted into his cell phone as Kylie's shield buckled and shimmered under the mayor's bombardment of blasts. She must have been trying to distract him to save them. Brave and foolish. It worked just long enough for the spell's effects on Tracey to wobble. She sucked in a great gulp of air and regained control. The animal shapes aiding them disappeared with the mayor's final attack and Kylie wouldn't last long against the Crocodile Man alone. Tracey had to act, but she was aching and exhausted. Sweat coated every inch of her skin. Sebastian, Jilly, and Jonny moaned. This was an impossible fight. They were going to lose.

"We have —" Tracey's voice gave out. She tried to roll onto her side but couldn't find the strength to do it. How could she help Damian and Kylie when she could barely swallow on her own. "Distrac —"

"How?" Sebastian whispered. It seemed that Damian already thought of it. Thundering footsteps thumped above them. The rumble grew louder as at least ten pairs of feet pounded down the stairs. Norm boy after Norm boy threw himself through the doorway, holding up shields of trash can lids and football push pads until the room was full of noise and movement; Laura darted in behind them, scooting around the madness to reach Kylie. The mayor's blasts grew rapid but thinner, his magic siphoned off in several directions, weakening with each blast. Shouting filled the room.

Tracey rolled until she could see Sebastian. "We have to stop him. He'll hurt them all."

"How? We can't fight him."

"He's distracted, but I need more time."

"What can I do?"

"Your illusion spell."

"I can't. I don't have the tools or ingredients —"

Tracey grabbed his hand and twisted her fingers between his. "I'm a superconductor. Take my magic. It's all you'll need."

His eyes locked onto hers. "It won't last long."

"I won't need it too."

Sebastian closed his eyes and began muttering softly. Tracey's gaze fell to his soft lips as she pushed her magic into his hand the way she did with her uncle to give him a boost. A heavy scent of smoke flooded the room. The fighting slowed as shouted taunts gave way to alarmed shrieks. Clouds of noxious smoke grew thicker and thicker, filling the small room and blinding them all. "Whatever you are going to do —" Sebastian said "— do it now." He released her hand.

Tracey rolled and pushed to her hands and knees, searching for the mayor through the thick smoke and panicked football players. She spied Laura tugging on Kylie's hand, encouraging her to evacuate. Kylie wouldn't leave without her brother and shoved Laura back. Tracey's eyes found Damian.

"Kick his ass," Damian mouthed at her. His smile was aggressive. All teeth. Anger. That was what she needed. Her friends were hurt, her family, everyone she loved. One man was responsible, and Tracey was furious at him. She threw back her head and screamed.

Her scream turned into a word and that word became a promise and an oath and a primal force. "No!"

She thought of the spell that locked the stones together. The one that stopped Tracey from accessing the Butterfly Stone while she wore the Serpent's Kiss. The one she'd broken in order to access the Butterfly Stone's magic again. She thought of the memory curse that affected each of the stone's creators and the one power the mayor seemed to control.

Memory.

He remembered.

The memories of his ancestor stayed with him. How? And more importantly … why?

Tracey screamed for the heart of her butterfly, the heart of change. It was the magic that belonged only to her. Magic that *was* her. She poured all of her power into the Shadowman spewing from her lips again who screeched, becoming a bolt of pure black, absorbing every bit of remaining light in the room. It swooped and dove directly into the mayor's eyes, forcing itself deep into his brain. Tracey drew magic from everyone. She took Millicent's power through Jonny's goodness and cheeky pranks, she took Jilly's determination and fiery passion, she took Sebastian's fear and rage and hope. And she took her own strength and memories and drove them all down into the mayor's mind. She locked onto

Damian and Kylie and drew on their love for each other and Damian's desire to keep Tracey safe.

The mayor's mouth opened in a silent scream. Tracey took it all. She took his voice and his power and his memory. She wrapped all of that magic up and dove into the mayor's mind with everything that she had.

The world fell silent.

Every tone and shade of green surrounded her in a spiraling swirl. She was in the green place. Inside the Crocodile Man's stone. This time she was in control and moved her body toward the glowing prison cell in the center. The mayor stood inside it, staring at Tracey in shock. "How did you do this? This is my place. My world. My sanctuary! It is mine to control. You cannot have power here."

"It's your prison now," she said coldly.

"You can't do this!" He bashed his hands against the bars of fluorescent green light keeping him contained.

Tracey drifted closer. "I did. You're trapped in here now. Break the curse on my friends and family. Unfreeze everyone and I'll let you go."

"You cannot hold me."

"You have no control here." She chuckled at the powerless man feeling only sadness swelling inside her chest. "Your spell — the circle and the runes — they gave me everything I needed to link the stones' magic and use their power against you. Now, break the spell on my family and friends or I'll do it for you and trust me, you won't like that."

"You've locked my magic," he reminded her. "And I wouldn't help you even if I could."

"Then I'll do it." Tracey knew how to unpick spells now. But how to do it on a grand scale. Oh. All of the stones were under her control. The mayor looked on, horrified, as she drew every bit of magic to herself. *Dreamer.* She found the spell weave attached to the mayor, a thick, oily, gray-green thread stretching out from his chest and took hold of it with her hands. She sent all of her magic into the thread and tore it from his chest. They mayor let out an ear-piercing shriek. Tracey felt the snap when the spell broke, like a broken rubber band that snapped back and stung her fingers.

The mayor fell to his knees, sagging back onto his heels, unable to stay upright. "How did you do that?" he muttered.

Tracey knew the spell that froze her friends, her family, the M-force agents, the prison guards, and the public caught in the cross hairs was now broken. She could feel it. She had freed them all. She could almost sense their confusion and fear at waking up in strange locations, places they didn't remember going to. She couldn't wait to see them all. Now she must make sure the mayor and Timothy could never use the stones again. "I have all of the stones now. I will destroy them so no one can ever use them."

"You can't," he cried out. "If you destroy the stones, you'll destroy the world."

She blinked slowly. "What are you talking about?" In her gut a bad feeling formed, hard and small and cold like a diamond.

"Can't you see it? Everything I know? You see I speak the truth."

"No, you're wrong." Tracey didn't look. She couldn't. "A weak attempt to change my mind. You can't. You lost," she said. "I won."

The mayor shook his head. "He has you now. Timothy. He will destroy everything."

"I control his stone."

"Do you? All of this has been at his bidding. He controls you, Tracey, can't you see that? He has always wanted power. Power to act from the shadows and to control the world. And now he has all of the stones."

"No, he doesn't. I do," she said.

She was in control.

She was.

"No," she said again.

"Then where is he?" the mayor asked.

Tracey gasped as realization dawned. The mayor was right. She didn't hear Timothy's voice and could no longer feel his presence. Had she stopped one monster, only to let another escape?

"How do I find him?" she asked.

"Let me out. I can help you."

Tracey straightened. "No. You're worse than he is. You had to be stopped and I'm not sorry that I did it. You're trapped in here, inside your mind where you can never get out and hurt anyone ever again."

"Don't leave me here."

Tracey focused on the Serpent's Kiss around her neck and threw herself into the black place shouting, "Timothy?"

He didn't appear.

She reached out with all of the power she now controlled. The inky prison echoed like a school hall during the holidays. Timothy was gone.

No! No! Tracey pulled her mind back and fell into her body, panting, kneeling beside the mayor's still form. He stared up at the ceiling, blinking occasionally. "Who am I?" He turned his head staring at Tracey blankly. "Who are you? Where am I?"

She knew where he was. The evil intelligence was trapped deep inside his own mind. He blinked at her slowly. She could see no recognition in his eyes. It was all a blank space. His memory was no longer there. Tracey pushed shakily to her feet. Jilly and Jonny moaned and twitched. Tracey turned her head. Sebastian was out cold.

How could she tell her friends that Timothy escaped while she was busy trapping the mayor's mind inside his own head? *What do I do now?* She had the stones. All of the stones. The power of all six was immense, and it was too much for any one person to possess. She couldn't let Timothy get his hands on them. And he would try. There was no doubt about that. Wherever he had gone, he would be back for the power she now controlled.

There was only one thing she could do. She could stop Timothy from ever being able to use the combined power of the stones.

Stumbling forward, Tracey grabbed the stone from around the mayor's neck and raised it high. The emerald stone was so bright its glow hurt her eyes. It had five cracks through it like claw marks. On it was the faint impression of a croco-dile, front claws dripping with painted blood. She stared at the Crocodile's Claw until all she could see was the weave of magic wrapped around it, holding it fast to the mayor's body.

Awareness dropped away until she couldn't hear or see or sense or touch anything in the room. Tracey could only hear her own breath and see the gleaming green strands of the spell's weave. She searched for the same spell woven around the two stones she wore and stretched her mind and power to find Jilly, Jonny, and Sebastian's stones. The spell weave around each of them, all except for Jonny, glowed brightly with every color; red, green, black, blue, gold, and silver. She looked closer, zooming her vision in until she saw the thread that linked the stones together. Not the colored weaves that kept each stone tied tightly to its Protector but the golden weave of the spell linking the stones together.

She snapped the golden thread, breaking the curse that tied the stones together. She barely felt the momentous moment, hearing only a tinny ping. But it was not over yet. She focused on the green spell woven around the Crocodile's Claw, keeping it tied to the mayor's body and shattered it with her mind. The thick chain holding the Crocodile's Claw to the man's neck broke and the stone came away, dangling from the chain in her hand. She climbed to her feet. The Crocodile's Claw was heavy and pulsed with power. Tracey shoved it deep into her jeans pocket and stared down at the still mumbling, broken form of the mayor. She turned to Jonny, found the purplish-blue threads around the Crow's Heart and wove them quickly around her friend, tying stone and boy together. "Tracey?" Jonny's eyes widened beneath his glasses, shocked, feeling something but unable to give voice to it. Tracey eyed each of her friends. "I'm so sorry."

Laura's stare was full of fear. She knelt near Kylie and the two girls watched Tracey warily.

"Tracey?" Sebastian's shocked expression changed rapidly to concern.

Damian stepped forward, his hands reaching for her. "Tracey?"

She found her shoes near the door and pulled them on. "I'm so sorry," she said again. She ran up the stairs and out of the basement.

Her friends shouted after her, begging her to come back, but she couldn't listen. She ran, leaving her friends and the scattered football team behind in the council building's basement. She ran out into the early morning light. *I can only do this next part alone.*

"Tracey?!"

One day soon I believe we will
be known and accepted by more
than merely our peers.

44

Tracey ran all the way home. Without her phone, she did not have any way to contact her family and confirm they were all okay.

She had left her friends behind.

Her head swam with too much magic and the implications of what she had done. The stone in her pocket was heavy, thudding against her thigh as she ran, causing bruises she would feel all day. She'd removed the Crocodile's Claw.

On her own.

With her own power.

She had to hide it. Timothy was free, out there somewhere, and though the stones were no longer locked together, individually they still held so much power. She couldn't let any one stone fall into Timothy's hands, not until she found a way to destroy them all.

The mayor's voice filled her thoughts like dripping tap water. *"You can't destroy the stones, it will destroy the world."*

Was he telling the truth? Would the world end if she destroyed the stones?

Until she knew for sure she would have to hide the Crocodile's Claw where no one would ever find it. She was the only one who could do it. The only one strong enough.

Tracey had destroyed the spell that tied the stones to their Protectors. That was huge. No one could know she knew how to do that. As long as the stones were locked to a Protector, then the Tiger's Eye, the Crow's Heart, and Sebastian's unnamed stone would be safe. Not even Timothy knew how to break that spell.

That left the Crocodile's Claw in her pocket to protect.

Voices whispered inside her mind, so many voices vying for her attention. She couldn't spare any of them any time.

M-force was after her too and she refused to let the Crocodile's Claw fall into their hands.

No one could be trusted. M-force couldn't remove the stones from her chest, but they could take the Crocodile's Claw from her hands. She made a quick stop to hide it and then ran all the way home.

Tracey crouched in the bushes around her front yard and threw out her search blanket spell to check for police or M-force agents hidden inside the house. Nothing pinged. Movement drew her gaze to the upper bedroom window and the familiar small shape pacing back and forth inside. Tracey climbed the tree at the side of the house and leaped onto the little roof space in front of Sarah's bedroom window. She tapped lightly against the glass.

Sarah's head twitched at Tracey's soft knock. Her eyes widened when she saw Tracey waving at her through the dirty glass. Sarah pushed the window open. "Tracey?" Her eyes and nose were red like she had been crying. "What? How? Come in quick before they see you."

Tracey climbed inside and pulled her sister into a giant hug.

"What happened?" Sarah mumbled into her shoulder. "Are you okay? Mom and Dad are frantic. The police were here and M-force. I don't even know how they got inside. I was in the lounge room with Mom and Dad and Grandma and the boys and I … I can't remember what we were doing, but you weren't there. No one could find you."

"Is everyone okay?" Tracey whispered. When Sarah nodded a weight lifted off Tracey's chest. It had been there for so long she hadn't realized what it was, but she felt lighter now, like she could flap her arms and actually fly. She held her sister tighter, inhaling her strawberry scented shampoo. Sarah's messy hair tangled with her own. "I'm in trouble, Sarah."

Her sister pulled back. "We should get Mom —"

"— no wait. What about Uncle Donny? And Tony, Dave?"

"They're all downstairs. M-force were here looking for you. They said you broke Agent Malden out of prison and that Doctor Chan escaped too? They said it was your fault they got away."

Tracey pulled loose from Sarah's arms and slumped down onto her bed, dropping her head into her hands. She bit back a sob. "I know. I — I can explain. I didn't really let them out. It just kinda happened and I was there and … it's not my fault."

The bed sagged, tilting Tracey toward her sister. "Then you have to tell Mom and Dad."

"I can't. I don't want anyone else to get into trouble."

"Tracey!"

"Shhhh." Tracey pressed her palm over her sister's lips.

Sarah mumbled beneath Tracey's fingers. "What happened?"

"Jilly, Jonny, and Sebastian are all safe."

Her sister's nose crinkled. "Who is Sebastian?"

Tracey laughed. "A new friend. We stopped the Crocodile Man." Sarah's face contorted as her confusion grew. "The bad guy," Tracey clarified.

The younger girl smiled. "No more scary fog?"

"No more scary fog."

"What are you going to do now?"

"What makes you think I'm planning —"

"You climbed in through my window, Tracey. You don't want Mom and Dad to know you're here. You're up to something."

"M-force are going to catch me," Tracey said standing up. She moved to the window and edged the curtain open to stare down at the empty street outside. It was only a matter of time before they found her. She was a teenager. She had no money and she couldn't drive. How could she go on the run on her own?

"Talk to Mom. Or Grandma. Maybe they can do something?"

Tracey knew her mom, dad, and grandma would do everything they could to help her, but they couldn't protect the stones. Only Tracey could do that.

The stones Jilly, Jonny, and Sebastian wore couldn't be removed. And as far as anyone knew, Millicent's stone was still in the UK. No one other than Uncle Donny and Prince Henry knew Jonny held it. Besides, Jonny couldn't remove the Crow's Heart now. She had made sure of it, and she'd hid the Crocodile Man's stone where no one could find it, leaving her with only the ones she wore.

And she couldn't wear them both.

"What are you going to do?" Sarah asked again.

Tracey raised her head and stared into her sister's eyes. Could she really do it? Could she force this choice onto her sister? Her little sister?

There was no one else in the world she *could* trust.

Sarah stared into Tracey's eyes. "What? What is it?"

Tracey thrust a stone into Sarah's hands. Sarah opened her palms and stared down at the Butterfly Stone. "What …?"

"You have to keep it safe, Sars."

Shocked eyes sprang up. "How did you take it off? Are you okay?"

"Promise me you'll wear it. Promise me you'll keep it safe."

"The Butterfly Stone?"

"It has to stay in the family, Sarah."

"What about you?"

Tracey pulled the black stone out from beneath her shirt. It glowed brightly under the bedroom light. The long red serpent cut into the stone sparkled. She could almost hear it hiss.

Sarah gasped. "Tracey, no!"

"Shhhh."

"You?" Sarah's eyes filled with tears.

"I can block him. I'm okay." She couldn't tell Sarah that Timothy was already gone.

"Are you sure?"

Tracey smiled broadly. "I'm sure. Really. But —" Tracey pointed at the Butterfly Stone in her sister's hand. "I can't wear them both. You have to keep it safe. Once it's on, they can't take it off you."

"But, Tracey —"

Their heads lifted at the sound of sirens outside. Several cars raced into the driveway, brakes screeching as they skidded to a stop. Tracey turned her stare from the open window to her sister. "Sarah, please."

"But —"

"I trust you."

Her sister nodded sharply. Shouting voices drifted up from the ground floor and feet in heavy boots thundered up the stairs. Sarah pulled the silver chain over her head and tucked the Butterfly Stone under her shirt just before the door was shoved open.

"Don't move!" Angry voices shouted. Sarah's bedroom quickly filled with men and women in dark police uniforms, bracelets glowing brightly red. Tracey and Sarah thrust their hands into the air. Tracey sighed. The stones were all safe. For now.

She was dragged off the bed as the voices shouted at her to freeze, to lay down on the floor, to raise her hands. *Already done.* Tracey didn't move.

Mom and Dad called from the hallway, saying they would fix things and ordered Sarah not to move. The world was full of noise but inside Tracey's head she was calm and quiet. She had done everything she could. She knew where all the stones were and the mayor couldn't get his hands on any of them anymore. Neither could Timothy. Tracey would be locked up and he wouldn't be able to reach her there. She had his stone and she had the majority of his magic. She didn't know what

Timothy's plans were but at least she had stopped him from getting the Stones of Power. She had done what she had to do.

Her hands were pinned behind her back by a strong female M-force officer. "You are under arrest," a woman told her.

"I'm ready," she said softly.

When that day comes, I know you will be as revered as I for your good works and knowledge of our arts.

EPILOGUE

"What are *you* doing here?" Tracey peered through the bars of her cell at the last person she ever thought she would see standing in front of her.

Meena approached the cell bars slowly. She was dressed in a black party dress and her skirt flared out slightly at the movement. Silver bracelets clinked together as she raised her hands. "I'm surprised too. But I had to come."

Tracey stood up. The cell's lights flashed and an alert blurted once to remind her to sit back down. She flopped down on the thin mattress and tucked her bare feet beneath her. "What are you talking about?"

"I dreamed of talking to you in a prison cell. When I heard that's where you were, I told my mother we had to come."

Tracey wished she could use her magic but the prison Mage-kind identification bangle was locked around her wrist and lit with that familiar horrible blue light. Her core was locked. She had no access to her magic and it was cold, oh so cold. These days all she ever felt was cold. Like her blood had been turned to ice. "I don't understand."

Meena snorted. "I don't understand it either. Apparently, my family are psychic. And so am I."

"That's why you've been so weird?"

Meena's eyes flashed. After a moment she shook her head, shrugged, and then nodded. "I guess so. I keep dreaming of you. That's what we call it. What my family calls it. The Dreaming. Tracey, there is a darkness in you. And it's gotten worse. You're going to destroy the world."

The cold in Tracey's skin turned icy. She shivered, sticking her hands under her armpits to warm them up. *Psychic? Dream? Destroy the world?*

Meena hummed. "I'm a bully, Tracey. I bullied you. At school I was horrible to you."

Tracey's mouth fell open. She couldn't believe Meena was actually acknowledging her bad behavior, let alone apologizing for it.

"At the time I didn't know why I didn't like you. But now that I've learned about my family's curse, I know why I don't like you. There's something wrong with you."

"There's nothing wrong with me," Tracey argued.

"Your heart is black," Meena said.

"What?"

"I can't explain it, but part of you is in shadow. Until you expose it to the light you will continue to be corrupted by it."

"Maybe the shadow is there for a different reason? Like it's bad magic or an evil spirit," Tracey said. It was what she desperately hoped. "Am I possessed by something?"

"No. It's you, Tracey. Just you. I see it every time I close my eyes. I hope now that I've come here and told you about it, I'll stop having the dream. I'm not here for you, Tracey. I want the dreams to stop."

Tracey sat in silence. After a moment Meena slapped her hands against her thighs and straightened her perfectly straight skirt. "I'd better go."

The door clanged shut behind Meena leaving Tracey alone in her quiet cell. She pushed Jonathan's book further up on her cot and lay down, pressing her head into her musty pillow. She stared up at the ceiling.

Fruit tingles.

TRACEY'S MISSION WILL CONCLUDE
IN THE FINALE OF

STONES OF POWER: BOOK FIVE

STAY TUNED!

ABOUT THE AUTHOR

Laurie Bell is a former teacher who has worked with children of all ages in the literary sphere. She is a science fiction aficionado who is regularly featured by publications such as the Antipodean Science Fiction E-Magazine.

Laurie maintains an active blog of science fiction, fantasy, and flash fiction pieces, and serves as a volunteer in her local theatre company.

Discover more about Laurie Bell at:

www.solothefirst.wordpress.com

A Thank You from the Author

I'd like to thank the following, without whom, these amazing books would never get written.

To the #auswrites crew — you get me. You keep me inspired with your words of wisdom and motivating calls to arms. I have found so many new writer friends on this thread and so many amazingly talented Aussie writers. I love the support, well wishes and monthly prompt ideas. #readmore-aussiebooks #auswrites

Australian Book Lovers!! Thank you for your support and for your incredible website and podcast. Veronica and Darren you are amazing. Thank you for everything that you do. If you haven't visited this website yet, why not? It is a font of information. If you didn't know about this website - I forgive you, but get onto it immediately! Go to www.australianbooklovers.com to find some incredible reads, podcasts and interviews. Aussie authors are the best! Love @australianbooks

Edmund and Linh for your CP & Beta-ery goodness! Every time I receive an email from you my writing becomes better. You are fabulous. Thank you for your valuable time. Keep on keeping on. I can't wait to read more of your words soon.

Mum and Dad who read each and every book. Thank you for reading. Wait until you see what happens next. Thank you for all your support! I love you both.

Nana. I love you. And I miss him too.

For all the kids I taught in the few short years I was a teacher — you will always inspire me.

To all the readers who have contacted me online to tell me about reading The Stones of Power and for those who share their reviews and photos and well wishes, I love hearing from you. I hope you love The Serpent's Kiss as much as I do. Do what makes you happy and sod anyone who tells you that you can't do something. If trying makes you scared, try it anyway. You CAN do anything. You can BE anything.

Hayley and Stefanie (BFFs forever and always.)

Lauren Lynne THANK YOU.

The Wyvern's Peak Publishing team: D.C. McGannon, Michael McGannon, and Holly McGannon — thank you for believing in this series and in Tracey's journey. Thank you for jumping onto the merry-go-round once more. Without you, this series would not exist. From the covers to the editing, the suggestions, ideas, thoughts and beautiful inner artwork and chapter teasers, you make all of this real. I appreciate you all. We are nearly there!

Thank you all for supporting local indie authors. Readers… get out there and support your local bookshops and booksellers! They are truly awesome people.

Oh, and to Libby, Elise, Lisa, Jen, Kathy, Luneah, Stefanie, Hayley, Justine, Blair, Amber, Anthony, Cathy, Brian, Caroline, Linh and Berny — sorry for making you wait so long.

Gerry. I love you.

Thank you! Keep dreaming.

Please consider leaving a review on your favourite bookish websites.

You can find me at www.solothefirst.wordpress.com

The end is coming...

For this and other exciting titles, visit:

www.<u>WyvernsPeak.com</u>

www.twitter.com/WyvernsPeak
www.facebook.com/WyvernsPeak

Sign up for our newsletter, get free stuff, and be the first to know when new books from your favorite Wyvern's Peak authors are released.

Follow Laurie Bell on Twitter
@LaurienotLori

Like Laurie on Facebook
www.facebook.com/WriterLaurieBell

Visit her website at
www.solothefirst.wordpress.com